WHO DISTURBS *the* KŪKUPA?

Praise for *Who Disturbs the Kūkupa?*

Kayleen Hazlehurst has produced a haunting tale of love and loss in wartime, made all the more memorable for its cultural inclusion and sensitivity. The adventures of Sonny Wirima, a Māori soldier on the run in German-occupied Greece, longing to be reunited with his great love, Atarangi Tahiri, are evocatively rendered without ever descending into cloying sentimentality. A great read.

PETER EWER. AUTHOR OF *FORGOTTEN ANZACS*

This is an inspired taonga by a gifted writer whose story joins the old world and the new during a time of turbulent change. A must-read for those who ever wanted to know more about those brave soldiers of the 28th Māori Battalion, like my grandmother's brother (Lt Hone Te Kauru Green, C Company, killed in action, 1941). Hidden gems of poetry give the book a spiritual identity you won't find in books on this era. Inspirational and emotionally gripping.

RANGI HAPI. CREATIVE ENTREPRENEUR, HAPIARTS

A truly heart-warming and pleasurable read that leaves persistent psychic vibes long after the last page has been turned. Māori practices and beliefs are knitted seamlessly into military events thousands of miles from home. Tender and descriptive though Hazlehurst's characterizations are, she does not shrink from stark wartime realism where necessary. It is a most impressive work.

JOHN CARR. AUTHOR OF *THE DEFENCE AND FALL OF GREECE 1940–41*

A unique and extremely precious contribution to our understanding of what happened during those events. The book informs future generations of the sacrifices that their tīpuna made.

MATTHEW MULLANY. HISTORIAN AND PUBLIC SERVANT, OF NGĀTI PĀRAU DESCENT

Cover artist: Sarah McBeath, 'On Taylor Road, Wharauroa/Kūkupa'

Also by the author: *A Caramel Sky*

'*A Caramel Sky*, Kayleen Hazlehurst's moving historical romance novel, is a heart-breaking love story set in wartime New Zealand and bookended by 21st century vignettes. Hazlehurst's prose is a love letter to this beautiful country. At its core, this is a novel that defines and redefines what it means to claim for oneself "a life well lived".'

MAGGIE TRAPP, KETE BOOKS, NZ.

'Taut, swiftly paced, engaging. Scenes beautifully textured and vibrant with dialogue, personality and mood.'

MARK SPENCER, FAULKNER AWARD WINNER, USA.

'*A Caramel Sky* is in one aspect a family saga, and in another a historical coming of age tale. [Hazlehurst's] interpretation and retelling of this period is truthful. I also enjoyed the fact that this novel is "real" and treats life with cool clarity, rather than rose coloured glasses.'

ESTHER PERRIAM, ELDERNET GAZETTE, NZ.

'This was a mighty read. I feel certain that such stories happened in real life. The war stories in the book are harrowing. The romance story was harsh at times. The writing had me lock, stock and barrel. I would recommend it to anyone that enjoys a good New Zealand story. It's a long time since any book has moved me to tears. I just loved this book.'

TERRY TONER, BOOK SHOW, RADIO SOUTHLAND, NZ.

First published in New Zealand in 2023
Revised Edition published 2026 by
Blue Dragonfly Press

National Library of New Zealand Cataloguing-in-Publication Data
Hazlehurst, Kayleen M, 2023
Who Disturbs the Kūkupa? / Kayleen M. Hazlehurst

ISBN 978-0-473-76800-3 (Paperback – International Edition)

Designed and distributed in New Zealand by
The Copy Press, 141 Pascoe Street,
Annesbrook, Nelson, 7011, New Zealand
www.copypress.co.nz

for information about bulk purchases,
please contact The Copy Press, Bookshop.

WHO DISTURBS *the* KŪKUPA?

KAYLEEN M. HAZLEHURST

— Māori proverb

— Harry Dansey

— Bahá'u'lláh

Artist: Kayleen Hazlehurst, 'Soldier with memory of fantail'

part one

Rangitakō Lands

1947

Miriama Wirima leaned on her hoe and gazed out to sea, aware of the pungent odour of seaweed rising from the overturned soil. Kūmara, carrots and greens lay beside her kit for the evening meal. Low clouds rolled over the darkening waters. Soon the sun-warmed cliffs that ushered travellers deep into Ngā Puhi country, and departing souls north on their spirits' flight, would be cooled by swirling yarns of white.

O chiefs of old. Ye have vanished from us like the moa bird …
O lordly tōtara tree! Thou'rt fallen to the earth.

She looked back along the cliff to gauge how light was falling on the village. Square wooden houses sat between the farmland and cliff like so many nesting seabirds—their faces set towards the sea, their backs against the pasture. Was this a protest against farming or was it just a preference of the heart? She smiled, knowing well the yearnings for the traditional ways of harvesting. *The sea will always have the strongest tow.*

Behind the marae were small farms that supported the local community. The paddock fences, which guided the cows to and from their milking, were fondly rickety and covered with lichen. There was occasional scorn from Pākehā neighbours when animals escaped or children meddled with things, but such derision was mutual.

Pockets of native trees occupied the crevices and folds of the surrounding hills, keeping her kinsmen anchored to the land. Further inland, the forested peaks of the Brynderwyns communed with the greyed roof of the world. Miriama watched a pair of wood pigeons, her kūkupa, winging their way from the forest to the pūriri tree at the back of the churchyard. They liked to feed there on the berries and to roost in the branches at night.

She worked in her garden, not only for the pleasure of cultivation, but also for the companionship of the sea. In manual labour a person found purpose, her father had taught her. A wise one discovered meaning in solitude. Miriama's quest was to understand the devastation, to piece together the stories. It was a need that ran deep into her bones. She must explain the losses. She must give assurance and demonstrate a future more certain.

They were happy times, before the war. There was always singing.

Kayleen M. Hazlehurst

~ 1 ~

The Tears of One Whale

1939–1940

Api turned the knob and the radio crackled to life. Tama, his youngest, was sparring with Sonny. The stocky middle boy jabbed back, producing a yelp from Tama. Api, tired from his day of lambing in the September wind and rain, did not intervene. Hēmi, the eldest son and tallest among them, commanded the most respect. He kept the younger boys in line, giving their father some peace.

'Oi!' Hēmi growled. 'Shut up, you two.'

'Yeah, see.' Sonny kicked out at Tama as a final assertion of sibling authority.

Mata and Heti, two visiting aunties, cackled over their tea. Miriama put a plate of scones on the kitchen table and flicked Tama's ear with her tea towel. 'Hush. Dad wants to hear this.'

Not everyone had a radio. News that something was afoot had swirled around the community, drawing people into the house like driftwood on an incoming tide. Two days ago, the Acting Prime Minister, Peter Fraser, had issued a statement to the newspapers that New Zealand was at war with Germany, declaring this was 'a dark day in the history of the world'.

Api waved his hands, palms down, to quieten everyone. Then he set his jaw to listen as Prime Minister Michael Savage addressed the nation.

Savage spoke about the evils of Nazism and of the country's loyalty to Britain.

Both with gratitude for the past, and with confidence in the future, we range ourselves without fear beside Britain. Where she goes, we go. Where she stands, we stand. We are only a small and young nation, but we are one and all a band of brothers and we march forward with union of hearts and wills to a common destiny.

'What do you think about that?' Mata asked as Api switched off the radio.

'Don't like it one bit,' Heti answered. 'It will be no better than the last one.'

'Worse, I think,' Api said.

The speech that left the adults dejected had set the younger boys on fire, making them jump and prance.

'Don't worry, Auntie.' Sonny smacked Mata's arm, eliciting a shriek. 'We'll chase those Germans back to where they came from.'

'Yeah.' Tama punched at his brother again. 'Kick their fat asses all the way back to Germland.'

Mata and Heti giggled.

'Tamati, watch your language.' Miriama turned her frown on the older women. 'Don't you encourage them.'

'Beat 'em from the bushes like hogs.' Sonny raised an invisible rifle in his hands. 'Pow! Pow!'

'Turn Kete and Turi on them, hey?' Tama responded.

Everyone laughed. Kete and Turi, mutts of uncertain lineage, and their favourite hunting dogs, were good at flushing out poaka.

Strength drained from Api's limbs. 'Auē! You boys don't know what you're talking about.' He remembered the bad old war that ended over twenty years ago, the faces of the men who returned from Gallipoli and France. Uncles and cousins who had come home maimed and lost of soul. The elders wept when they saw them. All their soldiers wanted was to return to Te Ao Mārama, the world of life and light. Now, another generation was being called to walk the path to Hinenuitepō.

'Time for bed,' Hēmi said. 'We've got work tomorrow.'

Miriama showed the visitors the door and Tama padded off to the outhouse.

Sonny cornered his father. 'We *can* fight them, Dad. We *can* drive 'em back.'

'Not if I have anything to do with it.'

     Kayleen M. Hazlehurst

'We're at war. The radio said so.'

'What makes you think you can fight them, eh? Those blighters are mightier than we are, and they've got some bloody big guns.'

'Yeah? They don't sound too clever to me.'

Miriama came back inside after saying her goodbyes.

'Mum?' The boy extended his hand in an appeal.

'No, Sonny.' She closed the door with a firm hand. 'Those troubles have nothing to do with us. The Ngā Puhi have no business in this Pākehā war. Besides, Dad needs your help on the farm.'

Api read out the newspaper article as Miriama stirred her soup pot. On Ringa Ringa Beach, in the far south, six small whales had dashed themselves to death on the rocks while the rest of the pod cruised fretfully beyond the breakers. Miriama spread a cloth on the table to slice the bread. *Poor lonely ones*, she thought. *Do not the tears of one whale raise the level of the sea?*

In the same month a large spot had crossed the sun until half of it was hidden. Api and Miriama had watched the darkening sky as a stillness fell over the land. Gulls flew to shore and sheltered in clusters on the dunes, as if expecting a storm. Cows fell silent and so did the horses, neither mooing nor nickering at each other. The dogs were asking questions. They were sitting on their tails and staring up at Api with their eyes bulbous and their lips drawn back. A fortnight later it was the moon's turn for a partial eclipse.

Miriama didn't like the signs. The children of Tangaroa, flinging themselves on the shore. Flocks of birds flying inland. The sun and moon obscured.

'This land is in trouble, Api.'

—ⁿⁿ—

It was another cold night in June and Miriama had not been sleeping. An arrow of moonlight ran across the floorboards and onto the dressing table, its tip pointing at the photograph of her boys. The younger ones were pressing her to let them enlist. Hēmi, though, was more cautious. At twenty-five, he had a sense of responsibility towards their poor father. *They are good boys. What more could a mother want from her sons?*

She moved the blankets aside and slipped away from her husband's prone body. Pulling on a shawl she moved soundlessly to the window, lifted her salt-and-pepper hair over the wrap and looked up at the violet-black vault of the sky. Clouds were closing in around a diminished crescent, its soft edges predicting rain. When the moon was full it acted as a beacon for vessels steaming up and down the coast. Tonight, there was barely enough light to separate sea from sky.

Miriama studied the stand of trees on the hill. Why were the kūkupa so restless? Over many nights she had heard the beat of their wings. This land she so loved now spoke to her of violation and danger.

A ship had passed Bream Head and was heading for the open sea. Out on the water she saw the glint of aft lights but could no longer hear the thrumming of engines. Soon the ship would disappear over the rim of the earth.

A column of light outlined the liner, followed by a dull roar. *Flash ... Boom!*

Miriama spun on her toes, bounded across the room, and fell on her knees by the bed.

'Api. Api. Wake up!'

'Wha— What?'

'I think the Germans are here!'

'What are you saying, woman?'

'A ship ... A ship blew up. I saw it.'

'How do you know it's the Germans?'

'A bad feeling.'

Api groaned as he climbed out of bed. From the window he could see a flicker of red. Out past the Hen and Chicken Islands something was burning. He was handed his woollen trousers and heaviest jumper.

'Dress warm,' his wife said, then she turned to light the kerosene lamp.

'Something has come to grief, that's for certain.' Api pulled on his trousers. 'She might stay afloat for a while ... Give us time.'

Miriama plaited her hair with rapid fingers. 'We'll have to get help.' She flung the single braid over her shoulder.

'I'll wake the boys,' Api said. 'They can take the horses. Hēmi and I will ready the boat.'

'Our boat's not very big, Api. How many people can we—?'

'Six or seven. There could be a fair few floundering out there.'

'I'll take a lantern, see who can launch—'

'Don't be long, Miriama. Get someone else to do it. Meet us at the beach.'

They were able to ride bareback just as swiftly, but their father had cautioned Sonny against it. In the dark, a horse might stumble. In ten minutes, they had saddled up and taken to the road. Men and their horses. Shivering streams of energy. Sonny in front on the dappled white, Tama close behind on the frisky brown.

Sonny's eyes grew round like an owl's, focusing on the pale line of earth but imagining he could see all around him. Most farmers owned fishing boats. As kids, they had often visited their Pākehā neighbours, driving them mad with their thieving of fruit or touching things they shouldn't. There were three households to rouse. Afterwards, the farmers would alert each other. Some of them had telephones. Angus Thompson was their nearest neighbour.

'I'll do this,' Sonny told Tama. 'You go on to the next one.'

'How do you know they won't shoot us?'

'They'll be curious, won't they? Watch how I do it.'

Sonny raised his fist to thump on the front door as his brother shrank back.

'Mr Thompson! Mr Thompson! Can you and your missus please come out? It's Sonny Wirima, we need your help … Hey, Mr Thompson!'

The dogs emerged from their kennels and set up a ruckus, but Sonny continued to hammer on the door.

'I can't do that.' Tama hung his head.

'Pretend you're a policeman with news someone's dead. You're allowed to shout at them in an emergency. Go on. Get on your horse. I'll catch up with you.'

Doors banged on the top floor. The farmer was swearing and his wife was answering in a squeaky voice. Angus Thompson clumped down the staircase and burst through the front door, red-faced and clinging to his pyjama bottoms. On the steps behind him in a nightdress was his wife, clutching the family rifle she'd obviously confiscated from her husband.

'What the *hell* are you playing at, Sonny Wirima?'

Tama sprang onto his horse and took off at full gallop.

Miriama hurried on the path to the beach carrying her lantern, two blankets and a kit of apples—the only supplies she could think of to satisfy both hunger and thirst. She slid one foot after the other on the crumbling clay. A canvas bag strapped to her waist contained ointments, bindings and a pair of scissors. Pieces of wood on the boat could be used for splints, if needed.

It was the kind of darkness just before the sky lightened. No one followed, but Miriama knew they would be coming. Mata and Heti had been assigned to raising the alarm. With the aunties on the job there'd be no more sleeping. A lot of organising would be needed before people turned up at their boats.

Below her, the figures of Api and Hēmi stood in the water holding the stern, and she swung her lantern as a signal she was on her way.

Hēmi leaned over to push aside deck-chairs, dunnage and other wreckage.

'Blasted sea fog,' Api muttered, as he steered them in a slow circle.

Miriama stared at the dark water. 'Look for a piece of wood. I'm sure I saw a man—'

'Can't see him, Mum. Your eyes must be playing tricks.'

'Whoa!' Api slowed the motor to a crawl.

'What, Dad? Did you see the ship?'

'Just shadows. I'm not going near that thing. We'll get sucked under.'

They were further out in the Hauraki Gulf than Api normally ventured. Long rising swells gave the sense they were approaching the mouth of the harbour. No white water. No foaming peaks to hint at shoals of sand beneath. This was deep water. Waves passed under the boat in wide, smooth rolls. They clustered close, staring ahead as puffs of low

     Kayleen M. Hazlehurst

cloud rushed past. Nothing could be heard above the heave and sigh of the waves.

The first sign of life came with a bobbing light.

'What is it?' Miriama asked in a trembling voice.

The light penetrated the mist again, waving left and right. Then another light … and another … and another.

'Lifeboats!' Hēmi yelled. 'They're lifeboats, Dad.'

'Over a dozen of them, by crikey!'

A stricken ocean liner loomed half a mile away. Smoke discharged from the hole ripped in its side and eighteen lifeboats were drifting in front under limp sails. Some survivors were attempting to paddle away.

Cries of joy went up.

Api looked behind and could have shouted for joy himself when he saw a tiny flotilla of fishing boats coming up in the rear.

Sonny and Tama watched from the shore as the boats came in. Everyone was there in the cool dawn, with their baskets and blankets, their horses and traps, in case they were needed to convey people along the beach to the road where the harbour master and his men waited with trucks.

The three hundred and fifty-one souls from the RMS *Niagara* were transferred by the fishing boats to a steamer that had come into the area after hearing the distress signal. Passengers and crew were on their way back to Auckland, everyone was told. From a quarter of a mile away the boatmen had seen the liner—stern up and angled for descent—plunge to the bottom of the sea.

Only one person noticed the ship's cat floating by on a piece of debris, its fur and whiskers spiky with fear and seawater. Hēmi reached to grab the feline before it went down with the wreckage. He grinned at his mother. 'Don't we need a cat?' he said as he wrapped the hissing, snarling creature in a towel. 'I'll keep it in the barn.'

It had been a good rescue. Every passenger was accounted for, nobody drowned, and only the cows were inconvenienced by a late milking.

—⁊⁊⁊—

The demise of the *Niagara* on 19 June 1940 filled the newspapers for days. This was the first direct attack on New Zealand. A German raider had been laying mines in the Hauraki Gulf. The ship's sinking gave the brothers a new avenue of appeal. The war in Europe had been going on for months and, so far, they'd made no headway with their parents. At the cowshed the pending 'invasion' became the main topic of conversation.

'Look at it this way, Dad.' Hēmi elbowed a cow's tail away as he put her to milking. 'What if those raiders come in here?'

'Yeah.' Tama jerked up his chin. When his father flashed a look at him, he lowered his head.

Api turned to Hēmi. 'We could keep watch from the cliff.'

'Then what?' Hēmi demanded. 'Grab our rifles and take potshots at them? We have women and children…'

'We have to stop the bastards from coming here,' Sonny told the udder in front of him. The formation of the Māori Battalion had been massive news in the North. The first draft of soldiers had been shipped out in early May, taking many of their cousins and friends with them. Now the army was looking for a second intake and he didn't want to hang back. 'It makes us feel ashamed.'

'Yeah. We're just the leftovers,' Tama said, testing their father's resolve. 'Manu and Ray caught the bus last week.'

Api grabbed the bucket to wash the teats on another cow, sloshing the water. 'That's exactly your mother's point. She thinks this war will be our greatest disaster.'

'Letting them destroy our land and animals would be worse,' Sonny countered.

Api nodded. 'You could be right, son.'

'I'd rather put a gun to their heads than have them put one to mine, wouldn't you?'

'Fight them on their own turf, do you mean? I'm sure I would, Sonny.'

Tama took the bucket from his father. 'One town sent a whole rugby team. Good, eh? Bet they'll be having games all over the place.'

Api gave a soft chuckle. 'I have to admit, that *is* impressive.'

Kayleen M. Hazlehurst

Hēmi had been long-faced as he listened to this talk. 'We're not going without Mum's blessing … How would you manage on your own, Dad?'

'I'd get a couple of youngsters to help. Don't you worry.'

Sonny stood to look his father in the eye, something he rarely did. 'Will you back us then, if we asked Mum again?'

Api straightened his back. 'Āe. I would. The land comes first. Your mother will see it that way.'

At the first streak of light, Miriama drew on her shawl and headed for the cliff path. She wanted to meet the sun as it rose above the ridgeline. No sounds of stirring animals. No cries from early birds. It was the time of day when words were not essential between gods and men. Her sons, once safe by her skirts, now stood proud and strong of arm. The conviction that they should leave to fight an unknown enemy had crept into their father's heart.

What sad spirits, to fall so far from their people.
To lie, forgotten, on some distant soil.
To not take flight over cliff and dune to that place where
sea kelp swirls and flax leaves twist and knot.

'I belong to this country,' Miriama keened to the wind, 'and so do my sons!'

The sea answered—surging, thumping, scraping back on the shore. 'Nay, I have spoken,' said Tangaroa. 'I am ready and I shall take them.'

Above her the black-backed gull cried, 'We all walk through the void of darkness.'

Higher still, the albatross displayed his feathered sail. 'I navigate the earth, and so do they.'

Kō tā Māui ki tōna ringaringa e kore e tāea te rūrū.
What Māui seizes he will not give up.

~2~

White Herons

The Wirima brothers were smoking fish with mānuka brush, a recent catch of tarakihi and hoki, when Atarangi Tahiri walked past them on the beach. She was a slight girl with a graceful step. Sonny loved the way the sun caught her black hair, thick and wavy down her back. Atarangi and Winifred Kahu, her best friend, had been playmates with the Wirimas. They had climbed trees and explored the hills since they'd run around barefoot as kids.

Atarangi never joined the boys when they went eeling. 'That's what brothers are for,' she would say. As older children Sonny noticed a change. The girls no longer swam in rock pools in their undies, they wore pretty dresses and smelled nice.

Sonny left the fish to his brothers and ran to catch up. 'Ata, wait.'

'Hey, Sonny.'

He took her by the hand and they strolled along, listening to the cries of seagulls and the ripple of waves on the shore.

'I've been looking for you,' Sonny said. 'Where have you been?'

'Practising my poi with Auntie Rea. She's teaching me a new dance.'

Atarangi was a favourite among the aunties, and little kids followed her around like bees. Lately she seemed to prefer the company of the old ladies. It drove him to distraction.

He stopped to study her eyes. Pools of still water flecked with colour, as if reeds beneath had tinted the surface with russet and green. His heart crushed against his ribs as he fell into them.

Atarangi Tahiri was 'sweet and uncomplicated', Miriama said. Not 'cloudy liquid' like the other girls. She was well born, and his mother was fond of high-ranking lines. 'Be careful with that one, Sonny,' she warned.

Kayleen M. Hazlehurst

When Atarangi turned sixteen she had agreed to go to dances and picture shows with Sonny. They held hands, shared ice creams. Every time he caught sight of her the force of his feelings stunned him, and now he had to tell her he was going away.

'I'd better go home. Nan wants me to help with tea.'

'Meet me after dinner under the pūriri tree behind the church.'

⁂

Earlier in the day a white heron had visited Atarangi, its plumes sleek in the morning sun. She had been sitting alone on the rocks, watching shivers of light playing over the bay. Cloud shadows swathed the waters out to the horizon, where the sea colours oscillated between cobalt and purple. It puzzled her that the Wirima brothers had spent the week fishing and preserving their catch. She shuddered. *They must be stocking up.*

This apprehension heightened when her kōtuku swooped down to land nearby. He positioned his delicate feet on the rough surface, bending and lifting his thin legs, raising his wings to shade pools and to confuse his prey—preparing her for news of other fishermen.

Chiefs once prized the wiry, white feathers of the white heron, her nan had told her. They wore them as signs of chiefly authority, of their rangatiratanga.

> *He huruhuru te manu i pai ai, mā te iwi te tangata rangatira et tū.*
> *As feathers adorn a bird, so a chief's status is maintained by his people.*

Atarangi knew to pay attention in the company of these message-bearers. Birds could be incarnations of both men and ancestors. They acted as mediums to the gods during prayer. The great chief Piki Kōtuku once placed his mind into herons and used them as sacred messengers.

She felt blessed when the ancients spoke to her, but other times she felt cursed. She foretold coming events and had an instinct about things before they happened. When she tried to understand the reasons for these visitations it left her light-headed. She slowed her breathing, turned inward to listen, becoming aware of her heartbeat and the flow of blood through her veins.

The aunties spoke of Atarangi as being a puhi woman, one of noble birth. They made her feel special and were teaching her the old ways. No man should spoil her tapu state, they insisted. As an infant, Atarangi lost her parents in a storm at sea and was raised by her grandmother, Nan. For her entire life she had relied upon the older women for help and guidance.

Sonny had been her exuberant companion since childhood. None of this rangatiratanga stuff for him. There was something calming about a person who cared more about everyday life than spiritual things. It was simpler, less complicated. In his youth Sonny had thrown himself into being her boyfriend with the same enthusiasm.

She looked along the beach. Winifred was dragging a stick, dallying beside the water, glancing up.

'Join me, Winnie,' Ata called out. 'It's so warm here.'

'I thought you were spending time with your people.'

'Only my old kōtuku is here.'

Winifred lifted her Box Brownie to snap a photograph. Startled, the heron flew off. 'Sorry. I frightened him.'

'He'll come back.'

Winifred found a flat surface for sitting. 'Why the sad face, Ata?'

'Everyone seems sad these days.'

'Maybe the whole country.'

Ata looked up. 'Do you often think about the whole country?'

'Sometimes. I was wondering what I could do to help.'

'How can you help?'

'Move to the city. Find work. Join the war effort.'

'You're such a modern girl, Winnie. I could never leave this place.'

'This is where you belong, Ata. Everyone would be sad if you left.'

Atarangi reached out to touch her friend's hair. 'You look pretty today. Are you meeting Hēmi?'

'We're going into town tonight. There's a film he wants to see.' She pulled a face. 'Something about the war.'

'It might be a love story. I hope you're not going on horseback?'

     Kayleen M. Hazlehurst

'We're borrowing Uncle Hoani's car. You and Sonny can come if you like.'

'You go, Winnie. I think Hēmi sees enough of his brothers.'

Sonny was waiting for Atarangi under the pūriri tree, as he promised. She was wearing blue slacks and a yellow jersey, with her hair pinned up in a roll. Girls wore trousers much more now. He recognised it as a show of solidarity with their menfolk. Everywhere women were joining the war effort. They appeared ready for anything, just like him.

He didn't want to be an ignorant country boy. The Wirimas were going places. They were joining the Māori Battalion. The army would teach them things. When he came home they could start a family, build a better community. Ata would share his dream.

'E ipo.' He kissed her cheek.

'What have you been up to?'

'Just fishing, taku whaiāipo.'

'Yes, all week. Have you boys got something against the fish population?'

He looked down, ashamed. 'You caught me out.'

'Oh, Sonny. You're going away, aren't you?'

'I'm sorry.' He put his arm around her.

'When do you leave?'

'We catch the recruitment bus on Wednesday.'

'Five days …' Her body began to shake.

'Kāore. Kāore, taku iti kahurangi. Please don't cry.' What a heel he was.

She smacked him on the chest. 'Don't you sweet-talk me, Sonny Wirima!'

He tussled her to the grass and smooched her face with kisses. 'Mm-m-m-m. I love you, my little treasure.'

After her shrieks subsided, they sat up.

'What will happen to us, Sonny?'

'We can marry the minute I come home. We'll have a dozen kids.'

'Never mind that. There'll be no one left to take me to the pictures.'

'Hey, I don't want anyone else taking you to the pictures!'

They ambled along the cliff path in the moonlight, passing by Miriama's garden until they reached their favourite grove of trees. One pōhutukawa bent seawards, its outer branches stretching beyond the cliff. Here, they made a nest among the roots and leaves.

Sonny opened his coat to pull Atarangi into his warmth. They lay with their bodies entangled, allowing the tree to shelter them from the elements of wind and time.

'The old people say this tree is over a thousand years old,' Ata said. 'There are grandfather trees like this all over the country.'

'They would have seen the first landings.'

'What will they see now, with this war?'

'You're my girl, Ata. Please say you will wait for me.'

'Of course, I will. Do you think I'll let you wander the earth not knowing where your home is, Sonny?'

He laughed. 'I love you, Atarangi Tahiri.'

⁓

People waited beside the river, heads bowed. Miriama stood with the other women in her long black dress and headscarf, her predictions unspoken. At this sacred place they had gathered to perform a blessing ceremony. Water rushed through the shallows, curling liquid glass over smooth grey stones. Specks of light scattered between the ripples, a myriad of fleeting souls.

Pure water was sprinkled over their fighting men. Sprigs of fern and woven flax were cast into the river to be carried away, along with the hopes of their whānau. As she lifted her voice in a karakia—a ritual prayer asking the Powers to divert troubles from the paths of young warriors and to assure them of victory—Miriama heard the sound of soft weeping.

On the morning of their departure, goodbyes were brief. The brothers kissed their mother in the kitchen and shook their father's hand.

Hēmi bent to give Turi's head a ruffle. 'See 'ya, old fella.' Kete got a stroke, 'You too, girl. Look after things for us.'

 Kayleen M. Hazlehurst

A battered yellow bus was parked on the roadside, its lower half caked with mud and dust from too many journeys on country roads. A small New Zealand flag fluttered from a side window. Heavy footfalls swayed the vehicle as nine more recruits mounted the steps to join the other keen men from the North. Mothers took out hankies, and fathers clung to rims of hats. In a contagion of excitement, younger children scooted about and girlfriends jostled to touch fingers through windows.

Miriama was glad Hēmi had chosen to sit at the back of the bus where he could keep an eye on the younger ones. Sonny was making jokes with his cousins while Tama fooled around as usual. The evening before she had reminded her boys they had descended from a long line of ariki and military leaders, giving assurance their tūpuna would be with them no matter what the circumstance.

'Lay down the cloak of your ancestors and use it as a mat to stand on,' Miriama had counselled. Then she made them promise to always look after each other.

The driver ground the gears. Miriama and Api raised their hands, and Hēmi gave them a wan smile as the bus pulled away.

On the trip south, Sonny watched the fields of home pass by. He wanted to impress into his memory every detail of this country. The way light and shadow contoured the hills. The morning mist that clung to the forests. The sheen on the backs of horses under the damp sky. Images he would keep close and take out on lonely nights in foreign lands, far away.

They had shared many adventures, he and his brothers. The end of summer was their best season for hunting. They would ride into the hills with their dogs and rifles, tethering the horses at the opening to the bush track. It was better to be on foot when going after pigs in the dense undergrowth. He admired the courage of the sows, the way they hid their young. The cunning of the boars in their attempts to mislead the hunters. Wild hogs were huge and aggressive, and he'd seen more than one hunting dog maimed by their tusks.

Adolescent pigs were the preferred catch. Seldom did they take sows when they were suckling. He loved the howl of the dogs on first scent. The thrill of pursuit on first sighting. After the hunt they carried their quarry out of the forest. Sonny with a disembowelled pig on his shoulders. Tama swinging a brace of pheasant or duck. Hēmi behind them, carrying the guns.

Overhead, autumn rays streaked through the upper canopy, catching the red and gold of deciduous shrubs, as they made their way back to the horses. They shouted jibes and insults at each other, their feet slipping and sliding on the damp leaves, as they raised the rich aroma of the forest.

Apart from his brothers, Atarangi was his closest friend. A ponytail was a handy thing for a boy to grab when he was doing the chasing. If she got away and scaled a tree, she would taunt him from her perch in the branches. He could have climbed higher, but it was more fun giving her the advantage.

When childhood games turned to courtship no one was surprised. Atarangi, now nineteen, and Sonny, twenty-two, were still friends. She was a virgin, and he intended to keep it that way until he came home from the war, but there had been some memorable kisses.

At her house, her grandmother had come to the door.

'Wait here,' Nan said. 'I'll get her.'

He dropped his knapsack and waited for Ata to come out. When she did, he saw her eyes were red from crying.

'Kia ora,' Ata whispered and wiped her nose with the back of her hand.

'Taku tama muna,' he remembered saying, as he enfolded her into his arms. 'Don't come to the bus, sweetheart. Kiss me now and we'll have said our goodbyes.'

   Kayleen M. Hazlehurst

3

Manoeuvres and Mock Battles

1940

The 28th Māori Battalion was a unique military unit, formed in November 1939. Organised along tribal lines, it had four rifle companies with a fifth company providing logistical support. When the first Māori volunteers converged on the Palmerston North showgrounds in January they were accompanied by their tribal elders. The old people, who said they had come to assist with the training, could not understand why the army sent them away.

At Trentham, the best men were groomed for leadership as officers and NCOs. Their commanding officer, Major George Dittmer, was a Great War veteran and strict disciplinarian. Over three months, Dittmer and his senior staff hammered a thousand soldiers into shape for the infantry. At 6am on 2 May 1940, they shipped the first intake to Britain on board the troopship HMT *Aquitania* along with the Second Echelon of the New Zealand Expeditionary Force (NZEF).

Training for the Third Echelon began in mid-May. Six weeks later, a few hours after the yellow bus dropped the brothers off at the Auckland Railway Station, Hēmi, Sonny and Tama stepped onto the platform at Palmerston North. Hundreds of eager young men were with them, clutching their suitcases, guitars, ukuleles and accordions, waiting to be scooped up by army trucks and taken to camp.

The Wirima boys had seen some big sheds in their shearing days, but nothing like the asphalt-floored sleeping quarters that awaited them. Elongated huts, with straw-filled mattresses installed on wooden pallets, each housed a hundred men. Nearby, a corrugated-iron building fitted with sinks and cold showers served as the ablutions block. Functional, but not quite the comforts of home.

Tama was holding his pillow and two blankets, staring at his bed.

Sonny threw his things down on the bed beside him. 'You'll miss your old kapok mattress, hey?'

'She'll be prickly with that hay poking through.'

Sonny pummelled the lumpy sacking with his fists. 'If we press her down a bit it's not so bad.'

'Bet that straw has fleas.'

'Nah. The army wouldn't do that to us. If it's good enough for a horse—'

'I can eat it if I get hungry.'

Sonny laughed. 'You'll get used to it, little brother. Don't tell Mum. She won't be impressed.'

Bell tents were assigned to those who'd missed out on a place in the huts. Opposite the tent lines, with a drill ground in between, were the tents of the commissioned officers, sergeants and warrant officers. A modern hospital occupied the brick building at the entrance to the grounds, and beside the Everyman's Hut and YMCA Hall was a marquee, where they'd been told to gather the next day.

They headed for one of the dining halls. The cookhouse was serving hot food from steaming trays and they were about to do justice to their first army meal.

Morning brought the issuing of uniforms and equipment. Long queues of Māori feet being squashed into Pākehā boots. Next were the medical and dental examinations. The army was keen on teeth. If you had any that were crooked, rotten or missing, the scheduling of dental work was inevitable. The brothers had better teeth than most. 'All those vegetables you've eaten growing up,' the dentist said. 'Your mother should be proud.'

Nobody wanted to be poked and prodded, but they couldn't get out of it.

In the marquee, with canvas flaps for privacy, Sonny was measured (five foot, eight inches) and weighed (ten stone, two pounds), made to cough while the doctor put his hand where he shouldn't, and then he was left alone with a bottle.

 Kayleen M. Hazlehurst

'Hey! E hoa!' A voice came from the other side of the canvas.

'What?'

'Can you help me out?'

'How's that?'

A hand bearing another bottle came through a split in the partition. 'I can't do any more.'

'Aw right.' Sonny took the bottle and topped up the urine sample. He passed it back to the waiting hand. 'Will that do?'

'Yeah. Thanks.'

A boy about Tama's age came out of the cubicle and grinned at him. That's when he met Pere Tupe from the South Island and made a new friend.

The Wirimas were placed in A Company, which included the Ngā Puhi and Te Aupōuri tribes. Sonny had no idea he had so many relatives. These men had come from every corner of the Northland—Hokianga, Moerewa, Whangārei, Ahipara and the Far North Peninsula. In former days they'd been shearers and fishermen, freezing workers and bush cutters. Hard men with true hearts who had driven trucks, repaired roads, split posts, shorn sheep and dug ditches. Men of contradiction—full of fight but ready with a song—and it felt mighty good to be among them.

The brothers enjoyed camp life. The rigid discipline and fierce training, none of this bothered them. In the evenings they coached each other on the manoeuvres they'd been learning. On one tough route march their friends Heketoro Hamilton and Rae Te Kanawa were with them. During the lunch break they were stretched out under a tree, recumbent as cows, when Sonny started to dream.

> He is running in a forest. Twigs and branches whip at
> his ankles. Light cuts shafts through the lower branches
> and falls in patches on the forest floor. Far off he hears
> the barking of dogs. It isn't a memory. During the hunt
> he feels elated, but not now. This time he is scared.
> Around him the woodland grows dark, more alien.

> Now he is half-carrying someone. The ground
> beneath their feet is freckled with snow and ice, and
> the barking is getting closer. They are the ones being
> hunted.

Heke was shaking him. 'Sonny, wake up.'

He sat upright, blinking. 'What?'

'You were having a bad dream.'

'Sorry. Was I yelling?' He ran his hand over his damp face.

Rae crouched beside him. 'What did you see?'

'I don't know. It was like …'

'What, Sonny?' Heke asked. 'Was something attacking you?'

'Chasing me, I think … Dogs. They'd set their dogs on us.'

His friends exchanged glances.

'Doesn't sound good,' Heke said. 'What do you think, Rae?'

'I don't like it. Have you had dreams like this before, Sonny?'

'One or two.' He looked at them, wide-eyed. 'What does it mean?'

Rae shifted his weight. 'Take it as a warning. That's what I'd do—'

'Yeah. Keep your eyes open, brother,' agreed Heke. 'Be on the
lookout—'

'And if you hear dogs—'

'Run like hell!'

When Sonny first considered going to war he had never imagined
this. Running through a bitter forest being chased by dogs.

Padre Haumate, the battalion chaplain, and Mr Berger of the YMCA,
did their best to uphold camp morale by organising church services and
sports programmes. After weeks of shooting practice, and hand-to-hand
combat, the fighting spirits of the young soldiers were becoming hard to
contain. Rivalry was tolerated, so long as it was limited to scoreboards
and not inflicted upon noses.

Hēmi was the best hunter of the three brothers and it was no surprise
he proved to be a crack shot on the rifle range. Sonny could strip down
a weapon faster than anyone. Even the sergeant was impressed. When it

     Kayleen M. Hazlehurst

came to sneaking up on a duck with a knife there was no one better than Tama. You wouldn't want to be around this boy when he had a bayonet in his hand. Straw sacks hung in tatters after he'd had a go at them.

Close to the end of duck shooting season a mock battle was staged. Field operations were to be conducted in the hill country of the Bunnythorpe-Feilding district, eleven miles outside of Palmerston North. Two companies set off on foot and the rest went in lorries. The boys were on the road with A Company and up ahead were the East Coasters, C Company, stirring up the dust. Those Ngāti Porou were a bit too pleased with themselves for the Northerners' liking, and more than a little cheek was exchanged between them before the vehicles came back to collect them.

The platoon commander and section leaders went over the plans. Half the battalion would be sent on the skirmish and the other half would observe from the ridge. Runners delivered orders and returned with fresh news. Rifles firing blanks and the occasional burst of mortar fire provided convincing sound effects.

They had been put into the enemy party and Tama was looking downcast. This changed when Sonny pointed out it gave them an opportunity to practise their evasion skills.

'You know, Tama, like the wild boars.'

They were spread in a ragged line along the contour of the hill, waiting for the attack. Several others from Rotorua and the Bay of Plenty had joined their group—Te Arawa and Tūhoe men from B Company. As fighters, they seemed hardy enough. Six of them shared a depression in the ground, with a lip of earth providing a natural firing platform for their rifles. From here, they could survey the surrounding hills, including the command post on the other side of the small valley. The advance party was climbing the incline, making themselves easy targets.

Tama ejected another blank cartridge. 'Hey, Sonny, think I winged one!'

Sonny flicked back his head. 'There'll be plenty more.'

Tama directed his eyes towards the observation area. 'Hope Hēmi's got a good view.'

'He'll have his eyes on you, brother.'

Ari Tangiora, 'Darkie', was beside them. 'He'll be telling those army bosses to chuck grenades at us, hey?'

'No, he won't. Shut up.' Tama gave Darkie a shove.

'Hee, hee, hee.' Darkie's squeaky laugh set them off.

Rua Hale leaned over. 'I don't trust those Ngāti Porou. Bet they're planning to attack us from behind.'

Sonny squinted downhill. 'They're still coming, Rua. I keep shooting the buggers, but they won't die.'

'What happens when they get here?' Rua asked. 'Are they supposed to take us prisoner?'

'Well, they're not catching me … Ai!'

In a flanking manoeuvre, D Company came leaping over the hill from above, as C Company rushed them from below. Punches were thrown in the scuffle. It could have developed into a full-scale brawl, had a mortified runner not pointed at the enraged commander dancing on the ridge.

At length they agreed to join the others on the promise of jam-and-cheese sandwiches, and the assurance that the mock battle was a tie. After lunch everyone switched places so they all had a turn at the 'assault-on-the-hill' exercise. Then the entire battalion was driven back to camp singing.

—〰—

Sonny had a sick feeling in his stomach. They were about to be shipped overseas. From his bed, trying to ignore the smell of a hundred sweaty bodies huddled under grey blankets, he thought about Atarangi. He remembered the dresses she wore, her moist lips, the promises they'd made to each other. *I wonder what it will be like with twelve kids.* He hoped his mother wasn't too sad and his father was managing on the farm. If someone had hacked off his right arm, he couldn't have missed home more. *Mum will be sending us protection and Ata will be sending us love.* With so many men leaving, the upper atmosphere must be crammed with messages going back and forth.

He was restless and found himself questioning everything. Āpirana

Ngata, the elder statesman, had urged every Māori soldier to overcome tribal tensions by 'sinking their political differences in the face of a dangerous enemy'. Sonny had a problem with this, it made him feel disloyal. If soldiering for the Empire brought a better future for the Ngā Puhi, it didn't erase the wrongs of the past.

Their tūpuna would be with them, he'd been told. It was annoying how sure the elders were about everything. *They don't have a clue what the army is getting into. Neither do the poor sods around me. Right now, I could knock someone's block off.*

The dream came to him in bright flashes—sparks of memory struck from flint.

> They hide in the long grass, fascinated. Old Man Petrovic, a Yugoslav, is harvesting honey. The farmer waves his smoke canister above the hives, draws out trays of honeycomb. They must creep up and grab a pot without getting caught. The man shrugs and pretends not to notice them. It is their game.
>
> Sonny hears the familiar hum, sees the flash and glimmer, the dart of young hands. Tama is careless. He comes in too close, tips over the table and disturbs the swarm. The farmer swears at them and they run all the way home, terrified of being pursued by a line of angry bees.
>
> As they climb the last gate, Sonny turns. No bees. In the paddock, their father is on horseback moving sheep and he waves to them. Then the horse screams and rears. Api is flung to the ground with the flank of the horse coming down on him in a dull, bone-crushing thump.

There was to be a ceremonial parade through the town. The unit was to march in dress uniform, wearing their lemon-squeezer hats. The ladies of Palmerston North had arranged a luncheon gala 'in honour of their departing Māori Battalion'.

The whole town was done up like Christmas. Flags and garlands hung from lamp posts and a banner bidding them farewell was strung across Main Street. Residents came out in large numbers to see them off. The battalion marched along smartly to lots of clapping. Cries of 'Good luck!' and 'God speed!' Hats raised by medal-wearing veterans.

During the town hall speeches the Ladies' Auxiliary announced they had created a patriotic fund for their boys. Food parcels and small luxuries would follow the battalion. Towards the end of proceedings, a group of soldiers delighted everyone with a concert of guitars and songs.

Back at camp a message was waiting for the Wirima brothers. The lieutenant wanted a quiet word. He held open his office door and invited them to occupy the three chairs in front of his desk. 'I'm afraid I have some bad news from home,' the officer said with sad eyes, and Sonny felt his pulse quicken with guilt.

Sonny and Tama gazed over the blue waters and lamented. On 27 August 1940, they were sailing out of Wellington Harbour to join the rest of the Māori Battalion—who were now three months ahead of them, undergoing advanced training in Britain. The bad news delivered to them after the parade was that their father had been crushed by a falling horse. Api was laid low with broken bones and a bruised spine. The doctors weren't even certain he would walk again. As a result, the eldest son had been called home to manage the farm.

'Our armies need to be fed,' the officer reminded them, 'and the government expects our farmers to produce food.'

With their father out of action, Hēmi now fell into a reserved occupation. Days before Sonny and Tama left for Europe their best friend and protector, their tuakana, was discharged from the army and sent home.

 Kayleen M. Hazlehurst

4

On the Shoulders of Tiki

Snow covered everything. The country looked like those greeting cards white people gave to each other at this time of the year. Fir trees stood in stiff pyramids, their branches weighed down by white drifts. Icicles hung from gutters and the swirly glass windows of pubs were frosted over. No sunshine. No pōhutukawa trees in full bloom. No trips to the beach. It was hard to believe it was Christmas.

Between these grey days the sun made an effort to come out, melting snow into muddy puddles. The residents rushed about the streets, smiles on their ruddy faces, uttering words of good cheer to uniformed strangers. To compensate them for their first English winter, the battalion boys were granted permission to lay down their earth ovens.

Four hāngī were dug in December, breaking a number of regulations to gather cooking stones, butcher animals and prepare the hard ground. On their first breakfast in England they experienced food rationing. Servings of porridge were meagre and they got one rasher of bacon with their fried bread. Butter, sugar and other provisions were scarce, but their hāngī was enhanced from local sources and a generous contribution from a pig farmer. The idea of pork cooked to juice-dripping perfection between layers of vegetables was enough to lift anyone's spirits.

British curiosity had been aroused when the first wave of the Māori Battalion landed in Gourock, Scotland, six months earlier. People asked why these men had travelled thousands of miles to protect the 'Mother Country' against the Nazi threat. German propagandists mentioned the Māori Battalion in their broadcasts, calling them 'cannibals' and 'headhunters', but the British public appeared heartened. Newsreel scenes of colonial troops disembarking with the Māori singing their battalion song had stirred many to tears.

As the boys were moved about the country there was some time for sightseeing. London reminded Sonny of an old lady. One who exhibited the same contradictions of age and grace, wisdom and decay, as many of the matriarchs he had known. The great city had a body too long lived-in, with a heart too stubborn to give up. After seeing her famous monuments, they gravitated to the markets and alleys where the real people lived and struggled. It was here they saw a nation under siege—road signs removed, windows boarded up, streets obstructed with barbed wire and sandbags. A grid of underground train stations was being used as a massive air-raid shelter for London. Everywhere there were men and women dressed in khaki, navy and blue. This was an old girl with her armour on.

Previously in September, Luftwaffe attacks were at their height bringing fears of an incursion across the English Channel. The Māori Battalion had been sent to defensive positions on the south-east coast. From Kent the infantry was able to glimpse RAF Spitfires and Hurricanes in aerial combat and hear anti-aircraft batteries firing shells at the bombers. How they longed to get off their own shots at the enemy. Then, as the October weather closed in, the threat of an amphibious invasion diminished.

They were to be moved again, and the news spread throughout the barracks. Months of training in modern weaponry and battle tactics had left them itching for action. Their destination was kept secret but many speculated it would be North Africa. Their last days were spent preparing their gear, cleaning their living quarters, fighting off an influenza epidemic, and extending final handshakes to new friends.

Most of the country boys had never ventured beyond their own regions before joining the army. They had come overseas to 'have a look around', as much as they'd come to fight. Now, the discovery of quaint villages and historic sites was wearing thin. The longer they were made to wait, the harder it was to fend off their yearnings for home.

In the dormitory, Sonny overheard their evening prayers and sighing. Tender invocations from the lips of young men torn from the love of

     Kayleen M. Hazlehurst

their whānau. The words 'Goodnight Mum' caused him more pain than anything.

He and Tama were cleaning their boots, not saying much.

'How're you doing?' Sonny asked.

'Aw right …'

'You homesick?'

'S'ppose …'

'Come on, brother. We'll be heading out soon.'

Tama blinked. 'You know, I even miss the cows.'

'Āe. I'd be happy to see those old girls again down at the cowshed. Who'd have imagined?'

⁓

Sometimes their mother would let them join her on her foraging. Sonny recalled those magical days. 'Pick those leaves, Tama,' Miriama would say, pointing to a flowering shrub. 'If you bind a poultice of koromiko to a wound you can stay the flow of blood.' In the forest she might take Hēmi's hand and rub it on the rough bark of the kohekohe tree. 'You're the tallest, Hēmi. Help me harvest this bark. I'll make a tonic for your father's stomach.'

On evenings she visited the river to seek blessings for her plants. She channelled the cool, flowing liquid into jars, preferring to make her medicines from living water.

'Fetch me that stone, Sonny,' she'd say. 'Āe, the round one by the water. I'll use it to beat the juices from these leaves.' She would speak of some ailment, or some patient in need, then she would begin to sing.

I am a traveller.
I walk upon the earth with other travellers.
We stand upon the shoulders of Tiki.

The soil gives her fruits, the sea his kaimoana.
The winds of Tāwhiri-mātea rage over the land.
The oceans of Tangaroa encircle the earth.

After Christmas the Māori Battalion marched onto a train at Farnham and journeyed through the night in unheated carriages. The following morning, they filed onto the *Athlone Castle* at the bomb-ravaged Liverpool docks. They were on their way to Egypt. All they knew to expect were pyramids, camels and sand.

The *Athlone Castle* was barely four years old. In less than a fortnight the luxury liner had been refitted to carry troops. She was spacious and comfortable. Everyone agreed there was no finer vessel. They left England on 7 January 1941, and not an hour too soon. The Powers must have known this, because it wasn't long before the Germans were bombing the waterfront again.

They sailed down the coast, anchored off North Wales and continued across to Belfast. In five days a convoy of twenty-one ships was ready for transit. It was an overwhelming sight. The Atlantic Ocean was a great pond of menace and the size of their air and naval escort indicated the dangers of these waters.

Once they were beyond the reach of aerial strikes their escort was reduced to two destroyers. A direct path to North Africa through the Mediterranean was no longer possible. Instead, the battalion revisited the route they had come, travelling by safer passage via Sierra Leone, Cape Town, and then up the east coast of the African continent to the Suez Canal. In the confines of the ships the spectre of influenza was upon them again, but as the days warmed some immunity developed among the men.

Despite these setbacks, George Dittmer, now a Lieutenant-Colonel, was determined to keep his troops in peak fighting condition. Deck D of the *Athlone Castle* was allotted to the Māori Battalion. Lectures provided an occasional relief from weapons training, bayonet practice and endless circuits around the deck carrying heavy packs. Dittmer flung himself into this task like a man possessed, along with Regimental Sergeant Major Wood. Sonny and Tama landed in Egypt, calloused and blistered, swearing that they had marched all the way there on their feet.

They dropped anchor in Tewfik Harbour. From here the boys were shovelled onto trains and taken through the desert. Helwan Camp was a sprawling settlement of tents, temporary buildings and huts. It even had its own hospital. During the North African campaigns, the No.4 New Zealand General Hospital at Helwan had been treating the wounded and attending to the usual ills that troubled soldiers—scabies, pneumonia, measles, appendicitis, dysentery and gonorrhoea.

Egypt was a stark land. No sheiks on camels, though they could see the pyramids right enough. The houses were dull and rough, as if they'd been moulded from the pale earth by bare hands. It was a far cry from the dewy pastures of New Zealand or the damp hamlets of England. However, they were on dry land and at last the mail had arrived.

Sonny opened their father's letter.

9 November 1940

Dear Sonny and Tama,

Well, it's Sunday. Time for me to put down a few words. We can't growl about the weather. Sunshine for most of the past month. Hēmi and I will be putting out the boat today. I haven't been fishing since the accident so I'm looking forward to it.

I'm on my feet again. The doctor has me on crutches. I'm no darn use to anyone, but I hope this will change. I miss the farm work. Hēmi and two of the local boys brought in the sheep for docking, keeping Mum busy preparing lunches and afternoon teas. Sal had her first foal last week and a fine little mother she is making. The young one trots along beside her, as confident as any stallion. He makes us laugh.

We look forward to your letters. Mum will write soon.
Keep well, my sons. Our blessings go with you. Love, Dad.

Tama leaned over, breathing on Sonny's neck.

'How's Dad?'

'Getting better … Here, read it for y'self.'

'You got some letters from Atarangi?'

'Hey. Piss off!'

Tama walked his fingers along the bed towards the other letters. Sonny snatched them away. '*Raho! Purari paka!*'

12 November 1940

Dearest Sonny,

I can't tell you how much I miss you. I find myself wandering along the beach visiting our special places and pining for you like an old sheepdog. Your mum says the dogs know something is wrong. Kete and Turi haven't been themselves since you two left. They howl for you at night. It breaks our hearts to hear them. I have to admit, I've done some howling myself. Sorry, I mustn't weary you with my misery.

I hope you are enjoying army life and seeing lots of exciting things. Winifred thinks I need an interest, though I don't know what to do. She wants to join the women's air force but says she won't leave as long as Hēmi needs her. Those two are holding off getting married. It's so sad. Which leads me to your lovely proposal. The idea of having twelve kids is beginning to have its charms!

I take the dogs with me on my walks. We wait for you on our hill, with our ears down and our noses pointing out to the sea. Stay safe, darling.
Please come back to me. Aroha nui, Atarangi.
(Nan sends her love.)

  Kayleen M. Hazlehurst

$\sim$5$\sim$

Our Home is Like Yours

1941

Shimmering waves rose off the land. Helwan Camp was twenty miles south of Cairo, and behind the camp was the desert. They watched as the mesmerising heat melded horizon with sky, making it difficult to judge distance. The sand magnified the glare but when the red orb of the Egyptian sun went down, and the grey-pink skies darkened, the desert became bone-chilling cold.

They had been told this was the season for sandstorms. Tents took off unless they were anchored with sandbags. Eventually someone had the idea of tying guy ropes to stones and burying them. Grit got into everything, and it was a daily trial keeping rifles clean.

Near the camp was the famous waterway of the Nile—a magnificent, murky river that the army doctors described as 'the world's greatest sewer'. To drink its unboiled water could give a person gippy tummy.

They were standing around in the sun, staring towards the river.

Pere Tupe kicked a stone. 'So there'll be fish on the menu?'

'Are there fish in the Nile?' Rae asked.

'Yeah, there'll be fish,' Sonny responded, 'but nothing you'd want to eat.'

Tama darted up. 'And camels floating along with their feet in the air.'

'Get lost, Tama.'

Rae pursued this. 'Anything else worth eating around here?'

'Corn, dates, lizards.'

'Not unless you want to end up like one of those camels.'

Sonny scowled at his brother. 'It might be easier to pinch a chicken, Rae.'

'Maybe the old people will send us some barrels of pickled kai.' Pere shifted his gaze to the blurred horizon. 'I'd love some tī-tī.'

'What's tī-tī?' Tama asked.

'Mutton birds,' said Rae. 'South Island tucker.'

The Cairo markets looked like a good place to explore—a clutter of shops and tents, hawkers and conjurers, and swarms of begging children. You had to check your change after buying things. 'Rotten fish in the sunshine', that's how they described the city's sanitation. The medicos and padre counselled them against Cairo's beer, and told them to steer clear of the town's other nightly temptations. Those who partook often paid the price with a visit to the army hospital.

Sonny heeded this advice. Ata would not be impressed if he came home with some shameful disease, and his mother would kill him. One day a group of them found they were covered in itchy lumps. When they lined up at sick parade everyone laughed. It was bedbugs. That was bad enough.

Nobody liked battalion parades in the scorching sun, so it was a genuine diversion when a reinforcement of three hundred Kiwis marched into camp. The boys staged a spontaneous haka in their honour. Nothing felt better than to welcome your brothers.

Some of the First Echelon were coming back to Helwan. They had been serving in the Middle East for more than a year and wanted to kick up their heels. The Australians were there too, and when the Aussies and Kiwis got together they had to beat each other at everything.

In town the troops were running amok and the army was getting wise to their antics. Officers said they wanted to toughen the men to local conditions. All leave was suspended and in its place a programme of desert manoeuvres was introduced. This included more infantry tactics, a practice night attack that had its interesting moments, and a seven-mile tramp over the sands that was no fun at all. Foot inspections were followed by applications of methylated spirits to blisters and corns.

The Māori Battalion had been issued with forty more tommy guns and they were all keen to be back at the shooting range. These submachine guns were light to carry and could be fired from the hip while running. Every man standing wanted to have a go with them.

     Kayleen M. Hazlehurst

The army engineers, the 'sappers', had put on an exhibition to extend their education. One display showed the fastest way to disassemble a tent. Another advised how to clean up a camp before evacuating. Sonny and Tama already knew about gas masks, how to dig weapon pits, and how to camouflage a site with netting. Drifting past these, they stopped to look at a diagram of land mines and a model layout of telephone lines for field communications. At the far corner of the exhibition the sappers were assembling a folding bridge and two canvas and spruce canoes for river crossings. They strolled over to see how these were being put together.

'Those look useful, Tama. Reckon you could hide one of them boats in your pocket?'

'I reckon.'

Then there were the tank hunters. The wild ones haring it out on the Sahara. Armoured fighting vehicles were buggers to stop, but they had one weakness. They couldn't level their guns at close targets and were hopeless at shooting downhill. Assault parties of three and four were being taught how to stalk tanks like big game. If you got near enough you could climb on board and throw a grenade down the hatch. Things that large fell hard.

Everyone wanted to be a tank hunter and the desert proved the perfect place for practising on the couple of beat-up Cruisers at their disposal. Off they went, hunched over or crawling along the ground, sneaking up on the tanks like they were bloody great rhinos.

'Ha!' said Tama. 'Those Jerries don't know what they're in for!'

The haughtiness of some British officers sparked clashes with the rowdier colonials. Battleworn Australians had threatened one or two with their fists. Kiwi officers tried to smooth things over, though even they might be challenged to a fight if there'd been drinking. In the heat of the day, a group of Māori caused offence when they were caught lounging in the shade of a truck, shirts hanging out and buttons undone. A passing officer, who objected to their slovenly appearance, complained to his superior that the soldiers had shown no inclination to stand and salute.

'Try waving at them,' General Freyberg cheerfully replied. 'That usually works.'

This gentle rebuke was typical of the Kiwi commander's manner. Word of this filtered through the camp, enhancing the popularity of the New Zealand general and Great War veteran. It had not escaped the notice of the foreign brass that Kiwis differed from the professional military. They were civilian soldiers, under the authority of their own commanders who answered to the New Zealand Prime Minister.

But the days of unruly behaviour were coming to an end.

That Sunday, Reverend Isaac Kapea was conducting Holy Communion for the camp, with his white vestments fluttering in the breeze. Most of the battalion boys attended the service, their voices sustaining rich harmonies during their favourite hymns of 'Piko nei te Matenga' and 'Au, e Ihu Tirohia'. They enjoyed the singing, but Sonny sensed in them a mixture of excitement and foreboding. Rumours were circulating. This might be their last peaceful interlude for a while.

The directive came down the next day. The New Zealand Division was to be sent back to the European war. In a special order, General Bernard Freyberg cautioned the troops not to underestimate the difficulties they would face. 'The German soldier is a brave fighter,' the general told them. 'Do not be caught unprepared.'

Freyberg's message carried a warning and a promise. There would be hardships and long marches. They would be attacked from the ground and bombarded from the air.

At last they were to meet the enemy.

—⁓—

Seven hundred and thirty men of the Māori Battalion arrived at Alexandria on 25 March 1941 to board the troopship *Cameronia* bound for Greece. They disembarked at the port of Piraeus on the 27th, near the three-domed church of St Nicholas. Their first march in full battledress was a nine-mile stretch to the staging camp on the pine-covered slopes of Mount Hymettus. Athens was a city like no other. Grey stone buildings, red tile roofs with avenues of trees and flowering gardens. On the skyline, Sonny recognised the dominating ruins of an ancient temple, the Parthenon. He'd seen a photograph of it at home in his father's well-thumbed encyclopaedia.

     Kayleen M. Hazlehurst

Cheering civilians lined the streets. People crowded doorways shouting 'Welcome! Welcome!' and 'Brávo! Brávo!' Greek men clutched each other and sang songs. Girls threw flowers in their path or gave soldiers a kiss. Sonny's cheeks warmed and most of his brothers had huge grins on their faces. What was a man to do, other than straighten his shoulders? For the rest of the march his pack felt lighter and his feet less sore.

That evening many went AWOL. It seemed everyone in Athens wanted to give the Kiwis a meal and a drink. When they stepped, bleary-eyed, from their tents in the morning they were met with the aroma of growing things. Mint, sage and the tang of pine trees. Once more they had foreign coins in their pockets and the leave time to explore a new city with its cafés and taverns, its pastry shops filled with honey cakes, its barrow merchants selling oranges and mandarins.

When they first descended the gangplank at Piraeus they had known little about the situation in Greece. Three hundred miles to the north, a friend of Hitler's was battering at the borders. At the battlefront, poorly armed Greek and Yugoslav soldiers were attempting to hold back Mussolini's Italians. No wonder the locals thought their saviours had come.

Now, the New Zealand Army was being moved to a defensive position called the Aliakmon Line. As the dilapidated rail coaches rumbled northwards they felt fire rise in their veins.

30 March 1941

Dear Mum, Dad and Hēmi,

Your letters were waiting for us in Egypt. After eight weeks at sea, the mail caused quite a stir. We had letters as far back as November. They camped us outside of Cairo. The desert wasn't so bad. Light sandy soil in some places with a skinny growth of brush and grass. With more water I reckon they could cultivate here. They gave us some desert training and one day they took us to see the pyramids. Thousands of years ago people around here got busy building things.

This week they sent us to Greece and the people of Athens gave us a fine welcome. It was embarrassing. Apparently we're heroes, the whole ruddy lot of us. Athens is a city of many old buildings. I've started collecting legends about Greek gods and heroes, Mum. So many of these stories are like ours.

Dad, we got a good look at the farmland as we travelled by rail through Greece. The farming methods are a bit primitive. They use bullock carts and donkeys for transport and there are few trucks or tractors here. Apart from that, the countryside reminds us of home with their sheep and goats, and their fruit trees and crops.

People have been kind, giving us bread and fruit. Most are poor villagers and farmers who are frightened by this war. We feel sorry for them. I hope this means us boys can make a difference and we won't be chasing our tails.

Dad, the best news was hearing you were on your feet again and going fishing with Hēmi. I could do with a feed of hāpuka myself. Eat one for me! Love to all, Sonny.

The fertile valleys of Greece in spring provided a spectacular contrast to North Africa. Wild flowers flourished between the orchards and vineyards, and olive trees grew in the coarser soil of the hills. The residents were curious. Whenever the train stopped in a village, tiny Greek women patted them like sons and wanted to know where they'd come from. Fathers swallowed hard as they reached to shake their hands. Girls in colourful dresses stood behind, watching them with shy, brown eyes. Their flickering smiles showed the boys how delighted they were that the soldiers were here.

The scarcity of fighting-age men became clear the further north they went. It seemed every able-bodied male had been sent to Albania. Sonny and Tama stood by the windows with the rest of A Company as the train rolled over the land. Scratching in the lonely earth were old men, and women with young children, in need of their protection. Scenes that reminded them of their own womenfolk toiling in the kūmara patches at home.

Every man present would have been thinking of the dear ones they'd left behind. It was enough to rip out a man's heart.

Rite tonu tō mātou whare ki tō koutou.
Our home is like yours.

     Kayleen M. Hazlehurst

~6~

Mount Olympus

Sonny cast around for a place to lay down his gear. He called Tama to a spot he found near the back wall. They had arrived at the coastal town of Katerini, north of Mount Olympus, where they were billeted in an empty hall. The unit's vehicles and ambulances were expected the following day.

Earlier he had asked around to get his bearings and studied the map he'd bought in Athens. On the eastern coastline of Greece, the Aegean Sea curved around to the city of Salonika. North-west was the Albanian border from where the Greek Army was in retreat. Civilian refugees were fleeing south. Villagers who had endured the bombings but were refusing to bow their heads to the coming invaders.

Sonny pulled out the mess tins and handed one to his brother. 'Get in line. I'll join you in a minute.'

A ragged group of Greek soldiers came in looking for a meal and were put at the head of the queue. They brought news from the front. Thousands of their troops had surrendered or were cut off in the north. Those men who improvised in getting away had to cover more than a hundred miles on foot—or they died trying, poor devils. They were starved and exhausted, with feet bandaged from frostbite. As they shuffled up for the food, Sonny smelled on them the odour of defeat.

In the ranks there was speculation about what was in store for the Allies. Their commanders had wanted to create a line of defence from the Aegean Sea to Mount Olympus. Three divisions of British, Australian and New Zealand troops were supposed to make a composite force in defence of Greece. When the British 1st Armoured Brigade didn't turn up due to vehicle breakdowns, the Anzacs regrouped.

They spent the first evening at Katerini composing letters home. Sonny licked the lead of his pencil.

31 March 1941

Dearest Ata,

We received the Christmas parcel you and Nan sent. Thank you for the Zig-Zag paper and pouch of tobacco. The tinned ham and plum jam were enjoyed, and the socks will come in handy. I bet you made those delicious biscuits, Ata. Thanks also for the jerkin you knitted. I will wear it under my uniform in the cold weather.

Can I join you on your hill? I loved hearing about Kete and Turi and can imagine the three of you sitting with your noses pointed out to sea. If I didn't know you were waiting for me, I think I would go stark raving.

The army stationed us near Cairo, and the trip from the docks to camp was through a desert. The train was packed with people, including their chickens and dogs, and their belongings and children. All cackling or arguing with each other. A fair few of our blokes got into trouble in the town. There was the usual mixture of Aussies, Kiwis, Tommies and South Africans on leave. They're a wild bunch when they get drinking and playing Two-up or Crown-and-Anchor. I bet the locals were browned off with the broken windows and smashed bars around the place.

I didn't realise how much I missed colours until we moved into Greece. Rolling paddocks. Fields of wheat and barley. Miles of purple and yellow flowers. I see your face everywhere, darling. I look, and you are there. You're as near to me as if you were down the road. Winifred was right. Find yourself something to do. Maybe an office job or teaching. You're good with children. I don't want you sitting alone feeling sad. Thanks for the photograph of you with your old kōtuku on the rocks. I will carry it close to my heart. Ko Tāwera te whetū marama ō te ata. Whakarite tonu tāku huia kaimanawa.

Love, Sonny.

After finishing with words from a love song—*Venus is the bright star of morning. No less beautiful is the jewel of my heart*—Sonny tucked the envelope into his jacket.

In the first week of April 1941 the invasion of Yugoslavia and Greece began. News came by radio that Hitler's army had broken through at the Bulgarian border. In three days, Salonika had fallen. Athens would be next, and the route to this prize was through the mountains.

Five days earlier, the New Zealand 5th Infantry Brigade had been moved to the northern foothills of Mount Olympus. The Kiwis were to hold the entrance to the Olympus Pass. They were told this would enable the Anzacs holding positions further north to withdraw to a new defensive position at Thermopylae, a hundred miles south.

The Kiwis from their side of the mountain, the 22nd, 23rd and 28th Battalions, had a good view of the fourteen miles of road leading back to Katerini. At their backs were the slopes and peaks of Mount Olympus, and to their left was the canyon of the Mavroneri River. This gorge began at the mill town of Skotina, winding for four miles towards the Katerini Plain. Skotina and its timber mill were accessible by a metal road linking it with the Pass.

To protect the left flank of the Māori Battalion, one unit of D Company was stationed near Skotina. The rest were in the Mavroneri Gorge. Everything they needed had to be carried in—stores, weapons, ammunition and full fighting kits. The cold was biting and the flysheets of tents were all they had for shelter. The rifle companies had not been trained for the high winds, or the sleet and snow of the mountains. *How is this going to work?*

Stories were circulating. Refugees from the north brought accounts of entire villages being abandoned. These were ordinary people fleeing for their lives. The residents of Skotina had been gathering their animals and leaving. But the mill owner, a German, seemed determined to stay. One day a scout heard cries down by the river. The mill owner had taken a stick to a hysterical woman, either his wife or daughter, who wanted to run away with the rest. Nobody intervened, making Sonny feel ashamed. If it had been him, he would have gone and told that man to quit beating the poor woman.

Sonny tried to picture this happening at home, but he couldn't. There was little in this landscape that was familiar to him. It was mountainous, broken territory, interlaced with gullies and streams. Oak, beech and broad-leafed plane trees grew in spaces between the ridges. At some point the lower slopes had been deforested and were covered in belts of oleander and chasteberry trees, or with the thick regrowth of thorn bushes, brambles and prickly pear.

Witi Parry said the area reminded him of Urewera country—if you replaced the town of Skotina with Ruatāhuna, and the judas trees with rātā. In Sonny's mind, Witi was grasping at straws. *Replace what you want with what. This will never be Ngā Puhi country.*

Sonny wiped his face and glared at the mountain, cursing that he'd ever joined the army. But why was he looking for reminders of home when he had his memories of growing up in Rangitakō? Did he not have the images of rolling hills and glistening forests as they drove down the country on the old yellow bus? Treasures he could pull out whenever he wanted. Like the snapshot in his breast pocket of Atarangi with her white heron. These were real gold.

Headquarters needed more information about the terrain so the Wirima brothers, with their bush experience, were sent to act as scouts. They followed the road to the other side of the Mavroneri Gorge and headed into the scrub. Below them they saw the Katerini Plain stretching out to the north-west. This site provided a good amount of vegetation for cover and was an excellent lookout. Unfortunately, it was also an ideal position for the Jerries to counter-fire on the Allies.

'Hey, Tama. Look at that.' Sonny pointed as a bronze eagle sailed into view.

'Nice.'

They watched the bird circle on its great wings above the peak.

'Where do they nest?' Tama asked, after a minute.

'On rock ledges. They build them with sticks and things.'

'Do you remember hawks, Sonny?'

'Yeah. Hawks were your favourite birds.'

'I loved seeing them circle around for rabbits. I've even seen them go for pūkeko. If I die, I'll come back as a hawk or an eagle. I will fly higher and higher until I touch heaven!'

'You're not going to die, Tama.'

     Kayleen M. Hazlehurst

Tama shrugged. 'If you could change into a different form, what would you be?'

'Something that could run far away from this place … Maybe a deer.'

'They shoot deer, and you still have to cross two oceans.'

'When I reach the sea, I will change into a whale and swim all the way home. How's that?'

'Good, Sonny! What kind of whale?'

'A humpback. I'll flick my tail and make the waves lash against the warships. When I reach New Zealand, I will turn back into a man.'

'Yeah. Hey, what animal would those Nazis be?'

'Mongrels … No, they would be centaurs.'

'What are those?'

'Half-man, half-horse creatures.'

Tama gaped at him. 'How do you know?'

'At our last train stop I saw two old people picking something near the track and I went to see what it was. The man spoke English, and I told him we had a similar plant called pūhā. We were very fond of it. He seemed interested and we shared stories.'

'Where was I when this was happening?'

'I don't know, Tama. Talking with girls, probably.'

A tender expression crossed Tama's face. 'Greek girls are so pretty.'

Sonny shook his head. 'The old man said centaurs were a warlike tribe who wandered about ancient Greece raping and killing. They were beasts hated by both men and gods.'

'Hated by both men and gods!' Tama shuddered. 'No Māori would want to be hated that bad. What do you think Mum would do if she ran into one of those horse-men?'

Sonny didn't answer. With her knowledge of mākutu, he knew exactly what their mother would do, but he didn't want Tama having thoughts of the dark arts.

'Centaurs are extinct now, Tama. Like the moa.'

'Nazis like wandering about killing things. I feel sorry for the horse part.'

'What?'

'It's not the horse's fault those whatchamacallits are so vicious.'

'No. It's not the horse's fault.'

'They must be very bad men.'

'Or have very bad leaders.'

'What did you call them again?'

'Centaurs.'

'Yeah, centaurs. Half-man, half-horse creatures. Good one, Sonny!'

—∿—

They could hear the thundering hooves of the approaching troops.

Smoke billowed from the burning oil fires and hung in murky clouds over Salonika. Refugees streamed south through the mountain pass. There was suspicion that a number of the Yugoslav and Greek soldiers were actually German spies.

'Any German can steal the uniform of some poor blighter he's killed,' Sonny told Tama.

They had all assembled at the Olympus Pass—the 28th Māori Battalion on the left, the 23rd NZ Battalion on the right, and the 22nd astride the road higher up—completing the New Zealand line. Mortar crews and machine-gunners from 27th (MG) Battalion straddled the spurs above them. Near the road, headquarters had pitched a tent to organise field operations, ammunition transport and stretcher-bearers. Close by HQ, the medical unit had established a dressing station.

The whole Māori Battalion was here, spread across a three-mile line. A and B Companies had dug in on the slopes parallel to the Mavroneri River. D Company was perched further west. On the western end of the ridge, C Company was positioned in reserve. From here the Ngāti Porou could come down to assist the other three companies when needed.

For sixteen months the battalion had been together, and this was their first confrontation with the enemy. All Sonny's mates were with him. He felt their presence and was sure they felt his. It was a powerful solidarity, knowing you would die for your brothers.

To prepare for the coming attack, Colonel Dittmer had hired Greeks to help the Kiwis carry in supplies. He turned up with half a dozen pack

Kayleen M. Hazlehurst

mules loaded with wire and ammunition. Concertina and barbed wire were run around their positions, weapons pits were dug, and telephone lines strung along the mountain tracks. After someone sabotaged their lines of communication a checkpoint was set up. Enemy infiltration had begun. On the paths, Māori code words were used to challenge strangers.

Sonny and Tama were assigned to reconnaissance duties. They were to clear the tracks and report back to HQ on the size and movements of the German formations. They did more than just bush cutting. By hacking low corridors, they made rabbit passages that might go unnoticed. Entry points were paced out and they practised using these secret routes after dark.

It was a comfort to know Australian and New Zealand units had been posted north of them. Now, with the Greek East Macedonian Army in disarray, the Anzacs were in danger of being engulfed. The Australians, along with the 4th and 6th Brigades of the New Zealand Division, were pulling back through the Olympus Pass. As the forward units hoofed it past them, the 5th Brigade found itself holding the front line alone.

The German Army would be storming through here into Greece. Sonny couldn't say it out loud, but he was sure everyone around him was feeling it—a thrill close to sheer terror, knowing nothing stood between them and the enemy.

The battalion knew what was expected of them even before their commander, Brigadier James Hargest, sent the order to hold the mountain pass 'to the last man and the last round'.

Padre Kapea held the dawn prayers.

All eyes were on the road. At first light on April 15 a thick black line materialised. A column of German tanks, armoured vehicles, troop carriers and motorcyclists could be seen stretching all the way back to Katerini.

On the Anzac side, eight field guns of the 5th Field Regiment had been winched on top of Petras Hill and covered with camouflage netting. A mortar platoon, some Vickers machine-gunners and Bren gunners, and an anti-tank battery were placed between the artillery on the hill and the

Māori infantry in the gully. Dispersed among the Māori riflemen were a few tommy guns, three-inch mortars and Brens.

'They'll never know we're here, Sonny,' Tama said.

'We will let them know soon enough.'

The big guns were at their backs. With a moment's notice, artillery fire could be turned in defence of the three fronts in the Mavroneri Gorge.

By mid-morning the Germans halted at the New Zealand line.

Kayleen M. Hazlehurst

First Encounter

Germans launched volleys of heavy-calibre artillery and mortar fire. Shells landed near HQ, setting an ammunition truck ablaze and injuring two men. Anzac field guns returned fire, scattering the enemy convoy. The battalion boys swore and crouched when they saw the flash-flash of enemy artillery. Then they heard the answering roar of the guns from Petras Hill.

Sonny scanned the opposite slope of the gully, staring red-eyed through the sights of his gun. Māori riflemen were peppered throughout the lower banks, their trenches well hidden by scrub and trees. Behind them were the Bren gun and mortar pits, with two men in each. All the men were restless, ready for a scrap.

He hated all this hiding and messing around. 'If those buggers had any guts, we'd have it out right here in the gully.'

Tama, Heke and Rae were on his right. Their mates, Rua, Pere and Darkie, occupied a trench further to his left. Sonny's helmet was hot and uncomfortable, and he wished he wasn't hemmed in by this earth and shrubbery. Maybe he could climb out of the trench and get a better angle.

'Come on, have a go,' he breathed through his teeth. 'Arā ka pēnei, tō kōuma āpōpō ka iri ki te pōhutukawa! And so it will be, that tomorrow your breastplate will hang from the pōhutukawa!'

'They're on the move,' Tama whispered.

Sounds were coming from the other side. German soldiers were scuttling down the slope and stalking through the trees.

Sonny put a finger to his lips. These Germans and Austrians might be skilled alpine fighters, but they were not stealthy enough to escape the sharp eyes of Māori pig hunters. He lifted his chin to Heke and Rae and they became alert. He caught Darkie's attention. Sonny pointed two fingers at his eyes and flicked out his wrist towards the opposite bank. His signals were acknowledged and passed on to the others. Colonel Dittmer had counselled them not to give away their positions, not to waste bullets unless they were certain of getting a good shot. They waited, remaining still.

The enemy's first charge was with automatic weapons against A Company. The Northlanders drove them back, forcing the attackers to take cover among the trees.

The noise was deafening—the crack of rifles, the rattle of Vickers and Brens, the thump of mortars. Sonny wedged his shoulder into the corner of the pit to steady his rifle and wasted nothing. Tama, Heke and Rae, sharp beside him, issued their own fury. United, they were a snarling beast of retribution. In fifteen minutes it was all over, and the surviving enemy fighters had melted back into the woods.

A twig snapped and Sonny whipped around to see young Hari, the platoon runner, wriggling towards them through the bushes. He was crawling at the speed of a snake with its tail on fire. Hari had come bearing a message. Cook's canteen had been hit and the quartermaster was sending out an invitation. Tins of condensed milk and bully beef were punctured and the contents needed to be eaten. Would they please oblige when they had a minute to get away?

It was an evening of strange bird calls and wavering shadows. Ngā Puhi fingers kept close to Ngā Puhi triggers. The river was the obvious place to cross, but patrols and listening posts as far west as D Company had produced no worrying signs. There was only one incident. Captain Harding Leaf, a veteran of Gallipoli known for his ingenuity, made his men string petrol cans along a wire as a precaution while they slept. That night the cans danced and rattled but the spies were chased off.

Morning brought low cloud and drizzle. Ideal conditions for concealment. Trees etched their skeletal branches against shrouding veils of mist. When the cloud lifted, they saw a hundred armoured vehicles facing them. German tanks and guns were stretched along the hill that Sonny and Tama had scouted three days ago. The invaders were not there to admire the eagles.

 Kayleen M. Hazlehurst

Enemy artillery blazed away at the ridge. The New Zealand Regiment's twenty-five-pounders hammered back in reply, knocking out five German tanks in the first round. A spotter plane droned overhead looking for targets, forcing the platoons to move in a hurry. Later, they were strafed by Stukas. These dive bombers with their screaming wings liked making a nuisance of themselves around mealtimes. They were not terribly good shots. One New Zealander was killed, but there was a lot of swearing and plunging head first into trenches when the men were most hungry.

While keeping one eye cocked skywards, the 28th concentrated on the gully, sparring with enemy soldiers as they flitted from tree to tree. An irritated B Company opened fire with rifles and Brens. C Company and the mortar and machine-gun sections added their support. By mid-afternoon, A Company had taken up the offensive again.

Bullets cracked and chipped nearby trees. Their uniforms were soaked with sweat and damp from the previous night's snow flurries. They'd had no decent rest for a week, no time to wash or shave.

Sonny and his mates hugged the earth as shells whizzed and exploded around them, leaving an acrid haze. In a strange way, listening to his heart pounding, he was enjoying this mayhem. It was an intoxicating soup of elation and fear. With all the flying shrapnel, they needed to keep their heads low. Helmets were poor defence against those shards of metal, but this didn't stop them from picking off targets when they could.

By the afternoon German mortar fire had become persistent, but they couldn't locate its origin. Someone sent up a distress signal. Green-red-green flares. The artillery came to their aid and a mortar nest five hundred yards across the river was hit.

All went quiet.

They were speaking in low tones as they climbed from the trenches for a smoke. There was exhilaration mixed with exhaustion in his friends' faces. He glanced at the next dugout and Darkie grinned back, giving him the thumbs-up. All of them over there were okay.

'I'll have a look around,' Sonny told Heke. 'Make sure those Jerries aren't coming back. You want to come with me, Tama?'

'Yeah. I'll be glad to get out of this hole.'

The brothers traced a quick route along the riverbank, looking for signs of activity. There were the usual camp noises, but no sounds coming from the hill on the other side. The assault force had withdrawn for the night.

After passing the camps, they came to a bend in the river. Here, a pool had formed, and the late sun was warming the surrounding rocks.

'God, that looks tempting,' Tama said.

Sonny regarded his brother with a smile. Tama was just a kid. Too young to be involved in a war. 'It'll be blasted cold.'

'I haven't had a wash for days.'

'Go on,' Sonny said, taking out a packet of Player's. 'I'll keep watch.'

While the boy stripped off, Sonny sat on a rock and rested his rifle across his knees.

Tama jumped into the pool, coming up again, and throwing his head back in a shower of spray. He let out a hoot. 'It's good, Sonny! Wanna come in?'

'Nah. Keep the noise down, eh?' Enemy scouts had been sighted on the paths around Skotina.

Waves rippled across the surface until they touched the rock edge. They'd swum in more than enough pools and creeks as kids. What he would give to amble along that dusty road and pat the horses as they came to the fence. To see the dogs stop in their tracks, then rush forward with their joyous barking.

Dad would come out of the cowshed to see what the commotion was about, wiping his hands on that rag he carried in his back pocket. 'They're home, Mother!' he'd shout.

Miriama would be at the gate observing their manner, deciding whether her boys were in good form.

Sonny wondered how Hēmi was doing, stuck at home, missing out on the war. He could neither pity nor envy him. *Someone has to look after things.* He observed the sun catching the water. *A myriad of fleeting souls.* That's

Kayleen M. Hazlehurst

what their mother called those specks of light. Perhaps they were. *There'll be a fair few spirits taking flight around here.*

'Hey, Sonny, look!' Tama took a breath and dived under to collect a handful of pebbles and weeds. Showing off like he used to.

'Okay, mate. You'd better get out now. Don't you want your dinner?'

Tama had barely got out of the pool when he went down.

Sonny heard the shot and pivoted to catch a glimpse of a figure on the higher track.

'Bastard!' Sonny fired at the hill and the man darted away. A second time he fired, but the sniper had gone.

Tama was clutching his right thigh. 'Shit, Sonny!'

'Sorry, little brother. I should have been watching.'

Sonny pulled away Tama's hand. A bullet had gouged a narrow channel through the flesh and the gash was bleeding. He removed his field dressings from his greatcoat pocket and tore open a pack with his teeth. 'This will sting,' he said, sprinkling sulfa powder on the wound.

'Aargh!'

'Here, press on the patch.' Sonny wound the bandage around the gauze. 'It's just a scratch, Tama. Pretend a horse bit your leg.'

'Bloody big horse.' Tama pulled on his trousers and jacket with Sonny's help.

'Let's get you back to camp. The medics will fix you up.'

'Ouch! Ouch!' Tama limped along with his arm over Sonny's shoulder. 'Don't tell Mum. She'll think I'm not a proper warrior.'

'Silly bugger. Serves you right for taking off your clothes.'

They could have been shot, there and then, but at least they'd have died laughing.

~8~

An Urchin Moon

An urchin moon cast a milky light along the river as it threaded its way through the gully. Sonny woke at four. Rae and Tama were curled up in the mud, sleeping. Heke was out on patrol.

Sonny heard a rustle in the bushes. 'Here we go.' But it was only a hungry rat. Heke slipped into the trench, quiet as a leaf, and Sonny raised his chin to him in a question.

'Nothing,' Heke said, putting aside his gun to light a cigarette. Holding it low.

Sonny kicked at a boot. 'Hey, wake up.'

Tama groaned. 'What?'

'It's our turn to patrol.'

The boy held down his lower eyelids, looking up at him like a dog begrudging a bone.

'Don't look at me like that.'

'Sorry.' Tama shook himself and started to stand.

Sonny forced him back into the pit. 'Idiot. Do you want your head shot off?' He handed his brother the last army biscuit he'd been saving. 'Here.'

'Thanks.' Tama crouched to eat the biscuit and took a swig from his water bottle.

'We'll go through the upper tracks.'

'Isn't it our turn to do the river?'

'Somebody else can do it. How's the leg?'

'Doesn't hurt.'

He checked the riverbank. 'Okay. Let's get going.'

They crawled out of the trench and through the bushes until they reached the trees. Hunched over their rifles, they trotted along the path towards the upper tracks.

Action began in the grey light of morning, with enemy probes intensifying during the day. Unable to uproot the Ngā Puhi, the Germans moved westwards where they met the Tūhoe and Te Arawa in the gorge. Thwarted by Māori defences, the enemy dispersed further west.

Sonny and Tama peered over the ledge to survey the length of the gully. They heard the echo of rifle shots being answered by the *rip-rip* of machine guns. Through his field glasses, Sonny scanned for enemy movement among the trees on the other side. It had been hours since they'd eaten and he felt his ribcage scraping the earth and his throat burning for water. Dread gripped his organs and he tried to feed off its energy.

In olden times, a rare lizard crossing the path of a warrior was interpreted as a bad omen. But there were green lizards all over these mountains. Earlier, a snake had slithered past Sonny's nose. The reptile monitored him with its jewelled eyes before taking off. He focused on the cascading music of a waterfall. If they moved upstream, they could get some fresh water. He tried not to let thirst distract him.

German soldiers were stealing along the riverbed, aligning themselves with the position of D Company on the ridge.

'We have to warn the Ngāti Porou, Tama. Can you turn around?'

Tama got out his knife to cut a detour through the undergrowth. Once out, they ran along the path where they encountered Corporal Jack Tainui, D Company's best scout. Jack was the one to tell when it came to the enemy massing for an attack.

Jack thanked them for the information, saying, 'Can you boys keep watch for us while we deal with this lot?'

'Sure, we can do that.'

'Cook's tent is over there. You fellas get yourselves some kai before you leave.' Jack then took his rifle and headed off to take a sighting.

After replenishing their packs with food and water, they plunged back into the bush. They wanted to return to the upper tracks where they could appraise the battalion's left flank. Here, they were closest to D Company, but cut off from their own unit.

—〰—

Death was stalking these mountains. The canyon rang with the sound of rushing water and the roar of German soldiers breaching the river in lines, ten deep. Hundreds of them hurled themselves at D Company's tommy guns, mortars, rifles, grenades and solitary Bren gun. The Māori had the advantage of higher ground, but their number was small. The enemy seemed to have men to spare and their officers were ordering them to take the battalion head-on.

The forest became alive with Germans. They scaled banks, threw grenades, cut wires and climbed trees to get better shots. They came at D Company wave after wave, putting 16 Platoon under the fiercest assault. Eleven men led by Corporal Harry Taituha were taking the brunt of the attack.

Bluish smoke dulled the air. Sonny and Tama had been asked to keep watch. With the battle unfolding at such a chaotic speed, what else could they do? They stared at the blurred shapes, their faces smeared with tears. A company of ghosts, as figures faded and noise grew dim.

The words of 'He Ino Tuku' rose like a crystal spring of hope, as they knelt to recite the battalion prayer for their friends.

> Almighty God with whom do live the spirits of just men made perfect after they are delivered from their earthly prisons: we humbly commend the souls of these Thy servants of the 28th NZ Māori Battalion into Thy hands, as into the hands of a faithful Creator and most merciful Saviour that they may in the end be brought to Life Everlasting through the Merits of Jesus Christ, Thine Only Son, Our Lord.

Their brothers had held their ground until they'd run out of bullets, until barrels sizzled and exploded, and until German jackboots overran the gun pits. Sonny prayed that the mothers of these men would one day know how bravely their sons had died.

—⌇—

Tama was shivering and had his legs drawn up to his stomach.

Sonny grasped his arm. 'What's wrong, Tama?'

'I don't feel so good. Think it's my leg …'

'Give me a look.'

They lowered the side of his trousers to the bandage on his thigh. The bullet wound was full of yellow pus, oozing and putrid.

'My ankle hurts.'

'Same leg?'

'Yeah. I ran into a thorn bush when we were scouting and saw the eagle.'

'That was days ago, Tama. Why didn't you tell me?'

Sonny pulled down the sock and lifted the trouser leg. Red dots ran along the skin from Tama's ankle to his calf. The area surrounding the thorn puncture had turned a bluish-green.

'Shit!' Sonny recognised it at once. *Blood poisoning.*

Tama turned away his head to throw up. He wiped his mouth. 'Sorry.'

Sonny touched Tama's forehead. 'You feel hot.'

'Can you find me that medic now, Sonny?'

'I'll get help once things go quiet.'

'I wish Mum was here with her herbs.'

'I wish she was too. She'd soon sort you out.'

The trees gave them some cover, but against the cliff Sonny saw an overhang of rock partially screened by bushes.

'Tell you what. I'll cut some scrub and make us a hut under that ledge. We'll be as good as gold.'

He hacked off some branches, weaving them into the shrubs in front. Taking their two tent sheets, he laid one over a bed of brushwood, and wove the other through the sticks to form a roof.

'It's only a burrow but should keep us dry for the night.'

'Don't leave me, Sonny.'

Who Disturbs the Kūkupa?

'Not on your life. I'll keep you warm.'

He pulled out a slender book from his jacket. It was a collection of prayers Padre Kapea had given him in Egypt when he'd shown interest in religious matters. 'You can call on Him,' the padre had promised as he pressed the book into Sonny's hand. 'God will come to your aid.'

'Shall I read a prayer for us?'

Tama turned away his head. 'Say one for Mum.'

Something twisted inside Sonny's gut. Tama knew he was dying.

Colonel Dittmer sent orders for the Kiwis to fall back. They were to join the Australians at the Thermopylae Line. The engineers had been told to destroy bridges and sections of the Olympus Pass road. The 5th Brigade were to have moved out before the sappers undertook their demolition orders at about zero hours.

To confuse a listening enemy, Lieutenant Bennett gave radio instructions in Māori and his messages were passed from man to man. One third of Major Dyer's D Company was assigned to hauling gear up to the road. The rest of the Māori Battalion were to hold off the hordes in the gully.

Companies peeled away like flesh from an onion. The machine-gunners and mortar crew of the 5th Brigade set off at sunset. The last to pull out were two units of the Māori Battalion, A and B Companies. But some men had been sent deep into the canyon and could not be found.

The ferocity of the Māori fighters resulted in a brief advantage. The Germans hadn't expected such resistance and their casualties were mounting. When black clouds threatened an imminent deluge, the attack was called off.

As the sky darkened, Sonny and Tama retreated into their makeshift hut on the upper tracks, unaware that they had just witnessed the fighting withdrawal of the entire Māori Battalion.

     Kayleen M. Hazlehurst

~9~

Are They Alone?

Atarangi was searching for a worthy carrier. A gull, on whose wing she might write an invisible message. A seabird, around whose neck she might tie a love charm with a thin strip of flax. Since Sonny went away her life had become food without seasoning, days without sun.

Even her old kōtuku had failed to visit her that morning. White herons were a pleasing omen but she sensed a reproach in his absence. She wasn't so grand a person who could leave her ancestral home to fight battles in foreign lands. She was a tiny bush bird, a fantail tumbling over and over, as she danced too close to the sun.

It was time to fetch the dogs for their walk. She brushed her skirt and meandered along the shoreline, stopping here and there to admire the shells. Then she turned towards the path leading to the sea cliff.

Hēmi was closing the gate on the rumps of the last cows when she reached the Wirimas' house. The herd ambled out of the yard and down the road. They knew their way back to the home paddock without the help of dogs. Kete and Turi were hanging around Hēmi's legs, begging for an ear scratch, when they spotted Atarangi.

'Here's your walk.' He laughed as the dogs bounded off to greet her.

Atarangi went to the yard and brushed her fingers over the moss on the gate. 'How's things, Hēmi?'

'Good, Ata. You?'

'Fine, thanks … Hello, Uncle.'

Api was leaning on his walking stick at the wooden railing. Every day he observed proceedings, giving instructions to his young nephews on the finer points of washing down a cowshed.

Api broke into a smile. 'Hello, girlie! I swear those mutts have been watching out for you since lunchtime.'

Kete and Turi got a hug. Ata loved their walks as much as the dogs.

'Guess we'd better go, hey?' she said in her dog-speak voice, and the animals sped away.

'Stop in for tea when you get back,' Hēmi called after her. 'Winifred's coming over.'

Atarangi turned to give him a wave.

The mussels Miriama had cooked up were scattered over a tray, and a large pot of potatoes and kūmera was issuing steam throughout the kitchen. At the centre of her table was a loaf of bread with slices folded back on the chopping board, a block of butter, some hard cheese, a jar of homemade pickles and three dishes of jam. A basket of scones sat on the sideboard. Winifred's contribution.

After dinner the girls collected the dishes and put out the mugs. Miriama placed milk and sugar on the table, along with her aluminium teapot and Winifred's scones.

Hēmi leaned forward to grab a scone. 'Winnie has started her new job at Wilson's Freight and Cartage,' he said with some pride.

'Is that right? So how do you like working in an office?' Api asked.

'I love it. They're teaching me to type business letters and one of the girls is showing me the filing.'

'You wouldn't think there'd be enough business for a cartage company in the North?'

'You'd be surprised, Dad. All sorts of things go up and down the country. Meat and wool, fruit and vegetables, machinery and equipment. Eh, Winnie?'

'The office is always busy, Uncle. Mr Wilson has five trucks on the road now.'

'What kind of trucks?'

'Bedfords, mostly,' Hēmi said, butting in again. 'Old Man Wilson got his hands on half a dozen before the war and he uses some for parts.'

Api beamed at his son's friend. 'Well, I dare say you'll be glad of a steady wage.'

     Kayleen M. Hazlehurst

Miriama had been observing Atarangi during this discussion. The girl appeared wistful and she leaned over to have a word. 'Have you heard anything from Sonny?'

Ata studied her hands and shook her head.

Winifred looked shocked. 'Aren't you getting his letters?'

'He sent me a few when he was in England. Since then I haven't heard a thing.' Ata's eyes sheened with tears. 'It's been weeks and weeks …'

Miriama placed a red chequered tea towel on the table and set a plate in the middle. 'It's just the mail, dear.' She piled the plate with leftover mussels, adding two slabs of buttered bread on top, and tied together the ends of the cloth. 'Here, take this home to Nan.'

Atarangi pulled the bundle towards her. 'Thanks. Nan loves mussels.' She drew in her eyebrows and turned to Api. 'Where are they now, Uncle? Do you know?'

'They sent them to Egypt last month for training, according to the newspapers,' Api said, his eyes bright with the desire to help. 'Then a few days ago there was a hoo-hah in the *Herald* about the New Zealand Division arriving in Greece.'

'That's in Europe, nē?' Atarangi was on her feet. 'Auē! Are they alone?' She spread her arms and glanced from one to the other. 'Is anyone there to help them?'

Api's face reddened. 'The Aussies are with them.'

Miriama came around the table to give Ata a hug. 'There now, you see. They're not alone. They have the Australians and the other New Zealanders with them. Don't fuss yourself, child.'

'But why … Why does it take so long?'

Hēmi shifted closer to Winifred and took hold of her hand. 'The army will take care of them,' he insisted and Winifred nodded.

'There'll be more letters, girlie. Don't you worry.' Api's voice wavered. 'I'll tell you the minute I hear anything, I promise.'

Miriama held the girl at arm's length. 'You can't let this beat you, Atarangi. There are other ways to reach our boys. We can safeguard our soldiers with prayers. We can send them love. Nothing is faster than that.'

'I know, Auntie. I haven't forgotten.'

Miriama produced her brave-smile-for-children. 'Tomorrow, bring your hoe and meet me at my garden. You and me and the sea working together, eh?'

The girl sniffed. She gave a little laugh and everyone responded.

'No more pining on the rocks with your old kōtuku,' Miriama scolded.

Atarangi looked at her with sad eyes. 'I think my old kōtuku has abandoned us.'

Miriama turned to Api. This was not good news for men at war.

———〰———

Jagged rods of electricity branched across the sky, followed by the growl of thunder. Between lightning flashes the sky was pitch-black. The best way for the battalion to retreat was straight up the Mavroneri Gorge. A northerly wind was lashing rain into their faces as they dragged themselves up the side of the cliff. Rivulets ran down their necks to mingle with the sweat of their backs. Even the Christians were muttering the gods had deserted them.

The lower paths were firm, their soil anchored by a network of roots. Higher up, the tracks became muddy and less defined, and the final precipice was jutted with rocks. The men grabbed branches and tufts of grass to haul themselves up, their feet slipping, aware that beside them was a drop to a river ravine.

During the five-hour climb, Captain Leaf, a robust man with legs like tree stumps, helped those who stumbled, lifting the weights from their backs. At one point the good captain, who had two rifles slung from each shoulder with extra packs hanging off their muzzles, was seen hoisting a struggling officer to his feet. Leaf regaled the soldiers with his jokes and threatened dire consequences should anyone's courage falter.

In this way they progressed upwards, single file, inch by inch, holding onto the bayonet scabbard of the man in front. Ahead, someone had laid a trail of white scraps—strips of calico, scraps of canvas, bits of cigarette paper—anything to direct them upwards and away from false trails.

Above them on the road, officers paced as they waited or trained their

     Kayleen M. Hazlehurst

binoculars into the gorge. Trucks had returned for the last of them. They were running behind schedule and should have left an hour ago, but two units were worth waiting for.

'Hoki mai! Hoki mai!' the officers called. 'Is anyone there? Can you hear us?'

No response.

Close to midnight there was a faint reply. 'Auē! Māori Battalion here. Wait for us!' Out of the darkness and driving rain came the tramping of boots and the faint sound of singing.

No one noticed the Wirima brothers were not among them.

———∿∿∿———

A black mountain moth fluttered by as Sonny poured more water into his brother's mouth. Tama was burning up, alternating between chills and fever. Sonny tried to stop him from thrashing and crying out. His mind oscillated from heart-thumping panic to the desperate hope that he could get them through the night. *Should I go for help? Should I carry Tama to the command post? Will we both die of exposure in this freezing rain?*

Sonny pulled two greatcoats over Tama, only to have them tossed aside. Between his brother's agony and confusion, there were moments of clarity. In one instant Tama had wanted to throw off his oppressor. In another he'd looked up in recognition.

'Save yourself, brother,' Tama begged, his eyes luminous with heat.

Sonny tightened his grip. 'I'm not going anywhere.' When Tama went limp, they slept the sleep of the exhausted.

Sonny sensed his soul reaching out …

> A deer bounds over the woodland floor, springing from
> rock to rock. At the top of the mountain it leaps down
> the slope to the far side. The deer runs, long-legged
> and graceful, over golden plains without fences until
> it reaches the sea. There, at the edge of the water,
> his love stands as still as a white heron, with her hair
> lightly shifting.

Atarangi sat on the grassy bluff above the cliff. In the young light of the morning an albatross had come to them, poised on an updraft of air, as if his presence had been commanded. Standing nearby, facing the sea, Miriama was sending out prayers for her sons. The old woman raised her voice in a karakia against the thundering waves.

'If your wish is to send messages of love and protection across oceans,' the tohunga had previously instructed Atarangi, 'an albatross is a far worthier carrier than a gull.'

He woke with a lurch. The storm had passed, leaving behind a blanket of cloud. Tama was sitting up, reaching out with his arms.

'Mum!' Tama cried. 'Mum! Mum!'

Sonny watched the leavening mist from the gully, trying to glimpse the apparitions visible to a dying man. When his brother exhaled and sank into silence, Sonny groaned and bowed his head. His tears pooled in the depression between Tama's neck and shoulder. His little brother, his teina, was lost to him.

'God keep you, Tama,' he whispered, remembering what he'd been taught. That beneath the surface of life there was a power, perfect and unchanging.

After he'd laid out the body he felt an urge to reach for the dog tags. *T. M. Wirima*. It was the last thing belonging to Tama. A token. Something his mother might like to keep. As he slipped away the cord, and blindly shoved the identity tags into his jacket, his last letter to Atarangi fell to the ground.

The plan was for the 5th Brigade to move to the other side of the mountain, where their retreat to safety might go unobserved. Vehicles were scarce and reserved for transporting casualties down the Olympus Pass road. Padre Kapea insisted he would stay back to help the wounded and to search for the missing. His intention was also to jot down the names of the dead in his small black notebook.

 Kayleen M. Hazlehurst

Major Dyer offered to acquire mules for Kapea, although the padre was told not to be too hopeful. The muleteers in their black-hooded cloaks seemed to have developed an aversion to the front line.

'You may have to walk out of the mountains like the rest of us,' Dyer said.

'If I can't get out,' Kapea replied, 'I will stay with the men taken prisoner.'

Sonny slung on his greatcoat and pack and sprinted down the trail. The paths were slick with mud and the trees around him were drenched. To keep himself upright he grabbed at branches as he ran. He had to find his unit. *My friends will say prayers and help me bury Tama.*

On reaching the lower tracks he edged along the river. The quiet was almost deathly. There were no sounds coming from where D and B Companies had been the day before. *It was a wild night, maybe they took shelter higher up.*

The camp site of A Company was also empty. No one at the river posts. No one in the trenches. There was scant evidence anyone had been here at all. *If the battalion bolted during the night, they'll be miles away by now.*

Water dripped from leaves as the lithe figure of Padre Kapea hastened through the pathways on his quest to find the lost. In previous days a detachment had been sent to defend the tracks leading to Skotina. Corporal Les Wipiti's section, a party of ten, and at least eight others, must not have received word of the withdrawal. The chaplain was determined to find them. Those who could still walk might be able to catch up, as long as they knew which direction the division was moving.

The padre's search continued to the west, coming to the position where D Company had carried out its last stand. The place where Harry Taituha's men had been rushed. Where the Bren gunners refused to run, and the mortar men died at their posts. Where Pere Tupe with his tommy gun had gone looking for trouble, and where Jack Tainui had strolled down the hill to offer the boys a hand. All dead or gone.

Kapea turned to the paths on the ridge. Battalion scouts had run the gauntlet through these woods to provide the army with intelligence. He could see the broken trails, the man-made burrows. After choosing a path upwards, he followed it to the top as if he was being guided. Hard against the cliff he came upon a rough shelter and was saddened to find a body inside. The boy had no dog tags, but when Kapea saw the peaceful face he was certain he recognised the young soldier.

After stopping to say a prayer for the departed, he reached to pick up a letter fallen in the mud. The envelope was unsealed, awaiting the army censor. The pencilled words were smudged, but the signature was clear. The padre replaced the letter back in its envelope and tucked it for safekeeping into his own vest. Then he took out his black notebook and wrote down the name 'Sonny Wirima'.

Sonny kept himself hidden as he checked along the river bank. The Germans were making morning preparations. Sudden shouting and issuing of commands signalled they had been alerted. Enemy scouts must have brought back the news that their adversaries had gone.

He heard barking. Tracker dogs were being released. German shepherds. He'd heard about these fierce animals. In one fluid movement, Sonny turned towards the forest and ran.

… He ran like a deer.

part two

~10~

Sympathy and Heavy Boots

Miriama had gone to the hills on a foraging expedition. Winter herbs were needed. There had been an outbreak of coughs and chesty complaints. Mr Wahapa was poorly from arthritis and required a tonic, the Kepa children had worms, and a new baby was due any day. She had taken Atarangi with her, in the hope this might distract the girl from her sorrowing heart. They rambled through the paddocks, their skirts growing damp from the wet grass. This morning her young companion was deeply reflective.

'Why are women weak, Auntie?'

'Women are not weak, Ata.'

'People say men are warriors and women stand back to watch a fight.'

'Someone has said this to you?'

'Mm-m-m.'

Miriama stopped to look down at the village, placing aside her basket. She folded her hands across her stomach and Ata slipped a hand into the crook of her arm. They leaned on each other, breathing in the fragrance of the land. 'This is true,' she admitted. 'Men go to war when provoked. Sometimes it is necessary.'

'So why do women stand back?' Atarangi lowered her head. 'Do we lack courage?'

Miriama knew her shame. 'No, dear. Women can be very brave. Some warriors are held back in reserve, even in battle. We would be a doomed people if we put our women and children in the place of greatest danger … Come. Let's go higher up.'

They gathered their skirts and baskets and walked to the crest, where the winter sun was catching the arches of the surrounding hills. Miriama swept her arm across the whole valley. 'Look at how expansive this is. See how the mountains reach up to touch the heavens.'

Atarangi flattened a circle of the grass where they could sit. 'I love coming here. I'm so glad this is my home.'

'Āe. We belong to the land, and the land will remain after we are gone. We must take the long view for the sake of our existence.'

'E pou, how does this help our existence?'

'Men are guardians of the earth and of practical endeavours. Women keep guard over spiritual things and the home. Remember, child, the spiritual world constantly speaks to us. It speaks to us when we are silent. It speaks to us through the land. We must see the signs and the warnings.'

'What happens if we forget?'

'When women forget who they are, dear one, their men become lost.'

Ata tossed her hair. 'So, men go to war and women must clean up the mess once the fighting is over?'

Miriama gave a slow smile. Young people were constantly jesting and simplifying things. This was not appropriate when she was imparting teachings. She raised a cautionary hand. 'Aro, Atarangi Tahiri. Heed me, child. Women must ensure the survival of the people. This is our purpose.'

The girl's face became serious. 'Then why are we sending our poor men to this terrible war? Why must I sacrifice my Sonny? Why must you sacrifice your sons?'

'*Ah,* this war. We send our precious warriors to help preserve the world. The elders agreed on this, and our men went with willing hearts.'

'Is the world in so much danger?' Ata asked, dismayed.

'Āe. I believe it is.'

'And we are protecting the land?'

'The land and people, the animals and birds … Everything we love.'

A slow tear passed down the girl's cheek.

Miriama lifted the young one's chin and saw her eyes were dark with inner quarrels. This girl had been the most promising apprentice. She had understanding. She had the gift.

'If there be fire, let it be virtuous, Atarangi. Let it cleanse the earth.'

A bird of heaven came into view. '*Kē-kē-kē!*'

     Kayleen M. Hazlehurst

Open country like this was hunting territory for harrier hawks. Tama used to love watching them from the hills. Something inside Miriama trembled as the kērangi circled up and up, ever closer to Rangi.

'*Kē-kē-kē!*' the bird screamed.

'*Mum! Mum!*' cried Tama.

In that instant, Miriama was struck by a crushing a sense of loss.

She had gone silent and the girl reached out her hand, as if to comfort her.

'Tell me about hawks, Auntie.'

Miriama turned to observe the bird wheeling in the space above them. *Surely the hawk is the envy of all humanity, how it soars and glides with such freedom.*

'The kērangi was one of the birds Tāne brought back from the twelfth heaven after he ascended to obtain the three baskets of knowledge. Since that time, hawks have acted as messengers between the gods and man.'

'What was in the three baskets, do you know? People have told me different things.'

'Āe. I have given much thought to this great mystery. My father held it was the sacred lore, the ceremonies, and all practical knowledge. If you reflect on this, you will receive your own guidance.'

'I think there was a fourth basket.'

'*Ai!* Do you, cheeky girl? And what was that?'

'The basket of music and poetry. My favourite.'

Miriama cackled. 'Perhaps Tāne went back to fetch that one.'

They raised their eyes skywards again, but the bird was gone. Most days they saw hawks swooping over the land. Miriama wondered what message the kērangi had brought her today, and why she was so overwhelmed.

'Auntie …? Auntie …?'

'Eh?'

'What happened after Tāne obtained the sacred knowledge?'

'Is this not obvious? It became the storehouse of the world's wisdom.'

Atarangi blushed from the admonishment and dropped her gaze.

Miriama sighed and spoke in a gentler voice. 'This wisdom was given so we could discern the difference between good and evil intentions.'

'Good and evil intentions … Do you mean in ourselves or in others?'

'I mean in both.'

'*E!* So with this wisdom we would know when to go to war and when to make peace?'

'This is so.'

'Then we must never lose this wonderful knowledge, Auntie.'

Miriama touched the girl's cheek. 'You're a special girl, Ata.'

'No, I'm not. Winifred and the others are doing far more important things than me. I'm just the girl who talks with the birds.'

Miriama bent her head towards the girl. 'We both talk with the birds,' she said, and leaning on each other they started to giggle.

—✺—

Sonny was running. Shrubs whipped at his legs as he avoided the pathways. He tripped on a root and regained his footing. Light streamed through the branches. The sound of dogs had faded when he stopped to get his bearings. Panting hard. Hands shaking.

The contour of the land was familiar, and his compass confirmed his position. He had ruled out tracking west along the Mavroneri River. Germans would be scouring Skotina for Allied soldiers, forcing the villagers to give them information. To the north-east the river wound its way to the Katerini Plain, an area now overrun. He was certain the New Zealand Army would be moving south. This was the direction he needed to go.

Many forest paths led to the Olympus Pass road. By keeping to the treeline, he could cross the mountain on the diagonal. Ascend slowly. In the forest he would remain undetected, although the steep gradient might hamper his progress. If he fell, there'd be no one to help him.

As he travelled, the woods thickened with plane trees and conifers and the forest floor became latticed with roots. Yet by keeping a consistent pace he arrived by mid-afternoon below the site where the 22nd Battalion had been. He could hear heavy vehicles on the road above him. The enemy had been stalled on the Pass, but now they'd broken through.

By the end of the day the trees thinned and animal tracks ended as he reached the top of the range. The last stage of his approach to the road was over a stretch of shingle. Traversing an open area of the mountain in daylight would make him an easy target for a marksman. He chose instead to rest under cover until nightfall. If he crossed the road into the next valley, he could look for an alternative route south.

Sonny wanted to get as far away as possible from the enemy. He trusted he could outfox the Nazis but he had a healthy respect for their dogs. Nothing stopped hunting dogs once they got hold of a scent, and his scent was the one thing he would not give them. *I'll travel as fast as I can without falling over a cliff and breaking my silly neck.*

Twilight. Time to move. After three sips of water and half a biscuit, he crawled from the scrub and onto the slope. The shingle, still warm from the afternoon sun, moulded his body and allowed him to move upwards with few stones sliding away. The edge of the roadside was solid, and he paused there to listen. No sound of vehicles or tramping feet. Cautiously, he raised his head.

A river of cloud rolled along the ridge and over the mountainside. Here he was at the top of Mount Olympus, among warring nations he didn't understand, thousands of miles from his own people. A piercing wind vaulted down from the snow-capped pinnacles, funnelled between the crags and crevices and flattened out into a low, cold moan. Part of him wanted to leap away from the foreignness of it all.

A flame of remorse rose up in his chest. He had left his brother in this desolate place. *This is what Mum asked us to guard against. How will Tama's spirit find his way home? How will he take part in the songs of the tangihanga?*

He hauled himself to his feet, bounded across the road and scrambled, crab-like, over the shingle on the other side. From here he headed for the sheltering forest. Away from the howling winds of the mountain. Away from the voices of regret.

———⁓———

He should have known to watch the animals. They always had good sense. Even goats didn't walk along mountain tracks in the dark. He damn near stepped over the edge. After three hours he scraped up an armful of branches and twigs to build a sleeping platform between two trees. It was safer to rest now, and to progress in daylight. The tracks on this side of the ridge were narrow and silent, except for the rustlings and sighs of a mountain forest. Had his mates passed this way with the other Anzacs in their exodus? *Tomorrow I will look for signs.*

On his bed of branches and leaves he had fallen dead asleep, not even hearing the nocturnal creatures, and opening his eyes only when the blue-glass light outlined the boughs of pines. As he watched the awakening sky, his thoughts turned to his beloved. He always assigned his first and last moments to her. If he did this, his memories of home would never fade. Whatever traumas this war might bring, he trusted this one conviction. He must never forget Atarangi.

Sonny had been moving along the curve of the range within earshot of the road. All morning he'd heard no grunt of vehicles nor rumble of wheels, until a cleft in the ridge forced him higher. This time there was something. Gentle voices.

He crawled to the verge and hid in the grass as a man with a boy, maybe a grandson, came ambling down the road. Following behind was a donkey harnessed to a cart. By the lilt of their speech he could tell they were Greek.

The cart was stacked with the spoils of war—their war, their spoils—concealed under a pile of sticks. He recognised the tins of bully beef and boxes of ammunition. In their hurry to get away HQ had left these behind in abundance. Scattered throughout this region were several remote villages. These hill people, mostly sheep herders and timber men, must have realised the fighting was over and were coming to scavenge.

When Sonny stood upright the Greek gave a sharp cry and collected the child under his arm. A scruffy unshaven Māori emerging from the grasses would have given any old fellow a turn. The Greek bared his teeth under his white bushy moustache and waved his donkey stick. A skinny old man trying to look savage reminded Sonny of one of his uncles. It was a sight that made him break into a grin. He lifted his hands to show he meant no harm.

 Kayleen M. Hazlehurst

'New Zealander,' Sonny said, pointing at his chest. He walked two fingers along his forearm to illustrate he was marching south.

Grandfather made a guttural noise. '*Ah, Neozilandós!*' He flapped his arms and uttered a stream of speech, growling at Sonny for frightening the life out of him.

Sonny persevered. Using gestures to enact a battle, he showed he'd been involved in the recent fighting. The man teetered back on his heels, and the boy made a gun with his fingers and ran around shooting invisible Germans.

Sonny wiped his forehead with his arm, rubbed his stomach, and went to the cart where he respectfully waited.

A glow of understanding appeared on the old wrinkled face and the man swaggered over to the wagon. After rummaging through his stolen loot, he came up smiling. Five tins of meat, a bag of biscuits and a second water bottle were loaded ceremoniously into Sonny's pack.

Sonny could have kissed the old rogue, but instead he saluted. The Greek swayed over his tatty boots and baggy trousers to return the honour. When the donkey brayed the child went to calm the animal.

Grandfather knelt to place his hand on the road. '*Germanoi! Germanoi!*'

Sonny bent to confirm the vibrations of approaching vehicles. He helped them rearrange the sticks, then he was directed to the verge of the road.

'*Fyge! Fyge!*' The Greek said in an urgent voice. He wanted Sonny to leave, and damn quick.

Sonny plunged down the slope and flung himself face down on the stones. While he lay there, he prayed the man and boy wouldn't be molested. On the road above, he could hear heavy vehicles trundling by, taking no notice it seemed of a peasant and his donkey.

As a shadow passed over him he rolled to look up. Gliding high against an azure sky was his eagle and he lifted his chin in a greeting. Tama was watching over him.

The next day Sonny ran into two Serbian soldiers who had come to the tracks from the Pass. Through simple signs and broken English, they indicated they had seen no Allies in these parts. All were gone. Sonny linked his fingers on the crown of his head and staggered in a bewildered circle. The Serbs studied their feet, kicking the soil with their heavy boots in sympathy.

The larger man grabbed Sonny's arm and pulled him into a crouch. He broke a stick and scraped a meaty palm over the track where he drew lines in the soil. Rough sketches to advise which paths to follow and which to avoid.

A mile or two back Sonny had noticed a river. He drew a wavy line and pointed at his chest. 'Me go down to river.'

The soldiers became agitated. 'No go to river. Germans!'

Sonny grunted, then he pulled out two tins of bully beef and four biscuits from his pack and offered them to the Serbs, looking apologetic. The Serbs made a fuss in their show of gratitude. They all bear-hugged, patted each others' backs, and parted as brothers—the Serbs taking the lower track and Sonny keeping to the upper. He had done the right thing. These soldiers may have saved him from capture. *We have to help each other. Greeks, Serbs, Kiwis. Everyone is hungry.*

Later, Sonny sat to consider his situation. Three days, that's how long he estimated his food would last. Hunting was one way to supplement his supplies. The mountain tracks were rough and slow, but if he used the road some of the way, it might save him a day's travel.

At home he would run through the forest with a wild pig on his shoulders, so there was no doubt he could hoof it down a road carrying an army pack. The highway was plagued by hairpin bends and sharp corners, sometimes with sheer cliffs on either side. He could make himself invisible, so long as there was something to hide behind, but to do this he had to see where he was going. *Daybreak. That's the best time for travelling in these mountains.*

Sonny was on the road again when he heard groaning. In the grass on the roadside he found a Pākehā who'd been shot in the face.

'Jesus Christ, you poor bastard!'

The soldier was young, not more than nineteen. His jaw was

     Kayleen M. Hazlehurst

shattered, his right eye was swollen shut, and he was turning yellow. He must have crawled here after the 22nd Battalion left him for dead two days ago.

Sonny knelt to dribble water into the lad's mouth. Moisture gurgled up and trickled from the split in his cheek. The soldier's gaze was pitiful, terrified. Sonny had seen that look before in the eyes of men expecting to die. He bent to listen, hearing a word slurred with 's' and 'th'.

Sonny checked the dog tags. 'Nathan Smith. Is that your name?'

The boy lifted his right arm and pulled it back in a couple of jagged movements.

'You're a gunner, hey? Sonny Wirima, rifleman. I'm going to get you out of here, Smithy. Don't you worry.' He took out his last bandage and wrapped it under Gunner Smith's jaw, tying it over the blood-sodden scalp. 'Sorry it hurts, mate. We have to immobilise your jaw.'

He stashed his pack behind some rocks and joined the stricken boy. Smithy needed a doctor. Sonny listened to the boy's shallow breathing and waited. An idea was forming. Better than the last one when he let Tama go swimming, he hoped. He had picked the mornings as the best time to travel, so he guessed the locals would too.

Among the trees near the river he had seen a terracotta-roofed building. The villa was isolated, with no surrounding structures. Was this a hotel or a mountain retreat? The Serbs had urged Sonny not to go there. They suspected Germans occupied the facility—but perhaps there was a doctor among them.

After a while Sonny heard the familiar clip-clop of a donkey and the scraping of wheels. Two men with their hands on a cart ascended the hill. More were coming in search of discarded ammunition and food. He emerged from his hiding place, allowing the strangers to notice there was a wounded man beside him.

'New Zealander,' he said as he got to his feet. '*Neozilandós,*' he repeated, trying out the Greek. These men weren't so frightened of him. They acknowledged him and came over to examine the injured soldier. Maybe the grandfather and child had related the story of their meeting, and word had got around. After some rapid-fire discussion and much arm waving, they signalled towards the empty cart. They were offering to transport Smithy somewhere.

With care, Sonny lifted the young Kiwi and gently placed him on the cart. Together, they walked back to the ridge until they arrived at a lane with the sign 'Petras Sanatório'. This was the way to a sanatorium. *Isn't that where they sent people with tuberculosis?*

'TB?' he asked.

They fanned out their hands.

'Is it a hospital?'

'*Germanoi*,' said one man, and he spat on the ground.

Whether once a sanatorium or now a German field hospital, the Greeks believed this was Gunner Smith's only chance. Sonny didn't argue. Halfway down the driveway the men stopped. This was as far as they were prepared to go. He thanked them and hoisted his new buddy on his back.

He didn't like the feel of this place. The drive was lined with a shaggy row of ash trees and the stone building at the end wore a cloak of desperation, with no lawns or flowerbeds for patients to sit by. It looked more like a prison than a hospital. A place where people came to die. The challenge of treating a soldier with a smashed face might bring some meaning to this sad place.

He bent to Smithy's ear. 'These people will fix you up, mate. See you back in New Zealand, hey? Visit me at Rangitakō when you get home.'

The boy palmed a light pressure of thanks on Sonny's arm. After propping him against the wooden doorframe, Sonny thumped twice on the knocker and then sprinted behind the shrubbery.

Inside, he heard questioning voices and a loud Germanic response. A young nurse looked out. She screamed and was joined by an older woman. A gush of high-pitched sympathy brought out a man in a white coat who started issuing instructions. The doctor hooked his hands under Smithy's armpits and hauled him inside, then the older nurse closed the door.

The good people of the sanatorium didn't look back once to see who had delivered the soldier to their doorstep. In the spirit of aroha, they just took him in.

 Kayleen M. Hazlehurst

~11~

Zeus and His Shepherds

Sonny had been watching a family of deer grazing, undisturbed by the birds arguing over their evening roosting spots. He had retrieved his pack from the place he met Gunner Smith and turned away from the road, plunging instead into the protecting embrace of the forest where he could breathe in the scent of pine.

It would not be long before he would see the foothills of Mount Olympus merging with the plains of Thessaly. This wasn't Egypt—that burnt, arid land. Its bright sun. The feeling of grit in your mouth. He wasn't alone in a desert. Nor was he stumbling in the sleet and mud of a gorge. The mountain slopes were teeming with woodland creatures.

A deer with a white tail sprang from rock to shelf, barely casting a backward glance. Squirrels darted up trees and scolded him from the higher branches. Birds and insects, he didn't know by name, fluttered through groves of mountain flowers. A minute ago, he'd seen a brown-and-yellow butterfly drifting on a ray of sunlight, and last night he'd even heard the howl of a wolf. *These mountains will not defeat me. They will be my friend.*

In the evenings he communed with the old people. His tūpuna were his lodestone, his consolation. Three grandparents and a dozen aunties and uncles had already passed on. He missed these favourite elders from his childhood and felt them drawing near.

His mother came to him in his dreams, and sometimes it was Atarangi. During the day the presence of his eagle brought him calm. The great bird was tracking his course through these ranges. *Has Tama reached his spirit place? Has he become the bird he wanted to be? Āe. Tama will be with me, circling against heaven, until I come home.*

He levelled his rifle and shot the deer clean through the head, feeling no regret.

—⁓—

It wasn't easy, predicting the topography of the mountain range without a map. He halted at a cliff top and examined the creases and folds of the land. A traveller would have to follow one of those ridges downhill. By now the German Army would have reached Athens, he calculated, making all roads south treacherous. The mountains, the forests and grasslands would provide safer routes for a man whose destination was the sea.

To cut a downward path, he retraced his steps and zig-zagged between the trees to prevent his feet from slipping. The stream at the bottom of the gully had a taunting freshness, reminding him of his grimy state. Before he changed his mind he knelt and plunged his head into the flowing water, rubbing his hair and beard and shaking out the excess. The stream was fresh and clear, and he drank deeply before refilling his bottles.

The mountain mist was turning to fine rain. He needed to find shelter. After crossing the stream, he climbed the rise and saw a strip of pasture running along the base of the cliff. In the dimming light he detected a line of hollows.

'Caves!'

Two children emerged from one of the openings, then he heard jingling. Fifteen or so goats with neck bells milled nearby. At this time of year sheep herders brought their animals to the higher meadows to feed on the spring grass. These tiny shepherds were guarding their flock. And the goats, each answering to a name, seemed accustomed to their care.

Sonny trotted towards the cliff, with the prospect of finding a refuge making his pack feel lighter. The boy and his sister cast him shy glances as he shuffled past to examine the sites further along.

The cave he chose had an uneven floor, but it was dry. If he scraped away the rubble he could make a sleeping area on the shelf near the back wall. Charcoal residue at the centre of the floor indicated its use by previous occupants. He was preparing a circle of cooking stones when the children appeared carrying sticks. They were quick at this chore and had built him

Kayleen M. Hazlehurst

a fire within minutes. He smiled his gratitude to the children, and raised his hand in farewell when they returned to their goats. A little later he took a haunch of deer, skewered it with his bayonet and set it against the embers. Once roasted, he would share the meat with his young neighbours.

—∾—

'Neozilandós, it is Theos!'

Sonny emerged to see two men inching along the cliff ledge. His shepherd friend had brought company. The stranger accompanying Theos was in his mid-forties, Sonny estimated. A black-bearded, powerful-looking man, whose face had been leathered from long exposure to sun and rain. A mass of raven hair fell from his cap to his shoulders. The visitor regarded Sonny with eyes more inquisitive than suspicious.

In the weeks Sonny had made this place his home, he had learned the ways of these mountain men. Soon they would share stories and the honey-sweetened corn mead that hung in skin pouches from their belts. He swept a welcoming hand across his threshold as might any gracious host.

Dimitri, the dark one, examined the grotto. Sonny had stocked his cave well. In previous days he had gone back to the road to comb through the belongings of the retreating soldiers. At one ration dump the packing cases were heaped high and covered with netting. Judging by the labels on the tins, these goods had once belonged to an Australian battalion. From this stash Sonny acquired beef stew with vegetables, peaches and creamed rice, evaporated milk, a quantity of tea and some cooking implements. A discarded camp stove was left behind because it needed fuel, but Sonny found a good supply of matches. He also took .303 bullets from the abandoned boxes of ammunition. As many as he could stuff into his coat pockets.

In their flight from an aggressive enemy, the Anzacs had left anything that would slow them down. Greatcoats, binoculars, army packs and even an officer's valise were cast along the roadside. A kitchen blade that might serve Sonny as a hunting knife was used to cut away a length of netting and a fair bit of twine. He hoped to fashion fish traps with the netting and planned to make snares with the twine. After he'd taken all that he could carry, the hillmen with their groaning mule carts had made off with the rest.

If the Anzacs had set fire to their possessions everyone would have suffered. Perhaps they couldn't spare the time or fuel, or perhaps they wanted the Greeks to get to the food and ammo first. As it turned out, the Germans who broke through the defences at the Pass were in an almighty rush to reach Athens. They either hadn't noticed the ration dumps or couldn't stop to scavenge. Each day Sonny sent up a prayer of thanks. There was famine in this land, and the Anzacs had made the right decision in sparing what they could not carry.

Theos and Dimitri were smoking near the ledge. Sonny joined them with his pipe, a gift from Theos. He surveyed the valley and reflected on his spell in the hills with the shepherds. They were teaching him Greek words and phrases and kept their speech plain. With the help of sign language and sketches in the earth they managed to get along.

Sonny enquired after their animals and the health of their families.

'Come to dinner,' Theos said, opening of his arms. 'We kill sheep. Come, join us.'

Sonny gave a broad smile. Since encountering the shepherd children, he'd been invited to the humble cottages of these hill people on several occasions. The women showed concern for him and he didn't object to their care. Before feeding him, they presented him with a bucket of warm water and a bar of handmade soap, insisting he have a wash. His hair was getting long and tangled. When he visited again he would ask for a rough hair cut with their shears.

On these visits he brought with him a portion of pig or deer, a rabbit or a couple of squirrels. They called him Neozilandós, and sometimes *o kynigós*, the hunter. Asking for little, and trading his meat for cheese and bread, or salt and lentils, he remained safe in his mountain retreat as the spring progressed.

Whispers were exchanged between villagers and shepherds in the marketplaces and on the roads. From these reports Sonny drew what he could. Outnumbered and outgunned, with no air cover, the Allied forces

     Kayleen M. Hazlehurst

had evacuated south en masse. German aircraft dominated the skies. They bombed the towns and countryside. They destroyed animals and crops. They strafed roads choked with fleeing refugees and soldiers.

Thousands had died and thousands more were taken prisoner. British, Australians, New Zealanders, Serbians, Greeks and even some distrusted Italians had been seen herded into fields and carted away in cattle trucks or railcars to prisoner-of-war camps in the north.

The war in Greece was over. The mainland had been overrun and the Allied withdrawal had begun. Confusion and despair might have consumed Sonny, had it not been for his friends. The shepherds persuaded him to remain in the mountains and to live to fight another day. He loved these people, but by helping him they were putting themselves in danger and he knew he could not stay.

⸎

A wild wind was blowing in from the sea. No bird would have stayed out in it. The rain was so heavy it could have sliced a feather from the bone.

Rumours of the events in Greece were causing great consternation among the tribes. Te Arawa Trust Board had sent a telegram to the Minister of Defence asking for authentic information about their boys. Meanwhile, Api kept a close eye on the newspapers. On 17 May 1941, *The New Zealand Herald* published a government letter of apology for the delay in providing an official account of the situation. There were assurances that messages dispatched from the field would be forwarded to the relevant families.

A trickle of intelligence about the fate of the New Zealand Expeditionary Force had been coming through. Some men believed dead, were reported as living. Others believed missing, were confirmed captured or killed. For families who received no news at all the uncertainty was crippling.

If anything might have caused an ache in a mother's heart, it was the thought that her son was trying to escape from his enemies to make his way home. On this day, no such message was delivered to the Wirima family. The two telegrams, sent on the authority of the Department of Defence, brought very different news.

When Miriama opened her door she saw three ladies were standing behind the postal official assigned the painful task of delivering the war telegrams. The women had spotted the postman and followed him. They were not going to let another mother be given bad news without someone being there to pick her up from the doorstep.

Miriama saw the distraught faces of her friends and she began to wail. The telegrams were snatched from the startled postman and the women stepped forward to grab her flailing arms as they bore her inside.

The Minister regretted to inform them that Pte Sonny A. Wirima had been killed in action and that Pte Tama M. Wirima was missing.

Api wrote to the New Zealand Army demanding to know if there had been some mistake. He couldn't believe it—not Sonny, not Tama. By return post he was assured that the information was reliable. Reverend Isaac Kapea, who in mid-April was taken prisoner at Mount Olympus with other members of the Māori Battalion, had recorded Sonny Wirima's death in his field diary. This was then communicated through the mail, collected by the Red Cross from the POW camps. In its letter, the army explained:

Tama Wirima was assumed to have died in the same battle as his brother, Sonny Wirima. In the ensuing chaos of retreat this cannot be confirmed. Great disruption has occurred during these months of fighting. These are troubled times. Thousands have surrendered and many more are missing. The Army is deeply grateful for your sacrifices.

Official news from the battlefields came in the form of a list released by the Department of Defence. The number of men killed and wounded had grown significantly. Not long after the arrival of their telegrams the latest Casualty List was published in the newspaper. Sonny was reported among those 'Killed in Action' and Tama among those 'Missing, Believed Killed'.

 Kayleen M. Hazlehurst

Reverend Noah Petera held a memorial service at the Rangitakō church. The ceremony was in honour of three local boys—Sonny Wirima, who had died on Mount Olympus, and Honi Wade and Kereti Anderson, who had died defending Greece. Miriama refused to allow Tama's name to be included, since his death had not been confirmed. The whole community and their far-flung kin attended, along with a few officials and local Pākehā families. After the service there was the laying of wreaths on the commemorative plaques for the fallen.

Miriama lingered near the inscriptions, gripping her stick as her body swayed from the weight of grief. *These empty gestures. The bones of my sons will never come home.* People were walking over to the wharekai, where a feast waited for the guests. She would have left the marae right away, had she not been concerned about the girl.

Miriama bent to speak with her eldest son. 'Hēmi, I want you to look after your father.'

'All right, Mum.'

'Where is Ata?'

'Over there, with Winifred.'

At the front fence a group of young people were standing in a huddle. Atarangi had her back to the church, with her elbows tucked in and her hands folded over her chest. In her stillness any casual observer might have been reminded of a statue of the Madonna. From across the grassed churchyard Miriama could read the true energy of the girl. Atarangi was a little bird wanting to take flight, tethered by the sympathy of friends.

'I'm taking Ata away,' Miriama told Hēmi. 'It's been too much for her. We'll be gone for a few hours.'

'Will you go to the sea or the hills?'

'We'll say prayers by the river, after that I don't know.'

'Good. Take her somewhere quiet. I'll ask Winifred to tell Nan.' Hēmi reached out his hand. 'Are you okay, Mum?'

'Āe.' She withdrew, regretful that she couldn't accept her son's pity, nor provide him with any comfort. 'Take care of Dad,' she repeated as she brushed past.

Miriama moved through the crowd, keeping her focus on Atarangi.

People touched her with their consoling eyes, but she ignored them. The girls saw her approaching and parted. After exchanging a few words, Miriama ushered Ata towards the lichen-mottled gate. The two of them slipped away on the mutual understanding that they needed the company of others.

<center>~~~</center>

Dimitri had offered to guide him. The shepherd was familiar with the remote passes and goat tracks of these hills and he wanted to set Sonny on a safe course to the east coast. This giant of a man, who was regularly seen carrying an orphaned lamb around his neck, had taken a liking to the Kiwi.

This was the day they had agreed to depart. Sonny was lying on a bed of cast-off greatcoats, listening to water dripping through the limestone, when Dimitri presented himself at the cave entrance bearing his antiquated rifle and leather sack. He wore the travelling attire of shepherds—fustanella and leggings, with a long sheepskin jerkin.

Dimitri swung his gun and sack to the ground and extracted a pair of trousers, a peasant's shirt and a hooded cape. 'No uniform!' He waved his hand in disgust over Sonny's ragged clothing and thrust the clean clothes at him. Then he took out his pipe and went to the ledge to wait.

Sonny changed into the new clothes and shoved the khaki remnants into a crack in the far wall. A man in a foreign uniform would be shot on sight, but Dimitri's wife had assembled a peasant's disguise for him. He stomped out the fire, heaved on his pack, and took his rifle to join his friend. The early sun had set the cliff ablaze, turning it fire-red and brushing the lower hills with pink and orange.

Dimitri scanned the terrain, muttering as he noted the landmarks. An eagle glided beyond the cliffs, and Sonny lifted his hand in a wave.

'My eagle!' Sonny said, jutting his chin towards the bird.

'Zeus!' Dimitri said, observing him through sun-narrowed eyes.

'What?'

'Eagle belongs to Zeus. What you say—'

'A symbol. Are you saying the eagle is a symbol of Zeus?'

       Kayleen M. Hazlehurst

'Is symbol.' Dimitri made an explosive noise and brandished his hand from the sky to the earth. 'So too, thunderbolt. *Hah!*'

'*E!*' Sonny enthused in the same spirit. 'Zeus. King of the gods!'

The Greeks had their own sacred mountains and Mount Olympus had been the home of many of these old gods. Zeus had sent a guardian to accompany Sonny through these ranges. Now he was leaving, the eagle had come to say goodbye.

When they descended the final slopes of Mount Olympus Sonny acknowledged the many friends who had sustained him. He had found kindred spirits here. The rocks and trees, the animals and birds, the generous hill people who were living as their ancestors had lived for centuries. One part of him grieved he was leaving, but another part was elated. As he swung his hips down the hill a waiata rumbled up from his chest. A song of homecoming.

I am troubled,
And I can stay here no longer.
I will go to another place to prepare my leaving.
My love, I hear you calling, 'Come back to me.'

The waves are breaking,
Soon I will sail on more friendly seas.
I will return and there will be a great homecoming.

Ah, to see the pīwakawaka,
As she flits and turns in flight.
How she fans her tail and mocks me with her spinning.

My love, I hear you calling. 'Come back to me.'

The day warmed as they left the foothills and entered the marshy wetlands—the ponds and streams, the reeds and rushes, the low islets covered with willows. So many aspects of this country were familiar. Around them, the birdlife was in the fledgling days of late spring. Even the silvery grass reminded him of wharawhara.

Dimitri pointed downriver, indicating there was a crossing. A traveller could not veer to the coast from here as Mount Ossa stood in the way. However, if he followed the road to Lárissa, keeping at a safe distance, an opportunity to turn east would come.

Sonny had heard about this town. Aerial bombings throughout central Greece had left many towns decimated. As if the hardships of war hadn't been enough, a recent earthquake had hit Lárissa. Fortunately, if there was any good fortune here, most of the residents had fled ahead of the army before Papatūānuku dealt her hand.

Dimitri arrested Sonny's attention by drawing another map in the earth. Sonny must keep to the wilderness and the coast. Nowhere else was safe. After eating their last meal of sour bread and cheese, the friends faced each other. They would part company before last light.

The shepherd gripped Sonny's shoulder one last time—this Greek who had been like an older brother, a tuakana, to him. There was only one way to thank him. Sonny laid his service rifle across his palms and presented it as a gift. Dimitri accepted the weapon, spending a minute to admire it. The shepherd then handed over his own relic and, laughing, they dug into their pockets to exchange bullets.

Without further comment, Dimitri turned and strode away. His broad back vanished into the haze of the marshes, giving the impression the man had never been here.

The air of the wooded hills was fresh and cool. Since leaving the mountains, wild goat and deer had become scarce. Birds were plentiful, but none were big enough to justify the use of ammunition. Special skills were needed to capture this elusive prey. Sonny set snares as his grandfather had taught him—the old ones had been forest hunters—yet the tiny bones of these birds provided sparse nourishment. His muscles were losing their condition. If he continued through these high woods hunger would strip away what remained of his strength. Ducks were his preferred quarry,

     Kayleen M. Hazlehurst

but to pursue them he would need to return to the plains.

Scavenging for food was hazardous and his mountain friends had advised him to stay away from the agricultural lowlands. With his beard, his traditional clothing and his antique gun, Sonny could have passed for any hill peasant. Beyond these hills he could see coils of smoke rising. One destroyed village was much the same as another, but a deserted farm on the outskirts might be a safer option.

He knew what he would find if he went down there. Exposed corpses. Rough graves. Murdered horses. Mules brought to their knees on the roads while they carried a family's meagre belongings. Bullocks stopped in their toil by a spray of Stuka bullets. *What a low order of beings these Nazis must be to kill innocent working animals.*

Below him was heartbreak. A place of ghosts. A living hell of bombed roads, ruined crops, starving animals—and centaurs with their dogs.

At a point where the trees parted an overhang promised him some protection for the night. With his back against the rock, he sat to eat a saved crust and to watch the stars rising. As the sky pearled and darkened, he began to wish Tama was beside him. Making decisions for them both had made Sonny brave. Now, who was he? He was nobody's brother, nobody's husband, nobody's father. Far below he saw no ant-like figures, no signs of moving vehicles. This was where his path would take him tomorrow.

Circling his arms over his knees, he swayed to the rhythm of his homecoming song.

Dear one, we are far apart.
My pen slips and breaks with longing.
If my words never reach you, know I have died for love.

Remember the promises we made.
The promises we made as we lay
like plaited straw under the pōhutukawa tree.

My love, I hear you calling, 'Come back to me.'

~12~

Safer Routes

Miriama was shaking with trepidation. At any moment her wairua might leap from her chest and race across the ocean in search of her lost children. It was only a mother's hope, people would say, but she was certain one of her sons was alive. She could feel his mauri in the world—he was alive and in peril. Her searing alarm was evidence of this.

She stepped from the garden and walked to the cliff edge to call on the Powers to help the lost and the fallen. Every atua and tūpuna who had ever been a guardian to her family, she summoned now to their protection.

—◦◦◦—

Sonny plunged through the water and clawed his way up the bank. These days it seemed he was always wet. This crop-growing area was laced with irrigation ditches that drew water from a myriad of creeks and springs. Huddled under the wooden supports of a bridge, he listened to the rumble of cart wheels and motor vehicles. He preferred to rest under these structures than to risk approaching strangers. Nothing much grew in the shade of bridges, but they provided protection and a dry dirt floor. Once the traffic stopped, he could build a fire to cook a snared duck, a speared trout, or an eel from his traps. Foraging for food was easier near water.

His routine was to sleep half the night, walk south-east under a waning moon, and find a new hideout before sunrise. During the day he hid among the willows and reeds that clustered along the banks of water courses. Here, he drank from streams, sampled water plants and sought game while observing the movements of Germans and Greeks.

This evening he longed for something more comfortable. He leaned into the bank and checked the surrounding fields. Greece was far from a wasteland. Over the centuries every inch of fertile soil had been turned to cultivation. The productive earth of a productive people. Half a mile away a stone building with a flat roof cast a square profile against the darkening horizon. *This might make a good shelter.*

After a quick appraisal, he gathered his things and sprinted towards the barn.

———∿∿∿———

Api was resting on the back porch, enjoying an ocean breeze, when he heard the patter of canine claws on the footpath. Atarangi must be coming for a visit. Kete and Turi often dashed out to accompany her back to the house. Naughty things. He had even seen them abandon Hēmi in the paddocks when Ata was approaching. The dogs had put 'looking after Atarangi' onto their list of duties after Sonny and Tama left for Europe.

'Uncle Api, are you there?' Ata called, as she came to the seaward side of the house.

'Yep, I'm here.' Api pulled himself up on the divan. A year ago, the doctors had said he might be crippled for life, but Miriama would hear none of it. She wasn't going to let his muscles desert him, she told Api, as she held his feet firmly to the floor. With her massages and medicines, his health had improved. Recently he'd discarded the crutches, finding he could use a walking stick. On good days he watched the milking and did a few jobs.

Atarangi handed him some flowers. 'I brought these for you.'

Api recognised them at once. Blue and orange wild flowers plucked from the dunes, a meeting place for lovers. She reminded him so much of the young Miriama. These precious puhi women who circled around him like the sun and moon, why had he been so blessed?

Kete was leaning against the divan and Api put down his hand to stroke her ears. This little girl was always quiet when her master was in pain.

'I'm glad you've come to walk the dogs. They need cheering up.'

Atarangi crouched to give the dogs a cuddle. 'Hēmi said they've been moping.'

'They're restless, that's all. Don't know what's wrong with them.'

'Yes, you do, Uncle,' she said softly. 'It's what's wrong with us all.'

His eyes blurred and he turned away. 'You go, girlie. Come and see me when you get back. We can have a long talk.'

<hr>

Wood grated on stone as Sonny heaved open the door. Oak, he judged, by its weight and thickness. The timber was scarred and cracked with age. On entering the barn there was the distinct smell of domestic pig. There were no signs of livestock and he assumed the owners had herded them into the hills for safety. The room had a single paned window, intact and dusty. In the corner was a greyed hump of hay. The farmer had been tidy. Grain sacks hung on hooks and the cobble stones were swept clean. Sonny forked a quantity of hay onto the floor and collapsed onto his new bed.

He woke with a beam of sunlight at his feet. It was well past his departure hour. When he looked outside the courtyard was empty except for six or seven chickens. The hens were surviving on garden scratchings and he instinctively searched for a handful of wheat to throw out to them.

During the night a shower of rain had passed over the fields. Droplets glimmered on trees and breaths of vapour rose from orchards. Pressed against the wall, a water barrel was collecting the last of the rainwater as it slid from gutter to pipe. He cupped his hands to drink from the barrel and to wash his face.

Worn-out equipment was scattered on the forecourt. A rusted threshing machine, harnesses and chains, a coil of rope, scoops for measuring grain. He considered the usefulness of a metal rod and a clean tin. If he sharpened the point of the rod with that file on the windowsill it would make a good spear and double up as a cooking skewer. Tin cans were good for boiling water.

A pile of kindling and a short-handled axe lay on a chopping block. The axe was compact, suitable for a woman's hand. An ideal size for a travelling man. Sonny said a brief prayer for the poor farmer and his wife, wishing them well wherever they were and asking forgiveness for the theft of their possessions.

 Kayleen M. Hazlehurst

In daylight it was unsafe to make a dash for the river over open fields. But here, at this farm, the surrounding foliage gave him cover to scamper around picking vegetables and fruit, the few eggs he might find, and a bag of grain from leavings in the barn. He had grown weak from hunger and recently felt phlegm gathering in his chest. *Can I risk hiding out here for another day?*

He eyed the chickens. One was lame, skinnier than the rest. With the prospect of roast chook for breakfast, it took him less than a minute to decide to stay.

———◠◡◠———

The marae was wakeful with activity. When it wasn't occupied with ceremonies or speeches, the meeting house was the place where the inner mauri was nourished. The women spread out their crafts on tables and floormats—they stripped flax leaves with blades of mussel shell, pounded and loosened the fibre and dyed it with raurēkau and tānekaha bark—each craftswoman inclining her head as they talked and laughed. Cordage was rolled on the women's thighs and pulled taut with strong fingers as they weaved and knotted.

Old friends had a talent for seeing the ridiculous in the smallest notion or incident. In such a manner, the women vied and teased, back and forth. They tossed their heads as another tale was told, their eyes brightened by banter, as they pursued artistic perfection. This was the day the ladies made beautiful things—baskets and mats, capes and cloaks, piupiu and tātua in the colours of red, black and tan.

At Rangitakō, the passion of the widows and senior women for arts and crafts was enhanced by the enthusiasm of the younger ones to learn the traditional songs and dances. Weekend classes were well attended and the aunties had been charged with making the children's costumes.

Atarangi, already a talented craftswoman, was unusual for her age. During these sessions she pestered the older women to teach her the oral traditions, the poetry and proverbs. The craft group ladies were feeling the absence of their youngest member. Touched by recent tragedies, they expressed their concern.

The girl had become vague and distracted since Sonny's death, they said. Some reported seeing her roaming the beach in the mornings or the dunes at sunset. Others had noticed her lonely figure on the cliff top or walking the hills. Miriama did not perceive these wanderings as boding ill. She loved Atarangi, but understood they were witnessing a young woman overwhelmed by grief.

Miriama studied the kilt she was weaving for the haka group, smiling up when there was an eruption of laughter in the hall. After the government had delivered its telegrams a space as wide as the universe had opened up inside her.

Passing on the traditions was a duty that weighed heavily upon the elders, and nothing was more sacred to a tohunga wahine than the maintenance of rangatira lines. Women were natural custodians of the genealogies. Right marriages must be struck. Arrangements must be made.

There was no doubt about Atarangi Tahiri's lineage. Her father and grandfather were of chiefly stock. Miriama had dearly wanted a Wirima to marry a Tahiri since the birth of her sons. Atarangi had shown high intelligence and a purity of heart, but this girl's mind was a rare and fragile thing. Now her mentor questioned how Atarangi would survive the loss of Sonny, a friendship she had encouraged since childhood.

'Time for tea,' Miriama announced.

It was early for morning tea, but nobody argued. The ladies dropped their work and closed the door against the leaves blown onto the porch. The day was blustery as they strolled arm in arm towards the dining hall. Not unusual for mid-winter. It was a chill that was easily dispersed by stoking up the wood range and the attendance of twenty ample bodies. The two women who'd gone ahead to prepare the refreshments had laid out four teapots, two rows of white cups, and plates of cakes and biscuits.

Years ago, Miriama had swept the young Atarangi under her wing after the loss of her parents. Her decision today wasn't difficult, but first she wanted to discuss it with the women.

Heti and Mata settled at the table with their tea and cakes.

'How is Ata?' Heti asked. 'She hardly speaks to anyone.'

     Kayleen M. Hazlehurst

Mata wrinkled her forehead. 'There's a strange look in that one's eyes. She reminds me of Granny King.'

'Granny King died of old age,' Miriama said, recalling the woman's dramatic deterioration following the death of her husband.

'And poor Hine,' insisted Mata. 'Remember poor Hine.'

Not long after her fiancé was killed in the Great War, Hinewai Rawhiti had taken to running along the beach in her nightdress. One night she disappeared. The men launched their boats in the morning to look for the girl. Her torn, half-naked body was found in the limbs of a mangrove tree. Since then, the name of the unfortunate one, 'poor Hine', was dredged up at any sign of deviance or madness in the young.

'Hinewai died of drowning,' Miriama rebutted again. 'I expect she slipped and cracked her skull. The tide carried her out and left her in the mangroves.' When she saw the concerned faces around her, she felt ashamed. The women only wanted news of their favourite daughter. 'These wanderings help Atarangi, and she always takes the dogs,' Miriama said as an assurance. 'Besides, she talks with Api.'

'Her heart is broken …'

'So young to have lost everything …'

'She's a lost one, that's for sure …'

Miriama tapped her fingers on the table while the women consoled each other and shook their heads. When she raised her hand, the nattering stopped. 'I have something to discuss with you … A proposal.'

'We're listening,' Heti said cautiously, not looking up.

'I think Hēmi and Atarangi should marry.'

Eyes widened. Someone gasped.

'Why?' Mata asked. 'Why do you think they should marry?'

'It is in keeping with the traditions. After a warrior falls in battle his brother may marry his wife. It is the honourable thing to do.'

'That was way back,' objected Heti, 'when men could have more than one wife.'

'No one has married anyone yet,' Mata said.

'Same principle,' Miriama persisted. 'Ka mate te kāinga tahi, ka ora te kāinga rua. When one house dies, a second house lives.'

'What about Winifred?'

'Āe. What about Winifred's house?'

'She's Hēmi's girlfriend.'

'Aren't they engaged or something?'

Miriama shifted uncomfortably in her seat. 'They've waited, in case one of them gets sent away.'

'I bet Hēmi will have something to say about this,' Mata protested.

'It's just a suggestion. Winifred has fancy ideas about going to the city.'

'She'll meet some Pākehā fella there …'

'Or a nice Ngāti Porou boy …'

'I have a nephew …'

The women collapsed together in laughter.

'Atarangi needs a strong husband. Someone she can trust.'

Heti frowned. 'Someone *you* can trust, don't you mean, Miriama?'

'If we don't make a good match, we may lose her.'

The aunties looked sorrowfully at each other, as if nothing could be done.

'Good luck making that one stick,' Heti muttered.

⁓

Twigs and leaves floated past him or rested beside the bank in whorls of scum. The water here was slow moving. Underwater meadows swayed to the motion of unseen currents. Sonny missed the comforts of the barn, but nothing was going to keep him from his brothers.

'Keep swimming,' he told the rat as it wove through the reeds.

The rodent moved at a relaxed pace between its hunting ground and burrow. Water rats were sleek, accomplished swimmers. Clean-living animals that preferred eating plants, water snails and tadpoles. After an hour of observation, Sonny could trace the domain of this round-faced creature.

In his stew pot the skinny carcass of a waterfowl was simmering. Once cooked, he would consume it, bones and all. He stirred the thin broth with his knife, adding watercress and a handful of leaves that tasted much like spinach. He'd eaten these wild greens before and they hadn't poisoned

   Kayleen M. Hazlehurst

him. Water lilies, too, were edible. The flower buds, young shoots and tubers. Some plants were bitter, and he wished his mother was here to advise him on which berries and roots he could eat.

The rat swivelled its ears and paddled to a jut of mud near the burrow. Sonny scratched his beard as he watched the industrious creature popping in and out of the water. Not a bad life for a water rat. He stirred his pot again and glanced over at his companion.

'Don't worry, little kiore. I'm not that desperate.'

Resolved to be friends, they contemplated the blue and gold of the day—the rat on its haunches chewing ends of stalks, Sonny nestled into the dry base of bulrushes—as glassy buds of water congregated against sticks, and sunlight ignited the iridescent wings of dragonflies.

Sonny continued south-east on his journey until he reached the expansive grasslands that skirted the base of Mount Ossa. This was poor farming country, sparsely populated. Goat trails hugged the stony hills and he set his pace at a trot, wanting to put more miles between himself and the tiny village he'd passed earlier. In the misty hours before sunrise a man's mind could slip back. At home this was the season for lifting the kūmara patches. *Are the fish running? How are the cows?*

A figure in tattered clothing came into view and they both halted, Sonny cursing himself for not having taken shelter. His experience of Greeks was limited. In this war-torn country, informers looked out for fugitives. This man was either a peasant or a wayfarer like himself. Sonny assumed he was a local man. An escaping soldier would have legged it by now. The man settled on a rock to observe the scenery, pretending he was unaware he had company. Sonny took his cue and diverted over a crest to allow the traveller to pass by unmolested.

He worried about these chance encounters. Men talked among themselves. This was a sign of things to come. The further he pressed south, the more likely he'd run into people. *Dimitri warned me about this.*

Mount Ossa and the coastal ranges contained stands of hardwoods and evergreens—maple, beech, oak, spruce and chestnut trees. At higher altitudes fir and pine were common, with groves of plane trees. Sonny surveyed the territory, accepting its ancient legacy. Not in the way of communicating with the gods and nymphs, but in acknowledging the first humans who had associated with these forests and sacred sites.

The spirits of this land would be aware of him passing through, as he was aware of them. Their rites and customs were unfamiliar, but he offered up his own chants and prayers in their honour, and for his own protection.

Far ahead he saw a vista of hills. *This must be the last range to the coast.* A dip in the ridgeline suggested a river ran between them, winding its way to the ocean. He planned to avoid the river as it would be the main travel route. Instead, he would make his way over the summit. In two days he'd surely be standing on the edge of the Aegean Sea. There, he would breathe in the salt air and be embraced in the arms of Tangaroa.

Sonny tramped the whole day and met no one. Close to sunset he came to a shepherd's hut butted against a rocky outcrop. Three stone walls, covered in a tangle of ivy and myrtle, supported a roof of gradually dislodging tiles. *Was this once a retreat for monks?*

Orthodox monasteries were plentiful throughout Greece, and wandering monks had been common in the years before the war. He searched the stony ground for a well and, discovering a flat stone at an opening, he lowered his bottles to the spring. When he hauled back the ropes he found the water was pure and cool.

The hut was one room, held up by the sturdiness of its chimney, with a useable hearth. The single window was broken, with a remnant of sacking nailed to its worm-infested frame. Lining the mantel were bottles and jars with peeling brown labels and over the floor were newspapers in different stages of disintegration. At the centre of the room was a table and chair, but no bed. A mattress, reeking of mildew and rat droppings, lay on the floor amidst broken glass and leaves. *God knows what lurks between its threads,* he thought, as he shoved it against the wall.

He would have preferred a clean cave, but looming clouds forced him to shore up the roof with brush and fallen tiles. After the floor was swept

     Kayleen M. Hazlehurst

with a head of brushwood, he spread his tent sheet over the newspapers, appreciating the insulation they provided. Within minutes he had built a fire in the hearth. When the flames died down he put his billy on the coals and sprinkled in a pinch of tea. Domestic tasks comforted him with memories of his mother. If the night noises made him nervous, he could draw on a few gems of paternal wisdom.

'It is a little-known fact,' Api once told Sonny, 'that even cows move around in the night.'

Splashing water and rapping branches were just the after-effects of a storm. Now he must sleep. The last five hours before sunrise was his time for travelling.

Breakfast was half a bag of broad beans stirred into a wheat porridge— the last of his supplies from the barn. He doused the fire and departed before lingering wisps of smoke from the chimney met the morning sky.

So, little flycatcher.
Will you come out to boldly challenge me
when I approach the place of Hinenuitepō?
Or will I be renewed like the moon and restored to life?

Will you laugh and dance
when I come alive in the sunlight?
Will you love me when I come to you at dawn?

Hah! And they said Māui would never return!

~13~

Reaching the Coast

A shot rang out from the old musket and echoed around the hills. Sonny had taken down a goat at sunrise. These stony grasslands, covered in yarrow, tarragon and wood sage, were home to the hardiest of animals—sheep and goats, foxes and other burrowing mammals. After gutting the goat and digging a hole to hide its entrails, he slung the carcass on his back. He would smoke the meat once he was well into the forest. This meat should last him until he reached the east coast. Through the coastal range he could scan the roads and seaways from higher vantage points and look out for a safe approach to the beach.

Sonny understood why men killed for a good pair of boots. Footwear was almost as vital as food and shelter. His own were worn and cracked from traipsing over this broken country. Holes were appearing at the toes and seams, and the leather was close to walking away from the soles. Infection was his greatest fear. More than once he had pulled a boot nail from where it had dug into his flesh. Cut, bruised and calloused, his feet were in much need of attention. The first thing he'd do when he got to the coast was soak them in the sea. Salt water was healing. His mother had taught him this. Afterwards he would seek a less arduous way of travelling. *Maybe I'll find a boat.*

'Yes!' he shouted when he reached the top of the range.

It had been months since he'd seen the ocean. Waves rolled to the shore in long, thin lines, softening the miles of coastline into a white haze.

On the second night he descended to a river. By keeping to the left bank, he was able to make his way to a village set above the salt flats. Moonlight sketched a line of road running north and south. Was it too much to

 Kayleen M. Hazlehurst

hope that this corner of Greece had escaped Nazi interest? As he slipped through the shadows, Sonny counted a dozen cottages with fishing vessels bobbing at anchor. Overturned rowing boats rested on the sand, with oars and nets stowed underneath. He left them undisturbed.

At the southern end of the village he found an empty building where a length of rope attached the door to a brass ring. No locks or bolts. This was public property. He pushed the door open. The musty hall was cluttered with chairs and trestle tables. Outside, the grounds were level and well cared for. *Enough space for stalls. A marketplace perhaps, where they sell animals or swap fish for cabbages.*

He dropped his pack against the wall, too tired to explore any further. For tonight, as far as he was concerned, the building was empty. After swallowing a mouthful of water, he collapsed on the horsehair couch and drifted away with the salty musk.

———

Hēmi placed the pail of milk on the kitchen table.

'Mum.'

'Thank you, dear … Dad feeding the dogs?'

'Yeah.'

'Dinner in ten minutes.'

Miriama added mint to the lamb stew and looked over her shoulder. Her eldest son had been quiet all week. With a pang of guilt, she remembered the shock on his face when she raised the proposal that he marry Atarangi. He had shaken his head and walked away. Since then, he'd been sulking.

She stopped to read his eyes. 'Well, what is it? Tell me.'

'Why must it be me who replaces Sonny? I don't see why it's so important.'

'Tradition.'

'Bugger tradition!'

'Hēmi!'

'Sorry, Mum.'

'Look at the poor girl. The state she's in. Don't you love Atarangi?'

'Not in the way I love Winifred.'

'Winifred has other plans. You've had a nice friendship, but she will leave, you'll see.'

'A nice friendship! Is that what you call it?'

The hammering of heels on the doorstep, and the sucking sound of feet being extracted from gumboots, announced Api's arrival home.

'Everything all right?' Api asked as he came in. He looked from his son to his wife.

Miriama turned back to the stove. 'Āe. Wash up, dear. Dinner is ready.'

The house was silent except for the breathing of sleeping dogs. Four hours earlier Miriama had listened to her inebriated son as he stumbled indoors. Hēmi had taken off after dinner and returned home late. *He'll be grumpy tomorrow.*

The dogs usually slept on the front veranda, guarding the door. When her eldest came home late, they sometimes followed him indoors and settled under the kitchen table. At other times they came into the main bedroom to occupy the mat under the window.

Miriama watched patterns of light on the ceiling. *Don't backtrack, old one,* she told herself. *Winifred will leave for the city and Hēmi will be heartbroken. He will see Atarangi is the right girl for him. Of course, they will marry. They're close those two.*

It started as a low growl, then a scraping of claws on the floorboards.

Miriama opened her eyes to see the bunched figures of the dogs. Kete was standing, her hair raised. Turi had lifted his muzzle. Alert. Listening. Miriama could hear nothing but the usual sounds of the night. She touched her husband's arm.

Api sat up. 'Is it possums?'

'I don't know, Api. Something is terribly wrong.'

—⌇—

Sonny woke to the shock of cold steel on his throat.

Outside he heard heavy vehicles passing. When the building stopped shaking his assailant relaxed his hand and let out a breath. Sonny slowly

     Kayleen M. Hazlehurst

twisted his neck to stare at him. *No one creeps up on me like this. I must be losing my edge.*

The youth was speaking in broken Greek and his hands were fluttering. Starving probably. Jittery with hunger. Under a worn cloak his khaki trousers were caked with dirt. He must have been on the run for a while. Still pointing the blade, the boy backed towards the pack.

Sonny kept his eyes on him, giving him enough rope while he jabbered. In perfect English, he said, 'What unit are you from, brother? And quit waving that flaming knife around before you hurt yourself.' Then he smiled as the young man fell to the floor.

'Bloody hell. You're one of us.'

'Quick as a lamb's tail,' Sonny replied dryly.

The soldier's face took on an expression of utter shock and relief.

'*Ah*, mate … You're a Kiwi.'

'Last time I looked.' Sonny eyed the knife. 'What are you up to?'

'Sorry.' The soldier dropped the weapon and waved his hand over Sonny's peasant outfit. 'You could pass for a fair dinkum Greek in that get-up. I was afraid you might give me away. Jerries are everywhere.'

Sonny slipped over to the window and flattened himself against the wall to look out. 'Why are they here?'

'Patrolling. Searching for soldiers or for the Greeks who are hiding them. They've executed entire families for helping our fellas.'

'Bastards!'

'Some Greeks have turned traitor. Be careful who you trust.'

'Informers?'

'Yeah, a nasty bunch of collaborators who think they're on the winning side.'

'Looks like the Jerries are passing through,' Sonny said, as the last two motorcyclists trailed after the troop carriers.

'They do the circuit to frighten people. Further down, the road turns inland.'

'What's after that?'

'The Pelion Peninsula, nothing but coastline for fifty miles.' The soldier sheathed his knife. 'To be honest, I haven't got a clue what to do next.'

By his accent, Sonny could tell his new comrade was an Australian. His teeth were crooked, and his arms and chest were muscular. A farm boy, he guessed. His hands were still trembling, and he was having trouble finding his legs.

Sonny went to his pack and opened an outer pouch. 'First things first,' he said pulling out two strips of dried goat meat. 'Get stuck into that. You can't think straight when you're hungry.'

In a second the younger man was tearing at the meat and gulping it down.

'Eat slow, trooper. Here, drink this.' He handed over his water bottle and sat on the floor to eat with him. 'How about telling me who you are.'

'I'm Freddy Peacock. AIF 2nd/8th. My cobbers call me Feather.'

'Sonny Wirima, Māori Battalion.' He accepted the handshake.

'*Ah,* Sonny. You're a walking miracle, mate.' Freddy tore off more of the leathery strip and ground it between his molars. 'Damn fine meat … I won't ask what I'm eating.'

'Leg of goat.'

Feather winked. 'Not leg of Hun?'

'Not yet. Where are you from, Feather?'

'South Australia. A little sheep station in the Curnamona region. A few of us went down to Melbourne to enlist.'

Sonny doubted any Australian sheep station was little, but he let Feather ramble on.

'We were fighting at Vevi. Then we pulled out of Servia to take up new positions. April 19th, I think it was. We were trying to help the British hold Thermopylae when your blokes came down from the mountains to join us.'

Sonny's heart went out to his friends. What a desperate state the New Zealanders must have been in after their withdrawal from Olympus.

'I tell you, mate. The Aussies were never more pleased to see a Kiwi than they were on that day.'

'What happened at Thermopylae?'

'Our field gunners held off the Panzers for a while, but without tanks or air support we didn't have a show. The Nazis were about to break

   Kayleen M. Hazlehurst

through, and the brass wanted to get us out of there.'

Sonny remembered how the Germans had tried to outflank them in the Mavroneri Gorge, and how D Company had stood their ground. Freddy Peacock was talking about another battle in central Greece that had come and gone.

'We knew they would be sending in the Luftwaffe,' Feather went on. 'At Thermopylae Pass we had ten thousand blokes and a convoy of vehicles cramming the roads. Bombers could have flattened us in one go. It was a nightmare!'

'How did you end up here on the coast?'

'As soon as we got out we were ordered to retreat to Athens. What with them strafing the roads, some of us figured we should head east. We've met many others since then—Aussies, Tommies, Serbs, Yugoslavs, Poles.'

'So where are you heading?'

'Our plan is to get to Turkey and make our way to Alexandria … There'll be a railway line some of the way, we reckon … We can walk to Salonika, or all the way around the flamin' Aegean if we have to.'

'Sounds like a long walk.' Sonny thought about the black plumes of smoke rising from Salonika, announcing the arrival of the centaurs.

'We'll keep an eye out for a boat. Hire a fisherman.'

'Fair enough. Watch out for those troops on the borders. Some Serbs I met said the Bulgarians are as vicious as wolves … How's your food supply?'

'Me and the other five go scouting for tucker and share what we find at night. We try to eat once a day, but that doesn't always happen.'

'So where are your mates?' Sonny asked Feather. 'There's six of you, did you say?'

'Yeah. They'll be waiting for me at our hideout.'

'Then we'd better go find enough to feed six hungry men.'

Feather took a step back. 'How're we going to do that?'

'Ever heard of fishing?'

The young soldier looked doubtful and Sonny gave him a clip over the ear.

'*Agh!* What was that for?'

'Come at me with a knife, would ya?'

Feather ducked his head. 'Sorry, Sonny.'

'Never mind. You'll keep.'

He stowed his gun and pack behind a stack of chairs and adjusted his clothes.

'If you're going to steal stuff,' Sonny explained to his new friend that morning, 'either be on good terms with the person you're stealing from, or make sure you don't get caught.'

'Will the people think they own all the fish?'

'Maybe not the fish, but they'll know they own the fishing gear. We have to borrow it politely and return it with interest.'

The sky had lightened, and they set off from the hall at a brisk pace. At the beach, three wizened figures were sitting on upturned boxes, puffing on pipes. These fishermen might be retired, but they knew who owned the boats. Sonny strolled over and bowed, adjusting his cap as he rose.

All eyes swivelled sideways.

He took out three strips of goat jerky and presented a piece to each elder. The Greeks accepted the gift and concentrated on the sea as they chewed. Sonny cleared his throat to regain their attention. Then, placing one hand on his heart, he gestured towards the boats where the nets were stowed. With a grand sweep, he cast out an imaginary net and deftly trawled it in. Then he made eating motions and touched his heart again.

The old men turned and nattered with each other.

Sonny beckoned them to follow him to the boats. He spread his arms, asking them to choose one.

There was disagreement, but one voice rose above the others. The victor, smacking the beseeching hands of the others, sauntered over to what looked like the best kept of the boats. Tipping it, he indicated that the net beneath could be borrowed. Sonny lifted out the net, folding it over and over as the fishermen settled back on their seats to watch.

Feather was knee-deep in the water with his trousers turned up, pretending to know what he was doing. A sheep station in South Australia hadn't

   Kayleen M. Hazlehurst

given him a lot of experience with sea fishing, but Sonny had shown him how to hold his end of the net and how to flick it.

Sonny stepped out of his clothes, folding and placing them in a pile on the seat. The Greeks fixed their eyes on him, their eyebrows up to their hairline, as he waded into the water in nothing more than his ragged underpants. He began dragging the net through the water, chest-deep, moving in a steady arc. There would be fish in these shallows—sprats, piper, herring—the sort of fish he'd once used for bait, but which still made a good fry-up.

That morning Sonny and Feather trawled in more than a hundred frylings, all jumping and silver in the net. A fistful for each gentleman, and the rest Feather bundled into a sack. Clothed again, Sonny returned the net to its place. He gave the fishermen his broadest smile and strode away whistling. Behind him he heard their animated voices but did not look back.

The elderly Greeks returned to the beach the next day. This time accompanied by their equally elderly wives, each bearing a modest bowl for the 'fish interest'. One woman brought olives and had two towels over her arm, another carried a basket of bread and cheese, while a third produced a pair of laundered underpants. The husband tipped his head towards the garment as it was presented to Sonny. In telling the tale of yesterday's encounter, the subject of the foreigner's underpants being threadbare and about to fall off in the water must have come up. The ladies averted their eyes as he swapped his old ones for the new pair.

Feather's compatriots had come along for the fishing ceremony, having enjoyed some of the previous day's catch. They hovered at the edge of a building, unwilling to come closer. Feather said they were ashamed because they were infested with lice.

The wives offered water and nourishment to everyone. Sonny rolled knobs of bread between his fingers and threw out the crumbs to attract more fish. On this net-drag the catch was more substantial. Everyone received a share for their bowls, and there was some giggling as the ladies patted the visitors dry with their towels.

It was time to leave. News would spread and more people might come to watch the sand fishermen. Maybe even one or two of those betrayers Sonny had heard about. There would always be men with treachery in their hearts. This was no surprise to a Ngā Puhi.

The Australians were ready to wing their way north and Sonny would fly south. In parting there were many things he wanted to say to his new friends, but he could not advise these proud men. Instead, he gave them an assurance that whether tramping around the great Aegean, or sailing over it, they could rely upon the kindness of Greeks.

Hands were gripped and shaken. Feather was given a playful punch on the arm. And they all agreed to meet up again for a drink in Cairo.

—⁓—

Sonny's aim was to travel the coast at night and shelter during the day in a sea cave. A suitable site protruding into the side of a cliff provided a platform of shells above the reach of the water. After a good sleep, he emerged in the afternoon to appraise his surroundings and to infuse the last of the sunlight into his bones. He stretched out in a warm nook, aware that every part of his body ached—legs, shoulders and lower back. It was as though he had never quite dried out since he'd left Egypt.

When Sonny first set out on this journey he had thought he was the last man left. Now, he saw Greece was swarming with Allied soldiers. Scattered men cut adrift from their units. They had come down from the mountains and assembled in the foothills of Mount Ossa. They had evaded capture at Lárissa and Lamia, or at the Thermopylae Pass. They had trekked to the coast from any point they were able. Each trying to make the best of it.

Sonny had himself walked the hills of Thessaly for weeks, with no news from home and no way of sending a message. In the wilderness he was protected, but this far south there was danger. Surveillance aircraft plunged from grey clouds without warning, enemy vessels patrolled the sea, and he was aware of a growing heaviness in his chest.

He was hungrier than he'd ever been and hot currents of apprehension

Kayleen M. Hazlehurst

ran through the wires of his nerves. Cold and hunger he could stand, but not this. Heartsick, he realised he was one of the lost.

Companionship with other soldiers made a difference to his state of mind. Their shared adversity as men on the run somehow gave him strength. If Sonny didn't know all these men by name, he could easily have told their stories. They had moved around in small bands, sleeping by day in olive groves, deserted buildings or holes in the ground. Some combed the countryside looking for any bullock cart, truck, or train that might carry them closer to freedom. Others, like him, preferred invisibility. At the end, every man longed to be gathered up by the Royal Navy and taken away from this tragic place.

It was heartening to hear that the defence of the three mountain passes in the north had given the navy time to evacuate so many of the Allied soldiers from the southern ports and beaches. Now mainland Greece was completely occupied, and the opportunity for evacuation had passed. Germans were staging raids along the coast, seizing diesel vessels and using them to ferry their troops. Fuel was almost unobtainable.

Men trapped behind enemy lines could only hope to find a sailing boat to convey them far into the Mediterranean, where they might be rescued by a British warship. Desperate dreams of desperate men. All of them straggling along in the same wretched condition.

There was something of the beached whale in their demeanour—as if their spirits knew they shouldn't be here but had no idea how to get off this land. Sonny felt pity for them. He wished he could summon a gang of strong warriors to heft them back into the sea.

~14~

Escape by Devious Means

It was a risky business, taking in fugitives. The Nazis were hostile when it came to dealing with soldiers on the run and particularly unforgiving towards the Greeks who helped them. *Better not to embroil innocent people in your troubles.*

It was a rare feeling. Sitting at the entrance of his sea cave, Sonny could almost convince himself that every sunset brought him closer to his loved ones. In an hour, he would take his knife and look for kina. He hadn't expected to find the prickly sea eggs—darker and smaller than those at home—but when he searched for food yesterday, there they were. He would set up a line at dusk, the best time for catching fish.

On Api's insistence, three fishing lines and a choice of hooks and sinkers had occupied a corner of his pack since he left New Zealand. Sonny wanted to thank his father for his foresight. Yet, how could he? He wiped his eyes with a rough hand. *What a mess. They will think I am dead.*

The cry of a seabird made him look up. Near him a gull was hanging on its wings with its legs dangling down. He sent a message of love to Atarangi, certain she had sent one to him.

—⁓—

Seabirds swooped and called. Atarangi had been listening to their love songs as she watched a fringe of water dampen the sand. The tide was turning, filling pools and crevices, sending in sticks and seaweed on the foam.

Winifred had come to the beach to join her. They were both miserable.

'Please don't take away my Hēmi,' her friend pleaded, almost in tears.

Atarangi's heart did a somersault. 'I don't want to take Hēmi from you, Winnie. Honestly. I'm waiting for Sonny.'

Winifred sighed deeply. '*Oh, Ata …*'

'I promised … I promised …'

'I'm not sure Sonny is coming back, e kare.'

'He must … You can't say that … You don't know anything!'

'You're right, I don't know a thing. I'm so sorry.' Winifred studied the water at their feet. 'Tide's coming in. We'd better move.' They took a spot further up. 'The thing is, Ata, I doubt many of them will be coming home. There'll be no one left for us to marry.'

'What should I do? They're all insisting …'

'Nan and the aunties?'

'Not Nan, the others. I'm the last of my line. I'm supposed to produce sons.'

Winifred brushed away her friend's tears. 'Well you can't do that on your own, now can you, poor girl?'

They turned to hug each other.

'I would never deliberately hurt you, Winnie.'

'I know.'

Ata hiccupped and pulled away. 'Perhaps we should both marry Hēmi.'

Winifred gave a short laugh. 'That would serve them right, wouldn't it?'

There were too many voices. Who were her muses now?

People kept telling her Sonny was dead, but she didn't believe it.

'Be careful, Atarangi,' they said. 'You could go mad with grief, like poor Hine …'

'It'll be better once you have your own child …'

'Hēmi will take care of you …'

Then there were the voices from her dreams. Her tūpuna. Those who spoke to her when she was alone. These were reassuring. Telling her to wait. Yet her soul burned as if a hot knife had passed through butter.

She loved the old ladies, but she wished they would stop pressing her to marry Hēmi. She couldn't bear to see Winifred so sad. The spiritual world would never lie. She trusted her people. She trusted her birds. *Why aren't I allowed to make up my own mind? Why is everything so urgent?*

Even his mother was puzzled. She told Ata she hadn't felt Sonny's presence during the dedication ceremony, nor had she sensed his spirit in his favourite places. 'Why hasn't he come home to say goodbye?' Miriama asked.

'Maybe he's trapped somehow.'

'Āe. We must pray for him.'

Atarangi knew Sonny was still alive. He had been sending her messages. She wasn't pōrangi. Her grasp of reality was better than anyone's.

Nobody listened … Too many voices …

Miriama was grubbing weeds when Hēmi's friend passed her garden on her way from the beach. 'Winifred,' Miriama called, 'these are for your mother.' She offered a fistful of carrots, the nearest vegetable she could tear from the ground.

The girl came over for the carrots. 'Thanks.'

'How's Mum?'

'She's good.'

Miriama went back to turning over the soil between the rows, finding it hard to meet Winifred's eye. 'I'm going back to the house. Will you come for a cup of tea?'

'That would be nice. Is Hēmi around?'

'I expect so.' Miriama pulled out a second bunch of carrots, shook off the soil, and added them to her kit.

They walked along the cliff path, one behind the other, not speaking. When they arrived at the house, Hēmi came out of the barn.

'This is nice. I wasn't expecting to see you.'

'Your mum invited me for a cup of tea.'

'Not working today?'

'I took the day off. Things to do.'

Miriama placed her hand on the doorknob, feeling a spark of remorse. *Those two light up when they see each other.* 'I'll bring your teas to the front veranda, Hēmi.'

'Thanks, Mum.'

In the kitchen she made clattering noises, excuses not to join them. Her husband was waiting for his usual on the back porch. After serving

     Kayleen M. Hazlehurst

the young ones, she delivered a single cup and a biscuit to Api, with a cursory greeting.

'Aren't you having one?' he asked.

'I need to get on, dear.'

Miriama hustled inside to where the kitchen window was set ajar. Alone at the kitchen table she sat with her tea to listen.

'I sent in my forms today,' Winifred told Hēmi.

There was no answer.

'They want support staff,' the girl continued. 'They're calling for recruits for the Women's Auxiliary Air Force ... Please say something, Hēmi.'

'The air force? Where will you do your training?'

'Auckland. Hobsonville, I think.'

'So you're going ahead with this?'

'I have to do something.'

He was silent again.

'Hēmi?'

His voice was low and gruff. 'When do you leave?'

'February sometime, I think.'

'You know they want me to marry Atarangi.'

It came as an outburst. An accusation. Winifred would be stung by this. 'Yes.'

'What am I supposed to do?' he asked her.

Then came the sobs. Winifred was crying. 'I love you both,' she said. 'But Ata is so fragile, and husbands are not thick on the ground right now.'

'What are you saying?'

'If you think it's the right thing to do, you have my blessing.'

'*Christ, Winnie!* Is that why you're leaving? To get out of our way?'

'I'm sorry ... No ... I don't know ...'

Miriama heard rustling. She was sure Hēmi had taken Winifred into his arms.

'I will miss you, taupuhi,' he said.

'I'll miss you too. You're my best friend in the world.'

The scream of the kettle voiced her own cry of shame. Miriama grabbed the kettle from the stove, spilling some of the boiling water. She cried out and held the scalded hand to her chest. *What have I done?*

—∞—

Sonny's thoughts turned again to the Māori Battalion. *How many of our men have been captured? How many killed?* It wasn't the first time an army had been routed and strewn to the four winds like hayseed. There was no disgrace in withdrawal before a superior army, Pākehā officers had told them. Greek history was full of such events. But Sonny's buddies would feel bad about this. Being chased from one end of the country to the other was not the Māori way of conducting a war. In traditional times the whakamā, the shame of defeat, would have been unbearable.

He detected a weakness in his limbs. A slow sapping of vigour as layers of fat and muscle melted away. His skin had become transparent, tissue paper pulled over bone. He was weary of crossing rivers, dog-tired from walking, sick to his soul with longing. *Homesickness can gnaw at a man's gut like a rat.*

In a warming flush, he reflected on his little river friend. If anything put him to shame it was that damn water rat. Not once did he see the creature give up. It kept swimming round and around gathering food, seeking out the next tasty meal of water snail. He remembered the sleek brown fur and chubby face of his companion in the days they had hidden together in the bulrushes. Like the rodent, he must adapt. *If I look for food when it's safe and sit in the sunshine when it's not, I will survive. What does it matter if I'm barefoot and hungry? So was Ratty and I didn't see him going belly-up.*

During his first days in Greece, Sonny had bought a map. He had studied the general terrain while he was in Athens and again when he was in Katerini. He wished his map had been linen like the ones the officers were given. Paper maps fell to pieces in the damp and his had long since disintegrated. At the time he had asked people to pronounce the placenames, committing to memory the location of major towns. Now, as he trailed along the coast, he had a sense of where he was going.

He needed a plan if he wanted to catch up with the Allies. Feather and

     Kayleen M. Hazlehurst

his friends were aiming for a neighbouring country, taking the long way around. On his map those north-eastern headlands had looked almost impassable to him. *They'll have to climb some steep cliffs, travel overland, and cross borders guarded by those vicious-as-wolves Bulgarians.*

In Sonny's mind, the safest route to Turkey was straight across the Aegean Sea. To the west there was the port settlement of Volos. Opposite to where he was standing, by his calculation. *How far have I travelled? Maybe a hundred and fifty or two hundred miles?*

A trek through the coastal hills should bring him close to this port. His first idea was to find a fisherman in Volos to ferry him to the island of Chios. Mainland Turkey wasn't far from there and he'd heard the Turkish port of İzmir had a railway station. *Who knows? Could be just a short hop to Cairo.* This seemed like a reasonable plan, until another band of travellers brought disappointing news. The Nazis had entrenched themselves in Volos and were watching the harbour.

His new companions were escaping prisoners of war. Allied soldiers were absconding in significant numbers, and this group had slipped away from their captors at a transit camp near Lárissa. POWs were sent in working parties to repair damaged roads and bridges, and these men had made a run for it along the gravel riverbed. They told Sonny it was their last chance to break free before they were transported to the more secure camp at Salonika. After that, it was the dreaded prison camps they'd heard about in Germany, Austria or Poland.

The escapers had hitched a ride under the carriages of a troop train. When they had alighted at Volos they found the place 'lousy with Jerries'. A Greek family had given them overnight shelter, and then taken them by bullock cart to the hills. It took them twelve hours to walk over the range to the east coast. With them came more bad news.

The southern port of Piraeus, where the Māori Battalion first landed in Greece, had been bombed. Many ships were destroyed. Even the *Hellas*, a large steam yacht recruited to evacuate five hundred hospital patients to Alexandria, had suffered a callous attack. The heat of rage rose from his chest to his face as he thought about those wounded men and their nurses, trapped and terrified in a burning, sinking vessel.

The hope they might escape through Turkey had its own problems. Hitler had threatened reprisals against any neighbouring countries who helped the Allies, and Turkey had declared they wished to remain neutral. The Turkish authorities might pass fugitives on to the British, or they might intern them and hand them over to the Germans. It would depend on who was on duty and whether they could be bribed. Much like the Greek police, you couldn't be certain of the reception you would get.

—❦—

It was a clear night and the dunes had retained the last heat of the day. After building a fire between the sand hills, the men had shared a mushy stew of six hard biscuits, a bag of oats, some dried beans, and the two fish Sonny had caught. It reminded him of his mother's boil-ups, but with army biscuits and oats.

'So, Ratty,' Sonny said. 'Escaping by slow and devious means was the best tactic after all.' The furry, brown companion inside his head had become a regular confidant on matters of survival.

'What's that?'

'Eh?'

The men cast their eyes sideways to check who Sonny was addressing. The Anzacs were relaxed. It sounded like a nickname for one of them. The other Māori boy in their group owned up to it and seemed glad. Maybe because he didn't yet have a nickname, or maybe because he didn't want people to think his battalion buddy was talking to himself.

Sonny saw his shining face and went along with it. After this brief lapse of concentration, Motu Paraki became known in the group as 'Ratty'.

Ruby leaned in. 'What were you saying, mate?' Bob Stone was a tall, red-faced Digger who hailed from a mining town in outback Queensland.

'If we should avoid the ports,' Sonny continued, 'what about a path through the islands?'

Mac looked uncertain. 'What are our chances of getting a boat?' Jock MacDonald was a hard-bitten New Zealand farmer from the South Island. A big man with a tangled beard and a shock of auburn hair, whose

     Kayleen M. Hazlehurst

humour and kindness belied a quick temper and ready fist when crossed. Sonny decided he was the sort of man who would be a loyal friend but a dangerous enemy.

Ruby drew a finger through the sand. 'We should strike out for Crete and find a way from there to Egypt. There'll be plenty of sailing boats. At sea we have a chance of running into a friendly naval ship.'

'Worth a try.' Sonny rubbed the back of his neck. Hurling a rickety boat onto the Mediterranean sounded daunting. 'We'll need food and water, some tools and blankets.'

Ratty knotted his brow. 'The people will help us, won't they?'

Sonny turned to the Greek. 'What do you think, Spiros?'

'Sure, sure they will help,' Spiros answered in his languid way. 'Is wonderful place, Crete. I have many relatives—'

'Will you do the translations for us?' Monty asked. 'My Greek's a bit rusty.' Monty Porter, a slightly built Englishman, was nursing an injured leg. Mac had carried Monty on his back during the worst part of the coastal path.

Spiros waved his hand. 'I come with you to Crete. I do all the talking.'

Later, as the others lazed under the stars in their sandy hollow, Sonny went to sit beside the Englishman. His last days with Tama had shown him the perils of not attending to flesh wounds.

'Will you let me take a look at that leg?'

'You can have a look. I'm not shy.' Monty pulled up his trousers and revealed an oozing tear in his calf.

'Hell. What did you cop?'

'A piece of shrapnel. Tore the muscle.'

'I can clean that for you, Monty. Do you mind taking a dip in the sea?'

The Englishman shuddered. 'Do I have to?'

'Mate, you don't want that thing going septic. If you wash the wound every day with seawater it will heal.'

'Freeze my balls off, don't you mean?'

Sonny laughed. 'Just enough to cover the wound. Hey, take your boots off first.'

Monty began to unstrap his boots. 'Blimey, I think they're stuck on.' He tugged at his socks and turned his face. '*Aw-w!*'

'Bit of a pong, eh? Never mind, a soak in the sea will fix that too.'

Monty looked at Sonny's bare feet. 'Where are your boots?'

'I chucked them away when I got to the coast. The mountains finished them off. There was nothing left of them.'

'Wait a minute.' Monty dug into his kitbag and pulled out a second pair of boots. 'These might fit you. They're too big for me.'

Sonny looked over the extra boots. He didn't want to enquire about their origin.

'They belonged to a friend of mine,' Monty said, as if reading his thoughts. 'He would've wanted someone to use them.'

Sonny acknowledged the lost friend with a sad smile. 'Thank you. These look like a fine pair of boots.'

'The best of British shoe leather,' Monty said.

They heard raucous laughter. The men were telling jokes around the fire and Mac and Ruby were having a game of cards on a flattened area of sand.

'Your turn,' Mac told the Australian.

'Anyone for a swim?' Sonny called out. They were standing in their underpants, ready to go in.

'*Oi!*' Ruby shouted.

Mac roared. 'Are you sure you want company?'

Sonny pointed at Monty's leg, indignant. 'We need to wash out this wound.'

'Yeah, yeah.'

'Come on, you smelly buggers,' Sonny retaliated. 'When's the last time any of you had a wash?'

'I'll come with ya,' Ratty said, stripping off his clothes.

Mac threw aside his cards. 'Righto. You're on.'

Ruby groaned. 'Suppose I can't inflict m'self on you lot any longer.'

'You Anzacs!' Spiros flung up his arms. 'All crazy people!'

In a few minutes everyone was naked and haring down to the water. Yelling their lungs out and plunging into the sea.

     Kayleen M. Hazlehurst

~15~

Damn Fools and Good Companions

They resumed their journey at midnight, etching footprints in the sand and using the luminous line of white water as their guide. Further on, the lights of cottages were the first signs of life—fishermen preparing to rise with the sun.

As they approached a village they encountered a lone man on the shore. Spiros shared a smoke with the stranger while the others waited on the beach. When Spiros came back, he was smiling. The man had a suitable sailing boat, he said. It belonged to a retired fisherman who was eager to sell. They searched their pockets for their last drachmas to buy the eighteen-footer with a short mast. The boat had canvas sails and a set of oars. The Greek happily took their money. Sonny didn't entirely trust the man, and he didn't entirely trust the boat.

Their success in obtaining a vessel had bathed them in a glow of promise. For their next venture it was proposed Spiros take them from house to house to beg for provisions. 'Greeks are generous people,' Spiros told them. 'They will give you what they can.'

Sonny volunteered to stay behind to guard their boat, saying he wanted to make sure it was seaworthy. He had noted two rotten side planks and intended to examine the hull for leaks.

'Can you find me a hammer and some nails?' Sonny asked Ruby.

'I'll try. Anything else?'

'Some wire cutters and a saw would help.'

'No worries.'

'Be quick. It's not safe to hang around. Just thank them and leave.'

Ratty wanted to stay back with Sonny. 'I can dive under the boat. Check the bottom for you, Sonny.'

Who Disturbs the Kūkupa?   119

'We'll get a better look if we pull her onto the sand. Let's swing her sideways. It will give us somewhere to hide if we see any patrols.'

The night before, Spiros had elaborated on the nature of Greek hospitality. It was tradition to welcome visitors and to never turn away a person in need. With this war many believed it was their duty to assist the brave men who had come from faraway to defend them.

The villagers would give away the last morsel from their kitchen tables, so care must be taken not to ask for too much. A small minority did not share this sentiment, Spiros warned. In their minds, a rabble of deserters had descended upon Greece like a plague of locusts. For a coin, bad Greeks would not hesitate to betray the Allies.

———⁓———

Pacific waves broke near the shore and washed onto the beach in white fans. The tohunga and her apprentice were discussing the sacred lore as they rambled over the dunes. In previous weeks, there had been little conversation between them. Atarangi missed her mentor's counsel, and the subject of her marriage to Hēmi had not been raised again.

They found a curved sandbank to settle against. Grey-green dune grasses, clumps of flowering shrubs and ground vines held together these sand hills. Beside them, tufts of cotton tails shifted on a light ocean breeze. Atarangi plucked nine of the fluffy heads and pressed them to her lips, aware the tohunga was watching.

'It is an eternal problem, Atarangi,' Miriama was saying. 'The battle of light and dark has been with us since the world was born out of chaos.'

Atarangi smoothed the sand by her leg, arranging the cotton tails into a sunny circle.

'This is a test for all of us. Especially for those who follow the wānanga teachings. In the ninth heaven there are entities occupied with drawing us away from our chosen paths.'

Ata searched her elder's face. 'Why would someone choose a pathway of darkness over a pathway of light?'

'It's no secret, there are those who walk in the light and those who do not. In the world there are two Schools of Learning—each with their

 Kayleen M. Hazlehurst

unique way of teaching, each with their own experts and priests.' Miriama turned her skirts right and left to free them from the grains of sand that had settled between the folds of fabric. 'These whare wānanga co-exist, child. In the greater universe it is a matter of balance.'

Atarangi stood to pick more wild flowers. These teachings were making her afraid for Sonny. *Why do people choose not to be good?* She placed the flowers on the older woman's lap and turned to face the sea. 'Explain to me the dark path again, Auntie. Why must it be?'

Miriama paused to admire the gift. 'Sit with me and I will tell you. The spirit realm is veiled from most of us. It is not for the faint-hearted to explore. The choices and decisions we make affect who we are in this life and what we become in the next.'

'Yes, but can you give me an example?'

'The elders acknowledge these opposites. We respect and honour the warrior, even if he comes to take our lives. The warrior is the bearer of death and sorrow. His counterpart is the light-bearer, the bringer of peace and life.'

'Why must he bring death and sorrow? Can't he also be a warrior of peace?'

'Because these two are not in accord. If in battle a warrior raised his head and shouted, "Peace, my brothers. Let there be peace!" what do you think would happen?'

Atarangi giggled as she imagined her reckless peacemaker, standing between two firing lines. 'He would be shot, of course.'

'Āe. But when the battle is over, then he may become a light-bearer. After those angry men have set aside their weapons, and he no longer feels the need to defend his people. A warrior who speaks of peace after battle will be heard because he speaks from experience.'

'The warrior has changed paths?' Atarangi said with a rush of hope.

'Everyone has the choice to change paths, Ata.'

'So these schools of light and dark each have their own priests?'

'Āe. Their own teachers and pupils, their own rituals and rules.'

'Like the army, do you mean?'

'Ka pai. The army is a whare wānanga that teaches the art of killing.'

'I don't like the idea of it very much.'

'Light and shadow bring depth and meaning to our worlds, Atarangi. We need them both. Priests of combative schools, leaders we now call them, also knew how to work their magic. Warriors have the final say in disputes between people, just as healers heal wounds. All forces have the power to cleanse, and even a dark prism reflects some light.'

'So I loved a man who chose to take the dark path, because …'

'Because this was the power required of him in war.'

'I'm not sure I can live with this.'

'*Ah-h-h.* Sonny was always a soul of mixed spirits. He has wavered between goodness and mischief since he was a boy. A mother observes these things in a son.'

Atarangi nodded. She too had seen this.

Miriama continued. 'Choosing between the two paths would have been Sonny's greatest dilemma.'

'What do you mean?'

'I have no doubt both forces have battled to claim him. Sonny would as likely die from trying to save others as trying to kill bad men.' She patted Ata's hand. 'I hope this is a comfort to you, dear.'

Atarangi's tears formed again. 'How I wish Sonny could come back to Te Ao Mārama one more time. I don't believe he's dead.'

'Āe, child. Don't we all wish … Don't we all believe?'

———〰———

Propped on its side with an oar, the boat provided them with shade as they waited. People on the beach passed them by, but there were no offers of help or food.

Ratty began to fidget. 'Why haven't they come back, Sonny?'

'They're getting to know the villagers. Come on. I need to get some pitch for these boards.'

They lowered the boat to the sand and set off at a good pace for the village.

'Don't speak to anyone,' Sonny instructed. 'Pretend you can't hear them.'

   Kayleen M. Hazlehurst

'Like I'm deaf or stupid?'

'That'll do. Try not to give y'self away.'

Ratty looked down, dejected. 'Okay.'

Sonny didn't want to be cruel. 'We'll get you some more clothes, hey? You'd make a nice-looking Greek boy.' He punched Ratty on the arm, making him laugh.

It didn't take long to find the others. Their voices could be heard from two streets away. In front of a taverna, Spiros was holding court with three men over a carafe of wine. Half-plastered, Mac and Ruby were telling each other stories. Monty, whose Greek must have been better than he'd let on, was having coffee and a conversation with a suited man whose air of confidence suggested he might be the mayor.

'There they are!' Mac raised his glass when he spotted them.

Sonny didn't like the attention. Fraternising with citizens in a public place had trouble written all over it. People on the street were scurrying past with their boxes of produce, or their donkeys and baskets. Some glanced sideways at the visitors, their foreheads furrowed. A sure sign the locals knew something they didn't.

He shoved Ratty into an alley. 'Wait here. Keep your eyes peeled. Come and get me if you're worried.'

The proprietor came out of the taverna for more orders. He stood with one hand on his aproned stomach, the other on the back of Spiros' chair like they were best mates. The chattering and gesticulations were becoming more excited and expansive.

Sonny pulled Monty aside. 'What are you jokers doing?'

'It's all right, Sonny. People are desperate for news. We're telling them what we know and they're buying us drinks.'

'Did you find some food for us?'

'Yes, yes. People were kind. The food is here and we got the tools you wanted.' Monty held open a sack for him to look inside.

'Good. I'll take this, if that's okay.'

'Sure, Sonny. You take it.'

He checked the street. 'Do you have any money? I want to buy some caulking to waterproof the boat. Sorry to ask …'

Monty took out a handkerchief containing a fistful of coins. He shook them into Sonny's palm before balling the dirty linen and shoving it back into his pocket.

'Thanks. Tell Spiros I'll wait for him by the shop.'

'Won't you join us for a drink?'

'Not me. And I suggest you get out of here.'

He was about to leave when a young girl tugged on his jacket.

'Eh?'

The child, aged about seven, had creamy olive skin. Her hair, the colour of a raven's wing, was tied with a blue ribbon. He had seen ravens in England and hadn't liked them. She observed him with her limpid eyes and pointed.

'What's she saying?' Sonny asked with impatience.

Monty crouched to listen. 'Her family have something to give us. Hey, Spiros, come here for a minute.'

Spiros came over to talk with the girl. 'Red Cross parcels, she says. One for everyone.'

'*Oh*, beauty.' Ruby clambered to his feet. 'Show us the way.'

Spiros offered his hand as the girl led him up the street. Ruby and Mac followed with their arms clamped over each other's shoulders.

Sonny glared after them. 'Damn fools,' he muttered. He took the remaining sacks they'd left beside the chairs.

Monty hesitated and turned back. 'You're not coming, Sonny?'

'I'll finish those repairs. Tell them I've taken everything.' There were men watching, and he didn't want them to notice he was anxious.

'Okay. See you anon.' Monty waved and took off after the others.

Sonny rounded the corner and jerked his chin at Ratty. 'We're leaving.'

'What's wrong?'

'Something stinks. How do you suppose a coastal town got hold of Red Cross parcels?'

'Did they?'

'I doubt it. Here, grab these.'

Ratty tested the weight of the two sacks Sonny had shoved at him. 'Is this food?'

     Kayleen M. Hazlehurst

'Food and tools.'

'Are we going back to the boat?'

'No. We'll head inland for a bit. We can keep an eye on the boat from the cliff.'

'Did you get what you wanted?' Ratty asked, as they headed off.

'The repairs can wait. What's that under your arm? You nick something?'

'Some clothes and a blanket,' Ratty said. 'I took them off a washing line.'

'Hell, why not? Let's have the whole ruddy town after us for looting.'

'You said I needed new clothes,' Ratty protested in a hurt tone.

'I was going to ask for them, not steal them.'

Sonny often thought about bad decisions and this one had dire consequences written all over it. They had to find a place to hide, and fast.

Traitors and Spies

Where the sea cliff curved back into the woods, they found a small hollow of matted spruce needles tucked away from the winds. Here, they dropped their gear and made camp. From the bluff they had a good view of the beach. Through his field glasses Sonny could watch the village entrance for the appearance of enemies or the approach of friends.

He stepped back to examine their sleeping quarters. Ratty had a real talent for making rough shelters. This one had been built between the forking branches of two trees, using their tent sheets as cover. Thick brush grew on the cliff edge and armfuls had been cut to make screens.

'Do you like it, Sonny?'

'Ka mau te pai, Ratty. People will walk by and never know we are here.'

As the sky darkened, they relinquished their post. Their companions must have found other lodgings as there'd been no activity on the beach for hours. That evening they dined on boiled eggs, a crust of bread and billy tea. The forest had grown dark, except for the rising embers from the fire. When they lay on their backs, they could follow the trail of sparks ascending through the lower branches. Visible beyond the treetops was a smattering of stars.

'I like it here,' Ratty said. 'Can we stay for a while?'

'Not long. They'll come looking for us.'

'Who will?'

'Those people who are holding our blokes.'

Ratty sat up on his elbow. 'Did that man on the shore give us away?'

'No question. Dozens will want to buy that boat from him. He had no intention of letting us have it.'

'What happened to Monty and Spiros? Where are Mac and Ruby?'

'Silly buggers fell for it, didn't they?'

'Were they tricked?'

'There were no Red Cross parcels. It was just a way of roping them in.'

'Fritz has got them?'

'I doubt it, but someone who wants to get cosy with the Germans.'

'Traitors and spies?'

'That's right.' He reached to give the fire a stir. 'They'll be locked in somewhere, maybe a cellar.'

Ratty got to his knees. 'Should we go after them, Sonny?'

'Not tonight. They'll be watching for us.'

'*Ai!* They're using them as bait.'

'Deception can work both ways, Ratty. If we don't turn up, they'll think we've scarpered. We'll be as good as gone in their minds tomorrow.'

Ratty slouched back. 'I bet some nice family has taken them in. They'll be tucking into roast chicken and potatoes.'

'So why didn't someone come back to tell us?'

'Yeah, no one came back.' Ratty stopped to think about this. 'How did you know it was a trick?'

'Hunter's reason. Set a trap … Wait for your quarry. Sending that girl as a lure got me suspicious. Where's the Greek hospitality in that, eh?'

Ratty jabbed the ground with a stick. 'I'd rather die than be taken prisoner.'

'Nah, they have what they want. They'll soon lose interest in us.'

'Maybe they've killed our blokes?'

'If there's a reward in it you can bet our men are still alive. We'll see if they reveal their hand.'

Ratty's eyes gleamed with defiance. 'They might lose interest in us, but we won't have lost interest in them, hey?'

'Mate, they won't even know we're here.'

Before Sonny fell asleep he found himself reaching out to the sea, listening to the waves. If all the world's oceans ran together then he understood why he was experiencing the tugging currents of love. On evenings such as this, as he'd walked down the coast with the assuring sand under his feet and the cobalt Aegean at his side, it was here that he felt the strongest connection with home.

At dawn Sonny adjusted the sights of his field glasses. Three new travellers had assembled around their boat, along with a figure in dark clothing.

'Are they ours?' Ratty asked.

'Kiwis, I think. I don't recognise them.'

'Is the other one that blighter who sold us the boat?'

Sonny focused on the fourth man. 'What do you reckon?'

They saw the soldiers dig into their pockets. 'Is he fleecing them?'

'Looks like it.'

'Bloody thief. Bet he plans to hand them over as well.'

Sonny agreed. By the end of the day they, too, would have disappeared. He scrutinised the far end of the beach. 'That's where he waits for us.'

'God, Sonny. If we can't trust the Greeks, who can we trust?'

'Most Greeks we can trust, but not this one. He's a miserable traitor who would sell his old granny for half a crown.'

<hr>

While the residents slept, Sonny slipped through the hamlet, his mouth dry from fear. He touched the bag of tools tied to his waist under his cloak. The dull thud of breakers behind him matched the pounding of his heart. If he listened to the reverberating waves, he could estimate how far they were from the beach. Short intervals of illumination between the long-shadowed darkness had produced no signs. There was a looming sense of failure and chaos in this venture.

Ratty had set a determined look on his face. He'd agreed to stay ten yards behind, under protest. It was pointless suggesting he should back away if there was trouble. Ratty's two brothers had died at Thermopylae, but the argument that he was his family's last surviving male didn't wash with him. Sonny understood. It wouldn't have washed with him either.

A cold wind drove the leaves in coils ahead of them. He was sure this was the way the child had lured their friends but could see nothing unusual about these buildings. Most of them were made of stone in

   Kayleen M. Hazlehurst

varying shades of grey, double-storeyed and butted against the cobbled street. They needed to narrow the search.

He heard a rumble. Then the atmosphere crackled and brightened. The elements might be with them tonight. *Zeus, some thunder and rain would be good.*

Sonny beckoned, and a figure slid in beside him. 'Hey, Ratty. Where would you hide people? Some place you could lock?'

'A barn or a police station?'

'I haven't seen any of those around here.'

'You said maybe a cellar.'

'So, there'd be a grille or window at ground level?'

'Do you want me to look out for grilles?'

'Yep. You take that side street and I'll take this one. Come back in five or six minutes. And Ratty …'

'Yeah?'

'If we lose each other, we meet back at the camp.'

'Sure. That's where the food is.' Ratty flashed a cheeky grin and dashed off.

He didn't have a clue how he was going to conduct the rescue.

There might be enough substance in Sonny Wirima to save a couple of soldiers, but was there enough to deal with a mob of treacherous Greeks? He and Ratty were an army of two, so an ambush was out of the question. His months in the wilderness had stripped away part of him, like green bark from a switch of willow. All that remained was the core of him. *I'll stalk the buggers like wild pig. It's as much as they deserve.*

'Anything?' Sonny asked when Ratty came trotting back.

'Nothing.'

'Okay. Let's keep going.'

Sonny hugged the edge of a building, glad he wasn't alone. *Come on. Where are you?* He leaned into the wall, hoping no one was observing him from behind a curtain. A drop in temperature suggested a shower was coming. When a bolt of lightning lit the street, his eye caught a gleam of white near the ground.

'Over here, Ratty,' he said in a loud whisper. 'That's Monty's handkerchief tied to the window bar. It has to be it.'

'What'll we do?'

'Go quietly.'

They knelt on either side of the grating and looked in. The cellar was inky-black, with no noises coming from inside. Ratty took a pebble and tossed it in.

'*Ouch!* Did you hit me?' A voice, reminiscent of Mac, had asked the question.

'Not me,' was the sleepy reply.

Ratty tossed in another pebble, this time with more force.

'Hey. Someone's chucking stones at us.'

Scuffling sounds brought three faces to the window.

'Bloody hell. It's Sonny and Ratty.'

'*Ah*, mate. Are we pleased to see you?'

Sonny gripped the bars. 'Good Red Cross parcels, were they?'

Ruby grunted. 'Pretty poor, actually.'

'Fancy a stroll on the beach?' Ratty added.

Mac laughed. 'Thought you'd never ask.'

'How many of you are there?'

'There's seven. Go easy. Someone's guarding the door. He's got a gun.'

'Can you reach this opening if we get it open?'

'We'll do our best.'

Another round of thunder, and Sonny walloped the grille with his hammer. It buckled but did not budge.

'Can you cut the bars?' Ruby asked.

'We've only got a wood saw. Is there anything metal down there?'

'Not even a pot to piss in, mate.'

Sonny handed Ratty the saw. 'Try cutting the top line. We'll turn them down with our weight.'

'What are *you* going to do?' Ratty asked.

'I'm going to look for something sharp and heavy.'

'I've got a knife.'

   Kayleen M. Hazlehurst

'Need something stronger. We may have to lever the grille off the wall.'

The first drops came, warm and teasing. Then Zeus opened the heavens.

Sonny darted up the side street beside the house. *How am I going to find a crowbar in the middle of the flamin' night?* He tried the side door. Locked. He pulled the fabric of his cape over his arm and elbowed the window, hoping the deluge would cover the sound of smashing glass. After knocking away a jagged chip, he put his hand through the broken pane and turned the key.

He edged along the hall, just missing a dresser. At the foot of a descending staircase he detected a sleeping figure. The guard was positioned in front of a cellar door. Mac had warned there was a gun. Sonny touched his toe on the top step, then slowly lowered his weight on the next run.

As he neared the basement the staircase creaked. Someone was scrambling to get up, turning on a lamp. Sonny was face to face with the man from the beach.

'I think you have something that doesn't belong to you,' Sonny growled in his deepest voice.

The Greek slid his eyes to a Mauser where it lay on the shelf. Sonny took the last two steps in one stride, butting the guard in the shoulder. They wrestled with each other but this ugly customer was stronger, better fed. He slammed Sonny against the wall and darted again for the pistol. Now the gun was in the Greek's hand and his finger was on the trigger. The man smirked as he started to drag the muzzle towards Sonny's chest.

Sonny couldn't hold off the gun much longer but still had some power in his legs. Those same legs had once stopped the rump of a horse from crushing him in a stable. He heaved against the man, thrusting the gun sideways and twisting the muzzle backwards.

The Greek's face contorted as his wrist weakened and his hand began to shake. Another thunderclap rattled the building as the bullet left the chamber and went straight to the heart. Sonny stood over the slumped body of the stranger he'd just murdered in his own home, and let the gun fall.

Muffled rapping from the other side of the wall reminded him he was in the house of a traitor. He hauled the body from the cellar entrance and pulled aside the bolt. Seven men were crowded behind the door with their mouths open.

'Let's get out of here,' he said as the prisoners tumbled out and clumped up the stairs. Sonny looked across the dim room to see Ratty staring in through the street grille. 'You can stop sawing now.'

'Good, because I wasn't getting anywhere.'

Heavy boots on the staircase had woken the household. As Sonny ascended he recognised the young girl on the upper landing. A woman in her mid-thirties hovered behind her in a nightdress. They were both very still.

'I'm sorry,' he said to the man's family. 'I'm really sorry.'

He went to join the others, but they were dashing through the rain towards the beach. Ratty had collected their tools and was waiting for him.

'Thought you went to find something heavy,' Ratty said with a crooked smile.

'Sometimes an old-fashioned thumping works faster.'

'A thumping, eh?'

⸺ɷɷ⸺

It was the day for craftmaking and weaving and Miriama had coaxed Atarangi to join them. At the tables the women chatted as usual, while those who had settled on the floor were listening to a narration on the first canoes.

Miriama told the story. 'Provisions for the voyage were stored in the hull of the canoes—kūmara, yam, taro and some of each to be kept for seed. Day and night prayers had been sent up, asking the spirits to ease the way.' She glanced at the listening faces. 'These events are recorded in our ancient waiata and laments.'

'Āe … Āe.'

Miriama went on. 'The ocean trails were once again calling our people to establish a heartbeat in another place. When they were ready, they looked to the star maps for direction.'

     Kayleen M. Hazlehurst

'The stars have shown us how to chart the seas …'

'They have told us when to do our plantings …'

'And when to bring in the harvest …'

Atarangi tugged on a thread of flax. She smoothed the woven fibre with her palms and lifted her mat to the light. 'I can see their patterns here.'

Miriama smiled in agreement. 'The stars—their rising and setting, and the cycles of the planets—all these help us commit patterns to memory. In any great venture we must be at one with the universe. There must be no disharmony. Those left behind—the grandmothers, the grandfathers and the very young—must have thoughts of love and peace.' She looked pointedly at the girl. 'You have the choice to remain unmarried, Atarangi. Nobody would blame you for this. High-born women often did not marry so they could become leaders of their own houses of learning.'

'I have always wanted to marry. Does this make me less noble?'

'Detachment from worldly things comes at a price. We must have our mothers and grandmothers. With so many men lost in this war some family lines will come to an end. This is an important decision for you.'

'I have wanted to marry Sonny since I was little.'

'If a puhi woman would marry Sonny Wirima, might she not consider marriage to his elder brother? I beg you, dear, think deeply on this.'

Atarangi sighed. 'Why do some stars shine much brighter than others?'

'It is true,' Miriama said, seeing beads of tears forming on the girl's lashes. 'Some stars fade, while others hold their brilliance until the first rays of the sun.'

'E pou, should we not take guidance from these brilliant stars and wait until the day returns?'

part three

~17~

In the Shadow of Waves

The night sky was clearing. Storm clouds had swept south down the Magnesia coast, leaving a breeze. A pale moon like this would hide a small craft in the shadow of waves, while providing ample light for sailors to get their bearings.

On the beach the three newcomers were in a panic to get away. They had flipped the boat upright and were preparing to launch.

Ratty stopped short. 'Sonny?'

'Don't worry. We'll find another boat.'

Mac and Ruby sidled over to talk.

'What do you think?' Mac asked.

'Let them have it. It can't carry all of us.'

'Can we ask them to take Monty? He hasn't a hope of doing more walking.'

'Good idea, Mac.'

Ratty squinted at Sonny. 'That means they'll have four and we'll have five.'

'That's about right.'

The two holding the boat were waving at the debaters. The third raced over. 'Is there a problem? We have to leave before someone finds the body of that Greek.'

'Malcolm, this is Sonny,' Ruby said, introducing one of his fellow inmates from the cellar. 'He's inspected the boat and says it will do.'

They exchanged nods.

'We could take two more,' Malcolm said.

'Can you take Monty? He's got a bad leg.'

Monty limped over. 'Did I hear someone using my name in vain?'

'We were saying you should go with these fellas,' Mac told Monty. 'It will lighten the load on the next boat. Are you all right with that?'

Monty hesitated. 'If it'll help.'

'Makes sense, Monty,' Ruby said. 'We'll not be far behind you.'

Sonny widened his eyes at Ratty. The boy dropped his loot on the sand and lifted out the blanket. 'Would Monty like this?'

'Good lad,' Mac said. 'He's a cold wee sod. Always complaining.'

Their British friend stared damp-eyed at the blanket.

'Go on, take it,' Mac urged. 'Sea wind can be freezing.'

Sonny took out three apples and his second bottle of water.

After accepting the gifts, Monty grasped hands with everyone. 'Thanks for everything … I've had the time of my life … I'll never forget you.'

'Get away with you before I start blubbering,' Mac said.

Sails were raised and lines snapped against the mast.

Ruby and Ratty both waded in to take hold of the boat as the men climbed on board.

Mac scooped up Monty, blanket and all, and deposited him on the rear bench. Then he gripped the stern.

Spiros was looking forlorn. 'Do you want to go too, Spiros?' Sonny asked. 'Get back to your family on Crete?'

'Yes. I go. I interpret for others.'

'Okay, but will you help find Monty a doctor? Can you do that for us?'

The Greek thumped his chest. 'Spiros is best mate. He find doctor.'

Sonny wanted them to leave before the patrols started. He calculated they had a head start of four hours. With this wind, they might get to safety before daylight.

'Spiros knows all these islands,' said the Greek. He flourished an arm towards the sea. 'We make it to Skiáthos, no worries.'

Ruby was now in seawater up to his thighs, barely holding on. '*Ah,* Spiros. What will we do without you? Get in, cobber, before this boat is ripped from my hands.'

'Ta-ta, sweetheart,' Mac said to Monty. 'Remember to write.'

Monty leaned to pull Mac's beard. 'God bless, you silly old bugger.'

Malcolm pulled the lines to unfurl the sails. 'Sorry we're stealing your boat!'

The passengers hooted and waved as a gust gripped the sails and the boat jumped away.

—ₐₐₐ—

The two women were sitting on the back porch in the sun while Api and Hēmi completed the afternoon milking. The canines had joined them, leaning against their legs, hopeful of an ear stroke.

'Have you finished your jobs for the day?' Atarangi asked the dog, Turi.

'They're lazy, those two,' Miriama said. 'They think they don't have to bark anymore. Hēmi opens the gate and the cows wander back on their own to the paddock.' Kete put a paw on Miriama's knee and she jostled the dog's ear. 'Yes, I'm talking about you.'

'They're thinking about their dinners.'

'Āe.' Miriama offered the basket of peapods and the girl took a handful. After settling the ceramic bowl in her lap, a favourite once belonging to her mother, Miriama let the green balls fall into the cracked and yellowed crockery.

Atarangi gazed at the horizon, a question trembling on her lips. 'E pou, where does evil come from?'

'This has been troubling you?'

'I don't understand. Who are these people forcing our men to war?'

'There are people in this world who are like the flounder fish. He flaps his fins to cause confusion, then hides in his own sandstorm. Ka huna te pātiki i roto i tōna anō puehu.'

'What about the poor warrior? Where does this leave him?'

'The warrior must stay alert. Deception can be used as a weapon. What he sees before him may not be real. To perceive the truth, he needs spiritual clarity.'

Ata slid her thumbnail along the length of a peapod, splitting it open. 'A good man has clarity.'

'That is so. A calm mind is most able to interpret the world, especially in a situation of turmoil.'

'But how will he know the truth if it's obscured from him?' Ata asked. 'How can he see through this sandstorm the flounder has made?'

'Caution is his best defence. First, he must observe the signs. Remember, it's not only people who cause chaos. All the elements may conspire against us. Even the gods …'

'*E!* Why would the atua deceive us?'

'They would, if we deserved it. Ask Tangaroa.' Miriama waved her arm to the strip of blue water beyond the cliff. 'The sea has been our livelihood since time began. It is admired and loved by all, and yet—'

'Yet there are dangers?'

'Definitely, there are dangers. The sea can be as shrewd and misleading as a troubled man's soul. The waters may toss and rage. We take our food from the sea and think nothing of it, but sometimes Tangaroa demands a sacrifice.'

'What if we approach Tangaroa with respect?'

'This would be wise. Supplications must be made before any significant endeavour, and the warrior must look for the signs.'

'The patterns you mentioned?'

'Āe.'

'I would like to learn more about these patterns. Can you show me?'

'Very well. Meet me at sunrise and I will show you. Bring your basket.'

~

The men watched in the moonlight as the boat sped down the coast, bearing south-east towards the islands.

'They've got a good wind,' Ruby commented.

'Aye,' said Mac. 'They'll do okay.'

'What will we do now?' Ratty asked Sonny.

'Dunno. We'll think of something.'

'All I know is we have to leave this place,' Ruby concluded. 'By morning it won't be safe anywhere along this beach.'

Mac grabbed his pack. He still had one. He was a large, aggressive man and his captor had given up trying to take it off him. 'Take us to this camp of yours, Sonny. We'll divvy up the grub and leave. Me and

Ruby. You and Ratty, eh? How's that?'

'Sounds reasonable.'

Ratty stood his ground. 'What about *our* boat, Sonny?'

'Forget it, brother. Right now, we have to disappear.'

⁓

The morning air was crisp and still—nature anticipating the coming day. Atarangi assumed the old woman wanted to collect herbs while the moisture was still on the leaves. It was the wrong season for picking fruit from the abandoned orchard and too late for gathering mushrooms. They walked along the dirt road from the farmhouse, through the gate of the cow paddock and up the gentle slope.

On the hillside they stopped to look back over the fields towards the blue arc of the ocean.

Atarangi hugged her chest against the cold. 'I love this time of day. It's when I feel closest to the land.'

'If you are sensitive, you can see that everything is connected,' Miriama said. 'The earth. The sun. Night and day. All are bound by the tides of creation. This is what the ancients have taught us.'

Early rays sliced shafts of light through the long grasses, catching the dew where it hung in droplets from every blade. Atarangi gasped. Cobwebs covered the paddocks. A net of silvery filaments as far as the eye could see.

'This is wonderful,' she said. 'I saw this once with Sonny when we were young. Are these the patterns you wanted to show me?'

'Āe. Spider trails are everywhere, though they're only visible at daybreak. These threads are crafted in exact proportions to give each web its form and strength. This is the spider's lesson, Atarangi. It is patterns like these that uphold the universe.'

'I see this now.'

'Can you think of other examples, Ata?'

'The patterns of the stars, and those we weave in our fishing nets.'

'And our whakapapa, dear. If we did not construct strands into form, how would we remember our genealogies? How could the grandmothers recommend right marriages? Broken lines between people mean—'

Who Disturbs the Kūkupa?　　　141

'Broken hearts—'

'You would know this, little one.'

They stood to witness the sun as it rose from the sea, silvering the water and bringing to the sky its first colours.

Atarangi linked her hand in her mentor's elbow. 'So, we are bound together, whether we like it or not.'

'Āe. The world is a single living being. If one part falls out of order, there will always be warnings. There will be signs in the land and forests, and signs in the rivers and seas. Even our animals and birds have something to tell us.'

'And these signs, they will help us find our way back?'

'Healers have always known this.'

Atarangi gave a soft laugh. 'If only the world and its flounders knew it also.'

Kayleen M. Hazlehurst

~18~

Setting off with Ratty

Spiros had told them more about the region during their evening on the dunes. Sonny took stock of what he knew. He'd already been warned not to seek transport from the port town of Volos, but had heard about an inland route. It wound through a gorge south of Pouri towards the village of Zagora. This too, Spiros cautioned them against. The sides of the gorge were vertical in places, offering few opportunities for escape if Germans were met on the path.

'Continue down the peninsula,' Spiros advised.

Despite its quiet coves, Sonny sensed the southern part of the coast was not a place to linger. Villages had spies. With the steep hills behind them, it would be difficult to melt away if they were detected.

'Our safest means of getting away from here is by sea,' Sonny told Ratty. 'What are our chances?'

'I'm sure we will, but not by going into towns and having drinks with villagers. Ruby and Mac will have to watch themselves.'

'Could we steal a boat, do you think?'

'If it looks abandoned. We can't take one from a man who needs it to feed his family.'

'What about an old dinghy?'

'That might work. How do you feel about doing some rowing?'

Ratty gave him a fierce glare. 'Anything to get us off this land.'

Āe, Tama. Like a beached whale.

The boat they excavated, half buried in sand, seemed dilapidated enough to be ownerless. The oars were covered with a torn and saturated piece of canvas. After scooping out sand and patching planks, they launched their old dinghy with the hope that it wouldn't be missed.

'The owner might have died,' Ratty said as they pulled away close to midnight.

'He might have …'

'Plenty of men around here would have joined the army …'

Sonny was silent. He didn't want to wish death on anyone just to possess his boat.

'How long will it take us, Sonny?'

'Five or six hours … We'll follow the shore until we reach the southern end.' Sonny visualised his lost map. He remembered the Pelion Peninsula turning west in the shape of a fish hook. 'Once the sea mist rises we should get sight of Skiáthos, to the south.'

The water in front of the hills was smooth and rolling. Wide seating at the centre of the boat allowed them to take an oar each. They slid powerfully through the shallows, matching their rhythm, with two arms working each oar.

'If we run out of darkness we can look for somewhere to hide. Take the crossing tomorrow night.'

Ratty was more confident, inspired by their good speed. 'Hey, Sonny, if we keep going I reckon we'll get to that island by morning.'

Miriama stood in her garden and looked out. Sometimes, it was as though she was standing on the edge of the world. She was solidly Ngā Puhi, with tribal associations spanning back generations, yet her vision stretched right across the ocean. She had sympathy for all peoples who wanted peace in their lives. Her father, who had never been one for quarrels, attributed this connection with others to a shared link between people and their gods. She agreed. Unless the gods themselves were at war, it was hard to resist this affinity with other humans.

On days such as this, she imagined herself in Greece. If she closed her eyes she could smell the orchards, hear the fading battle cries and running feet, the small unattended voices of the dead. What heart would not feel for them and send out a prayer?

     Kayleen M. Hazlehurst

A whoosh, whoosh, whoosh of kūkupa wings brought her back to the embracing silence. The wood pigeons were returning to their roosts in the pūriri tree. She harvested the last of her evening vegetables and stepped from the garden for home.

✧

Sonny and Ratty swung out to the Aegean, heading straight for the faint outline of Skiáthos. Sonny was sure they could row this distance. The channel between them looked no further than some of the offshore islands of his youth. His aim was to land somewhere on the northern tip, or to tuck in behind it, as long as Ratty's crumpled socks did the trick on the leak that had sprung up at his feet.

This was the first day of the long voyage they must make through this island chain. They rowed with a kind of madness, churning up the dark water with their oars and helped along by a bold new ocean current.

The priest, who liked to roam the cliffs, looked below to the inlet.

Skiáthos Island was seven miles long and four miles wide—not too far for a man of his vigour to walk across in one morning. Below the cliff, the turquoise waters and rock formations of Lalária Beach shone white in the morning sun. He never ceased to be in awe of its beauty, but today brought something he had not expected. Below him, two men lay face down on the pebbled beach.

The war had not yet reached Skiáthos, although the priest knew it soon would. The British Navy had rescued thousands of Allied soldiers from the beaches and ports near Athens, but countless numbers had been left behind. He had heard about the suffering of those stranded soldiers. Many were now trying to escape through the Aegean in trawlers, caïques, schooners, yachts or any seafaring vessel they could find.

The means of transport for these two men, a mere rowing boat, was shifting at the edge of the waves. The priest took out his old telescope for a closer look. The poor condition of both boat and men suggested that it was a miracle they had made it here. He tried to discern their origin. Their clothing was mismatched and oddly worn. Some of the items must have been acquired from the seaside villages, others from the mountain peasantry.

The priest observed the castaways, willing them to rise from their stupor, praying they hadn't drowned. Laláría was a secluded beach and there was no path to the foreshore to help them. Then, lifting his cassock, he rushed away to fetch a boatman. If these wayfarers had made it here by Divine intervention, who was he to question their worthiness?

The sky had been charcoal-grey when they collapsed on the beach, scarcely conscious of the white water raking over the smooth pebbles beneath them. Now, as the sun baked the surrounding stones, blood returned to cold limbs.

While Ratty collected firewood, Sonny inspected the dinghy. The planks were pitted and swollen with seawater. It had served them well, but this was not something simple repairs could fix. He felt parched and feverish. The old illness was upon him again. After a fit of coughing, he accepted a sip from Ratty's canister.

'We'll have to find water,' Sonny croaked.

'I know … Hey, what's that noise?'

They heard the chug-chug of a diesel engine. With their own boat in tatters and their supplies all gone, there was no point in running away. Instead they waited, allowing themselves to hope. It sounded like the modest thrum of a fishing boat, not the roar of a sleek patrol vessel.

A slim blue boat nosed around the cape. The boatman waved his arms and spoke to them in a stream of Greek as he beckoned them on board. Soon they were skimming over the aqua waters on the eastern side of the island. Their rescuer—content in his environment of cray pots and tackle, his face tanned from a lifetime in the sun, his trousers held in place by a knotted rope—sustained his excited discourse as lagoons passed them by. There was a familiarity about this. Sonny couldn't help recalling happier days on the bright Hauraki Gulf with his father and brothers.

Glossy red-brown pines and a variety of other trees grew on these hills, all the way down to the shore in places. As they progressed, the wooded landscape gave way to orchards and green, sloping spaces.

Sonny leaned over to Ratty. 'There'll be building industries on this island with all those pines.'

   Kayleen M. Hazlehurst

'Could they fix our boat, do you think?'

'No mate. Our boat has had it.'

Ratty looked doleful and Sonny gave him a friendly punch.

'Come on, brother. We'll find something else.'

'I hope it doesn't need rowing. I thought my arms would drop off last night.' Ratty gave the boatman a quick glance. 'Where's this maniac taking us?'

As they entered a bay the boat throttled back and motored towards a wharf. Beyond the beach, a dirt road branched off towards the interior. Sauntering down the hill, with the skirt of his black robe hoisted over one arm, and the other leading a beast, came a man with a grey bushy beard. He looked like somebody's grandfather.

The priest strode to the end of the wharf with a broad smile. 'Good afternoon. I presume you are English?'

Ratty was on the pier, staring. His mouth open, like a hāpuka.

Sonny thanked the boatman with a firm handshake and climbed the wharf steps to join them. 'We're New Zealanders, Sonny said. 'Infantrymen with the 28th Māori Battalion.'

'*Ah.* Soldiers of the Empire.'

'How did you know?'

The priest scratched his beard and eyed their clothing. 'Your apparel is all in a muddle,' he said, breaking into a laugh.

'How is it you speak English?' Ratty asked, now finding his voice.

'I was born here, but I did my seminary training in America after the Great War. My name is Father John Christos. You can call me Father John.'

'I'm Sonny Wirima and this is Motu Paraki. Ratty for short.'

The priest put out his hand. 'Welcome to Skiáthos. You'll be hungry, I expect. I will take you to the chapel where you can rest. It's a long ascent, but I brought my donkey in case you boys were tired.'

Ratty's eyes lit up. 'I've never ridden a donkey.'

'You go first.' Sonny filled his lungs for the next round of exertion. 'I might ask you to swap with me halfway up.'

The Monks of Skiáthos

Ekklisia Taxiarches was a stone church, situated between the town of Skiáthos and the hill top monastery of Evangelistria. The church was set back in a wooded area with a pond, fed by a spring that discharged from the base of the building. Nearby, a handpump provided water for weary travellers and the two resident priests, Father John and Father Antoni the Elder.

As they entered under the dome of the cross, and through the heavy chapel door, Sonny and Ratty were struck by the coolness of the interior. Inside, a single window provided daylight, while the rest of the area was lit by candles.

The wafting fragrance of incense failed to chase away the mustiness of the chapel. Images painted on board hung below the ridgeline of the polished wooden ceiling. Sonny and Ratty were gazing at these pictures with their arms crossed over their chests.

Father John came over to speak. 'Have you been inside an Orthodox church before?'

'This is my first time. What about you, Ratty?'

Ratty gave a respectful nod.

'You will find religious icons all throughout Greece,' the priest went on.

'When were these painted?' Sonny asked.

'In the third and fourth centuries. What we call the Byzantine period.'

Ratty, looking awestruck, ventured a question. 'Are they sacred?'

'Oh, yes. They represent Bible stories, images of saints, and depictions of heaven. They bring sanctity to a place. We do not worship them, but devotees use these icons as objects of prayer and veneration. Early

Christians believed they were reflections of the perfect world that existed behind the world we know with our five senses.'

Sonny recognised the idea behind the image. He recalled the ornate carvings and panels of the wharenui that portrayed the power of the gods and the heroism of the ancestors. 'My people would understand this,' he said.

'Not idolatry, then. Something greater than this.' The priest moved closer. 'Our histories may be different but I was wondering … have we not all come from the same antiquity?'

That evening Sonny fell into the grip of a fever. Father John sat with him, alternately sponging his body to reduce the pouring heat, or covering him with blankets to stop the violent shaking from the chills.

Ratty slept fitfully on a corner bed, scrambling to his feet when asked to draw more water from the pump in the courtyard. He paused to sit beside the spring, watching the pure liquid turning silver in the moonlight. He didn't feel alone, hearing whispers and soft laughter, or maybe it was the rustle of leaves and the echoing splatter of droplets.

Back at the parish house, Ratty found the patient sitting up, his eyes glistening with the heat of delirium. Sonny reached out with his hands to a presence only he could see.

'Dad, look out for the rocks. Throw out the anchor. I'll dive in and pull us away. Watch out, Dad! You'll strand us!'

Then his tone changed from panic to dismay.

'Tama, I'm so sorry. I'll take you home, little brother … Look, there's Mum. She's waving … Don't go, Tama. Don't go. Take me with you.'

At first light Father John saddled his donkey and rode five miles into town to fetch the doctor. Father Antoni, equally troubled, was preparing to hurry away to the monastery to offer prayers to the Virgin Mary.

'Please help him,' Ratty begged, his eyes starting to fill. 'Don't let my mate die.'

In his broken English, Father Antoni assured Ratty that the monks at Evangelistria, the Monastery of the Annunciation of the Virgin Mary, had a veritable pharmacy of herbs in their garden and he promised to bring back their most powerful medicines.

By late morning, Father John had come back with his companion. Doctor Marinos bustled in and removed a wooden tube from his bag to listen to Sonny's back and chest. The doctor spoke a rough form of English for the benefit of the young soldiers.

'Coughing? Trouble breathing?'

'All through the night,' Father John reported.

'Phlegm?'

The priest indicated the yellowed, blood-streaked rags beside the bed.

'You must burn those, Father.'

'I've had this thing for weeks,' Sonny wheezed. 'This time it's worse.'

'Well, it has advanced to pneumonia. Your lungs are inflamed, and the air sacs are filling with fluid. You're lucky to be alive.'

Father John lost his colour and put his hand to his forehead. 'Pneumonia.'

The doctor plumped the pillows at Sonny's back and asked for another. 'You must sit up or you will drown. Drink lots of water. Cold flannels to reduce the fever.'

'I can administer a steam inhalant.'

'Yes, with a good measure of lavender and garlic. For the throat, an elixir of thyme and honey. Tonight, a goose grease and mustard compress applied to the chest to improve the breathing. I trust the monks will help you with these ingredients?'

'Father Antoni is at the monastery fetching medicines.'

'Very good. I will call in tomorrow to see how the patient is doing.'

At the doorway the men exchanged a few words in Greek, then the doctor left.

The monks of Evangelistria had ten hives in the valley and could be relied upon for honey. For centuries their order had cultivated gardens and they were keepers of geese. In preparing compresses, goose grease could be procured from the monastery, along with medicinal wines and herbal tinctures. While medical supplies were scarce, herbs were not. The

     Kayleen M. Hazlehurst

doctor, notwithstanding his training, cleverly incorporated traditional remedies into his treatments.

Father Antoni returned with his arms laden with promise. He had twigs of lavender, thyme and marjoram for decoction, and leaves of peppermint for tea. Under this bundle of clippings was a hessian sack containing a pot of honey, a jar of rendered goose fat, and a bottle of tonic wine made by the monks for respiratory conditions. Most important was the straw-woven string of garlic slung around his neck. Everyone knew garlic cloves had curative powers bordering on the miraculous.

When the priest stumbled up the path with his burden of cures, Ratty uttered a cry and raced out to give the astonished man a hug.

Sonny woke to the wafting tang of peppermint and thyme. Something was simmering in the kitchen. Father John entered the bedroom carrying a bowl, with a towel over his shoulder.

'Sit him on the side of the bed, please.'

He struggled to put his feet on the floor, supported on one side by Ratty and on the other by Father Antoni. A tray was placed on his knees bearing a bowl of hot water. In it, torn leaves and twigs floated alongside slices of garlic.

'Bend over and breathe in the steam.' With a flick of his towel, the priest covered Sonny from his head to his knees. His shroud further darkened when a second covering was pitched over him. Inside this tent there was nothing for him to do but breathe in the pungent vapour.

New openings seared through his nose and throat and his breath expanded. In his hand he accepted a fistful of rags for the liquefied mucus.

'Now cough,' the priest ordered after removing the covering. 'Cough deeply, my son.'

Sonny hacked into his lungs while the others watched on. When he dragged forth an admirable globule of green phlegm it was met with as much cheer from the priests as if he'd given birth. Poor Ratty was reduced to tears.

Father John dipped his fingers into the rich yellow fat and looked satisfied.

'A good consistency.' He rubbed the fat on Sonny's chest and back. 'Goose grease is a fine insulator for bronchial conditions.'

'How does it work?' Ratty asked.

'It drives heat back into the body where it is needed to dry out the damp lung. Infection cannot survive in high temperature. Fever can be a godsend.'

Sonny gasped again. 'As long as it's not too high, Mum told me.'

'Your mother is a doctor?'

'A healer. Runs in the family.'

'*Ah*. Then you will recognise the things we are doing.'

Ratty, who had been watching this procedure, waved his hand in front of his face and wrinkled his nose. 'Whew, what a pong.'

The priest lifted a spatula to apply the paste of mustard powder, flour and water to muslin cloth. 'This will loosen your congestion. We must ladle the mixture onto cloth so it won't burn your skin. You will feel the heat.'

After the compress had been packed around Sonny's chest and back, his greasy torso was wrapped in layers of brown paper, with twine used to secure everything.

'You look like a Christmas parcel,' Ratty said. 'Perhaps we should mail you home.'

'Wish you would.'

Father Antoni brought in the tonic wine and looked at Sonny with kind eyes. 'Two spoons of this and you'll be ready to sleep.' He administered the delicious beverage and piled on more blankets.

'I feel like a cooked goose.'

Father John laughed. 'That's exactly what you are, Sonny. We're cooking the sickness out of you.'

———〰———

Two weeks passed. Once out of danger, Sonny was left on his own between mealtimes. Mostly he slept, but sometimes he sat outside listening to the songs of woodland birds and the music of water running into the pond. During his convalescence Ratty visited the monastery to help in the gardens, saying he wanted to repay the monks for their medicines. Sonny could see his friend was drawn to the herbs and wanted to learn more about their healing properties. The monks were also teaching him their Orthodox creed. When Ratty returned in the evenings, his face was glowing with newly acquired knowledge.

'How was your day?' Sonny asked.

'My day was excellent. You look stronger, Sonny.'

'Āe. I think I'll get up tomorrow.'

'Did you know there are no young men left in the monastery? Those old men could do with a hand.'

'Do you want to become a monk, Ratty?'

'What would you say if I did?'

'What about your family?'

'Both my brothers are dead, but I have cousins. My family line won't end if I die without children.'

'And the army?'

'Do you think they'll miss me?'

'I doubt it, but I would.'

'Become a monk with me, Sonny.'

'Thanks, but there's someone at home I want to marry.'

'You will move faster through these islands without dragging me along. Doctor Marinos has offered to take me on as an apprentice.'

'Then you should stay. Study the healing arts, Ratty. They could be useful to the soldiers passing through here.' Sonny looked with fondness at his friend, a young man who had surprised him with his gentleness and courage. 'Hey, I can see you as a monk with a bushy beard and robes!'

'A nice Greek boy, eh?'

Sonny ducked his head. Those had been his words on the day Ratty had stolen his civilian clothing from someone's washing line. 'You're a good man, Motu Paraki. Now that you've joined the monastic life, I suppose you'll be given a new name.'

'I suppose. Here, take my rifle, Sonny. We can put your old shepherd's gun with the other relics. A monk doesn't need a gun.'

'Are you sure about that?'

Geese scattered before them as they approached the gatehouse. Father John, who had suggested Sonny might like to see where his friend had chosen to stay, offered to accompany him on his first visit to the monastery. Ratty, who now regularly joined the monks for dawn prayers, could be found working in their gardens by mid-morning.

Evangelistria Monastery was topped by three domes and had its own Byzantine church. Passing through the refectory, Sonny was shown the doors leading to the cells where the monks slept and prayed. In other rooms there were collections of rare books and manuscripts, and religious artefacts and icons from distant eras. Sonny could not imagine himself living in this place.

Ratty, being Catholic, seemed right at home here. He rushed ahead of them, chattering and opening doors. 'There's something I want to show you. I think you'll be impressed.' They were escorted into another room dominated by a large weaving loom. 'The first Greek flag, which was woven on this loom, was raised on this roof in 1807.'

Sonny turned to Father John for explanation.

'It is true. Many fought against the yoke of Ottoman rule during our War of Independence, including some famous warrior monks. The Orthodox Church has always fostered just causes. These nine stripes on the flag represent the phrase *Freedom or Death*. The fire of liberty burns bright in the Greek breast.'

Sonny stood tall. 'Then we are honoured to fight alongside such heroic people.'

The priest gave a courteous sweep of his arm. 'Be assured, all of Greece is thankful to you and your fellow warriors.'

Sonny grasped Ratty's arm in a hongi. 'Ka mahue koe i au ki konei i runga i te rangimārie. I'm proud you're with such a noble institution. I leave you here in peace.'

'Kia ora, Sonny! Ka inoi au kia āhuru tō hoki ki te kāinga. Good luck, Sonny. I will pray for your safe journey home.'

     Kayleen M. Hazlehurst

~20~

The Teacher of Skópelos

A tea of flat-bread and honey was served on a wooden table that had been scoured over the years into ridges of grain. A green painted dresser covered with plates and cups stood against the panelled walls. After tea, Father John took Sonny to the roof of the monastery. It was early summer, with few clouds above the sapphire ocean.

'This cluster of islands is called the Northern Sporades.' The priest pointed ahead. 'That's Skópelos, our nearest neighbour, and to the east is Alonissos. The outline you see in the distance is the northern tip of Evia. It is our second largest island, after Crete.'

'Do people live on all these islands?' Sonny asked.

'All but a few uninhabitable rocks. Before the war, trade flourished between the islands and the mainland. What will happen now, we don't know. I expect merchants will continue to come and go with supplies.'

'That's reassuring.'

'A hundred years ago we had a prosperous shipbuilding industry. Anything that sailed we could build.' The priest gave a regretful tilt of his head. 'Much of this craftsmanship has been lost. Today, our fishing boats and caïques are our main workhorses.'

'Maybe I could hitch a ride with a fishing boat.'

'If you can find one. The Germans have seized many boats for themselves and they are watching the sea traffic.'

'I will travel at night.'

'On Skópelos I have a friend in the village of Glossa. Adrian Petros, a schoolteacher. His mother was English. I can give you a letter of introduction.'

'Thank you. How do I get there?'

'I'll ask the bargeman to take you. We mill timber here and barge it
to the boatyards in the ports. But you must go quickly, dear boy. I fear
the invasion is upon us.'

⁓

Sonny eyed the shifting logs. He was sitting on the floor of a flat-bottomed
boat with his back against the wall, absorbing the throb of the engine
beneath his out-stretched legs. Sailing from Skiáthos Harbour to the
closest landing point at Loutraki took nearly two hours. Ten miles in a
slow, chugging barge.

This was the first stop on Skópelos, and it suited the bargeman to drop
off the foreigner. It was clear he preferred not to have an Allied soldier
with him, even one well disguised.

At the wharf Sonny helped the shoremen unload their allotment of
timber. When he went to thank the skipper, he was already reversing the
vessel.

'Glossa! Glossa!' the bargeman shouted as he waved towards the hill.

Sonny began his slow walk from the bay to the high village of Glossa,
taking note of the fruit trees and vines on the wilder side of the hill. As
he explored the lanes, climbing hundreds of steps as he went, he sensed
this place had been built on an ancient settlement.

At the top he gazed back over a cascade of tiled roofs to the cradle
of the bay. Stone towers—lookouts from earlier times that once warned
citizens of pirates and other seafaring assailants—were surrounded now
by a muddle of houses. Newer structures were wedged between the old.
Balconies dangled from upper levels, creepers lined the eaves, flowers
hung from windowsills, and cats slept in the shade of potted shrubs. *Is
this all about to change?*

It was hard to decipher the layout of the town. Folded at the back of Father
John's letter was a rough map. Nowhere could Sonny see a schoolhouse.
He stopped to lean on a wall. Who could he ask for directions? If he was
going to survive he would have to speak more Greek. But when would he

     Kayleen M. Hazlehurst

be anywhere long enough to learn? He wished he had paid more attention to the phrase book he'd bought and lost along the way. He hadn't expected to be wandering Greece in search of his lost brothers. This was not the war he had imagined.

A boy of about fourteen ambled up the street towards him, carrying a satchel and wearing a round cap and baggy trousers. The youth appeared friendly and Sonny decided to try out some of his Greek. He displayed the letter to the boy and drew himself up to show it contained a message of great importance.

Sonny excused himself and mentioned the name of Adrian Petros. '*Sygnomi. Adrian Petros, se parakaló.*'

The youth looked delighted. '*Ton Kýrio Pétro, o dáskalós mas.*'

'Mr Petros is your teacher?'

The boy nodded and waved his arm, inviting Sonny to follow.

—⁓—

The teacher of Skópelos was unlike any tutor Sonny had known. Scholarly in his knowledge and gracious in his views, Adrian Petros was the wise man of the village. In his living room he imparted learning to the young during the day, and at night the adults gathered to air community concerns. Like Sonny's mother, Mr Petros was skilled at guiding people to understand difficult problems.

Adrian, who did not appear to have a wife, threw a raw leg of mutton on the table, lifted a cleaver, and proceeded to debone and chop the meat.

'In his letter, Father John has asked me to find someone to take you to Evia. If you're dropped off on the eastern side, he says you can walk south and enter the Cyclades from there.'

'Does he say what trouble I might run into along the way?'

'No. But our goodly priest has knowledge of this area from his pastoral visits. That side of Evia is remote and inaccessible by road. The beaches are cut off and the land is steep and wooded. Sea patrols are unknown along this strip of coastline. The Fascists have arrived in the Aegean, but the Italians are slack in their supervision of the coasts and the Nazis have other fish to fry.'

'What fish might they be?'

'I've heard rumours about Crete.'

'Can I help you prepare dinner, Mr Petros?'

'Call me Adrian. You can scrape the potatoes for me.'

Sonny was shown a sink piled up with dirt-encrusted potatoes.

'My intention is to pass you off as a local resident,' Adrian said, handing Sonny a paring knife.

'Can you find a fisherman to take me to Evia? It looks a fair distance.'

'It's sixty miles to the centre of the island. Some of our fleet hunts for fish in this area. I'll make enquiries.'

'Thank you. What are you cooking?'

'Moussaka.' Adrian knelt beside the wood range to stoke the fire box, speaking over his shoulder. 'It's a traditional Greek meal.'

'I ate a lot of mutton growing up. On Sundays Mum made a roast.'

'*Ah*, roast lamb. We Greeks are very fond of it ourselves.'

'With roasted veggies.' Sonny held up a potato.

Adrian tossed the meat into a hot skillet and added diced garlic, onions and herbs, along with lashings of olive oil. 'So you're a country boy, Sonny?'

'Oh, yes. A country boy at heart. What do you farm around here?'

'We cultivate many things on Skópelos. According to legend, the island was founded by Staphylus—the son of the Greek god of wine, Dionysus. His mother was Princess Ariadne of Crete. It is believed Skópelos was colonised by Cretans who introduced viticulture here.'

'Viticulture?'

'Winemaking, Sonny. Greece has the finest soil for grape growing. Some of our vineyards are the oldest in the world.'

'Were there people on Skópelos before the Cretans?'

'Ah. You want to know about the first inhabitants?'

Sonny hesitated, wondering whether he should mention this. 'I felt their presence in the land as I walked through Greece.'

Adrian cut a pear-shaped vegetable into rounds and placed them on a roasting tray.

Sonny touched the shiny purple skin of the plant. 'What is this?'

     Kayleen M. Hazlehurst

'This is an aubergine and it's going into our moussaka.'

'A strange name for a strange plant.'

'I think you'll like it,' Adrian said. 'In ancient times neolithic peoples inhabited Greece and the Aegean Islands. This was thousands of years ago. Long before the emergence of Greek culture, or the discovery of bronze. They were hunting and herding cultures, named by the classical writers as the Pelasgians.'

'Do you still have any of these early peoples?'

'Enclaves of these early ancestors may have survived among the waves of migrating populations. Whatever we were, or whatever we have become, Greeks have always been people of the sea.'

'The sea is in our blood as well.'

'Then, as you travel through these islands be assured you will be in good company.'

That evening, Sonny slept more soundly than he had for months. He wasn't wet or cold. He was comfortable in a bed at the home of Adrian Petros. As sure as mist rose from rain, the teacher's conviction that he would achieve his purpose had touched his soul.

—⁓—

In the cool of the morning they descended the hill through the orchards, their feet slipping and sliding on the dewy grass, as they passed by grazing sheep and groves of olives, almonds and plums. They had woken before dawn so as to meet the fishermen when they came in for their first coffee. Adrian had insisted Sonny take a set of clothing from his wardrobe.

'We can watch for the boats from here,' Adrian said, stopping at a high resting point. 'We're looking out for the one that belongs to Geórgios Stavros. He's the oldest of the fishermen and tends to come in last. Geórgios will know what to do.'

A green lizard scuttled on the gravel path towards the bay. Since Mount Olympus, Sonny had learned these reptiles were common in Greece. He turned his eyes skyward to disperse any sense of foreboding. On the foreshore he had seen two black shags and a grey heron. Now he searched for a familiar gull that might bring him tidings of Atarangi.

They sat in silence until Adrian asked, 'Do you mind travelling on your own, Sonny? You're not afraid?'

'No. I prefer it. I am never alone.'

'You have your companion spirits with you?'

Sonny paused. 'Don't you?'

'Sometimes. This was the belief among followers of the old religion.'

'And now?'

'*Oh*, we Greeks are a superstitious people and Christians are very fond of their saints.' Adrian pointed to a high seabird flying towards the bay. 'That's an Audouin's gull. They hunt for fish at night and sometimes escort the boats home. There'll be flocks of smaller gulls following the boats, scavenging for scraps as the fish are cleaned.'

Sonny watched the larger bird and sent loving thoughts with the gull for Atarangi. His longing for home still dogged him. He turned to study Adrian's face. 'Why did you ask me if I was afraid? Do you expect me to meet something strange in those wooded hills of Evia?'

'Like what?'

'Some beast I should be warned about. A half-man, half-horse creature.'

'A centaur!' Adrian laughed. 'None I know of.'

As the sky wakened, small shapes emerged from tones of yellow and grey.

'You said the Māori Battalion fought at Mount Olympus?'

'Yes. We tried to hold back the invasion on those first days.'

'Then, on behalf of all Greeks, I commend your battalion.'

Sonny pulled at tufts of grass, not speaking.

'A famous centaur named Chiron once lived on Mount Pelion.'

Sonny turned back to the teacher and tilted his head.

'Yes,' Adrian went on. 'He was famous for his skills in archery, music, healing and prophecy. The Olympian tradition cast Chiron as the first among centaurs. He was a wise and revered teacher, not violent and unruly like the other centaurs. Achilles was tutored by Chiron, as were the warriors Heracles, Jason and Phoenix. I must tell you this, Sonny. Not every member of an evil species may be evil.'

　　　Kayleen M. Hazlehurst

'Like the Nazis, you mean?'

'I mean like the Germans,' Adrian corrected. 'They are not all bad. This sage was friend to many warriors and heroes. Chiron welcomed the Argonauts into his home before they sailed with Jason on his quest for the Golden Fleece.'

'You're telling me this because I might run into this Chiron fellow?'

Adrian laughed. 'Only in your heart, should you need courage.'

'I'll remember that.'

'*Ah,* the boats are nearly here.' Adrian scrambled to his feet. 'Come, we'll go down to meet them.'

Sonny was stirred by the sight and smells of the boats. The fishermen with their nets and their boxes of fish. On the wharf, the teacher was conducting an animated conversation with an older man. Adrian waved his arms northwards, towards Mount Olympus. The fisherman lifted his palms to the heavens.

A deal was struck with a handshake, and a wad of cash was transferred from the hand of Adrian Petros into the ready hand of Geórgios Stavros.

~21~

Geórgios' Boat

Sonny set out for the bay before sunrise, with his knapsack and gun on one shoulder and Adrian's packed lunch under his arm. By the time he arrived at the wharf most of the fleet had already left. Leaving later than everyone else was a privilege accorded to the elderly skipper, Geórgios Stavros.

Night winds were more favourable for reaching the fishing grounds, Adrian had explained. The best catches were at sunrise. Deep-sea fish that were not nocturnal came nearer to the surface as the water lightened. In these summer months the first nets were cast in the dark. Some fish were more active when the water was cold. After a good haul, it was a quick run back to land before the flesh spoiled.

Sonny agreed to help with the nets before being dropped off on Evia. He was looking forward to the fishing, but was under no illusion about why he was tolerated. Adrian had hired Geórgios' boat for the day. The two of them had to communicate by hand signs. Sometimes the fisherman forgot this and yelled his instructions in Greek, as if Sonny was deaf.

There was something troubling about the boat. While it was equipped with the usual set of sails and auxiliary engine, it was showing its age. The paintwork was chipped and faded, and the planks pitted and worn. When the motor spluttered on starting Sonny feared vital repairs had been overlooked.

Evia was also disturbing. The eastern side of this long, narrow island was harbourless. Was there anywhere for a boat to pull in? Sonny had been told that its mountainous centre, and the territory further south, would become increasingly inhospitable. He could survive on the shy foxes and long-eared hares, but what he couldn't live without was clean

Kayleen M. Hazlehurst

drinking water. Nor was he willing to approach the coastal hamlets to the west that were closest to the mainland. He had no knowledge of the loyalties of those who lived there.

A man walking sixty to ninety miles through rough terrain might experience many dangers. He could be injured and delayed for months. The more Sonny thought about Evia, the more he believed it was a place to avoid. Anywhere that kept him from his journey through the Cyclades was a trap, and every mile he could travel by sea would save him hours on foot. How could he convince Geórgios Stavros, a man clearly displeased with his company, to take him far from here?

—∿—

An incoming squall was difficult to see in this early light, but Sonny detected the sudden drop in air pressure. To the east a bank of cloud was developing. They were drawing up their catch when a hump of water pitched the boat to the side, knocking them off their feet.

'*Travixe ta dichtya. Prépei na fýgoume!*' Geórgios' instructions were hollered with an upward sweep of his arms. They must pull in the nets and leave right away. Sonny's father would have done exactly the same thing.

They were on the sea in a flimsy vessel with a storm barrelling down on them. Ahead of the dark clouds were streaks of white. Sheets of rain were raking the water and coming in their direction. Sonny raised the nets on pulleys as Geórgios lowered the sails, leaving a minimum of canvas for steering. The skipper knew how to outrun storms and his deftness was impressive.

The Greek restarted the motor and Sonny took his place beside the wheel, giving nods of encouragement. They exchanged quick grimaces and Geórgios shouldered the boat into the waves. Within fifteen minutes they were scaling five-footers and slapping down on the other side, hoping the bow wouldn't bury itself in the next rise as they slid into the trough. When the boat stalled Geórgios managed to prevent it from doing a cartwheel.

Now the wind was driving them forward. They were running blind on a high sea, with only flashes of lightning to illumine the way. Their greatest danger was being smashed into matchsticks on a protruding reef. At the southern end of Evia they arched right, looking for shelter behind the tip of the island. Geórgios raised his arm and stabbed his finger at the sky.

Sonny examined the clouds. Something was different. More bad weather seemed poised to batter them from the opposite direction. *Has the storm combined with a second squall?* A fierce ocean current was tipping and spinning the boat. *Are we facing west or south?*

Rain slashed down, soaking everything, running across the deck and escaping through drain holes. The grey bluff of Evia faded behind a wall of fog.

No good came from fighting the wind. Whenever they tried the boat broached, sending boxes and equipment flying. Swearing and calling on the names of saints, Geórgios gripped the wheel and continued to hold a steady course. Standing side by side, staring straight ahead and enthralled by the high rolling waves, they listened to the straining vessel. The whine of the rigging, the creaking of boards and the single steering sail cracking against the mast.

Streams of mist slithered past them. The rain had stopped and slowly the sky lifted, revealing a scene of white-capped waves and patches of glowing sunshine. This place was unrecognisable to Sonny, since nothing beyond Evia had ever been described to him. Interrupting this vast seascape was the distant profile of a pointed rock.

Cheerful now, Geórgios rejigged his sails. As they neared the rock, it became an island. An island among a group of islands—two to the east, two to the west, and a sprinkling of others to the south. The archipelago of the Northern Cyclades.

Straight ahead, the half-moon bay of the smallest island was sandy, but its hills looked barren. Little more than wilted shrubs and dry stony ground. Sonny fretted again about obtaining fresh water. *This must be why we're stopping.*

There was a strange quietness in the bay. No boats at anchor. No orchard groves or grazing animals. No people coming down to greet them.

'Where is everyone?'

     Kayleen M. Hazlehurst

The fisherman lifted his shoulders. 'Gyáros,' he said, looking sorrowful. A few yards from the shore he turned the boat and cut the motor, letting the stern drift to shore.

Glad to be on land again, Sonny threw over the anchor and tugged on the chain until the boat halted on the sand. Geórgios handed him the water bottles, propped his feet on the side, and took out his pipe.

Sonny trotted towards the point, looking for rock pools recently filled with rainwater. The first pool he tasted was too salty, so he dipped his finger into one closer to the cliff. *This will do.* After scooping away the froth, he slanted the bottles on the surface. He turned to wave the full bottles at Geórgios, who responded by raising his pipe.

At the sea ledge he stopped to admire the waves of light glistening over the shallow stones, concentrating on the water as an octopus swam past with a languid sway of limbs.

The skipper was tending to something inside the boat, so Sonny ducked behind a bank to relieve himself, noting signs of nesting birds on the cliff face above. When he came out, he saw his gun and pack had been deposited on the beach and the fisherman was lifting the anchor.

'Hey! Hey!' he shouted as he jumped down from the rocks and raced towards the shore.

The Greek swung himself onto the deck and kicked on the motor.

'Geórgios, what are you doing?'

A hand net was flung towards the beach and Geórgios jabbed a finger to the sea ledge where Sonny had previously been standing.

Sonny threw himself into the water in disbelief. 'Please, Geórgios!'

Was he going to be left on this deserted island? He waded into the sea as the boat pulled away and headed for the grey clouds in the north.

Sonny watched the boat recede in a trail of white. Minutes later, he realised he should get out of the water. His clothes were soaked to the waist and a chilling wind was blowing them against his skin.

The hand net, a token of guilt, was moving back and forth at the water's edge. Sonny was tempted to walk past it, but felt his father's hand upon him, urging him not to be proud. Swearing under his breath, he picked up the net. It was a three-foot round band, attached to a pole. He assumed the net was used for scooping up marine life as it swam past the rocks.

What had caused Geórgios' cowardly departure, he asked himself, and why was this island unoccupied? *Gyáros. Isn't that the word the fisherman used? Is this the name of the island or does it mean something else? Do people avoid this place because it lacks water, or for some other reason?*

Sonny collected his things and considered which way to walk. Birds were his best guides. They knew where to find food and water. He would go back to where he had seen them nesting and follow their line of flight. Despite being dumped in this inhospitable place, his mood was lifting. He pictured the sunburnt eyes, the lined and pitted face, the black coat and mean little cap with its twisted cord and decided he had also had enough of Geórgios' company.

There were plenty of fish. Birds came here to breed, so there had to be something to live on. On the question of wildlife, he still had some bullets, a good knife, and string for snares. *Perhaps a rabbit or goat?* He adjusted his rifle and pack, grasped the hand net, and started to trudge along the beach. *I bet that grumpy old bugger is cursing me all the way back to Skópelos. He didn't want to come this far south. Well, his loss is my gain.*

When he saw a flock of long-winged seabirds gliding above the water, travelling in the same direction, Sonny took heart. He was not alone.

—◦◦◦—

His mother would have instructed him to look out for the signs. She spoke to him now, reminding him that good men were tested by the gods, and not to forget he was protected. He could see signs of human habitation— thyme bushes, stunted cypress trees, stone walls long since collapsed. There was sorrow here. The ghosts of sad men. Had Gyáros been a place of exile over the centuries? A night beside a fire in the company of his guardian spirits would keep away this misery.

He continued around the bays looking for shelter. After an hour he

 Kayleen M. Hazlehurst

found a crevice backed into the cliff before it gave way to a north-facing headland. In front of the cave an outcrop of rock provided pools rich with limpets and shrimp. With his knife, Sonny had flipped off shellfish for his hooks before casting out his line. Then he returned to the task of making camp. He had two canisters of water, a hand net he wanted to try out, and an armload of driftwood for his fire. In these unfished waters, he had every reason to believe a catch would be simmering in his pan by evening.

Close to sunset, he took out a mirror and rubbed his palm over his face. With his razor blade long since blunt, he would have to be content with a beard trim using his scissors. He jutted out his chin and swished the beard upwards before starting on his neck. Tomorrow should bring him to the other side of the island. *If there's grass on those hills I might find some game.*

> Sonny sits on a high cliff, where the thick roots of a pōhutukawa buckle around him and continue to run down the cliff. A sallow moon lights the sea in a shimmering path. He watches the path. Sees it shudder and break as the humped back of a whale broaches the water.
>
> The wind is in the east as a waka crosses the harbour. He stands and reaches out to his ancestors, hears the swish of the paddles, but they pass onwards and do not pause. Yet he is certain they have seen him. Like the whale, they want him to know they are waiting.
>
> He hears the voice of his mother. 'Come home, dear. Come home soon,' she calls, and he wakes to the sound of his own weeping.

Gyáros and the Seals

Sonny stripped off his clothes, hesitating at his underpants. They could do with a wash. In the weak morning sun he decided to leave them on. He entered the sea, whooping at the coolness of it and rubbing his skin to increase circulation. The water was so clear it was easy to search for sea eggs, or anything else that was edible. He rolled over and looked up at the surface. *Hello, I have company.*

A seal was passing over in a relaxed motion of flippers and tail. Sonny circled away so as not to frighten the graceful mammal. He climbed out of the water further along the beach and saw the seal sunning itself near his cave. That this creature showed no fear made Sonny believe the seal colony lounging on the rocks and sand were unfamiliar with people. With their enormous eyes and flared nostrils, they did look curiously human. *It's nice they think I'm one of their kind,* he thought as he picked his own spot in the sun. *I wonder what Mum would say about this.*

In preparing to explore the eastern side of the island, Sonny had taken his pack, his water bottles and some hunting gear. There was no point dismantling the camp on the off-chance of finding something better. The real reason, though one he was not prepared to admit, was that he'd just acquired a family of seals.

The other coast was even more isolated. Here, the steep hills were the home of birds of prey. Buzzards, falcons and eagles. Aerial hunters that lived off insects, reptiles, mammals and small birds. He sat to watch the lazy sweep of a pair of falcons above the crags. It interested him that Gyáros provided a breeding ground for migratory birds. Yet, still he saw no goats. There was scarce food for foraging animals and the rocks were covered with lichen. An adult eagle could easily snatch a young goat. Maybe they grazed on safer pasture across the top of the island.

He was about to turn back when he saw a stand of reeds growing behind a bank. Stealthily, he circled above it and looked down to see a promising assembly of ducks. A natural wetland between two slopes was being fed by a rivulet from an upper pond. Sonny filled his water bottles at the mouth of the spring and crept into the reeds to set his snares. Tonight, with any luck, he would be a happy man. A couple of Adrian's potatoes to add to his roast duck would have been nice.

—✺—

Every morning his seal wife came to visit. For three days he never attempted to touch her grey silky fur, but it wasn't long before he noticed her size and discomfort. This little girl was about to give birth. It crossed his mind that she was planning to whelp in the cave, so he set about preparing the nursery. His belongings were pushed against the far wall, and he scooped together a layer of sand to make a platform.

Early on the fourth day, he heard steady scuffling as she made her way up the beach. She stopped at the entrance and regarded him with liquid eyes.

'Sorry.' A little abashed, he stepped outside so she was able to gauge the comfort of the birthing chamber.

For two nervous hours he sat and waited—standing and sitting, trying not to disturb her as she struggled. With a last groan a head emerged, followed by a *squish* and a three-foot long pup with brown fur and a white belly-stripe.

After the mother nuzzled the pup into life, a pair of teats descended from her belly for the infant to suckle.

'I'll be damned!' Astonished, Sonny had to wipe away a tear.

That afternoon he placed a fish by her nose. A nursing seal likely stayed with a pup in the first days after birth, but she seemed hungry and ate his small offerings. He felt trusted enough to stay and prepare his own dinner. He remembered sharing his sleeping quarters with a hundred men at training camp. A straw bed now seemed a distant luxury, but sharing a cave with seals was much more intriguing.

In subsequent days he stayed close, living off the sea like his seal family, and watching the pup grow. This was his job as a seal husband. He never did get a chance to go after those elusive goats, nor was he troubled any more by ghosts or dreams.

One day the seal flippered off to catch her own food and the pup, left curled and mewing, did not seem to mind his touch.

Another storm broke while the seal mother was gone.

It rolled in with unexpected force from the north, swelling the waves and heaving them up in peaks of surf. When Sonny saw the lapping waves he knew the cave would flood. Tucking the seal pup into his backpack he jumped out before the next surge. In the hills behind them he had seen some overhanging rocks.

Rainwater had carved channels through the clay and stones, making this poor ground for climbing. When he slipped and stumbled, or when he landed face down in the mud, there were moans of complaint from the rear. Apart from his bloodied knuckles, they arrived safely at the top.

The best shelter he could find was a hill facing south. As he shuffled along the crumbly bank, he appreciated the protection it gave them from the blasts coming in from the ocean. With this advantage, and his trusty tent sheet, he and the pup snuggled into the earth under a small ledge.

Seaward, he could see the wind thrashing the Aegean. On the horizon, lightning strikes lit the inky water. Not a good day to be out in a boat. With the warmth of a young seal against his chest, the prospect of being stranded on a deserted island no longer seemed so desperate.

By morning the weather had calmed. The pup lifted its head and looked around, curious about its surroundings. Sonny jumped when its whiskers brushed his cheek.

'Hello, little fella. Are you hungry? Shall we see if Mum is home?'

The water had receded, leaving the beach littered with debris. But these were sea creatures after all, so what to them was a bit of misplaced sand or seaweed? Back from her excursions, the seal mother looked

   Kayleen M. Hazlehurst

relieved to see her pup when Sonny laid him down to suckle.

There was nothing more Sonny could do for this little family. Saddened by the loss, he shouldered his pack and rifle and strode south.

—✺—

The tempest had left its mark along the foreshore. As Sonny walked towards the bay where he first landed he had to pick his way through dead fish, kelp, weathered planks and other wreckage thrown up from the ocean floor. The sea was still unsettled, but swooping seagulls told him things were returning to normal. His intention was to circle the island from the south, hoping the eastern cliffs would prove more passable from that side.

As he rounded the point where he'd first collected the drinking water he saw a smudge on the skyline.

He watched for almost two hours until it was apparent the object coming towards the island was an old fishing boat. The vessel's movements seemed aimless, propelled by the ocean currents. It twisted and turned, surfed forward, and then stalled. *It could have drifted like this for days.* As it came closer he saw a chain drooping and swaying from the stern, like some sea beast had torn away the anchor. One side of the vessel looked broken and the mast was shattered and charred.

'Geórgios' boat!'

Sonny ran to the end of the point and called a warning to Geórgios that he was approaching the rocks, but the boat just proceeded on its ghostly path. He tore off his outer clothing and dived into the sea. With a powerful stroke, he swam to the back of the boat to grab the dangling chain and pulled with all his strength.

Halted, the bow pointed skywards and slapped down, tearing the chain from his fingers. Then the boat turned sideways and slid along the point with the flow of the waves where it thrust itself onto the beach amidst streams of foam. Sonny swam to the bay and dragged himself panting from the water. He placed one hand on the stern and looked in.

There was no sign of the skipper. Only a jagged line left by a lightning bolt, as it had seared a path down the mast and out through the side. The force could easily have flung a man overboard. Geórgios would have been dead before he hit the water. If leaving an Allied soldier on a forsaken island was uncharitable, Geórgios had paid for it dearly. In his haste to return north, he had sailed into the fury of the first storm.

Sonny wished he could see that tired old face again and thank the man for getting him this far. With enemy patrols on the hunt, it would be risky to ferry Geórgios' boat back to Skópelos. Maybe after the war he could make amends. He had to keep moving. In the future there may be times when he'd think shamefully about this incident, but not today.

With a large wave, Sonny heaved the wreck a little further up the sand. It was in a sad condition. During those ten days at sea, it was a miracle it hadn't sunk. He climbed onto the deck and started sifting through the scattered items. Everything was wet—coats, fishing gear, the box of tools. What he could dry he laid out in the sun. Tools were placed on an upturned box, then he stood back to take an inventory.

There were three fish knives, a saw and a crowbar, a claw hammer and a tin of nails, a mallet and a tangle of rope and string. To these, he added his own tools from his pack. The pulleys and hoist were still fastened to the floor, but the engine had been split apart.

Sonny would have to make the fishing boat seaworthy for the trip to the next island. A distance of about fifteen miles, judging by the visibility of the land mass. If the enemy was on the move again people would know their location. All he needed was one kind person to draw him a rough map of the Cyclades and to suggest a safe route.

With the cabin tidied and wiped down by an old towel he left the boat to dry. He lifted a wooden panel, thinking he might find some more rope. Tucked at the back of the cupboard was another sail. It was a smaller canvas than the one Geórgios had used during the storm and was later vaporised by lightning. This emergency sail would be enough to get him going, although the problem of a mast still needed to be solved.

Sonny examined the boat's splintered side. How could he make it watertight without an oilcloth or some proper caulking? Caïques sat low in the water and this was more than a crack. *If I borrow planks from the seats or skirting ... Hang on.*

     Kayleen M. Hazlehurst

He jumped over the side and started to run, remembering he'd seen some planks of wood on the beach. A different storm. A different wreck.

'These will help.' He grabbed any planks that weren't ridden with sea worm and cast around for a longer piece for a mast.

'I'll think of something.'

After sawing, chiselling, hammering and filling seams with bits of sacking, tufts of wool, twists of string and some tree resin, the vessel was as watertight as she was going to be. From the hillside he felled a scrawny cypress. This he lashed to the base of the shattered mast, securing the sail as best he could with ropes.

Sonny pushed out the boat, satisfied to see it floated. After stowing his belongings and saying a prayer for a safe crossing, he heaved in his stone and rope anchor and pushed off with the single oar. As the sail billowed and caught the wind, he looked back at the island where the gods had tested a man.

He heard a splash. Above the water his seal wife followed his retreat with her large eyes, her whiskered face enquiring and calm. Beside her, darting among the waves, was her pup. 'Thank you,' he said.

~23~

Sýros and Father Jacob

Sonny enjoyed the slanted light coming in the kitchen window, as he waited for his clothes to dry. A man in the black robes of a Catholic priest had draped a prickly wool blanket over his bare shoulders.

'You must have seen some marvellous things in your travels,' said the priest.

'I've seen a thing or two.'

Father Jacob took Sonny's socks and began to scrub them with laundry soap in a bowl. 'I'll give these a darn this evening.'

'You don't have to,' Sonny said, embarrassed. The water would be black from sweat and dirt.

'Oh, but I like darning. I was taught how when I was young. It was understood my family would dedicate their first son to the Church, and a priest needs to have extra skills. My mother was proud of me. She said no one could see where my thread began and where it ended.'

Sonny looked at this rare man. Only yesterday he had steered into the bay north-east of the cluttered port town. The good citizens of Sýros, who had come down to help when they saw his boat limp in, had rushed to tell the priest of the soldier's arrival. Father Jacob turned out to be fluent in English and accustomed to speaking on behalf of strangers.

The caïque with its odd tree-mast was covered under an oilcloth and hidden among the other boats. Sonny had been hurried up the hill, shielded by darkly clothed figures, to a cottage on the seaward side of an imposing Catholic church.

A barley and maize porridge with stewed figs was put on the table in front of him. 'You know the Fascists are here?'

Sonny lifted his spoon and faltered. 'They're on this island?'

Kayleen M. Hazlehurst

'The Italians arrived in the Cyclades Islands a month ago. It appears Mussolini wants to make Sýros his footstool.' The priest scuttled outside to hang up the wet socks on the line and to test the other laundry. 'Almost dry.'

'Is there anything we can do, Father?'

Jacob glanced around before coming back inside. 'Escaping soldiers must be very careful,' he said in a lowered voice. 'We will assist you, of course we will, but famine has gripped the mainland and who knows how much longer we can withstand this misfortune.'

Sonny looked guiltily at his breakfast.

'Come now, you must have boots for me to mend.'

He searched his pack for Monty's boots where they'd been stored during his time with the seals.

'My father was a cobbler.' Jacob mounted the first boot on an iron last and poked critically at places where it was coming away.

Sonny had never seen a shoemaker at work. The sole was loosened and removed cleanly with a tool similar to a pair of pliers. A piece of hard leather was taken down from a shelf and matched to the boot. From this, a new sole was cut with a knife. Jacob trimmed the sole, tapped it into place and hammered it down. The rest of the boot was re-stitched along the edges with a hand-wheeled sewing machine. The skill and natural grace of the man intrigued him.

He was handed the repaired boot with some rags and a smear of grease.

'Give this a polish,' Jacob said as he readied the second boot. 'Catholic and Orthodox Christians have lived in friendship on this island for decades. We share many festivals. That these invaders are also Catholic has not made it easy for us.'

'I don't understand the difference between the Catholic Church and the Orthodox Church. Can you explain it to me?'

'It would be my pleasure.'

'You see, a friend of mine has joined an Orthodox monastery.'

'And this friend was a soldier?'

'A member of my battalion.'

Father Jacob swept his hand over the land, in much the same way Miriama would have done when speaking in broad terms. 'You are aware that Christ's apostles founded the ancient church in the first century?'

'Yes.'

'Very good. After our Lord's ascension, bands of followers moved throughout this region preaching the gospel and nurturing the people. You will find many baptismal fonts and catacombs dating back to the third and fourth centuries. The Greek Orthodox Church descended from these early communities.'

'It was the ancientness of the Orthodox Church that attracted my friend. He believed it was pure, untouched by civilisation.'

'Your friend had good instincts. The Roman Empire grew so vast that its administration was eventually divided into two. The Western Empire was to be governed from Rome and the Eastern Empire was to be governed from Constantinople—the city you may know as Istanbul. The Cyclades became part of this Byzantine Empire. This schism between the Eastern and Western Church has never been healed, you see. But here on Sýros we are very fond of our Orthodox Christians. They are a hardy people.'

Sonny went to the window to watch the fluttering garments on the line outside the washhouse. He pivoted back to Father Jacob. 'So what can we do about these invaders?'

'My son, many foreign nations have tried to conquer us over the centuries. Our mission is to survive as we have always done. When we bring our joys and sorrows to each other and the Holy Church, we become strong. Your mission is to find your battalion. There is nothing here for a lone soldier unless he plans to be a martyr.'

Sonny did not believe in submitting to bullies but agreed he needed to move on.

Father Jacob extended his hand in an apology. 'But I'm sorry, I have spoken too much. Please tell me about your own religion, Sonny. I imagine your people have carried the light of sacred knowledge since antiquity.'

Sonny gave an amused grunt. 'I'm not sure you'll want to hear about my pagan beliefs.' *Remember Mum's stories, Tama? How Tāne journeyed to the*

Kayleen M. Hazlehurst

twelfth heaven to bring back those wonderful birds for his forests. How he moulded the first woman from clay and breathed life into her.

The priest studied him for a long moment. 'We are all children of God,' he said at last. 'What humble scholar would not be interested in the stories of Creation?'

Sonny smiled. 'Then tonight, as you darn my socks, I will share with you some of our stories.' He glanced out the window again. 'Any chance of getting back my clothes? I want to go down to the port.'

Half an hour later Sonny was given his dried shirt and trousers, along with fresh undergarments.

'I'll get something for your feet.' Jacob dashed down the hall and returned with a pair of sandals. 'Army boots are too conspicuous.'

'Thanks for taking care of me. You've been very kind.'

'I'll come to the Port with you. It's safer than on your own.'

'As long as I'm not putting you in danger.'

'Who would not trust a Catholic priest with a friend?'

'Many people, I expect.'

Father Jacob lifted his head and laughed. 'You might be right, Sonny. Now that Italy has designs on our islands.'

—~~~—

They turned towards the port, feeling the sun on their shoulders. The path from the Catholic quarter of Ano Sýros snaked past a line of houses and stone walls, iced white like Christmas cakes.

Before the war the commercial port of Ermoupoli had been a major stopping point for ships between the Mediterranean and the Black Sea. Would he be noticed among the well-dressed residents and merchants of Sýros? Now, with the Italian military on the island, what exactly did he expect to find? Men who would have sympathy for a stranded Allied soldier, or men who would report him to the authorities?

Halfway down the hill, Jacob broke their stride. He seemed to be having reservations and suggested they stop.

'This is not a good idea, Sonny. There are almost fifty Anzacs hiding on Sýros and many of them are trying to find passage through this port. I fear the Italians will soon learn of it. What are your plans for the caïque?'

'The boat is useless. It needs a new rudder and mast. One side is leaking, and the engine is dead. The old tub wouldn't stand up to high seas the way it is.'

'Let's take a different path. I know the owners of a boatyard, two brothers. They are skilled craftsmen.'

'Do you think they will help me? I have no money.'

'Nobody has money these days. Everything is done by favours. We'd starve if we didn't share what we have. The boat was abandoned, you say?'

'It was wandering the sea on its own.'

'And the owner?'

'Killed by lightning, I think. The boat was empty.' Sonny was still heartsick at the way he had acquired Geórgios' boat.

'Don't be ashamed, my son. You did not steal this boat. God put it into your hands for a purpose. I would say it is your duty to repair it. Let's see what old Elias and Nicholas have to say. They love a good challenge.'

They veered down a path that was no more than a track through the grasses. Few people came this way. The usual access to the bay below was by water. The path narrowed to a bank, leading to the seafront, where two elderly men sat smoking beside an iron-roofed shed. Planks and timber offcuts lay in untidy piles on the ground. The open doors of the shed faced a jetty with hoists for pulling boats onto a slipway.

Sonny stood aside as the boat builders greeted Father Jacob as an old friend, holding back so they could eye him from a distance and negotiate. After a short while the boat builders ambled over to say that if Sonny provided his labour, they would fix his boat. Through the priest, Sonny related his delight at being apprenticed to such skilled craftsmen.

Elias wiped his hand on his sawdust-streaked trousers, spat on his palm and extended his hand to seal the deal. Nicholas, his droopy eyelids not concealing mischievous eyes, warned Sonny that his older brother would likely work him to death.

As an enticement, Father Jacob promised the brothers a box of vegetables, to be assembled from donations made by his hinterland

Kayleen M. Hazlehurst

parishioners. The box could be collected on Sunday, he said, if the rogues would make their way to the church service.

Chastened, Elias and Nicholas agreed.

—*∿*—

Father Jacob and Sonny were instructed to meet the brothers on the beach at midnight to help with the launch. The boatyard was two coves away and Elias and Nicholas had promised to bring a rowing boat and plenty of rope. The task of restoring the damaged craft to its former glory would begin the next morning, and Sonny couldn't help wondering what Geórgios Stavros would have thought about this.

Priest and soldier stretched out their legs on the dry sand while they waited. A calm night and a dark moon were predicted that evening. At home, Sonny hadn't really liked the Catholics. Or rather, it was more a case of the Catholics not liking his family for adhering to pre-Christian practices.

His mother was often ridiculed for being old-fashioned. Sonny remembered being teased at school about her facial tattoo, her moko. Her fury over the Tohunga Suppression Act of 1907, where the government had tried to turn Māori away from traditional practices, was far more serious. Sonny's grandfather had been a man filled with the spirit of the gods, she said, and this legislation had hurt his heart. Although many ignored the new law, Miriama had never stopped growling about it.

Father Jacob was different. This clergyman had put himself in harm's way for the escaping soldiers. Who knew how many he had helped? For this reason, he had won Sonny's respect.

All of a sudden, Jacob sat up. 'Look, a shooting star!'

'Tāne told the Milky Way to guard the restless and troublesome stars. He instructed the minor ones to stay close to the cluster for their protection.'

'Tāne?'

'Tāne-mahuta is the god of forests and birds. He is an offspring of the original parents.' Sonny moved his hands to indicate the sky father, Ranginui, and the earth mother, Papatūānuku.

'I'd like to learn more about these deities.'

'Tāne is a primary atua who helped bring light to the world so humans could flourish.'

'Do your people have many gods?'

'Āe, a great variety—Tangaroa, Keeper of the Sea. Tāwhiri-mātea, Keeper of the Winds. I grew up with them all around me.'

'Similar to the pantheon of gods from Greek antiquity. Do you worship these gods, Sonny?'

'Maybe not in the way you understand worship,' he answered cautiously. 'I acknowledge their authority and call on the Powers when I need them. My spiritual connections help me navigate my way through the world.'

'Some might call these forces angels and saints.'

'Angels and saints are like our guardian and companion spirits.'

'I see. And these elemental gods, where did they sit?

'Under the reign of Io, the Primary Creator.'

Jacob sat back, slightly astonished. 'Was this widely known?'

'Not at all. The Supreme Being was so sacred, only the initiates of our Schools of Learning were acquainted with His name.'

'Your Supreme Being was called Io?'

'He had many names. The Crown of the Heavens, the Parentless, the Many-Eyed, the Unseen.'

'This sounds so familiar. Christian theology also struggles with a multiplicity of concepts. *It is not the sun that is our Lord*, Saint Augustine said, *but He who created the sun*.'

'Christianity wasn't difficult for our people to accept.'

'How does the modern Church cope with such a richness of belief?'

'There is a blending of rituals and customs. Anglicans and Catholics carry on their services, with Māori participation. It seems to work.'

'I don't think our Pope would be very pleased.'

'I don't think your Pope has a say in the matter.'

Father Jacob's shoulders shook with suppressed glee. 'I cannot comment.' He turned back to the stars. 'Divine revelation, surely this provides the clearest evidence of a constant link between the physical and spiritual worlds? Christ's teachings.'

     Kayleen M. Hazlehurst

'I do not doubt there is a link. I live this connection.'

'So you do, Sonny. Civilisation owes much to the religion of the ancients. Ritual purification. Mysticism. Concepts of the soul and of the afterlife. These are our common roots.' Jacob leaned forward. 'You will know about our warrior class of Sparta and their codes of honour?'

'I don't know much about them, but some of our men fought at Thermopylae Pass.'

'*Ah.* Our Spartans held that passage twenty-five centuries ago. Their fierce hand-to-hand combat caused terrible harm to the Persians. I expect this narrow gorge made the Allies an easy target for German Stukas?'

'I met an Australian who fought there. Freddy Peacock. He said it was a terrifying place. Officers wanted to get our soldiers and equipment moved out of there as quickly as possible.'

'Indeed. The Battle of Thermopylae Pass illustrated the importance of warriors being noble-hearted. *Now, Oh Greeks, is the moment when, freed of quarrels and fighting, we should rescue sweet Eirene and draw her out of this pit. This is the moment to drain a cup in honour of Agathos Daimon.* Agathos Daimon was a companion spirit of the old religion.'

'Who was Eirene?'

'Eirene was the goddess of peace.'

'I like that.'

After a long pause, Jacob asked, 'And what about your people, Sonny?'

'Our war parties were dedicated to Tūmatauenga, and those chosen by Tū were blessed with spiritual authority. Ihi, the psychic power granted to fighting men, was the vital force felt ahead of arriving warriors. In battle this force petrified the enemy, especially when our men had a blistering sense of justice.'

'The bringers of righteous fire?'

Sonny tilted his head. 'You could say that.'

'Have you known these spiritual powers yourself?'

'Since I was a child.'

'Are those who serve the will of the gods also sacred?'

'Āe. They are highly tapu.'

'And to treat them with disrespect incurs spiritual retribution?'

Sonny held the man's gaze. 'I have seen it many times, Father. This is why I believe the Nazis will ultimately fail. They are cruel and fight without honour. They kill civilians and innocent animals. Their crimes will bring down the wrath of the gods.'

'Amen to that!' Father Jacob said.

They heard the swish of dipping oars and walked to the water's edge where Sonny's ruined caïque stood ready. Under the starlit sky, they caught a glimpse of approaching boatmen.

The wreck slid off, Elias cursing at the oars and Nicholas answering as he guided the dark frame with two ropes.

'I wish I could help them,' Sonny said.

'They'll manage.'

'Perhaps I should swim behind and push.'

'No need. They'll be halfway across the bay before you catch up. I've seen them do this before.'

'They're tough old birds. I'm looking forward to working with them.'

'Come.' The priest took his lamp and guided Sonny towards the path. 'You'll need rest before Elias cracks the whip tomorrow. I'll tell you more about the Spartans as we walk.'

   Kayleen M. Hazlehurst

~24~

Sífnos and Julian's Arrowheads

He woke to the sound of bleating. Through slit eyes he saw a spectacular pair of horns rising above the crest of a hill. A herd of goats jostled down, making it evident that this was their island. Sonny knew about goats. They would eat anything you left on the ground, including Father Jacob's straw hat. This gift from his friend to keep the sun off his face was something he valued. *I must have slept on this sand for hours.*

A brown-and-white buck stamped his foot and regarded Sonny with menacing yellow eyes. Sonny grabbed the hat and backed away. A billy's horns could do serious damage. A group of nannies with their kids were eyeing him. He could stalk goats all day in their own environment, but it was hardly fair play to kill an animal that had come down a hill to greet him. He searched his mind. *How did I get here?*

On Sýros, the elderly brothers and Sonny had slaved on their project until they'd brought Geórgios' boat up to scratch. The hull was rebuilt, a nice piece of spruce was retrieved from under the shed for a new mast, and a better sail was obtained. There was no replacement for the broken engine. In any case, asking around for scarce fuel would have drawn unwanted attention.

Before he continued his journey through the Cyclades, Father Jacob invited three other stranded servicemen to join Sonny on his boat—Brian, a British ambulance driver, and two Kiwi soldiers, Colin and Keith. The priest had secreted them away with Catholic families. Sonny would have taken more of the stranded men, but Elias and Nicholas advised him not to overload the boat until the repairs had been tried and tested.

On the night of their sailing, he was led to a safe house for their first meeting. The escapers were thin from weeks of travelling, but in good spirits. After an emotional farewell to their friends, they meekly followed Jacob and Sonny down to the beach.

To help him on the next stage, Jacob had provided Sonny with a map of the central and south-west Cycladic island groups. The priest had listed the names of each island and estimated the miles between them. Based on this, Sonny decided to head straight for Sífnos, sailing past Kýthnos and Sérifos. While the winds were favourable, and the boat was holding up, he would take the longer hop. If they came to grief on these open waters no one would ever find them, but he kept this knowledge to himself.

The lovely island of Sýros faded into a thin line. After six hours of sailing south to south-west, the sea softened from a grape-purple to a silvery blue. The four of them stood bewitched as they witnessed strange patterns on the water's surface. Streaks of yellow, made luminous by reflected light from deepwater plankton. Little by little the eastern cliffs of Sífnos rose to meet them.

The profile of a castle appeared at the top of a jutting point, and below this they found a bay to moor the boat. As they started on the road above the inlet they debated aloud who might help them. Entering any new village was risky. After a short walk they came to an opening in the scrub. Here, a man was seen scraping a clay bank with a trowel. It seemed only polite to put down their packs and observe the activity. Brian, who could make himself understood in Greek, stepped forward to offer a greeting.

The man, Julian Nicolaides, introduced himself and conveyed in a jumble of Greek and English that he was looking for artefacts. Sífnos had a long history of settlement and this retired schoolteacher liked to comb the island for treasures from the past.

'Artefacts like this are scattered everywhere,' Julian said, showing them some broken tiles in a wooden box. 'An hour ago, I unearthed these from the Roman period.'

The men gaped at the newly discovered fragments.

'Stone Age hunters and gatherers lived here first. Then came the pre-Hellenic tribes, the Carians and Leleges. The Leleges were mentioned as

 Kayleen M. Hazlehurst

allies of the Trojans by Homer in the *Iliad*.' Julian lifted his shoulders in an apology. 'History blends with mythology.'

Brian was having difficulty with some of the translations, but they got the gist of it.

Julian extracted two silver coins. 'In the millennium before Christ, Sífnos enjoyed remarkable wealth from its gold and silver mines.'

Brian patted Julian on the back as a fellow defender of the arts, and before long they were all invited back to the fortified village of Kastro to look over Julian's collection.

At his home, the custodian of ancient things drew away a sheet covering rows of cabinet boxes. The display included stone axes and bone needles, chipped ceramic tiles, broken pottery cooking pots, an assortment of old coins, terracotta animals, and figurines sculptured from stone.

Julian selected a black, chiselled arrowhead. 'This is made from obsidian. It was mined on our neighbouring island of Mílos. Thousands of years ago different cultures knapped volcanic rock into blades and tools. It was a valuable item of trade throughout the Aegean.'

Colin touched the hard tip. 'It looks like black glass.'

'One day people will see the importance of these,' Julian declared. 'Sífnos will have its own museum and they'll be glad of my findings.'

Sonny had seen enough alabaster statues and pagan idols to know Greece was very old, but Julian's artefacts were quite different. *What ancient people crafted such beautiful things? If they're still around, I'd like to meet them.*

A chill passed through his body as it occurred to him that many of these objects were taken from graves.

Events unfolded rapidly at Julian's house, propelled by the arrival of a fisherman. Gossip rippled from boat to boat through these islands, and from house to house after the boats docked. Because of his expeditions, the retired schoolteacher was a familiar character on the island, and his door was the first to be thumped on in a crisis.

'Crete has fallen! Crete has fallen!'

A messenger in gumboots had pitched his arm against the doorframe, breathless from running.

'Come in, Jace … I have guests … Tell us everything.'

They gathered to listen around the kitchen table.

'The Allies have been defeated!' Jace cried. 'Overpowered by the Germans in a brutal air and sea assault!'

The host fetched three loaves of bread, a dish of olive oil and a glass each of ouzo.

'Poor Crete. What does this mean for us?' Colin asked.

Brian's answer was brusque. 'It means the end of our fellas leaving by this route.'

'Crete was our last hope for escape,' Keith said. 'And, now …'

'Now it's prison camp for us,' Brian muttered.

Sonny bent close to Brian's ear. 'They have to catch us first.' He leaned back on his chair. 'It's the people I feel sorry for. Are they really overrun, Jace?'

'Completely! The Luftwaffe have been sinking ships and attacking fishermen and trading vessels. Our boatmen don't know what to do.'

Julian gulped down his drink. 'It must be hell.' He turned to Sonny. 'You boys will have to be careful. Nowhere in the Aegean is safe.'

This was the last time Sonny saw his comrades. Brian, who shared an interest in ancient art, was taken in by Julian Nicolaides. For the other three, Julian suggested they pay a visit to the breadmaker. Two miles from Kastro was the town of Apollonía, named after the Greek god Apollo. The baker and his wife who lived there might offer them shelter.

'We'll stick with you, Sonny,' the Kiwi boys said. 'You can count on us.'

'I don't know,' Sonny answered, as they walked on to Apollonía. 'If these people will take you in, maybe you should work in the bakery until it's safer to travel.'

It was not unusual for Allied soldiers to fall into the bosoms of kindly Greeks. A family, whose husband or son was absent, might appreciate the strength of a man who could chop wood or hoe the ground.

'What will you do, Sonny?' Keith asked.

'Don't worry. It shouldn't be hard to hide a boat among this nest of islands.' After the fisherman's news, Sonny was even more determined to continue on to Crete.

And there it was, his lost memory. With Brian lodged with the tenacious Julian, and Keith and Colin tucked away in the baker's basement, Sonny recalled going back to the bay. His plan was to sleep on the boat and cast off early.

He had food for his supper. Julian had replenished his water bottles, and the baker had given him two loaves of crispy lagana bread. Over the coming days he wanted to restock his supplies. Tinned beef and hard biscuits. Army food, or anything else that would stay fresh on a long sea voyage. Now where was he going to find something like this?

———∿∿∿———

Sonny addressed the majestic animal with the horns.

'Your Highness, apologies for the intrusion, but I don't suppose you know of any food of no interest to goats?'

King Billy belched and one of the nannies moseyed over to sniff Sonny's knee.

'No, I didn't think so.' He shooed off the teeth nibbling at his trousers.

If he'd lost his appetite for goat meat, on an island ruled by goats, maybe this was a sign he needed to move on.

He focused on the nearby island shimmering in the midday sun. Strange, also, was the taste in his mouth. Was it liquorice or cinnamon? The last thing he remembered before falling asleep was drinking the water provided by Julian—except it wasn't water.

In New Zealand he might have had the occasional beer with mates, or with the battalion boys in Egypt, but since then he'd seen no alcohol. The glass served to him while they were lamenting the fall of Crete had been his first experience of ouzo. One of his water bottles was empty and he gave it a sniff. He should have known it was liquor, but not that it was so potent.

Sonny rubbed his temples. On the shoreline his boat was washing back and forth with the small waves. That would explain how he wound up on a strange beach, with a sore head, surrounded by meddlesome goats. *I must have sailed here in the middle of the night, blind drunk.*

The next hop was short and he decided to risk it in the daylight. A wind caught his sail and he made the crossing in half an hour. In a bay a man was drawing in a net from a small boat. Sonny fastened his sail and threw out his anchor so they could speak.

The boatman's face cracked into a smile as he pulled in his oars. '*Ah*. You have been visiting Polýaigos, the Island of Goats. I saw you sail over.'

Pleased he was understanding more Greek, Sonny tried a phrase or two himself.

'*Kali méra.* Where am I, sir?'

'Ah, young man, you are most fortunate. This is the beautiful island of Kímolos.'

 Kayleen M. Hazlehurst

~25~

Kímolos and her Maidens

Kímolos was undeniably beautiful. After he left the friendly boatman, Sonny sailed around the coves. Silica-white sands and strange rock formations glistened above the waters. But the land was parched. Straw-like grasses and prickly pear covered the hills, confirming the sparseness of this place.

As he hugged the coast he looked for signs of vegetation or evidence of damp. Water flowed to the sea, and orange-stained banks pointed to possible water sources further inland. After sailing past one or two derelict cottages, he came to a secluded bay. There, etched into the white cliffs, was a row of caverns jutting into the sea. One of them, high enough to take his mast, had a shelf leading back to the beach. *A good place to hide a boat,* he thought, as he nudged into the cave and drove his anchor into its chalky walls.

The first thing he needed to do was set his fishing lines. Starvation, and the madness that followed, would render him incapable of making sound decisions. Shellfish and sea eggs were plentiful for bait. A freshly opened kina might entice an octopus or a lobster into his traps, and he'd look around to see what else would be good for netting. While sailing here he had seen ground birds and field hares in the hills. On the shore there were cormorants and shags, although it was too late in the season for their eggs. He'd even seen an eagle, but he would never harm such a sacred bird.

Three hours before sunset Sonny stood at the foot of a slippery bluff and cupped his hand under a dribble of water to test its purity. He touched the wet moss, finding it warm, and sniffed his palm. Sulphur. Before he left Sýros, Father Jacob had explained the last islands in the western group were volcanic. Sonny wiped his forehead and lifted his water bottle to his lips. Julian had fortunately had the presence of mind to fill his second bottle with water. Now it was half gone. If these hills refused to offer him drinkable water he'd have to leave Kímolos.

The next island was less than a mile away and appeared greener. Milos was the last in this island chain and bordered on the Sea of Crete. *There must be artesian water there and people who can provide farm produce.*

He trudged uphill with his hunting gear and positioned himself above the bank where he'd seen the run-off. As he laid his snares, weariness and hunger made him wish he'd obtained some meat while he was on the Island of Goats. *Sentimental fool.*

Aside from its dryness, he liked Kímolos. The scarcity of water would mean fewer people lived here. How did Jason and his mariners survive as they voyaged through this region all those centuries ago? What food did they bring with them? What did they hunt? Had Chiron, the wise centaur, given them good advice? Sonny wouldn't mind asking Chiron a question or two himself. Jason had been searching for a trophy. What was it Adrian said, a golden fleece? *So many gods and heroes. So many stories. Perhaps I should leave those myths to their misty shades of the past.*

Talking about mist …

In a gully, between two hills, clouds had formed above a cluster of trees. As he neared, he saw brushwood screening the grove. He pressed through a gap, stepping unsteadily onto a spongy depression. Vapour curled through a dark passageway of branches and the smell of sulphur confirmed his suspicions. As he came back into daylight, he discovered a small waterfall and a pond encircled by sudsy white clay. He tested the water temperature, removed his clothes and eased his aching, sweat-soaked body into the thermal spring. With an exquisite sigh, he sank into the soft bank and raised his eyes to the violet-blue sky.

'Tama, I wish you were here to share this hot pool with me.'

> Through the haze of steam a woman appears to him. A
> maiden wearing a long, white veil and flowing garment
> hovers and melds with the air above the pond. She

          Kayleen M. Hazlehurst

speaks to him in a soft language that, somehow, he
understands. There will be crossroads, she tells him.
He will have to make choices. As a gift, she offers him
a life of prosperity and pleasure, or a life of struggle
and valour. Along the way he will be tempted, but this
is part of his training. 'Be not afraid,' she says. 'You
are not alone.'

Sonny rubbed his eyes. He was on the boat with no memory of how
he'd got back there. Had he been dreaming, or had he finally gone mad?
Closing his eyes again, he surrendered to the rise and fall of the waves.

That night he dreamed of Atarangi. Their souls met, and she flowed
into him like the swell of water into his cave.

———෴———

Sonny wished he didn't have to leave this place. Kímolos felt safe. In the
Māori world wairua had been known to warn people of dangers through
visitations and dreams. Was the white maiden a spiritual being seeking a
warrior's help for the people of this land?

He doubted he had enough strength to handle a boat across the Sea
of Crete, let alone to fight in a war. If he was going to die here he dearly
wanted to honour the ancestors of this land with supplications. To spend
some time with the rocks and the trees. To make his peace with the spirits
of the animals and birds he had killed.

He hoped the morning coolness would give him energy as he followed
his previous track. The contour of the land suggested an underground
stream ran through this gully. Moisture from the hills flowed through here
and terminated at the thermal spring. *Where there is water, there is game.* The
first two snares were empty but checking the third he found the plump
carcass of a partridge waiting for him. As he tied its skinny legs to his
pack he whispered a prayer of thanks.

After a longing glance at the grove with the pool, Sonny started up
the second hill. At the top he rested his back against a boulder, cast there
by the same thermal activity that still smouldered in the ground beneath

him. The bright blue panorama of the Cyclades reminded him of the coast near his village—the view from his father's porch, and from the cliff where his mother gardened. He gasped at the force of his loneliness and tried to drag his eyes away from the scene. *I need to get home. Mum will know the meaning of my sacred dream.*

The lady of the veil said he would have to make a choice. His instincts told him this had little to do with soldiering and everything to do with his lineage. Since he was a boy, Miriama had impressed upon him the responsibilities he had inherited, and he'd witnessed how the spiritual world assigned difficult tasks to his grandfather and mother.

'A noble woman has spoken to you because you are of rangatira stock,' he heard his mother saying.

He put his head on his arms and let his tears fall. If he was to select the path of light over the path of darkness, he hoped this did not mean he would never see Rangitakō again.

A grey-and-brown flat-headed viper emerged from behind the boulder and darted at his leg. Sonny howled as its fangs pierced the skin of his ankle. He took a stone and threw it at the reptile as it slithered away. The army had never taught them how to handle a snakebite. *They should've known we'd be going to places with snakes.*

His first inclination was to return to the shore. He hurtled down the hill, feeling his heart pumping as venom coursed through his veins. When he tripped and fell into the long grass, he vomited from the spreading pain. Panic was making things worse. On his feet again, he considered sweating out the poison in the hot pool. *Not clever. What if I pass out? ... Okay, it's the boat ... If I sicken, I'll need shelter.*

His vision had blurred by the time he stumbled along the ledge to the boat, but he managed to lift himself up and roll onto the deck. He looked at the affected limb, expecting to see the fatal signs. There was swelling where the viper's fangs had punctured the ankle and his leg had turned a horrible purple-yellow. He was as sick as a dog, but there was no telling line of red dots on his skin. He didn't have blood poisoning.

All he could do was curl up into a miserable, snake-bitten ball. *So this*

   Kayleen M. Hazlehurst

is it? Death by snake, alone on an island in the middle of a foreign sea? I'd rather have taken a bullet.

> He stands with Tama on the hills above Rangitakō,
> watching two hawks as they manoeuvre themselves
> above an upward draught. They admire the finger-like
> feathers, the slant of wings. The birds circle and turn,
> all the while scanning. Scanning the land for food.

Sonny was startled awake by cold water. He was naked in someone's outdoor bathtub. The boatman he'd met earlier, and an elderly woman with a girl, were standing around jabbering in Greek. The woman issued an order and hustled towards the cottage.

The other two continued to scoop water over his body and to rub him over with rags. After helping him out, they dried him and tied a towel around his waist. There was no sign of his clothes. Barefoot, with his bad leg buckling under him, he leaned on the boatman's shoulder as they escorted him to the house.

The woman welcomed Sonny into a room with an earthen floor. There, he was urged to lie on a cotton mattress arranged on a low pallet against the wall. On her wood stove she had an iron pot simmering, and the aromas of lavender, thyme and oregano, with stronger tangs of bark and roots, filled the room. She spooned half of the herbal liquid into a white bowl, adding some olive oil. The rest she set aside. *It must be an antidote.*

Nobody took their eyes off him. The couple, Albertos and Cosima, were kindly. The girl, perhaps a niece or a grandchild, seemed more curious. Shamefaced and clinging to his towel, Sonny looked up at the older man for guidance. The boatman's wrinkled face split into a yellow-toothed grin, and he rushed off to fetch a blanket.

Cosima issued clucking noises at the sight of Sonny's leg and spoke in soothing tones as she stroked a sea sponge loaded with the herbal oil over his swollen skin. She instructed the girl to prepare a paste of charcoal from the fire, adding to it crushed leaf. This was applied as a poultice to the snakebite and bound with a piece of cloth. The healer then poured the last of the liquid into a teacup. Sonny accepted the medicine, realising he so hungered for human compassion that he would have drunk just about anything.

After a shared meal, the girl placed two loaves of bread on the table and covered the rest in her basket with a cloth. This was her job. Uncle Albertos rowed Sirena, the bread seller, around the island to help with her deliveries. When they had pulled alongside his boat earlier in the day they found Sonny in a coma.

Later Cosima handed him some of her husband's dry clothes. She muttered as she poked his ribs and squeezed his arms, signalling to Albertos how thin he was. As she tenderly patted his face and fussed with his blanket, something inside him broke.

His last image before falling asleep was the old woman sitting beside her hearth as her fingers moved along a rope of coloured wool and beads. She was chanting prayers in a strange and ancient voice. As he listened, Sonny thought he heard the distant echo of a karakia.

 Kayleen M. Hazlehurst

<h1 style="text-align:center">~26~</h1>

<h1 style="text-align:center">Albertos and Cosima</h1>

Albertos and Cosima had hens and a vegetable garden. A barn stood at the back of the yard and, beyond that, the stalks of a recently harvested field of barley. Volcanic soil was good for growing things, and it appeared that inland Kímolos was not as dry as its coast.

Above a stone mantelpiece were the usual trappings of a religious household. A cross, a wooden image of Christ, a painting of a guardian saint. Most people who lived on Kímolos made their living by fishing or farming. And where there were Greeks, there were chapels.

The farm work here was hard. A horse-drawn plough was used to turn over the field and sowing was done by hand. After a few days in the couple's care, Sonny went out to the woodpile to split some logs. An old couple could never have too much stacked firewood. After an hour it became too much for him and he had to rest.

The following morning Sonny took an amble in the barley field, noticing some leftover grain on the stalks. He located a scythe in the barn and gleaned some of the remaining barley, bringing back bundles to be scattered in the yard. Cosima put her hands on her hips and cackled at the excitement of feathers and wings as the hens scrambled for the grain. On another day he weeded the garden.

In the evenings, Albertos played haunting melodies on a pear-shaped instrument with a stringed body and neck. Sonny learned this was an oúti from the lute family. Sometimes Cosima joined her voice in song with Albertos. Other times she told them stories—tales Sonny scarcely grasped about brave voyagers and noble warriors.

When she was in a good mood Cosima showed off her finger games with threads of wool, hurtling them into laughter when Sonny was all

thumbs. The games reminded him of those played by Māori girls in the
school playground. When his hosts needed to converse with him they used
simple sentences and gestures. With Albertos and Cosima as his patient
instructors, Sonny was learning new words and phrases every day.

After a week Sirena returned. Sonny was in the barn sharpening the
scythe in the light of the window when she came in. He saw a glint of
silver dangling from her ears. Her long black hair had been loosened to
fall around her shoulders, and she spoke to him in a caressing voice.

Such enhancement of her charms made Sonny pull away. The idea
of friendship with this girl was both thrilling and frightening. Sirena was
beautiful, but she was not his to have, and he was not hers. When she
placed her hands on his chest, Sonny felt Atarangi falling away from him.
He stared hard into her eyes, taking her wrists to turn them back.

'What is it?' she said, her eyes glistening from the rejection.

He did not have the words to explain the reason. Albertos' tactful
cough and the clomp of hooves in the yard propelled Sonny outside,
where he took the bridle to bring Heracles in for stabling. This encounter
with Sirena had left him desperate.

I mustn't let this girl delay me. I mustn't be trapped in this way.

Albertos was sitting outside the cottage indulging in an afternoon pipe
when Sonny came to join him.

'My boat ...' Sonny said, moving his hand like a boat on waves and
pulling down his lips. 'I am sad ...'

Albertos patted Sonny's arm. 'No worry. *Oi psarádes diatiroún skáfi se
spilaia ólo to cheimóna.*'

Sonny tilted his head, not fully understanding. Something about
fishermen and boats being wintered in caves.

'Is good,' the old man said, waving his arms. 'Sonny's boat is good!'

Sonny pointed to his mouth. 'I sail to Mílos. Need food. Tools.
Dressings for wounds.' He mimed the use of each item.

'Uncle Albertos go with Sonny to Mílos. Is safe. We buy lentils, beans,
dried tomatoes, figs, raisins. I have friends.'

     Kayleen M. Hazlehurst

Sonny agreed, a guide would be helpful in finding provisions.

'We men go to alehouse, eh?' Albertos slapped Sonny's back and tipped his wrist to his lips. 'Thank Sonny for his hard work.'

A cranky voice came from behind them. 'Did you tell him there are Germans on Mílos?'

Sonny recognised the words 'Germans' and 'Mílos'. He turned his head to see Cosima leaning from the window.

'Don't frighten the boy, woman. Look at him. He looks like a Greek.'

Cosima came to the door carrying a pair of scissors, a bowl of water, a cut-throat razor and some soap. She plucked at Sonny's hair with her fingers.

'He'll be a real Greek once I've finished with him.'

The sun was hot and summer days were long. Perfect weather for drying meat. Eating the food of these generous people was shaming Sonny. He would head out with his gun. Half a goat for Cosima's stew pot and the rest he would dry for trade. If wild goats weren't plentiful in these hills, he knew of an island where there was a horde of them.

———〰———

Albertos was a strong oarsman. He rowed to the southernmost point of Kímolos and crossed the short channel. The artefact collector, Julian Nicolaides, had said Mílos was the centre of Cycladic culture during the Bronze Age. There were the ruins of a city near Pollonia, the fishing village where they intended to land. Albertos was certain no attention would be drawn to a small boat resting high on the beach. For centuries, the wealth of Mílos had been extracted from the earth. The multicoloured seams in the cliffs revealed their volcanic origin. Obsidian for tool-making, later ceramics and pottery, and more recently the mining of minerals.

As Albertos rowed, he related how the Italians had arrived in the Cyclades in May, followed by the Germans. When Sonny first set out for the Greek Islands he believed he was well ahead of the Axis invasion. How little he had known. Now, he saw it moving from island to island. The Occupation was here.

Albertos was vehement that the Mílosans had stood firm. Many had raised the Greek flag outside their houses. These were forcibly torn down and replaced by flags bearing the swastika. Albertos' outrage at this indignity stirred an unease in Sonny. On the mainland he had seen what the Nazis did to resistant populations.

By late-morning the cool ocean airstreams had been sucked away. After their boat was pulled up to a safe spot, Albertos had taken Sonny to the house of a friend to discuss their business. Vasos Kafatos lived at the top of the street, partially shielded by trees, with a view over the rooftops to the beach.

It was hard to see how anything other than juniper and cypress could flourish on these islands at the height of summer. But the lunch Vasos served showed that Mílos produced many crops of grain, olives, grapes, oranges and melons.

The grapes yielded a rough red wine, a glass Vasos shared with them, and dairy cattle gave them enough cheeses for trade with neighbouring islands. At Tripiti, an old windmill worked a waterwheel for milling flour. Out of compassion, Albertos had brought Sonny to the home of a merchant who spoke four languages, including English. It was a relief for them both to have someone to do the translations.

For over an hour Sonny entertained them with stories of his life. He spoke of leaving his beloved people to sail by liner to England and then on to North Africa. At Olympus Pass he explained how the Māori infantry had faced the might of the German Army in order to delay its pillaging advance into Greece. Blinking back his tears, he related how he and his brother were separated from their battalion, and how Tama's death so affected him after that stormy night in the mountains.

Groans and laughter erupted at appropriate spots as Sonny carried them along with his tales of the kindness of shepherds and priests, of being left by a wicked fisherman on a deserted island, sharing a cave with a seal and her pup, and ending up drunk under the malign gaze of a herd of wild goats. Furthermore, a snake would have done him in, had it not been for Sirena, the lovely bread seller, and the special care of Albertos and Cosima.

     Kayleen M. Hazlehurst

At the end of his storytelling, Sonny saw beards quivering and eyes bright with tears. His sole aim, he concluded, was to be reunited with his comrades.

Albertos and Sonny got down to business. As a man of commerce, Vasos Kafatos was undoubtedly the person to know. He could kit Sonny out without them going from house to house begging for charity. They asked Vasos' advice on what food would be most nutritious, and what would keep the best in the summer heat. Sonny offered his dried goat meat in payment.

Vasos drew himself up. 'How can I take payment from a soldier who has come so far to protect us? You have given everything to Greece, Sonny Wirima. I would consider it an honour to provide all your supplies. Come, I will take you to my cellar.'

As they went towards the staircase, Sonny noticed a dusty chip of black glass on a shelf. 'Is that lava?' he asked.

'Obsidian, yes. Have a look at it, if you like.'

Sonny picked up the flint and turned it over. It had been knapped to fit into the palm of a hand, with edges that were hard and sharp.

'Keep it. I have plenty more.'

'Thanks. I'll use it as a cutting tool.'

Vasos handed Sonny a square of linen. 'Fold it away in this. I have drawn a map of Crete on it for you.'

Sonny tucked the obsidian and map into a pocket.

Within an hour, they had stowed two sacks of supplies at the back of the house, to be retrieved later. Alberto wanted to spend his modest coin on their drinks. With the old man's insistence, Vasos agreed to join them at the alehouse.

Sonny needed more information and hoped this might be forthcoming over a glass or two of beer.

A red brick building fronted the street with a billboard announcing its trade as a drinking establishment. The lower halves of the windows on either side of the door were curtained to prevent wives from staring in.

On the upper level of the tavern there were rented rooms looking out on the street, and a fire escape that zig-zagged to a deck at a reachable drop to the pavement.

Inside, two barmen wiped chequered cloths over a wooden counter and served beer in ceramic mugs. A blackboard listed a modest selection of food—beans on bread, sausages with mushrooms, chicken skewers on rice, seared red mullet, lamb cutlets with cos salad. The board was dusty and smeared. Some dishes had been crossed out. Few customers could afford to buy meals. Most came to the tavern for companionship and the ale.

They chose a table near the far wall, watching the men come and go. The patrons looked shabby—clothes draped about them, hair and beards untidy. Ordinary workers on their way home after a day's labour. Vasos in his suit was the best dressed among them.

Men sat quietly, heads bowed, as they drank and talked. It had not always been this way, the merchant said. Greeks were a cheerful and friendly people. It reminded Vasos of the years before the war when he had lived in Europe. There was a distrust then—a fearful watchfulness as Germany re-armed, while the rest of the world seemed oblivious to the growing ambitions of Adolf Hitler.

'Can you tell me more about Crete?' Sonny asked.

Vasos was slow to respond. 'I can tell you what I've heard, and what I suspect. The Navy evacuated soldiers of every nationality to Crete, all weakened from the Greek campaign. But it became obvious Hitler wanted the island for himself. German soldiers were dropped by parachute over Maleme and Chania. People described paratroopers falling from the heavens like a thousand poisonous mushrooms.'

'What happened to our soldiers?'

'Many of them have been taken prisoner. I imagine those who have escaped will be hiding in the hills. Some may have joined the Resistance.'

They all scanned the room to check nobody was listening.

Sonny dropped his voice. 'There's a Resistance?'

Vasos chuckled. 'Greeks don't lie down while we're still able to fight. Some of those fighters may be your countrymen, Sonny.'

'I'm *damn* sure they are.'

     Kayleen M. Hazlehurst

They lifted their heads at some rowdiness at the door. A group of German officers swaggered in to take the central tables, hastily vacated by the locals. One soldier was left to guard the door, looking grim. Peaked caps were dropped on tables and jackets were loosened. The officers shouted for drinks, sending waiters scurrying over with loaded trays.

The hair on the back of Sonny's neck bristled. He'd never been this close to a German without a gun in his hand. Albertos gripped Sonny's arm, warning him not to react.

'No sudden movements,' Vasos said. 'We speak only in Greek.'

The alehouse customers lifted their drinks and sipped, calmly creating a fitting atmosphere for enemy soldiers in recreation.

As Albertos and Vasos talked, Sonny pretended he understood every word, but he could not resist the force of the Māori proverb that came to mind.

Whāia te iti kahurangi ki te tūohu koe me he maunga teitei.
Seek the treasure you value most dearly.
If you bow your head, let it be to a lofty mountain.

He would not bow his head to these Nazis, but neither would he endanger his friends. The best place to hide was in full view.

When Greeks started to leave the tavern, Sonny whispered to Vasos, 'I'll go ahead. Tell Albertos I'll grab the sacks and meet him back at the boat. Give me a head start.' He winked at their astonished faces and crossed the room to join the departing men.

With his arm over the shoulder of one inebriated patron, Sonny staggered out, slurring Māori words to the tune the Greeks were singing. The scowling guard could not shoot them while his officers were in a state of merriment. One Jerry had got to his feet and was singing a rousing German song and his comrades were joining in the chorus.

Sonny followed the flow of people until the alehouse was well out of sight. Then, veering up a side street, he made his way past a group of shops where proprietors were shuttering windows and drawing curtains. People were closing for the day.

Who Disturbs the Kūkupa?　　　201

The thought of food got his saliva going, and he extracted a strip of dried meat to chew. He was looking forward to returning to Cosima's kitchen and the meal she would have prepared. If he hurried, he could be at Vasos' house in ten minutes to retrieve the provisions.

He halted outside a house where a swastika fluttered from a homemade mast. *It's one of those households forced to remove their national flag.* Part of him shared Albertos' outrage. He took out his knife and slashed the cord, seizing the Nazi flag, and stuffing it into his shirt. This was not his time to do battle, but he would not forget these good people when that time came.

~27~

The Sea of Crete

Miriama was sensing an absence of light. The marae was not a happy place. People hastened between houses and halls, wavering when friends approached, unable to look into their faces to see the new sorrows.

In the North every household mourned the loss of a son, brother, nephew or cousin, or had heard of someone else's loss.

Where are the young men
to be inspired by the feats of their ancestors?
Where are the leaders who will shape their lives
by the virtues of the great chiefs?

'Died on the battlefields,' Miriama answered aloud. 'Lost or enslaved, far from the arms of their dear ones.'

Church on Sunday would be well attended. More names would be read out, more prayers formed on lips, more memorial services planned. She would go with the rest of them to hear those names, those prayers, those plans. In these dark days she reminded her people that Light came from Nothingness. This was small comfort to offer the grieving. Later today she would make her own supplications.

Atarangi was lingering outside the gate. With so many deaths, the girl could no longer bear to enter the church grounds. Atarangi was young. She might know about the co-existence of the natural and spiritual worlds, but was yet to learn the wisdom imparted to old women. The spiritual world comes closer as you age.

'I'm riding to the mountain this afternoon,' Miriama told Atarangi. 'Will you join me?'

'If you'd like me to.'

'Āe, I think you need this, dear. Come first for lunch. Winifred will be there.'

Close to midday, Api and Hēmi came inside, beaming.

'We nipped out in the boat after church,' Hēmi told his mother, holding open a sack. 'Five snapper!'

'You did well. Prepare them for me and we'll have them for lunch.'

While the fish were taken to the garden table to be scaled and filleted, Miriama mixed up her flour-and-water batter. She had been simmering a mutton stew with dumplings for their Sunday lunch, but everyone preferred fresh fish.

Hēmi tapped on the kitchen window. He handed the fillets through on a chopping board, then went off to wash his hands.

'Let me know when the girls are coming,' she called after him.

Api came in and eyed the kettle. 'Anything I can do?'

'I'll make you a cup of tea in a minute, dear. Clean up first.'

She cut each fillet into two and dipped them into the batter. A pot of potatoes had been boiling on the stove. She drained the potatoes in the sink using her steel colander, a gift from Api to spare her from a scalding. She sat there, waiting to hear the dogs. When they barked and bounded off she knew they had sighted Winifred and Atarangi. As usual, Hēmi had forgotten to tell her. Muttering, Miriama scooped two spoons of dripping into the skillet and set the fish to frying.

Few morsels remained on the table at the end of the meal.

'A lovely lunch, Auntie,' Winifred said. 'Thank you.'

'You can thank the men for the fish. They caught them this morning.'

'We feel spoilt, don't we, Ata?'

'Very spoilt,' Ata agreed. 'Did you have to go far?'

'We stuck to the coast. Must have run into them at the turn of the tide.'

After a short silence, Winifred asked, 'What are you doing now the cows have dried off, Uncle? Are you expecting lots of babies this spring?'

 Kayleen M. Hazlehurst

'I hope so. Butter-fat prices have been going up and most of our girls are in calf. We might even increase the herd.'

'Wonderful. What are your plans, Hēmi?'

'I'll find some casual work for a couple of months if Dad can spare me. Timber milling, I was thinking, or some scrubcutting or fencing. I know a man in Whangārei with a fencing crew. He makes those southern farmers pay through the nose for our labour and we could do with the cash.'

Winifred looked at her lap. 'Let me know if you're going away. I'll miss you.'

Hēmi shot her a look. 'I'm not the one signing up.'

'Well, maybe you should be!' Winifred got to her feet.

'*Hey, hey!*' Api raised his hands. 'She's following her conscience, son. You can't fault her for that. We should be proud of our country girls offering themselves for war service.'

'Āe. That was unkind, Hēmi,' Miriama said. 'You mustn't strike out at your friend.'

Hēmi's face flushed. 'I'm sorry, Winnie, I didn't mean to hurt you.'

Atarangi's eyes filled with tears as she looked from one childhood companion to the other. 'Winnie, please don't leave. Spend the afternoon with Hēmi. Your time together is so precious.'

Miriama wondered what had just happened and why she hadn't stopped it. She turned to Winifred. 'I'm taking Atarangi into the hills. Would you like to join us?'

'No thanks, Auntie.' Winifred glanced at Hēmi. 'There's someone I'd like to keep company this afternoon, if he will have me.'

Hēmi's face glowed even more. This time Miriama saw it was from shame.

⌇

The horses trotted through the paddocks, heads high, sniffing the wind.

They progressed sturdily up the first slope and down into the next valley. The air was sharp and clear, freed from winter gales, but not yet laced with the seed-head smells of spring grasses. Miriama and Atarangi rode along the bank of a stream as it curved beneath the Brynderwyns, until they reached the lower edge of the forest where the brothers used to hunt for poaka.

This area, called the Piroa by the local iwi, bore spiritual significance. The women dismounted when they came to the foot of the highest range.

'We'll tie up here,' Miriama said, looking over the dense forest and the grey-green cascade of ponga. She unstrapped her leather saddle pack and extracted two bottles of sweetened lemon water. 'Rest now, we have plenty of time.'

Atarangi flattened an area of grass for them. 'I'm sad for those families, I truly am, but I can't face any more services for dead soldiers.'

'Maybe later.' Miriama handed her a drinking bottle. 'It's essential to revere every hero who passes, so new life can come forth.'

'I know, but all this death is so hard …'

'Mm-m-m. Which god invented that, I wonder?'

'Whoever it was, they should think of something better.'

Miriama cackled. 'But consider this, without death wouldn't there be more fighting over land?'

The girl lifted her shoulders. 'Unless people stopped fighting for its own sake.'

'*Ah*, and what would make them stop fighting?'

'If they realised our separation from each other was an illusion. Scientists are saying the universe is made up of these tiny specks called atoms? It was in the newspaper.'

'Why is this news? Our wise ones have always known this. All things have life. The rocks and trees, the rivers and mountains, the animals and birds. Our bodies may die, but our mauri lives on. We are all sacred. See how the wairua roams the heavens while we sleep. In our dreams the truth of things is revealed to us, and we solve many problems.'

'So, the Pākehā now agree with our seers?'

'They do, if they have found tiny specks called atoms. Maybe one day they will also discover that every speck is connected by pure energy.'

The girl looked at her with a desperate expression. 'E pou, how can we stop this killing?'

     Kayleen M. Hazlehurst

'We must ask the mountain. Today we will placate Tāne and beg for guidance.' Miriama patted her saddle pack. 'I have brought offerings.'

Atarangi looked longingly at the forest path. 'I am looking forward to being with Tāne and his birds.'

'Āe. The song of the korimako and the chatter of the kākāriki will lift our hearts.'

'When I was a child, I used to collect the red and green feathers of parakeets.'

'Then, as a child you were blessed.'

⸻〰⸻

The pole swung sideways and slapped him in the chest, sending Sonny hurtling across the deck. He recovered enough to grab the rope. He wasn't accustomed to the new boom. It had been installed before he took the boat out of hiding on Kímolos and set sail for the Sea of Crete.

Still he kept on, driven by a yearning to find his friends. He'd started out two hours before sunrise, passing by Mílos and leaving those occupied shores far behind him as the sky lightened. A portion of this ninety-mile journey would be done in daylight and it made him nervous. He turned his mind inward and prayed for a swift crossing.

Warriors and sailors needed to be alert to the capriciousness of the elements. His atua could be quarrelsome, but they also gave him strength. He looked over the dark blue sea that gave no hint of its depth. A wind toyed with the water, disturbing the surface but allowing him to cut a smooth path. He was heading south to south-west, though not too far west or he would end up in the Mediterranean.

Seabirds were his best compass when the atmosphere was too shrouded to pick out any features of land. By observing the fishing excursions of birds, and their return flights, Sonny was convinced Crete was dead ahead. In about seven hours he should make landfall.

The salt air, the low whistle of wind in the sail, and the majestic gannets plunging into schools of fish gave him a strange clarity. A weightlessness induced by childhood memories. Eeling in streams with his brothers. Their grandfather weaving cray pots on the beach from flax and reeds.

He could hear the steady strokes of the oars as their koro rowed them to favourite fishing spots. The boys' laughter as they pulled in the flashing, snapping beauties.

Sonny dared not think too much about those pleasant days. Instead, he angled the sail towards a sunlit spot where he saw birds working. The boat was now in full flight, yet what was the point of being at sea without doing a bit of fishing? He took out his fish trap and attached it to a long rope. A shallow pass might yield a basket of smelts or whiting. The catch could be eaten raw or dried in the sun during the hottest part of the day.

He threw his trap over the stern, holding it taut with one hand while gripping the tiller with the other. After it sank below the wake, he watched the silvery eruptions of jumping fish.

Look, Tama. I am the wind! … I am the sea!

Something hit the side of the boat. It was more of a bump than a blow.

The first thing Sonny saw when he woke was the position of the sun. It had passed its zenith and was sliding down the scorching white dome of the sky. *The heat must have got to me. How long have I drifted like this?*

He pulled himself to his feet, gripping the ledge as his knees buckled. Straight ahead was nothing but open sea. He spun around. To his left was a grey hump of land. The western coast of Crete, he guessed, unless he was hopelessly lost.

A swishing, blowing sound caught his attention. Two dolphins were trailing alongside. The closest one gave the boat another nudge. Sunstroke could be lethal. He had seen its effects on the water at home and in the heat of Egypt. Had the friendly creatures not woken him, he might have sailed right past the largest island in the Aegean.

'Hello, you two. Are you hungry?' He reached for the small fish he had no memory of trawling in and threw out a handful before the dolphins dived away.

He took a long swig of water. 'Right, I'd better get this boat turned around.'

He steered the boat back towards Crete, keeping well away from the

          Kayleen M. Hazlehurst

western cliffs. Here, the land rose straight up from the sea, but as it curved around to the north he saw hills that were dry and steep. Vasos Kafatos had convinced him that the escaping soldiers would likely be in the central region, hiding in the mountains. That would mean a lot of walking.

If he risked sailing along the northern coast, coming in at an inlet beyond Souda Bay, this should put him closer to his friends. He knew nothing about this port town, other than that Hitler had sent his troops to take it over. A tiny boat out at sea should raise no interest.

Out of the clouds came the sound and shape of an approaching aircraft. It wasn't a Spitfire or a Hurricane. It wasn't British.

'Luftwaffe!'

The fighter began to drop down.

'*Shit!*' He shinned up the mast and pulled out the Nazi flag he'd stolen when on Mílos. The plane was close enough for him to see the outline of the pilot. Sonny waved and held up the swastika, and the sod waved back. Then the plane banked away towards Crete.

A rock shouldn't have been there.

Sonny had slid around the bulbous peninsula and along the front of the bays. He thought he was still in deep water—until he ploughed into a solid mass. After the collision there was a graunching sound and the boat shuddered to a halt. *Is it a reef?*

They were pinned onto something big, and the boat was beginning to list. Water rushed through a hole in the floorboards. Sonny grabbed his pack and jumped into the water. As he swam away, he turned to watch Geórgios' boat slowly breaking up. The last thing that went under was the mast with the Nazi flag.

He was just a head bobbing along, swimming breaststroke, while he scanned the beach. The place was empty. To the left he spotted a cluster of tall reeds at the water's edge, and above that a scrubby bank.

He would be like a pūkeko. The clever swamp hen stalking through the rushes on slender red legs, hidden from hunters with guns and hawks with sharp beaks.

His pack was so waterlogged it was a wonder he hadn't drowned. Among the reeds he took breath to consider what had just happened. The obstacle that ripped open his hull must have been the twisted steel of a submerged trading vessel or barge.

He looked out at the harbour. Souda Bay was choked with the carcasses of bombed and sunken ships.

Kayleen M. Hazlehurst

part four

~28~

Alena and Makos

The place was crawling with Germans. After losing his boat, Sonny had to make his way through the bomb-cratered streets of Souda. Even slinking among the demolished buildings dressed like a Greek, he stood out. Soon he found himself at the wrong end of a gun.

He was arrested, stripped of his pack, and hauled off to a transit camp near Galatas. Almost everything he needed to survive was taken from him, but the loss he felt most was his anonymity. They took his name and gave him a POW number. It was like walking into a nest of snakes with 'bite me' written on his forehead.

Dulag Krete was a foul place. The smell of fear and vomit hit Sonny before he reached the gate. A patch of sandy ground strung with barbed wire served as a temporary cage to hold prisoners before they were shipped to the high-security stalags in Germany, Poland and Italy.

At the camp, people slept among the vermin with no shelter. There were trenches for latrines and little food and water. A group of Allies had recently been transported and the debris of discarded clothing, dented cooking tins and scraps of tenting surrounded the wretches who remained. Men hovered near the gates, waiting to see if any of the new captives were from their units.

In this heat and filth, it wasn't surprising wounds turned septic. Men suffered from exposure and malnutrition and were plagued with stomach problems. Some deaths were unavoidable, but what left Sonny seething was the casual viciousness of their captors. Not long after his arrival, he saw a guard clubbing a weakened soldier, a Kiwi, with the butt of his gun.

'English swine!' the guard snarled. 'Why are you killing Germans?

We are not at war with your country. Have you come here for sport? I should kill you too!'

'I'm just a soldier,' the Kiwi answered. 'I go where I'm told. Please stop.'

'What the hell do you think you're doing?' Sonny yelled as he charged over. This was not the way to treat a POW. A jolt of alarm shot through him when he recognised the soldier. Jock MacDonald, old Mac. The once large man was shrunken and bent.

Sonny flung himself between the assailant and his friend, grasping the gun with both hands to halt the blows. The distraction gave Mac time to crawl away, but there were shouted warnings from the other prisoners. A second guard had come up on Sonny from behind.

The two guards knocked him to the ground and started dishing out the same medicine until an officer called them off. Sonny would not forget this incident, and he would not forget those guards.

The attack left him with bruised ribs and jagged wounds across his temple and cheek. The dent in his skull was giving him headaches, but this did not outweigh how chuffed he was to see the South Island farmer again. In the evenings, they talked.

'After you took off, Mac, how did you fare?'

'A merchant ship picked us up south of Skópelos. Our boat wasn't up to much. We would've come to grief at sea if we hadn't been rescued. What about you and Ratty?'

'This might be hard to believe, but Ratty joined a monastery on Skiáthos. He wanted to help the monks look after the Allied soldiers as they came through. I agreed, a monastery was a good place for doing that. After we parted I carried on through the islands.' He laughed. 'Got nabbed by Germans near Souda, of all the stupid things.'

'Did you hear anything of the others?' Mac asked.

'Afraid not. Spiros was from Crete, wasn't he?'

'Yeah. He was busting a gut to get back here.'

'Where did your ship drop you off?'

'On the south coast. Sfakia was in a shambles after the evacuation,'

     Kayleen M. Hazlehurst

Mac said. 'We got caught up with the soldiers left behind. German troops were everywhere. They rounded us up, robbed us of our rings and watches, and marched us back to Galatas.'

Sonny looked around. 'So where is Ruby?'

'He died a couple of days ago,' Mac answered in an unsteady voice. 'His malaria came back. Got it in Egypt. Bastards wouldn't give him medicine. That's why those guards were bashing me. I'd been pestering them for quinine.'

'I'm sorry. Ruby was a good bloke. You stuck by him the whole way, Mac. You're a good mate. Did many of our men get away?'

'I saw a few take to the hills. The rest of us barely had the strength to walk back through those bloody mountains.'

Sonny lowered his tone. 'I'll join those fellas in the hills once I get out of here.'

'*Ah,* laddie.' Mac looked at him hard. 'If you say so, then I reckon you will.'

Shortly afterwards Mac's wounds became infected. Sonny stayed close by him for three nights, cradling his friend as he cried out in pain. At the third dawn, two Kiwis from the camp came to take the body away.

In captivity, minds dwelt on escape. Some dreamed of a luxury liner, like the *Athlone Castle,* bearing the soldiers home. Others imagined a graceful yacht whisking them off to a safer coast. Prisoners spoke of sparkling rivers, clean beds, and the gentle company of wives and girlfriends. Everyone longed for food. Cream cans packed with preserved mutton bird, pipi or other seafood. Fried fish and chipped potatoes, with a bottle of beer. Sonny decided a stone pillow on a rough hillside would be better than these taunting dreams.

Security at Dulag Krete was slack. There had been many attempts to break out. He held back to observe the risks, letting those men who had plans go ahead of him. The guard posts set around the perimeter made going under the wire dangerous. He would bide his time, wait for a better opportunity. At night he withdrew to a place with light where he could be alone with his whittling tools.

During his travels, Sonny had concealed bones in the lining of his coat, along with his flake of lava. His obsidian tool. The strongest candidate was the leg bone of a deer, but it was too long. After this, there was a goat's femur. It was small enough to hide, yet strong enough to sustain a good thrust. While crossing the Sea of Crete he had split the bone and pared away the shaft. Now, using regular strokes with his obsidian, he was sharpening the end of the bone to a point.

When his time came to leave, Sonny joined the line of men being loaded onto open army trucks to be taken to the Souda docks. He positioned himself as the last man on the last truck. Two armed guards—his sworn enemies, who had beaten Mac and caused his agonising death—accompanied fourteen prisoners who sat on benches with waist-high boards at their backs. The gravel road had been worn down to the dirt by military vehicles. Ahead, three more trucks were stirring up thick clouds of dust.

Some prisoners watched the guards and the others scrutinised the floorboards. Those looking down might be willing to sit out the war in captivity but the watchful ones, like Sonny, had something else in mind. The slow pace of the vehicles, and the screen of dust, provided them with their chance. Two prisoners sprang on the first guard and snatched away his gun. Before the second guard could raise his weapon, Sonny plunged his bone knife into the man's neck.

※

Beside a pair of dilapidated boots, four hooved feet stepped elegantly backwards, pushing a cart in his direction. The man leading the donkey tapped his stick on the wheel and pointed at the hay. He'd seen Sonny hiding under the shed and was offering to save him. Prisoners from the truck had scattered, and soldiers were shouting orders as they conducted a search of the streets. Shots were fired.

Sonny crawled out on his elbows and scrambled head first under the hay, with the furtive help of the cart man. The donkey circled around and took a different route. A path, Sonny prayed, that would take him far from Dulag Krete and far from the guards who wanted to get their hands on those who'd murdered two of their own.

 Kayleen M. Hazlehurst

After what seemed like a three-hour climb, the cart stopped. This was the way to the high grassland of Lefká Óri, the White Mountains. Omalos Plateau was up here somewhere. With luck, he would be closer to his friends.

'Alena! Alena!'

A woman came to the cart to sweep straw away from Sonny's face. Her eyes flooded with tears. 'Holy Mother, he's just a boy.'

Sonny tried to smile. He must have looked a sorry sight—his battered face, his trousers stuck to his leg with blood from where he'd been grazed by a bullet.

'Let's get you inside.' The man bundled Sonny into his arms.

'Look at him, Makos. How thin he is. I could carry him myself.'

Sonny was swinging his fists deliriously at an invisible enemy. 'I'll fight those Nazis. They'll never catch me!'

The man made soothing noises as he laid Sonny on a couch and covered him with a blanket, while the woman went to milk the goat tethered at the door.

'Don't think of those devils,' she said, coming back inside. 'You are safe here with us.' She slipped her hand under Sonny's head and put a cup of warm goat's milk to his lips.

Alena and Makos Ambrosia cared for Sonny with the tenderness of grandparents. Over the next weeks they had coaxed him back to health on a diet of bread dipped in olive oil, eggs and vegetables, and bean and onion stew spiced with rosemary and garlic. When meat was available, their young soldier was given the largest portion. In the walled garden behind the house, under the shade of a walnut tree, they applied themselves to teaching him the Cretan dialect. Sonny became an ardent student, making himself understood after a while.

'I am looking for my brothers from the Māori Battalion,' he told Makos.

'*Ah*, your comrades.'

Sonny learned that bands of rebels had sprung up across the island. Makos did not know of their exact locations, but occasionally armed men came down from the mountains to trade meat for information and supplies from the remote villages. Makos was a patriarch in this region. Families were known to each other, and many were related. Sonny's presence was kept hidden, but it came to his attention that other Kiwi soldiers were joining the insurgents.

'I have an idea where we might find your friends,' Makos said. 'I will ask around.'

At regular intervals Makos went off with his donkey. Sometimes he hoisted a wooden saddle over the beast's back and tied on two baskets. Other times he took his cart. When Makos had the cart, he was collecting produce from local households. When he had his baskets, he was making deliveries in the high country. One morning, Sonny asked if he could accompany him on his next trip.

Makos shook his head. 'The climb is hard,' he said. 'Wait until you're stronger.'

Sonny might have sulked, had Alena not taken pity on him.

'Come into the hills with me tomorrow,' she said. 'If you intend to live in the mountains, you must know how to find nourishment. There are plenty of wild greens to eat if you know where to find them.' She unhooked two hand-baskets from the rafters.

'I wish I had my gun,' Sonny said. 'I could get us some meat.'

'Mm-m-m. I'll talk to Makos. He will know how to get you a gun.'

'What is good for hunting around here? Goats, I suppose?'

'Yes, there are kri-kri. But also hare and grouse and sometimes a partridge.' She eyed his worn thin clothing. 'Bring your coat. It turns cold higher up and I see your boots are falling apart.'

Boots needed to go the distance. Sonny knew this from his Mount Olympus experience. At the prison camp, survivors of the walk through the White Mountains had told him it was a territory of daunting summits, deep gorges and stony ridges. A place of entrapment for too many of the war-fatigued men as they had pressed on to the coast for the evacuations.

He shrugged and looked at his cracked and worn boots—the best of

     Kayleen M. Hazlehurst

British shoe leather loaned to him by Monty. After Father Jacob's repairs on Sýros, they were still holding up.

'You should have seen the boots I threw away.'

After sunrise, Alena and Sonny were preparing to leave. They had turned over the vegetable garden, fed the hens, and forked fresh straw into the nesting boxes. Makos had departed with the setting moon, saying he had a long way to go.

They walked for a while with a slight wind at their backs. Alena lightened the miles by singing songs and pointing out features of the landscape. This was rough country with no fences, and with animals that made themselves scarce when people were around. Crete was a long island, Alena explained. One hundred and fifty miles in length, nipped in at two waists. One in the south-east on the road to Ierapetra, and the other south-west of here, on the road to Sfakia.

Sonny felt the power of this haunting white range and remembered the retreating soldiers. 'Those poor blighters were half-starved when they were forced to march back over that mountain to the prison camp.'

She gave him a sympathetic smile. 'I wish we could have helped them.'

The rich scent of the earth rose up to meet them. Oleander and alpine flowers—crocuses, blue irises and white daisies. They were here to forage, not admire the scenery, but when Alena parted the grasses to reveal artichoke stems and wild asparagus growing among the stones, his wonder at the mountains only increased.

'Cretans eat almost everything,' Alena said, laughing at his astonishment. 'Even what donkeys won't eat. See that thistle with its prickly burrs? It may look uninviting, but it has edible roots.' She stopped to pluck a white flower. 'Black nightshade. We eat the shoots, but the berries will make you sick. This is milder than its dangerous cousin, the deadly nightshade.'

He believed her when she said a hundred varieties of greens burst into life on these hills in springtime.

She listed a few. 'You can find bitter dock, borage, nettles, fennel, prickly lettuce, nasturtium, arugula, savory and lavender flowers.'

'How do you prepare these greens?'

'They're boiled or eaten raw in salads with olive oil. Horta, we call it.'

'What do you eat in the winter?'

'We grow pumpkins and root vegetables and store them in hay over summer. Potatoes, parsnips, carrots. And there is something else.' She folded back a leaf to reveal a gold-and-brown shell. 'These are a delicacy.'

Sonny drew back at the sight. 'You eat snails?'

'We rinse off the slime and boil them in salt, oil and thyme. They are delicious in a garlic or wine sauce.'

He listened without comment and she turned to regard him more closely.

'If the Germans keep stealing our food, a hard winter will be upon us, Sonny. Snails may be all that stand between us and starvation.'

'I understand what you are saying,' Sonny said, turning his gaze to the rim of a hill. 'Are those herb bushes up there?'

'Rosemary, thyme, marjoram and laurel. They all prosper in this country. We use aromatic herbs—'

'For cooking, I know. But also for healing.'

'This is true. I see you are very observant. Another important medicine is mountain tea. A herb called dittany. It grows on the wildest gorges and mountainsides. It has a pink flower with a grey-white velvety leaf. This special herb has been used to treat sickness for a thousand years. Look out for it, Sonny. One day dittany may save a life for you.'

They lingered to watch the sky change to the colour of persimmons, then walked on making good time. Where the path forked, they saw the form of a man with a donkey.

'It's my husband,' Alena said.

Makos beckoned them onto a second track behind a cluster of shrubs. In one of the donkey baskets Sonny noticed an army pack, probably discarded. He hoped it was for him. He needed to replace the knives and fishing lines he'd lost when he was captured.

Makos grabbed his wife by the arm, and she let out a yelp.

'I've been waiting for you. This way. Hurry. Hurry.'

'What's wrong, Makos?'

   Kayleen M. Hazlehurst

'There's a German detachment on the lower tracks. They've been looking for men on the run, threatening the villagers. We've come to warn people.'

'We?' Alena looked around to see they were not alone.

Two adult males and a boy of about fifteen stepped onto the path. The men were the toughest-looking Cretans Sonny had ever seen. Hawk-eyed hillmen with long moustaches, faces greyed with dust, knives tucked into their belts. *Outlaws who would cut your throat, sure as look at you.*

Sonny bowed deeply, but stayed silent.

Alena gasped. 'What should we do?'

'Go home, Alena. Remove any evidence we've been caring for a soldier. Stay out of sight.' He swung his attention to Sonny. 'It's no longer safe for you in the village. You must leave tonight.'

'But Makos,' Alena begged, 'where are *you* going?'

'We'll go down to the lower tracks to discourage them.'

Sonny noticed the fighters responded with a slight curl of lips. While the two rebels went to the edge of the path to listen, the younger one with the beginnings of a moustache and wearing a red bandana lifted his gun from his shoulder and cradled it across his arms.

'If you mean to pick them off,' Sonny said, 'I'm coming with you.'

With one sweep, Makos withdrew a fifth rifle from the gun case strapped to the donkey's body and threw it over to him. 'You'll be needing this.'

~29~

Ruhi and Whetu

Three ducks crossed the pale sky as he gazed at the curtain of mountains. Already, the peaks bore a light powdering of snow. Overnight, he'd been keeping guard, thinking over the evening's conversation.

Two battalion boys, Ruhi and Whetu, lounged on greatcoats and blankets alongside the three rebels who had taken them in. Stacked against the back wall was a cache of weapons and sitting on an upturned box was a wireless transmitter nobody knew how to operate. Around the embers of a dying fire, Sonny had been listening to their stories of the battle he had missed.

Ruhi, a rifleman from D Company, began by describing the Allied evacuation from Greece to Crete. Whetu, an excitable youngster from A Company, filled in the details.

'They sent the *Glengyle* to take us off the mainland,' Ruhi explained. 'Weird-looking ship with two derricks and landing craft instead of lifeboats. We had to climb the rope nets they'd slung over the side, swinging back and forth. We were so exhausted we didn't know if we'd make it. The decks were covered with sleeping blokes—Greeks, Cypriots, Palestinians, Yugoslavs, Tommies, Aussies and Kiwis—all weary and downhearted from the defeat.'

Ruhi's face seemed to have lost its roundness and his civilian clothes hung from his body in folds. He couldn't have been more than eight and a half stone.

'We were well out to sea by daybreak,' Ruhi said, 'under the escort of a destroyer and cruiser, when the Luftwaffe arrived.'

'Nine dive bombers,' Whetu added.

Ruhi rubbed his hand over his face. 'The navy threw up some lead and

I followed it with a prayer. If one of those Stukas went into a screaming dive—'

'We'd be toast!' the younger one chimed in again. 'Stukas carry some big bloody bombs. Big enough to demolish a ship.'

'Yeah, we'd be finished.' Ruhi resumed the story. 'Then out of the blue another plane came through the clouds. A lone Blenheim, one of ours, and it went straight for the Huns.'

Sonny glanced at Ruhi. 'Where did the Blenheim come from?'

'Don't know. Sometimes the RAF shadows the troopships. Or maybe the pilot was passing. Anyway, put the wind up them.'

Whetu gave Sonny a wide grin. 'The Luftwaffe turned tail and left. Everyone on the ship was cheering and slapping each other's backs.'

'Bet they were. So, you landed safely on Crete?'

'Āe. They ferried us to shore and put us on the road to Chania. We felt small and insignificant among those crowds of the larger units.'

'There we were, the little 28th Māori Battalion, tramping along a dusty road towards the capital.'

'Halfway there we came upon a wonderful sight. A line of lads from the Welch Regiment were handing out hot tea, cigarettes, chocolate and oranges. Boy, were they good.'

Sonny was surprised to hear this. 'The Welsh were there?'

'Yes. They seemed as astonished to see the Māori Battalion as we were to see them. We had a good chat before we left them. That night we slept under trees beside a stream, with our own canvas tank of drinking water. Later they handed out blankets.' Ruhi's voice took on a reflective tone. 'For a couple of weeks, we were on two-thirds rations. Bathing in the sea every day. Doing a few exercises, nothing too strenuous.'

'Hey, we'd started to enjoy ourselves,' said Whetu.

'Then word came down that Crete was about to be invaded.'

'And there we were thinking we were on our way to Egypt.'

Ruhi picked up the thread. 'They split us up. The main units were left to defend Souda Bay and Chania, and the rest of us were sent to the three airfields. Maleme, Heraklion and Retimo. The Māori Battalion was positioned between Maleme and the village of Platanias, to guard the beach and help defend the aerodrome. We were mixed up with the rest of the Kiwis from the 5th Infantry Brigade under Jimmy Hargest.'

Whetu gave his scalp a vigorous scratch. *Lice.* According to Alena, olive oil and onion juice did the trick. Sonny would have included garlic juice. His own mother said scrunched Eucalyptus leaves under bedding discouraged fleas. Maybe this would work with lice.

'We were pleased with our position,' Whetu commented. 'High ground, with a ridge behind. The surrounding land was covered with olive trees and grape vines in full leaf. It bugged us we didn't have enough rifles and machine guns, and most of our mortars had been left behind in Greece.'

Ruhi frowned. 'No big guns at our backs like Olympus, Sonny. The dive bombers came early. Ack-ack fire showed the areas they were hammering. We could hear the whine of planes and see the glow of burning buildings above Souda and Chania. Every day for a fortnight the Luftwaffe had been bombing us like this, so we thought it was a normal day.'

Sonny raised his eyebrows. 'Hell. That was normal?'

Whetu gave Sonny a quiet smile. 'Yeah, but not what came next …'

Ruhi drew in a sharp breath. 'We were all standing around, scanning the horizon, when we heard a drone. A dark line was moving towards us like a flock of birds. Hun troop carriers. The sky was full of them.'

'As they got closer we could see the black crosses on their sides.' Whetu widened his eyes. 'And what do ya' reckon, some of them were towing gliders! All we could do was watch as those little planes rose and fell at the end of their cables.'

Sonny turned to give their Cretan friends a rough translation and related back one of the questions. 'They want to know how many men in each glider.'

'Twenty, wouldn't you say, Ruhi?'

'More like ten or twelve.' Ruhi paused. 'After the bombing there was this eerie silence. Then these black dots fell from the planes. Long strings of parachutes. Waves and waves of them, floating down like coloured umbrellas.'

'We stood there gawping, until somebody yelled we should shoot the buggers before they hit the ground.'

     Kayleen M. Hazlehurst

Sonny was himself open-mouthed. 'Your bullets reached them?'

'We were picking them off like berries, Sonny.' Ruhi turned to study the night sky beyond the cave. 'Somehow, it didn't feel right.'

Sonny came to Ruhi's defence. 'Yeah. But who had the bright idea of flinging a whole army into the air?'

'Not our blokes,' Whetu said.

Each man returned to his own thoughts. Two went outside to check around and came back with more firewood.

Ruhi put a branch on the fire. 'More Jerries poured into Maleme the next morning. Paratroopers were firing but most were just hanging there, dead or swinging around, trying to avoid our bullets. We shot those who slammed into rocks or got tangled in their own harnesses. The ones caught in trees were the easiest targets. On the road we saw some jump up to grab their weapon boxes. We'd had our eyes on those guns for ourselves. A few landed further west and got away.'

Sonny told their Cretan friends about the weapon boxes, and they pointed with pride at their collection of German knives and guns.

'We thought we'd beaten them, Sonny. But Fritz had got hold of the north-west end of the runway. Two of our men did a recce and came back with orders. We were to help the other New Zealanders recapture the airfield. That evening B Company went off to join 22nd at Maleme and a few more of us come along. We hid in an olive grove and went at them with everything we had. Vickers and Brens. Rifles and grenades. Even the Spandaus and Schmeissers we'd pinched from dead Germans. Hearing the rattle of their own machine guns must have given them a turn.'

'I'll bet.'

'Those bloody Māori,' said Whetu, spitting out his words. 'They're using our Spandaus against us!'

They all rollicked with laugher.

Ruhi became serious again. 'All day it carried on like this, and the airfield was littered with burning planes. Smoke and dust. Gliders busted-up on the ground. More Junkers trying to land on the runway.'

Sonny contemplated the embers. 'How many of our men did we lose?'

'A fair few,' Ruhi answered, his voice wavering, as if the storytelling had become too much for him.

For a while they sat in silence, until Whetu told them about a commotion coming from behind the hill.

'Gliders were landing on the dry riverbed and our gunners from D Company had gone out to deal with them. Matiu Bailey was running through the vines like a madman, using his Bren like a tommy gun, and John Whare was annihilating the Germans nearest to him. When the two of them were brought down they were riddled with bullets.'

Sonny dragged a hand through his hair as he thought about the raw courage of these men.

Whetu got to his knees. 'Did you hear our CO, Harding Leaf, went missing? Two boys from A Company went looking, but no one could find him. We hoped he'd been taken prisoner and nothing worse.'

Ruhi interjected. 'The thing is, we were expecting an order for a second counter-attack. We waited all night but the order never came. Something had gone wrong. Around three in the morning the other Kiwis buggered off and we were the only ones left.'

'The 28th?'

'Yeah. It took some nerve to stay. They were throwing tracer bullets and trying to drive us back with mortars, showering us with dirt and sand. By the second morning, German transporters were making drop-runs of new troops and equipment.' Ruhi raised his shoulders.

'Maleme was lost?' Sonny asked.

'Dead in the water, mate. Some Ngā Puhi boys came over. "We're supposed to withdraw. We should stick together," they said, and we agreed.'

'Ka pai.'

'One of our men was badly hurt. "You fellas go without me. I don't want to hold you up," he told us. So we made him comfortable, hoping the medicos would find him. Then we broke up our guns, jumped over the stone fence and escaped through the vines.'

The men had dropped off to sleep where they lay—the Cretans comatose

    Kayleen M. Hazlehurst

and snoring, the Māori mumbling and twitching. Sonny was exhausted himself, but the nightwatch gave him time to think. He mulled over what their soldiers had suffered in this battle to save Crete, and what it meant to leave the Cretan people at the mercy of such a vicious opponent.

At sunrise, Ruhi joined Sonny with two bowls of millet and goat's milk.

'Where did you fellas go after you left Maleme?'

Ruhi chose a place to sit. 'The Anzacs, what was left of us, pulled back to the east to form new lines between Platanias River and Galatas. We'd been fighting for seven days and were dead on our feet. All we wanted was to give our blokes a chance to withdraw.'

Sonny had heard about these rearguard encounters. The prisoners at Dulag hadn't stopped talking about the desperate stands taken in the town square of Galatas, and again on a dirt road named after the 42nd Field Company of Royal Engineers. In both places the Australians and New Zealanders charged with fixed bayonets, giving the parachute troops a serious mauling.

Sonny stroked the matted hair on his chin. Shaving was now a luxury and, since a full beard was normal in these parts, he'd stopped bothering. 'So how did you get away, Ruhi?'

'They told us to head for the south coast to this fishing village called Sfakia.'

'Through the White Mountains?'

'Fifty bloody miles. More of our fellas were linking up, coming in from Maleme, Souda Bay and Chania. Stukas spraying us with bullets. Having to hide. Queues of men at dirty water holes. One army biscuit a day, with one tin of milk or sausages between five of us.'

Sonny walked to the edge of the cliff and checked the track below. 'All clear,' he said, then he came back.

Ruhi looked at him, hollow-eyed. 'The mountain plateau was a sea of stones, and Imbros Gorge ran between sheer rock walls. Burned-out trucks pushed over the banks. Kits and clothing thrown along the road. We were more tired and footsore than we ever thought possible.'

'Where were the Germans?'

'We heard guns in the distance and figured they were engaged. The Stukas had gone off somewhere else.'

'Must have thought you'd gone another way.'

'Yeah. May have been checking the south-east road.'

'What happened to our blokes?' Sonny asked.

'Over a hundred were at the rear. Half a dozen British and Canadian Commandos, along with the Māori Battalion. A and B Companies, with a few stragglers from D Company. Major Dyer led the rearguard unit with Captain Logan and the other officers. Captain Rangi Royal from B Company told us it was our job to slow down the German advance. I tell you, we were in no mood to be messed with. If those buggers had caught up with us we'd have given 'em hell.'

Sonny grinned at Ruhi.

'On the last ridge to Sfakia, Captain Royal put up his hand. He'd seen a tuatara crossing our track. "This is a sign from Tū," said the captain. "I'll take you no further on this path." He pointed straight down the cliff. "We're going that way." And down he went, with the rest of us slithering and sliding behind him.'

'I didn't know there were tuatara on Crete.'

'There aren't. If the captain saw that lizard, then it was definitely an omen. The cove below was covered in pebbles, but it had a good slope.'

'Good for pulling boats into the shallows?'

'That's right. But there was hardly anywhere to sit or stand. I'd never seen so many men crammed together, all jostling to get in line for the next navy ship.'

'What did you do?'

'We moved to the end of the beach to where we could rest and share our last food.' Ruhi shifted his weight. 'Someone handed me a hot cuppa. I swear it was the best tea I've ever tasted. After drinking half, I felt guilty and gave the tea to a wounded Welshman lying on the shingle beside us. "What's your story, young fella?" I asked. He told me that most of his Regiment were captured or wiped out at Souda Bay. All those good men who'd given us chocolate and oranges on the road to Chania. I'll never forget them.'

     Kayleen M. Hazlehurst

Sonny gave a deep nod. 'Losing all your brothers like that ...'

Ruhi went to scan the valley. 'We're running out of food. Tomorrow we'll have to go down to the villages.'

'I'll go hunting. Dry us some meat.'

'Good. The old people are saying it will be a hard winter, but I'm still glad to be here.'

'I don't understand. Why weren't you taken away with the rest of the army?'

'There wasn't room on the ships. Each battalion had to pick their stayers and goers, and by dusk we'd picked ours. A hundred and fifty men of the 28th, including six officers, stayed to fight right up to the surrender. The Suicide Company, they called the unit. We handed over what weapons we could, and our last tins of golden syrup and jam. One chap gave them a baby rabbit he'd caught that day. After our farewells, we watched the unit move off into the dark. Around midnight we heard the engines of a landing barge.'

'Did you ever see those suicide blokes again?'

'No. We never did. Though what we saw that night was terrible disappointment. Thousands of men were packed on the beach waiting to be evacuated. Not talking. Not smoking. Raising their heels in waves as they looked out for the dim shape of another destroyer. Some were standing on the water's edge, others were up to their knees in the sea   listening to the rattle of the anchor chain as the last rescue ship sailed away.'

<h1 style="text-align:center">~30~</h1>

Goat Meat, Oil and Beans

Api read all the newspapers. He hunted down every source of information and wrote so many letters to the authorities he was becoming a nuisance. The press told of the tragic happenings in Greece and Crete. The Royal Navy, in its daring evacuations of their men from these sad shores, had been a source of hope.

People had been receiving telegrams saying their boys were safe in Egypt. The Minister of Defence would inform the Wirimas this was all a terrible mistake. Sonny had been wounded but was still alive. Tama had made a courageous escape from a prison camp to join the others. Something of this nature, Api assured everyone.

News of the brothers' fate was taking so long to reach them it was making Api despair—he had failed everyone in trying to discover the truth. His wife became so concerned that she promised to return to the hills to make a special petition. Miriama vowed to call on the living wind of Tū to blow their sons home.

Atarangi looked ahead at the fringe of forest and breathed in the air. They were visiting the Piroa Ranges to make offerings and prayers on behalf of the brothers. Beside her, the old woman swayed in her saddle as they walked the horses inland. These high forested hills were sacred and needed to be approached with respect. Not only because they drew energy from the earth, and were the birthplace of rivers, but because powerful mountains were the places where the tūpuna had been turned to stone.

'Why are mountains special, Auntie?'

'Mountains are the oldest form of Papatūānuku. They were fished

 Kayleen M. Hazlehurst

up from the sea aeons ago. Evidence of this can be seen in the shells and bones of fish found in the highest peaks.'

'Scientists think some mountains were thrown up by volcanoes.'

'Fished up or thrown up, what does it matter?'

'Could not both be correct? If there are traces of shells and fish in high places, these early life forms must be our ancestors?'

Miriama halted the horses so they could speak. 'You may be right, dear. These are questions for future generations. I can only tell you what is known.'

'The ancients must have been deep thinkers to have considered such questions.'

'This is so. Mind journeys taken by our teachers and healers, or by our great-souled chiefs, were for the purpose of obtaining knowledge. Should we be astonished that our ancestors were intrigued by the same mysteries as modern people? Those who trod the path of life before us would share their wisdom, if we invite them. We are all bound by the same silken threads of time.'

The women nudged the horses forward, their eyes fixed on the exposed peak as a hawk passed over.

'So, the role of the tohunga is to maintain these connections?' Atarangi asked.

'Maintaining the connections between past and present is one skill. Enabling the atua to speak through you is quite another. The true role of the tohunga is to have a soaring mind.'

⸻ ⁓ ⸻

A zinc mist rolled down the side of the mountain, dragging with it dark strings of rain. The men had thrown more sticks on the flames and shrunk further into the cave—their shadows stretched and flickering on the walls behind them.

Sonny was sitting under an eyebrow of rock, a natural overhang that kept him dry, as he surveyed the valley. Nothing stirred in the landscape. No cry of birds. No drone of crickets. It seemed the land had been holding its breath since the invasion.

Who Disturbs the Kūkupa?   231

He rested his rifle across his knees while he considered the new dangers. Those twelve days in May must have been savage. He admired the Cretans for defending their land. From what he had heard, they'd been in the thick of the fighting. Any hapless parachutist who fell too far from his unit was likely to be killed. Ruhi had seen it himself. Mobs of Cretans had streamed down to join the Anzacs, taking up knives, shovels, pitchforks, scythes, shotguns and even old blunderbusses against the 'umbrella men'. In the neighbourhoods of Maleme and Chania, the Kiwis had to aim high so as not to hit the attacking civilians.

Sonny took out his pipe, lit his last wad of tobacco, and recalled another cave and other shepherds. It was comforting to think of his friends on Mount Olympus, Theos and Dimitri, and to smoke a pipe in their honour.

He perceived he was not alone. Someone was observing him, reading his mind. Could it be the ghosts of dead soldiers or the ancient ones of these mountains? *This is a bad situation, Tama. The Cretans fight with a fierce spirit, but who will protect them now that our armies have left?*

The Nazis were quick in exacting their revenge. On 2 June 1941, the day after the Allies surrendered, twenty-five men from Kondomari were taken to an olive grove and executed by firing squad. Their women had refused to turn their backs on their husbands and sons as they were murdered in front of them. Sonny knew his own mother would have done exactly the same.

The following day the citizens of another village, Kandanos, were massacred and their homes were razed to the ground. News of the reprisals spread within hours. It brought terror, as intended, but it also brought the swirling storms of shame and rage. Across Crete there were strong bonds of allegiance between the clansmen, ties that could not be suppressed. Guerrilla bands were becoming the backbone of the Cretan struggle. Sonny was sure civilian support would not waver for the soldiers on the run, or for his rebel friends, Deacon, Deo and Paulos.

After a morning downpour, the sky stained the clouds with crimson and orange. Paulos said he would take Whetu to acquaint him with the alpine route to the Lasithi Mountains. This mountainous spine, which led to the

     Kayleen M. Hazlehurst

guerrilla headquarters in the remote south-east, was a maze of goat trails interrupted by deep crevices and gullies.

Deacon and his son, Deo, said they wanted to replace their food stocks and Sonny and Ruhi were keen to accompany them. Kri-kri, impressively horned mountain goats, inhabited this high country and their valued meat could be traded for eggs, lentils, beans, oil and cigarettes. Sonny planned as well to search for some of Alena's wild greens.

On their way to the villages they discovered leaflets strewn over the tracks. Deacon told them this propaganda had been dropped by low-flying planes. Sonny snatched up one from a thorn bush to read.

SOLDIERS OF THE ROYAL BRITISH ARMY, NAVY, AIR FORCE! MANY OF YOU ARE STILL HIDING IN THE MOUNTAINS, VALLEYS AND VILLAGES. YOU HAVE TO PRESENT YOURSELF AT ONCE TO THE GERMAN TROOPS. EVERY OPPOSITION WILL BE COMPLETELY USELESS! EVERY ATTEMPT TO FLEE WILL BE IN VAIN! THE COMING WINTER WILL FORCE YOU TO LEAVE THE MOUNTAINS. ONLY SOLDIERS WHO PRESENT THEMSELVES AT ONCE WILL BE SURE OF AN HONOURABLE AND SOLDIERLIKE CAPTIVITY OF WAR. WHO IS MET IN CIVIL CLOTHES WILL BE TREATED AS A SPY.

THE COMMANDER OF KRETA

Sonny threw the leaflet down in disgust.

'We, too, are the enemy,' Deacon responded in his soft Cretan voice. 'Notices have been posted threatening the death penalty to anyone caught sheltering the Allies.'

'It breaks my heart, Deacon. I'm so sorry we couldn't help you.'

'You are helping us now, even though you must long to be with your own people.'

On the path further ahead, approaching a bend, they glimpsed a slight figure leaning on a stick. A boy of about twelve was tending to a herd of goats.

'There's Tobias.' Deacon picked up his pace. 'He will tell the villagers we are here and let us know if it's safe to come in. This is a guarded track.'

The young herdsman was using his animals to block the path as they grazed.

'Wait, Papa …' Deo put a hand on his father's arm.

Tobias had his back turned to them, concentrating on the lower track. He signalled them to stop.

'Hurry. This way.' Deo pointed to the upper bank.

Above them was an outcrop of limestone fronted with scrub oak and gorse.

'What is it, Sonny?' Ruhi asked.

'Dunno. Follow Deo.' He shifted the heavy weight of the carcass from his shoulders. 'Here, help me with this bloody goat.'

They needed to be vigilant. Groups of enemy soldiers had been combing the hills, trying to hunt down the 'hotbeds of banditry and rebellion'. The men scanned the grasslands below. A small settlement of shepherd huts could be seen nestled among the boulders at the base of the mountain. This was the first point of contact for the rebels of the central-western range. An updraft of air carried the laughter of women as they slapped their washing on stones by a stream. Their menfolk who'd left for the pastures at daybreak would soon return with the flocks.

Tobias' eyes were focused on a curl of dust rising above a crest. It was too slight to be a party of soldiers. When a man and his donkey emerged on the path, everyone was delighted.

Tobias beckoned them back to the path. 'It's Makos with his supplies,' he called.

The shepherds knew these mountains. How to withdraw into them, and how to reappear when welcome visitors arrived. Soon enough sprouted bread, boiled beans and knuckles of mutton would be prepared to feed everyone.

Once Makos had unloaded his supplies and conducted some business, he and Sonny sat together to enjoy a cup of mead on the porch of a stone hut.

'It's wonderful to see you again, Makos.'

 Kayleen M. Hazlehurst

'Did you find your brothers, Sonny?'

'Two of my battalion, Ruhi and Whetu, although I believe there are many more.'

'The rebels have been good to you?'

'Treating us like kings.'

Makos' moustache twitched. 'And you are happy?'

Sonny clenched his hands and stared straight ahead. 'One day I would like to go home.'

'So you will, my friend.'

'And how are your people?' Sonny asked.

Makos gave a sad nod. 'Everywhere there is hardship. German patrols trouble the households near the roads. There have been reprisals and arrests. Grain stores and animals have been confiscated.'

Sonny felt his temper rising but said nothing. After he'd simmered down he asked after the Anzacs.

'You got away from Galatas just in time, Sonny. Prisoners keep breaking out and the guards are getting wise. The Germans have been shipping them more regularly to the mainland.'

'And it's no longer safe for families to take them in?'

'Our people have been hiding your men in the gullies, bringing them food and medicine. If they reach us in the higher villages Alena and I do what we can to find them shelter.'

'I truly miss you both. Please tell Alena I am harvesting the hills as she taught me.'

Makos made an approving sound in his throat. 'She will be pleased to hear this. We often speak of you. Will you and your comrades be coming our way?'

'Is there something we can do for you?' Even in the best of times, life was difficult unless people had peasant relatives.

'Bring us more meat, Sonny. There's a terrible need. And we would always relish a few snails.'

Sonny laughed. 'Snails! How could I forget? I'll gather as many as I can for you.' Sonny had heard people speaking about the 'Miracle of the Snails'. The mysterious abundance of these creatures since the

Occupation, a secret source of food, had convinced the women that God was intervening to save the Cretan people.

The merchant broke away to discuss some needed items with an elder. Makos had many clients, having lived his life as a courier on a trade route that spanned generations. Foreign invaders found the mountainous regions hard to manage and left them mostly to the wild men who inhabited them.

Sonny sought out Deacon and Ruhi, wanting to discuss some ideas. Winter might be the perfect time for the rebels to improve their lines of communication, and to restock their food and weapons. Deacon agreed. The increased movement of people and provisions could alleviate scarcities.

Makos came back to resume their conversation. 'What are your plans, my son?'

'We have been talking among ourselves, Uncle.' This seemed the proper term of address in such a fond relationship. 'If you bring our men up to your village, we will take them away with us. The mountains are a safer place for hiding. They can work as goat herders and hunters, or they can help with the spring crops. Those who want to fight can join the rebels. We will take care of them.'

The merchant pumped Sonny's hand. 'God bless you and your friends for your service in our struggle. Germans are big men behind their machine guns, but with Christ and the Virgin's help we will rout them.'

'May our warriors choose the path of light over the path of darkness,' he replied, using his mother's words.

Makos returned his gaze, as if wanting to fathom such a fine sentiment.

Sonny beamed and kicked the carcass at his feet. 'This is a good-sized beast. If you will take this billy goat off my hands, I'll have some of your oil and beans.'

~31~

Preveli

Sonny expected to reach Preveli Monastery by morning. The south-west coast interested him, and he had slept for a few hours at Sfakia after talking with some fishermen. A generous donation of a gaff and some fishing tackle was followed by promises of dried fish for the needy villagers, to be collected on his return journey. Sfakia, with its white houses stacked against each other, dated back thousands of years. Its residents once worshipped a snake goddess, information he tucked away to share later with his mother.

He trained his field glasses on the dark sea as he neared Preveli. Something was moving on the water. As far as he knew, there was nothing out there but whales and green turtles. High winds had made boating hazardous, yet a tiny craft was emerging from the ocean like a sea nymph and making progress towards land.

He looked again. In the pallid moonlight, a lone man was working his oars on a swell. Behind him was a long silhouette. *Is it …? No, it can't be … A submarine!*

'What have we here, Tama?' It wasn't a question to his dead brother, more an observation, as the slick black form gracefully turned and sank beneath the waves.

Sonny waited, partially hidden by a bank, as the rower pulled in his oars and stepped onto the pebbled beach. In Egypt, the sappers had shown the boys collapsible canvas boats for crossing rivers, but nothing resembling this seafaring rubber dinghy. After the boat was stowed high on the beach, a sturdy figure in a dark suit and white roll-neck jersey, with hobnailed boots, picked up his duffel bag and strode towards him. Sonny raised his arm in a greeting. With his beard and rifle, and a bandolier slung across his chest, he looked every inch the image of a mountain man.

'The name is Poole,' the man said in flawless Greek. 'Royal Navy. Do you speak English?'

'Sonny Wirima. Māori Battalion, New Zealand Infantry. I speak English and Greek.'

'Just the fellow,' Poole said. 'I have come here to help.'

How a single naval officer could make a difference in the Cretan struggle was unclear, but it appeared Lieutenant Commander Francis 'Skipper' Poole really *had* come for this reason. Not wanting to delay, Sonny invited the commander to accompany him to Preveli Monastery. The monks would know what to do with him.

In the refectory of the Holy Monastery of St John of Preveli an evening meal of boiled potatoes, salted fish and white beans simmered with herbs was placed before them. Sonny thanked the monk who was pouring him a mug of red wine, and the man solemnly bowed his head. Seventy monks lived at this fourteenth-century monastery, some being absent on pastoral duties.

Three visitors were receiving the absorbed interest of the ten monks at their table. A partisan leader, Michael Alexandros, had joined Poole and Sonny for the meal. This black-eyed rebel with an earring reminded Sonny of the Romanian gypsies he'd seen in Britain. All kinds of men had been washed up here since the war. With a surname like Alexandros, he was probably Cretan or Greek.

Sonny inclined his head towards the crowing rooster in the back garden. 'I see you produce your own crops. These potatoes are full of flavour. What is your region like for growing?'

The monks, circumspect in their modest robes, answered in sequence without introducing themselves.

'The climate is sunny and dry most the year …'

'With some rain and bluster in between …'

'You will find this a warm coast …'

'We have excellent soil. Our gardens and orchards do well …'

'Of course, we don't cultivate everything ourselves …'

'No, no. Not at all …'

     Kayleen M. Hazlehurst

'We get olives from Ierapetra, wine from Malevisi, cherries from Amari ...'

'We bring in oranges, plums and nuts. Something from every fertile valley north of the mountains.'

Sonny widened his eyes. 'Such abundance.'

Abbot Agathangelos Lagouvardos, sitting at the head of the table, stroked his beard. 'Haven't you heard? God Himself was a Sfakiot.' He laughed. 'This is more belief than myth in these parts. Crete has always looked after herself.'

'Until now,' muttered the last monk.

Michael Alexandros was listening to the prattle in brooding silence. As horticultural topics dwindled, conversations returned to the war and voices took on an urgent tone. The monks related the pitiful state of the stranded soldiers, and the horrifying reprisals being taken against the Cretans. Both the monastery and the local leaders had been able to arrange shelter for the foreign defenders. Every remote village concealed from five to twenty 'English'. Hundreds more were believed to be hiding in the nearby hills. The rebels had the paths under surveillance, and the fugitives were hurriedly moved when German patrols were seen.

For the benefit of everyone at the table, Commander Poole described the current state of hostilities in Europe and North Africa. Tobruk had been under siege since April. While they hung on his every word, the monks were reluctant to ask the Englishman his purpose here.

After dinner, the residents went off to their devotions, and the commander was ushered into the library to discuss his business with Abbot Agathangelos and Michael Alexandros. Sonny was not invited, so he sought out a large chair beside an impressive stone fireplace. *What role might a naval man, a monastery and a few rebels have in this? I suppose I'll eventually be told.*

One of the monks came over and introduced himself as Father Ioannis. He was middle-aged with a round face. 'I'm glad you liked our potatoes, though humility prevents me from claiming they are mine.'

'You are the gardener?'

'I am one of them. I confess, the gardens are my favourite place.'

'Also, for my mother. Mum took more comfort from talking with her birds and trees than she did from talking with people.'

'Birds and trees are very good company. You are, perhaps, your mother's son?'

'I've never thought of myself this way. My mother is a spiritual leader in my community. She inherited her gifts from my grandfather. The two of them gave me much to think about when I was growing up.'

'An enquiring mind, this is a fine attribute in a man and a soldier. All Greeks know this. But you are tired. I can see you have travelled many miles. Let me fetch you a bowl of hot water with sea salts to soak your feet.'

Father Ioannis placed a steaming bowl of water beside the chair and started to untie Sonny's bootlaces.

'You don't have to do that,' Sonny mumbled.

'*Ah,* but I do.'

The monk cupped his palms under Sonny's soles to draw his painful, grime-encrusted feet from his boots. Each foot was gently lowered into the bowl where the water soothed the flesh with its heat, and stung cuts and blisters with its astringent salts and herbs.

'Now you will do well,' said the monk.

Tension drained away as Sonny drifted to sleep. When he woke, his attendant had finished patting him dry with the towel spread over the knees of his cassock. The monk took from his pocket a bottle with a glass stopper. From this, he poured some golden oil into his hands and proceeded to anoint each foot.

Oatmeal and barley porridge, soaked overnight in a copper bowl, provided a nourishing breakfast, along with slabs of black bread. The monks entertained each other with stories of their day. This was a pleasant change from the troubles murmured over hearths in the north. Sonny requested an audience with the abbot. He wanted to ask the senior monk whether there were any messages for him to carry back.

'I am glad you've come to see me,' said the imposing man. 'Have you spoken with Skipper Poole and Michael Alexandros?'

Kayleen M. Hazlehurst

'Not since last night. Are they still here?'

'I'm sorry, they left at daybreak. Michael said to tell you he was taking Poole throughout the country to meet the partisans.'

'Why take the risk?' Sonny asked, alarmed. 'Why show one Englishman the hideouts of all our fighters? What if he's captured?'

'Because this Englishman is with British Military Intelligence. A Middle East Headquarters has been set up in Cairo, and they will be sending us help and more agents.'

Sonny felt blood drain from his face. 'Do I need to know this? Secret agents sound like the sort of people Nazis would love to torture and kill.'

'We are all in this together, my son. It will mean more resources for us. The English will be making aerial drops to our fighters in the mountains. Weapons, equipment, food, supplies …'

On hearing this, Sonny backed down. The abbot was a good man who would do anything to help the Cretans. 'How will they find us?' he asked.

Abbot Agathangelos walked to the windows facing the sea. 'Arrangements will be made by wireless transmissions with Cairo.'

Sonny remembered the radio in their cave. What they needed was someone who knew how to operate it.

The abbot continued. 'Our job is to find ways of getting the lost soldiers off this island. Commander Poole is here to organise the evacuations. Sonny, we want you to carry this message to your brothers in the White Mountains. Tell them to be ready. They will be contacted.'

'Only the White Mountains?'

'And east to the Kedros and Psiloritis Ranges. Michael will handle Dikti and the Lasithi Plateau. Do you have guides?'

'Yes.'

'This is a herculean task but I'm sure others will help you.'

Sonny stood to go. 'Then I suppose I'd better head off.'

'Stay another night, Sonny. I'm conducting High Mass this morning, but I'll explain more to you later. In the meantime, Father Ioannis has much he wants to discuss with you. He is a student of antiquity, and your traditional background inspires him. We are an ascetic order here, but I see no harm in it. Perhaps you can help Father Ioannis in the gardens today.'

A lifetime ago, Sonny had set his mind on being a farmer like his father. War changed all that. Learning about himself from residents of a nation thousands of miles from his homeland made him feel vulnerable.

'Ancient things also interest me, but there is a more urgent purpose in my visit.'

'What is it?'

'There are villagers in the north close to starving and our band has been searching for new sources of food. I'll stay one more night if the monastery will supply me with your list of growers. Any orchards or garden plots that have survived the war may be worth locating.'

'We bless you and your brothers in this endeavour. Helping us endure is vital to our people. Yes, we will give you our contacts, and tomorrow we'll saddle up our best donkey so you can carry away a share of our food.'

Father Ioannis reached into his vestment to take out a paring knife. They were sitting in the shade of an apple tree. Two baskets rested near them on the grass, one of freshly dug potatoes and the other of gathered apples. At the monk's feet, a carafe of water was wedged between two ceramic cups, and over his knee he had draped a white napkin. The monk lifted a red and green apple and peeled its dappled skin with his knife. Sonny was looking forward to sampling this fruit. It had been months since he'd seen apples.

While labouring that morning, Father Ioannis had asked many questions about 'Classical Māori Society', as he called it. How was tribal life ordered? Were leaders appointed by birth or were they elected? Did beliefs continue alongside Christianity after the Europeans arrived?

Sonny did his best to answer. He observed how the monk lit up when he discovered Māori parallels with ancient Greece. He seemed to think Sonny was a spokesman for those times.

'Tell me about the specialists among you. What were their roles and skills?'

'The most powerful were those gifted in sacred knowledge and the healing arts. Our tohunga summoned the gods and performed all the

     Kayleen M. Hazlehurst

ceremonies necessary in life and death. They were our priests and our guardians.'

'Were there other experts?'

'On the land we had master carvers and builders of canoes. There were also those who predicted the weather and advised when to plant and when to harvest.'

'And on the sea?'

'Some studied the ways of birds and fish by watching their migrations. These people advised birders where to place their traps and fishermen where to cast their nets.'

Father Ioannis shifted forward, his eyes bright with curiosity. 'Your sea voyagers must have been exceptionally skilled.'

'Our ocean navigators read the sky maps. They took their bearings from the sun, moon and stars. They looked for signs in the clouds, interpreted the shapes of waves, and observed the sea currents to help them find land.'

'Astonishing, and you had no written script?'

'Not in traditional times. Knowledge was passed orally from teacher to pupil.'

'Your people must have had superb memories.'

'Our teachers did and our chiefs were great orators.'

'Like the Athenians! Are you sure you didn't originate from Greece?'

Sonny smiled. 'I think the origin of these ideas was local. Many still exist in our communities.'

'As they do in ours.'

'There were always those who specialised in weaponry. I am told your Spartans were skilful in hand-to-hand combat.'

'*Ah*, yes. Our Spartans. What about you, Sonny? Do you consider yourself part of a warrior class?'

'I am just a volunteer soldier, that is all.'

'A benevolent soldier doing the will of the gods in a savage war?'

Sonny did not reply.

'You may find some kinship in Athena, our goddess of war and wisdom,' Father Ioannis continued. 'She was a fierce deity and the favourite daughter of Zeus. Athena urged the study of war strategies, but she was also our goddess of civilisation. She designed tools for artisans and craftsmen, she introduced the plough and weaving loom. She even invented the first chariot and ship.'

Sonny paused to appreciate such wisdom. 'Certainly, a goddess to have on your side when you're fighting on Greek soil.'

'Indeed, she is. And here's what is significant. Athena did not actively seek to do battle, yet when defence was necessary she inspired men to fight with honour. All Greek heroes have sought her advice.'

'Tell me, Father. Are there omens or events in nature that signal Athena's presence?'

'Her bird is the small brown owl and her tree is the olive. When the goddess is present arts and crafts flourish in society, but when she is not there is tyranny and oppression.'

Sonny lowered his head. This he understood. This he had seen.

Through the monastery windows he heard waves breaking on the pebbled beach. From his narrow bed, Sonny thought about his trip home the next day in the company of a donkey named Caesar. Donkeys were cantankerous beasts. He had never liked them. *Give me a horse any day. I'll take the animal straight to Makos and Alena. They know how to care for donkeys.*

This led him to think about other journeys he needed to plan. Deacon and Paulos were familiar with the eastern routes. The mountain rebels would help him spread the message that British Military Intelligence was ready to back the Cretan Resistance. As he drifted away, hazy images of monks and donkeys, of goddesses and owls, flitted through his dreams.

> He is on Mount Olympus. He recognises the
> Mavroneri. The rarefied atmosphere of the peaks.
> There are shepherds wanting to cross a river with their
> flocks before the sappers blow up the bridge. Kiwi
> soldiers are trying to help them. It seems urgent that
> they should. Why? Is the battering wave of the enemy
> almost upon them?

     Kayleen M. Hazlehurst

His first dream fades and another begins.

Now he stumbles along a shrouded path, unable to find his companions. His steps falter as white clouds wrap around him. He cries out in his blindness. It has been so long since he has seen his family. And here, a new season is upon him.

Where is he going? When will he return?

He hears the tinkling of goat bells and sees ahead a dark figure at a junction on the path. It is a man in a black cassock carrying a lamp. The monk beckons him forward and points to a higher track. 'Come, my son. This is the path to take. The shepherds will guide you.'

He turns to thank the wayfarer but the monk and his light have vanished.

~32~

Clandestine Landings

Winter came early to the mountains. At the cave opening they had built a stone barricade and padded it with brushwood. This makeshift barrier kept out the baneful winds blowing in from the north-west but did nothing to stop icicles forming on the ceiling. Clouds blotted out the sun. Around a spluttering fire they shivered in their greatcoats, wondering aloud how long they could stay in their lair or whether it might be all right for them to winter lower down. Many men had been forced from the mountains—the sick and the hungry, and those who had surrendered.

Sonny's sleep was restive. Thirty or forty minutes at a time before guilt intruded. Food on the land was hard to come by. Foxes, martens, hares and ground birds had withdrawn into their dens and burrows. He was loath to ask for anything from the shepherds who had to live on their own meagre stores. For the cave dwellers, only the hardy kri-kri could be relied upon.

Domestic livestock were becoming less evident. Some households hid their pigs and hens, while others hung their canisters of flour and dried beans on ropes over precipices. In the moonlight it was not unusual to see a hundred villagers scouring the hills, oil lamps in hands, searching for snails under every leaf and twig.

Many husbands and sons had not yet returned and everyone was anxious for word from the front. They begged for stories about their brave fighters and asked when the British were coming back with their great warships and planes.

News filtered through from BBC broadcasts and spread from person to person. Thousands of souls throughout Greece and the Aegean Islands were dying from starvation. For hearts as tender as those of Cretan women, the idea of abandoned children perishing in the streets of Athens was

Kayleen M. Hazlehurst

beyond their comprehension. Sonny's defence against their tears was to work harder and longer hours. He and his companions were good at feeding people.

Deacon's cave organised foraging parties. They hunted for game and cajoled fishermen to throw out extra nets. They stole back domestic animals from the plundering troops when this could be done on the sly. With more Germans retreating to the eastern coast for the winter, the villagers were now able to obtain meat and fish in exchange for cheese and eggs, re-soled boots, leather belts and goat-hair vests.

No matter how far Sonny travelled, he could always come back to his cave. Hidden above an embankment, it had no access except by an arduous climb. In the occupied towns and villages below, there was only tragedy and despair. For every five Cretans there was one Axis soldier backed by an arsenal of weapons.

Sonny was at peace in the mountains. He was never alone in the foothills of the central White Mountains or the Ida Ranges. The sighing winds, the clacking branches of oak and chestnut and the small forests of cypress and pine were his constant companions. Between the cooler heights of the alpine pastures, and the lower grasslands visited by the goat herders, he was completely at home. Even after the cold had silenced the birdsong.

Above the timberline, he appreciated the stark contours of the limestone slopes and ridges. The scat of wildlife on the paths and frozen waterways, animal footprints in the snow, and the constant presence of the dawn maiden—the mist that appeared without fail. His respect for mules and donkeys had grown in recent months. The Cretans had shown him how these animals were sure-footed enough to take on the upper tracks, and he was looking forward to their help in the spring.

True to his word, Commander Poole made his headquarters at Preveli and began his work with the partisans to rescue stranded Allies. On a moonless night, 28 July 1941, the second day after his arrival, Poole's submarine returned. HMS *Thrasher* came inshore at Limni, a secluded beach below the lower part of the monastery, to evacuate an assembly of survivors.

Sonny had slept through the whole thing. He did not hear about this flight to freedom until long after he'd left with the donkey. Nevertheless, he now understood why he hadn't been told of the operation and why Skipper Poole and Michael Alexandros had left in such haste.

Three weeks later, in August, another submarine was about to surface off Preveli. Tobias, the young shepherd boy, arrived in a sweat at the mouth of Deacon's cave with a message. They must bring the lost soldiers to Preveli for evacuation the following evening. The battalion boys knew where some Anzacs and British soldiers were hiding. Deacon and Deo said they could locate a few Cypriots and mainland Greeks.

They set out with their rifles, and knobs of bread and cheese wrapped in scraps of cloth. Along the way, they ran into other guides with parties, joining up with them as they traipsed from village to village. Within eighteen hours, Sonny and fifteen well-armed men led a motley assortment of fugitives to the rendezvous point, where a crowd from Preveli had also gathered. Among them walked the monks serving water and oranges.

From the cliff overlooking the bay of Limni, someone with a lamp was sending coded signals out to sea. HMS *Torbay* surfaced a hundred yards from the shore. Moving forward, the submarine came to a halt about fifty yards from the beach. Two commandos in a folboat, a folding canoe, could be seen battling gusty winds to paddle ashore, uncoiling a thick rope as they came. This lifeline was then tied to a large stone and tugged tight.

'Take off your clothes and boots, lads. Leave your gear on the beach.'

A procession of near-naked men waded into the water, using the rope to haul themselves through the waves towards the metal railings on the *Torbay*. Most did this well and without complaint, but the non-swimmers were struggling to keep their heads above water. Sonny stepped forward but felt a hand on his arm.

'It's all right,' Deacon said. 'They're helping them.'

Looking down the line again he saw the commandos, and others familiar with the sea, assisting those who weren't.

Lots had been drawn, nobody knew the exact number the submarine would take, but in the early hours the captain sent word he would take

     Kayleen M. Hazlehurst

everyone. Close to eighty evacuees, somebody mentioned. Once the last man was packed in, the submarine slid noiselessly from the bay.

In Sonny's heart there was a hollow feeling. On shore he had seen the emotional farewells between the departing men and their Cretan friends. Whetu had wanted to leave, but Ruhi was anxious they remain at the side of the Cretans. In the end, it was Skipper Poole who resolved the argument. 'Unless you plan to marry a Cretan girl, Ruhi, you would serve us best by rejoining the Māori Battalion in Egypt.' So Ruhi and Whetu left with the rest of them, leaving Sonny to wonder whether he would ever see them again.

Nobody asked Sonny to go. He rested his rifle on his shoulder and stepped back among the rebels who were keeping guard over the rescue and the stash of weapons they'd acquired from the leavers.

—◦—

Submarine incursions could not be kept secret for long from the bad Cretans. Five days later the Germans sent parties of soldiers to Preveli. The farm was stripped of crops and animals. Barrels of olive oil were knocked over. Everything in the lower building was broken or stolen, and the empty monastery was put under surveillance. A German post was sited over Limni Harbour, making this stretch of coastline no longer viable for clandestine landings.

Forewarned by their own spies, the abbot and his monks had gone into hiding. Defiant in the face of arrests and execution, many monks took up arms and joined the guerrillas. Sonny could relate to this impulse. *A place that was once sacred to them had been desecrated. Didn't the warrior monks fight to throw off Ottoman rule eighty years ago?*

Early in October, Sonny and his friends were trudging inland from the central south coast, having seen off a party of six Australians, five British, three Greeks and one New Zealander on a naval launch bound for Egypt. The two travellers on the path ahead looked oddly out of place. One had an unusual gait, and both were fair-haired with ruddy complexions. The stout man was clean-shaven and wore glasses. The taller one had the first signs of a beard. Deo and Sonny stood back while Deacon spoke with the Englishmen.

The man who introduced himself as 'Yanni', and his friend and radio operator, 'Siphi', both answered in Greek. The secret agents had crossed over from Alexandria by submarine the previous morning, making landfall on a beach near Tsoutsouros. Bewildered by the crowds who'd come to greet them, they were delayed a day by the feast held in their honour. Now they were heading for a large house situated above the shepherd village of Asi Gonia on the eastern end of the White Mountains.

'It is the home of Colonel Papadakis,' Yanni said. 'A retired officer from the Greek Army.'

'The colonel is well known in these parts,' Deacon replied.

Siphi pointed at Yanni. 'Papadakis helped our captain after he escaped from prison camp.'

'Andreas Papadakis has opened his home to many escaping prisoners.'

Sonny intended to avoid Papadakis. The colonel was a proud man, with many powerful friends. He suspected the Germans knew this as well and would one day pay Papadakis and his family a visit.

'Why have you returned?' Deacon asked Yanni.

'Cairo asked us to meet with the influential people of Crete to see what can be done. We heard Papadakis was uniting the leaders under a national alliance.'

'Ah, yes. The Higher Committee of Cretan Freedom.' Deacon sighed wearily. 'Did you hear he had appointed himself as its leader?'

'This organisation is not widely recognised?'

Deacon raised his shoulders. 'It is recognised by Papadakis' closest circle, which barely extends beyond Chania. Leaders in the remote territories have deep roots with hundreds of supporters. Their lands and livestock are jealously guarded. There are constant quarrels. You'll never persuade those clan chieftains to work together.'

Yanni looked serious. 'I agree, it won't be easy to get them to sink their differences.'

'So, the British want to get behind our Resistance?' Deacon asked pointedly.

     Kayleen M. Hazlehurst

'Yes. Our first mission is to establish an intelligence network. Accurate information will tell us how to give you our best support.'

'Now, this *is* possible.' Deacon's voice took on a deeper resonance, as if someone had finally spoken sense. 'Have you heard of the Cretan telegraph?'

As Sonny walked the criss-crossed mountain trails, memorising the routes in the same way as the locals did, he saw that every settlement and every cheese hut had its own connections. Families linked by trade and marriage produced webs of clansmen who could navigate the pathways by day and by night. News travelled at astonishing speed along these lines—as it would have in Ngā Puhi country. *Invisible spiders' webs cast over the fields.*

Since the invasion the Germans watched the Cretans.

And the Cretans … Oh, yes. The Cretans watched the Germans.

33

A Pilgrimage to Lasithi

1942

Deacon wanted to visit the guerrilla headquarters in the Lasithi Mountains. He planned a spring pilgrimage and was only waiting for the snow to melt on the upper track, so it no longer filled their boots.

They would pass by the northern fringe of the Messara Plain to buy milled wheat and corn, as much as Sonny's gold-and-brown donkey could carry. Caesar would be borrowed back from Makos for this task. The animal had remained with Sonny's friends for fear he would be seized if he was returned to Preveli.

The bulk of the flour they transported would be presented as a gift to the leader, the rest mixed with stream water to form a dough for cooking on a skillet. Sonny remembered his mother making flatbread like this.

—◦◦◦—

How quiet it was up here. They had been walking east through the central high country of the Rethymno region, skirting the snow-clad peaks of Psiloritis. At dusk their path began to curve downwards. Deacon led the way, followed by Deo and Sonny with the laden donkey. Cold and hunger were driving them to find shelter.

They paused to assess the dangers a short distance from a settlement tucked between two hills. The light of a lamp swayed back and forth as it progressed towards an outlying hut. Confident all was well, they walked on until the lamplight stopped and quivered. Then the figure of a woman came running towards them.

'Antos! Oh, Antos, I knew you would come!'

'Alas, it is us,' Deacon called out in his milky voice.

They rushed forward before disappointment overwhelmed the poor woman, but she had already dropped to her knees and begun to weep.

'*Ah*, my dear,' Deacon said, as he advanced. 'You have been waiting for someone?'

'I thought … I thought it was my son coming home. He left months ago …'

'With the 5th Cretan Division?'

'They sent him to Albania when Greece was invaded. I've heard nothing …'

Deacon placed a gentle hand under her arm. 'Let's get you to your feet. Soon you will hear.'

'*Avrio. Meth avrio*,' confirmed Deo. 'Tomorrow, or the day after tomorrow.'

Sonny kept his doubts to himself, remembering the pathetic sight of the defeated soldiers coming back from the Albanian front. Any soldier could be taken prisoner. Any soldier could be trapped behind enemy lines. He bent to retrieve the fallen lantern, looking into the mother's anxious face as he handed it back to her. 'There are sons everywhere trying to make their way home,' he told her. 'I have seen them myself. I am sure you will see your Antos again.'

The woman wiped her tears. 'You are honourable men,' she said. 'But where are my manners? My name is Kassia. I see you have travelled far. Come, come. You need your rest.'

Her dwelling was the size of a shepherd's hut. Thick black beams supported the shingled roof, and a stable housing chickens and goats shared the western wall.

Kassia lit a second lamp as they entered a cosy room furnished with a lounge chair, a rough-hewn table, four kitchen chairs and a colourful woven mat. An open fireplace had been built into the alcove of a solid stone chimney. Displayed above the mantelpiece and on the walls were the images and totems Sonny had seen in other Orthodox homes.

In this simple place, Kassia lavished her attention upon her three guests. Supper was half a mug of goat's milk, two boiled eggs with bread, and a sweet milk pudding eaten to a chorus of appreciation. All were given blankets for the night. Deacon took the large chair, Deo settled beside the hearth, and Sonny made himself a bed of straw in the stable. There were protests from Deacon and Deo at his choice, but Sonny said outbuildings provided the quickest escape in a raid. Jibes were followed by queries as to whether he might return to rescue his friends.

In the company of sleeping animals, Sonny reflected on the wasted lives and sea of grief that engulfed ordinary people in wartime.

Caesar didn't complain as they reloaded his saddle, having enjoyed a warm night in the stable. After breakfast, Kassia muttered a prayer and made the sign of the cross. As Sonny filled her containers from their flour sacks, he saw how empty her shelves were. The widow had given them everything. *These souls who show such generosity to strangers, are they the last of their kind?*

At her doorstep, she kissed them goodbye and watched as they trod down the track. 'Go towards the good,' she cried after them. 'May God and the Blessed Virgin guide you.'

—∞—

Darkness was settling when they arrived at a spot below the highest ridge of the Lasithi Mountains. From here it was a two-hour climb to the guerrilla encampment.

'We'll sleep in that sheepfold and make the ascent at sunrise,' Deacon said. Nobody argued.

Sonny listened as Deacon talked over a fire about the legendary partisan leader, Manolis Bandouvas. People in the eastern highlands spoke of a long history of feuds over wife stealing and property ownership. Every family had colourful stories about cattle and sheep being taken. The wise knew the origins of these quarrels, and where they still lingered. The character of Bandouvas may have been shaped by sheep rustling, but he was now a notable patriarch and owner of vast flocks.

Bandouvas had become a popular figure during the war. The patriotism of this fierce leader was beyond question. 'The struggle needs blood' was his famous motto, and many were responding to his summons.

'Do not underestimate the influence of this illiterate shepherd,' Deacon warned. 'Some may think his views extreme, but he never fails to stir the passions of our fighting men.'

Sonny knew how a powerful orator could instil courage in the heart. 'What is the strength of this camp?'

Deo pointed to the ridge. 'There are one hundred and fifty armed men up there, with extra men in the sentinel camps below us.'

'Impressive,' Sonny said. 'But is it enough to defeat our enemies, or only enough to provoke the colossal shedding of Cretan blood?'

Deacon spoke again. 'Bandouvas has many loyal followers. He claims he can bring together two thousand fighters, and the British have promised to supply us with more guns.'

'You mean those agents we spoke to?'

'Yanni and Poole.'

'They also warned we are staring down a force of forty thousand Germans and thirty thousand Italians. This doesn't sound like good odds to me.'

'They'll be better odds once the Allies return. With your warships in the harbour and our fighters at their backs, those Nazis will be in trouble. We are night fighters and know this island better than anyone. We will outwit them.'

Sonny smiled at Deacon. 'War strategies, eh? Isn't that what your goddess advised?'

'Athena!' Deacon hooted and slapped his knee. 'Yes, Athena did advise us to plan our battles. Though I never expected a Kiwi soldier to remind me of this. You are thinking like a Cretan, Sonny. Perhaps you've been here too long.'

In the night Sonny was roused by the call of an owl.

The sheepfold smelled of dung and straw, and he had chosen to sleep outside. The humped body of the sleeping donkey beside him gave off more heat and wind than any man could have wished for.

He leaned back against the wall. Further down the slope, two dots of light glowed in the dark. The fires of sentinel camps. He'd seen few trees suitable for nesting this high up the mountain. *Why did I hear an owl? Is someone about to die? Was I dreaming?*

How much he missed home—the cry of seabirds, the sunlight playing over the fields. Weeks had turned into months. Months had turned into years. Deacon was right, he had been here too long.

He woke when a hand touched his shoulder.

'How was your night?' Deo asked.

Sonny patted the rump of the donkey. Caesar snorted and kicked out a leg to show his displeasure at being disturbed.

'Good, thanks. Last night I heard an owl.'

'There've been no owls around here for years.'

'Well, I heard one.'

'That's strange. What do owls mean to you, Sonny?'

'It means my ruru is calling me home. Owls are guardians of my family.'

Deo regarded him in silence, then he examined the sky. 'Sun is rising. Time to go.'

After a long and winding trail, they arrived at the top of the rock face. Here, the track folded back onto the Viannos Plateau where the air was miraculously still, except for the singing of nightingales. Below them the cliffs were brushed with early light. To the north-west they could see the peaks of Psiloritis and the wooded foothills they'd travelled through. The east coast was not familiar to Sonny. It was a terrain that caught the eye with its slash of sea colour and its agrarian haze, but which also concealed the garrisons of the Italian Army.

Sonny tugged at a torn piece of shoe leather. 'A day of idleness would be nice.'

'Nearly there,' Deo said, tightening the donkey's girth strap.

They proceeded over the ridge, and around a bend, to where the land levelled onto a table of rock. Dotted over the stony ground were huts made from woven straw and branches, plus a few acquired army tents. A grouping of boulders appeared to be guarding the entrance to the settlement. The travellers waited, not quite knowing how to announce their presence, until Caesar brayed and another donkey answered deep in the camp.

     Kayleen M. Hazlehurst

Suddenly the stones moved. Sonny froze as three whiskered men swished off their kapotis—hooded cloaks that disguised them as conical rocks—and stepped from behind the boulders. On their belts they carried an array of pistols and curved daggers.

Definitely bandits.

Dark eyes crinkled as Deacon opened his arms to the watchmen. 'Kiriakos! … Grigori, my old friend! … Petraka, how are you?'

Kisses on both cheeks were followed by friendly slaps on the face. Even Sonny was embraced. Under rebel protection, or possibly under guard, they were ushered into the headquarters of Manolis Bandouvas himself.

—∞—

The largest guerrilla band on Crete provided a magnet for the disillusioned, the idealistic and the marooned. Sonny recognised two priests, a few monks, and soldiers of different nationalities. Deo pointed out a huge Russian, who he suspected had escaped from a local prison. Also visiting to speak with the leader were three town officials, the chief of police, a teacher with four schoolboys and rebel leaders from various regions.

Bandouvas was conducting audiences under the shade of a venerable ilex tree. While a young couple sought the patriarch's blessing for their newborn, Deacon went to converse with the other men.

Deo and Sonny sat waiting for their interview with the leader.

'How do they survive?' Sonny asked.

'Villagers bring them news and supplies. The wealthier patrons donate money. Apart from that they barter or buy what they need, like everyone.'

'The band seems well set up.'

Deo bent to answer. 'They're almost self-sufficient. They have their own baker and carpenter, cobbler and tailor. They also have their own armoury and, of course, plenty of sheep.'

It was a simple life. Meagre in provisions and probably under-defended, yet Sonny saw something else. High spirits permeated the camp. Not just in its daily running, but at the heart of it. He was sure this was due to a shared belief that they were on the side of the angels.

The splendidly moustached man seated in front of them was flanked by his younger brothers, Yiannis and Nikos. His piercing gaze exhibited the intelligence of a natural leader.

Bandouvas' manner was relaxed, with one boot crossed over the knee of his breeches, but Sonny noticed the rifle propped close to his right arm, and the ammunition belt around his waist. This was a man ready for action. Under his leather vest and goat-horn buttons, the leader wore a clean white shirt as if he was expecting important company.

When Bandouvas saw them waiting in the crowd, his face brightened. 'Deacon, my old friend! You have travelled many miles to visit us. Come, sit with me.'

After a robust greeting, Deacon asked, 'The invaders are not bothering you, Manolis?'

'Oh, no. The Italianos are lazy and they fear the mountains. They think we will pick them off, one by one. Now, would that be courteous?'

Deacon laughed. 'No doubt you would.'

'We watched the Nazis bomb Heraklion with great sorrow for the citizens, but the Italians are different. Lieutenant Tavana detests the Germans. He boasts he has caused the death of not one Cretan. Spies have informed Tavana that Bandouvas is itching to get his hands on Italian guns, but he does not care. So, in answer to your question, the invaders have left us alone at Lasithi. We hear this is not the case in your region.'

'The Germans seize our livestock and take our food. They threaten execution to anyone helping the Allies.' Deacon lowered his voice. 'And I am afraid some of our people are no longer patriots.'

Bandouvas answered with a deep growl. The kapetans were conducting their own war against collaborators. This month alone, Bandouvas' band had killed six traitors. These were weak men who could be bribed. Released criminals who preferred drinking or who lusted for reward. The most dangerous were the bad Cretans, aggrieved persons who informed on other citizens. Their deeds were no secret, and guerrilla justice was swift. Bullets were never wasted on betrayers.

'There's only one way of dealing with traitors,' Bandouvas said quietly, as he stroked the sheathed knife at his side.

 Kayleen M. Hazlehurst

Deacon hung his head. 'I know.'

The leader opened his arms and gave Deo and Sonny a warm smile. 'I hear your excellent men have been helping the defenders get off the island.'

'Yes. The British have been sending us torpedo boats and motor launches. I've lost count of the number we've seen off.'

'Over three hundred,' Deo chipped in.

'Keep it up. It's safer for them and it's safer for us.'

'But the villagers are panicked, Manolis. Not because they nearly starved last winter, but because they fear some ambitious captain will embark on another murderous campaign.'

The leader leaned forward, unblinking. 'The secret is to know how to exploit the exploiter. They have guns, and we know how to steal them. They have explosives, and we know how to put them to the match. Our fighters will make such a murderous campaign a horrible experience for such a captain.' Bandouvas raised a fist. 'Our anger will become the fuel for good!'

Deo sprang to his feet and brandished his rifle. 'We will eat them!'

'Spoken like a true patriot!' the leader bellowed, sending up cheers and shots in the air.

Deacon's beard quivered as he waited for calm to return. 'But *will* we overcome them, Manolis? Have you heard anything? We need weapons, ammunition ...'

Bandouvas beckoned to one of his men. 'Stay the night, Deacon. Kiriakos will find you shelter. I am expecting some visitors you may like to meet. Join us tonight for a meal.'

Deacon bowed his head. 'We would be honoured.'

At sundown, Sonny walked to the edge of the cliff to observe the curves of the western foothills. The emerald heads of the evergreens and lighter growth, rendered tawny in this low-angled light, gave no sign of fruit trees. No soil bursting with edible life.

The eastern side of the mountain was said to be covered with old orchards. Mulberries, pomegranates, figs, plums and almonds. If Deacon decided to stay another day, Sonny thought he would like to take the donkey and explore those lush slopes. It had been a while since he'd sunk his teeth into the flesh of a plum and felt the red juice running down his chin.

Deo interrupted Sonny's daydreaming, calling him to an open space where several fires burned. Sparks were rising, and he was greeted by the aroma of sheep fat dripping into the flames of roasting spits. The whole band had assembled for the meal.

Senior men and their guests were seated on mats, their copper and ceramic plates before them. Earlier, Sonny had seen two men slip into camp accompanied by the renowned shepherd guide from Asi Gonia, George Psychoundakis.

The kapetans—Manoli Bandouvas, the wealthy sheep owner, George Petrakogiorgos, the olive oil merchant and Antoni Grigorakis, notoriously known as 'Satanas'—were speaking in low tones with two strangers. Sonny and Deo concentrated on the faces of these esteemed leaders, trying to read their lips.

The visitors were British officers, they were told. Young and lean, without the gauntness of having suffered a famine. The fair one, dressed as a poor shepherd, spoke in the Cretan dialect. He was taller and broader than most Cretans, and his easy manner reminded Sonny of the Australian officers he'd seen in Egypt.

The second man, cloaked and daggered, had the watchful presence of a loner who lived beyond social constraints. It was rumoured he had arrived in Crete with explosives strapped to his body. With his swarthy appearance he could have been taken for a Cretan, but Sonny detected something more exotic in his origins.

By the end of the evening, Deo had his own questions.

'Who were those men, Father?'

Deacon ushered them aside, checking no one was listening. 'They are intelligence agents. The fair one is O-Tom and the dark one, Aleko. They're here to establish radio stations to transmit information to Cairo.'

'What sort of information?'

'Rescue rendezvous points. Co-ordinates for parachute drops.'

'This is good news, Father. Did you tell them about the radio in our cave?'

'A runner will fetch it. If the radio doesn't work they will use it for parts.'

	Kayleen M. Hazlehurst

'Where is their hideout, do you know?'

'In the Psiloritis Ranges. Mount Ida, probably. Sleep now. We go tomorrow.'

Caesar was chomping hay as they saddled him for the home journey. Deacon had gone to offer thanks to their hosts, saying he would meet them by the camp entrance. Sonny felt hair rise on the back of his neck. Someone was staring at them. He turned to see the large Russian lumbering over in their direction.

The Russian put a possessive hand on Caesar's rump, using his bulk to appear menacing. 'Leave donkey!'

He returned the stance with a hard stare. 'I can't do that. He's not my donkey.'

The Russian's face reddened, and he spat out his words. 'He's ours now. *Leave* him.'

Sonny took a handful of straw and examined it before handing it to Caesar. In one slow motion he reached into his pack, pulled out his hunting knife, and began to clean his fingernails. Softly, he said in English, 'You want to take me on, mate?'

The man started and pointed at Sonny's chest. 'Australian?'

'New Zealander.'

In this brief stand-off, Deo darted in and snatched Caesar's lead. 'No donkey today, Mr Sergio. Next time we bring donkey and plenty of food. Maybe even some tobacco, eh?'

The man bared his nicotine-stained teeth, and they hurried away before he changed his mind.

They stood beside the rocks—that sometimes were men—and waited for Deacon.

'Would you have killed him, Sonny?'

'I don't know. I've got nothing against Russians, particularly.'

'Good thing we didn't leave Caesar. *That* Russian would have roasted and eaten him.'

34

The High Spy Route

Paulos intercepted them on the track with a warning. They had guests. More men on the run were appearing on lonely paths in the hills, and in recent months the noose had tightened. Troop incursions had brought more arrests and abductions. Villagers were becoming cautious, fearful of the betrayers among them.

'Who are these men?' Deacon asked Paulos.

Sonny understood Deacon's concern. The Resistance could only be served while their cave site remained concealed from all but a few trusted shepherds and runners.

'Escapers,' Paulos said. 'An Australian and a New Zealander. One of yours, Sonny.'

Sonny gave him a doubtful glance. 'Are they strong enough to hunt?'

'They've been feeding themselves. After Dulag, they headed straight for the hills. Didn't hang around the towns begging for food. If you're not satisfied, Deacon, I'll take them to the Amari Valley. We can go on twisted routes, so they won't remember how to find us.'

'We'll see.'

The visitors waited at the foot of the escarpment, clutching two grouse and a marten. As Deacon's men neared, the taller man with sandy hair held up the marten as a peace offering.

'Furry bugger fought like hell. Hope he's worth eating.'

Sonny studied the Australian. 'That's a marten. Makes a good stew.'

'Glad to hear it.' The man took a step back to look over Sonny's clothing. 'You're a Kiwi. I'd never have known.' He put out his hand. 'Moseley Holland, 2nd/7th, Australian 19th Brigade.'

'Sonny Wirima,' he reciprocated. 'Māori Battalion, New Zealand 5th Infantry Brigade.'

The West Australian turned to his spiky-haired friend. 'This is Norm Milton. A country boy from somewhere in your North Island who can run like the wind. Luckiest bastard I've ever met. I once saw a bullet pass clean through his tin mug without leaving a scratch on him. Hey, Lucky, meet Sonny from your part of the world.'

They all shook hands and Sonny did the translations. The man called 'Lucky' had been with the 22nd NZ Battalion on Mount Olympus. Sonny acknowledged the skinny Pākehā with a tinge of sympathy. This was a wiry one. Lean and sinewy, slung low to the ground, with an apologetic look about him. The man reminded Sonny of another Kiwi soldier, Gunner Smith. Had the doctors at the sanatorium on Mount Olympus repaired his smashed face? Like the smaller Cretans, Lucky was a survivor who would do well in these mountains, Sonny thought, although he wasn't so sure about the rambunctious Australian.

'So, your name is Moseley?'

'Yeah. It was my mother's maiden name. Couldn't bear to part with it, she said.' He laughed. 'There's a place in England named after me ... Call me Mo.'

'Okay, Mo.' If the Digger was courageous enough to handle an angry marten, Sonny reckoned they should give him a chance.

Deacon welcomed everyone into their cave with his usual graciousness. As band leader, it was his job to discern the character of any new members. When Deacon's eyes met Sonny's over the marten stew Sonny gave him a quiet nod. This confirmation was all he could give without overstepping the authority of their proud leader. In a day or two, Deacon would decide whether the Anzacs could stay.

After their meal they spread out on the cave floor. Long distances sapped the strength from a man, so there wasn't much talking.

Deacon wanted to bring news of their visit to the camp of Manolis Bandouvas to the other partisan leaders. The Amari Valley stretching between the Kedros and Psiloritis Ranges was one of the last hideouts for wanted men. From here, fighters came down to confront enemy patrols, or to unnerve army garrisons with sudden attacks and swift withdrawals. British agents also roamed through this mountainous territory. They'd come to bolster the rebel bands and to help formulate plans for sabotage.

Civilians were asking whether subversive activities were worth the loss of life and property, yet Sonny could see the pay-offs. Enemy troops loathed venturing into the remote regions in pursuit of outlaws and spies. Behind every bush and boulder was a potential ambush.

A network of clandestine highways had been built throughout the mountains. From Lefká Óri to the Kedros and Psiloritis Ranges, and all the way to Dikti and Lasithi, there were escape routes, rendezvous points, safe havens and lines of communication linking west to east. For men like Mo Holland and Lucky Milton the high spy route was a godsend.

Sonny rolled over on his brushwood-and-blanket bed and gazed out to where the dark sky dripped with stars. Below them he heard braying. The donkey was not sleeping well on the stony ground. Tomorrow he would be returned to Makos, but for tonight he'd been secured to a tree beside a stream. Neglected and missing his friends, Caesar was displeased.

News of the operation came quickly on the heels of their return from Lasithi. Rebels targeted the airfield compounds of Heraklion, Kastelli and Tympaki in June. Twelve commandos landed by submarine to be part of a combined force, which included both the RAF and Kapetan Petrakogiorgos and other civilian fighters. This secret army destroyed twenty-six grounded aircraft, detonated an ammunition dump, bombed a storage facility, blew up a depot of aviation fuel and killed four German sentries. The message to the enemy was plain. *Covert attacks will continue until Occupiers are driven from Crete.*

German reprisals were sweeping. Fifty hostages, wrongly assumed to have organised the airfield strikes, were taken from the greater Heraklion region. The ex-mayor and ex-governor were shot, along with many others.

It was clear the Nazis had set their sights on the leaders of the Resistance. Deacon warned his men to brace themselves for more troop intrusions. To everyone's delight he also declared the two new men, Mo and Lucky, had joined their band.

—⁂—

An old woman hustled up the path, carrying a basket and waving her hand. A minute earlier they had witnessed her throwing a warning rug over the stone wall at the boundary of the village.

'Fly my child, there are Germans here!'

After an urgent exchange between Deacon and the villager, she thrust on him a limp chicken wrapped in a linen napkin and rushed away.

'Problem?' Sonny asked.

'Here, put this somewhere. Keep it covered.'

Sonny saw the fowl had been plucked and cleaned. It looked naked. *Why do they call them dressed chickens?* He shoved the scrawny carcass into one of Caesar's baskets. 'If we find a few potatoes and carrots, I can make a soup …'

'Later,' Deacon said, gesturing for Sonny to follow. 'We'll take the track above the shepherds' fields so we don't run into anyone.'

They had fetched the donkey from Makos and Alena, and were now on their way to join their mountain brethren. Paulos and Deo had left earlier, taking Mo and Lucky with them. In September, George Psychoundakis had arrived at their cave with a message from O-Tom. The runner told them the kapetans, Petrakogiorgos and Bandouvas with several others, were gathering for a supply drop.

'Bring your men and mule and meet us on the Nida Plateau in two days.'

Sonny had thanked George and given him some water and walnuts. He'd regularly seen the slight, agile figure dashing over the goat tracks, carrying his messages. Deacon had made the right decision in letting Mo and Lucky stay. The Anzacs were good hunters and might one day prove to be good fighters.

The Nida Plateau, between the eastern and western peaks of

Psiloritis, was a high and difficult place to reach. It involved a long walk for Bandouvas and his men. But as a location for a British airdrop it was ideal.

Twenty rebels had assembled by the time Deacon and his men arrived to set up camp. The partisan leaders were keeping the operation quiet. They had brought enough menfolk to help them with the retrieval of the hoard, but no more.

The signal pyres, built from branches and dried shrubs, were ready to be lit on the second evening. They waited, listening for the drone of an approaching plane. When the fires flared, a frisson of excitement raced through the crowd.

Against the grey light they saw, not a single aircraft, but a formation of eight bombers.

'Germans!' someone shouted. 'They've come to bomb us!'

Men ducked and scattered.

The squadron swerved sharply towards the coast, but one plane dropped down. Those who had stood their ground recognised it right away. The Blenheim circled to get a measure of the field. With one passing swoop the pilot released his load, wagged his wings at the cheering men, and carried on.

All eyes followed the disappearing aircraft as boxes and crates drifted to earth under the pearly canopies of small parachutes. A few nights ago, Deacon's band were given a spine-tingling view of the Souda Bay bombings. From their cave they could see red lines where jetties had been set alight. Flames on the harbour showed that a ship was on fire. Now, deeper in the mountain range, a dull glow hung in the sky above these newest bombings.

Mo and Lucky asked if they should start retrieving the containers. Most of the boxes had landed on flat ground, but a number had tumbled over a bank. Deacon seated himself to consider the wisdom of this. He looked every bit the worthy leader in his dark cloak, rough-woven shirt and waistcoat, and loose breeches tucked into high leather boots. About his person he bore a deadly armoury. Two pistols and three knives were secured between his belt and shirt, and crossed over his chest was a double bandolier.

Sonny watched Deacon as he assessed the mood of the assemblage, noting how the tassels of his sariki headscarf quivered as each emotion passed over his face.

'Leave the boxes until morning,' Deacon told them. 'Rest now. There is nothing more to do tonight.'

Actions seen in daylight were less likely to result in accusations of theft, but right now hearts were high on success and the celebrations would go on well into the night. Raki and ouzo flasks, strong spirits, had already been drawn out. Two musicians with lute and lyre wrestled to stay in tune, and voices were raised in song.

Slowly, young men began to circle—cross-stepping, slapping their heels, and linking their hands with handkerchiefs.

By mid-morning the cargo had been gathered and piled into the middle of the field. O-Tom had descended from his Mount Ida hideout to attend the drop. It was he who had organised the supplies and radioed Cairo with the drop zone co-ordinates. With him was a new arrival, an English officer he introduced as Michali. The second agent resided in the village of Vaphé, deep in the White Mountains. The two had come to help the bands divide up the spoils. In the company of such hot tempers, perceptions of unfairness might lead to bloodshed.

Kapetan Bandouvas was feeling bold that morning, declaring that the supplies were solely for the benefit of his Lasithi band. Several men reached for their rifles. Petrakogiorgos raised his hands for guns to be lowered. At this point, O-Tom stepped forward to declare that the air drop was the property of His Majesty's Government, and he would decide its distribution.

'Have you brought us here to tease us?' Bandouvas growled. 'We will seize the lot by force. Stand to your arms, men!'

There was a tremor of confusion. The men who loved Bandouvas also had a healthy respect for the British officer who'd generously provided these goods.

During their hesitation O-Tom scrambled up the pile of boxes and perched himself on the top. Unfazed, he opened his arms. 'Go ahead, gentlemen. Shoot an unarmed man!'

After spluttering words of condemnation of the 'brave fool who had so brazenly defied Bandouvas and his guns', the guerrilla leader put his hands on his hips and roared with laughter.

Relieved, everyone joined in.

A barrel of flour had split open upon landing, scattering its contents like snow. The rest of the crates and boxes were laid out and opened. Some contained stocks of arms—twelve Smith & Wesson .32-calibre revolvers, ammunition, explosives, fuses and limpet mines. In the food boxes they found tins of bully beef and ham, packets of biscuits, lentils, beans, rice, chocolate and tea, along with tobacco and cigarettes.

The British agents had been sent a new transmitter, two spare batteries and a battery charger. In the three crates of clothing there were English cavalry breeches, similar to those worn by Cretans, linen shirts and new soles for boots. Sonny discovered a sack of gold sovereigns tucked in with some medical supplies, probably for bribes, and he handed the money to O-Tom for fair dispersal.

A share of the drop was given to each group according to its size. Deacon was allotted a hundred bullets, one pistol, a quantity of the medical supplies and some clothing, tobacco and food. Their band also received five sovereigns—more money than any of them had seen in years.

As they were preparing to leave, O-Tom came over to help them load up Caesar. Sonny wanted to question the agent more about the war.

'Why are they bombing Souda Bay?' he asked. 'Is it because of what's happening in North Africa?'

'Yes. Jerry has been building his strength on Crete,' O-Tom explained. 'Sending out reinforcements. Using the island as a supply centre for warships and aircraft on their way to Libya. We're trying to put them out of commission before they can give our chaps more hell.'

Sonny yanked on Caesar's girth strap. 'We should smash the lot of them!'

Kayleen M. Hazlehurst

'That's the plan. We'll pull the plug on this cesspool one way or another. Your Greek is good, Sonny. We could do with a man like you.'

Deacon shuffled his feet to urge caution at the implied invitation.

Sonny glanced at his leader and then back at O-Tom. 'Are you saying you want me to become an intelligence agent?'

'We would give you special training.'

'I'm just an ordinary soldier, Mr Tom. Nothing fancy.'

The man gave a quick snort. 'When you're not being a Cretan guerrilla!'

'Yeah, well. Some time, I want to go home. There's a girl there I want to marry. We need to get on with producing twelve kids.'

'I'll be damned!' O-Tom extended his hand. 'Good luck, old boy. I hope you do.'

Sonny broke into a broad smile. This felt like a blessing to him, and in this strange life of his he would take any blessing he could get.

Sonny had been struggling to understand how the North African campaign affected them on Crete and his talk with O-Tom had helped. With the enemy on Egypt's doorstep, communications with Cairo were becoming intermittent. There'd been long silences. The rescue boats sent to Crete had slowed to a trickle. For the foreseeable months, British and Commonwealth forces would be battling it out in the Western Desert.

Left to their own devices, a number of Allied soldiers had been making independent escapes. Some hired caïques, while others pirated boats once stolen from Greeks. The more desperate patched up dilapidated dinghies. Nobody heard the outcome of these dangerous expeditions. Had dark waters flowed past them like silk, or had mountainous waves torn them apart? Had they been rescued by a British warship or captured by an Italian cruiser? For all he knew, they'd all drowned. Still, Sonny wished the escapers well, and asked himself whether he would have the courage to battle high seas in an overcrowded little boat.

Back in the moonless dark of Deacon's cave, Sonny thought about what he had seen on the Nida Plateau. Recent images swirled around him—the wildness of the high country, the warmth of comradeship around a shared fire, the nostalgic singing of untamed men. Before sinking into an exhausted sleep, he prayed he might one day find a way off this intoxicating island that had somehow seduced every fibre of his being.

In a flash he sees her. Atarangi is standing on the edge of the sea cliff with her arms outstretched, as if she is about to take flight. A large seabird sweeps by. The girl falls onto the back of the bird and they climb.

He narrows his eyes to stare through the lashing spray. Against the rolling clouds and shrieking winds, a white speck falls and rises, harnessing the shoulders of the gale in rhythmic arcs. As the boat pitches and spins on the ocean swells, an albatross sets her strong bill and curved wings into the maelstrom.

The flight of the great seabird is a display of such serene mastery that he forgets the stinging elements and commits himself to imitate her resolve. From now on he will let no storms, no encompassing chaos, unsettle or deter him.

He stumbles from the stern to the bow as the albatross passes over. An invocation to the gods rises from his throat. A chant his mother once taught him. Reaching up, he adjusts the sails to follow the storm rider in her direction towards land.

~35~

Finding Dittany

They were sitting on a sand hill watching the morning sea turn silver, and listening to the news of gulls regarding fishermen and passing ships. Miriama wanted to speak again with the girl to give her reassurance.

'It's important to remember our ancestors who set forth on the great seas always had guidance.'

The young one drew her finger through the dry grains of sand. 'Crossing great oceans in little boats must have been terribly dangerous.'

'Ocean-going canoes were not so little, Atarangi. They had double hulls for balance and were skilfully handled, and our seafarers had other helpers. Birds have always understood the secrets of the land and sea. Sharp-eyed seabirds could see the outlines of the seafloor, valleys and mountains hidden underwater. Our ancestors followed these sea trails in much the same way as birds have used the contours of hills for navigation.'

'Seabirds helped our ancestors in the great migrations?'

'Āe. And for that reason, we must treasure the wisdom of all species. Without them, how would we survive?'

'I don't understand. Why did these voyagers leave their homes in the first place? How could they abandon everything they loved?'

'Some took flight ahead of waves of bloodshed, some ahead of hunger and disease. They journeyed under the protection of their atua and had no fear of death.'

Atarangi looked down. 'I do not fear death. I only fear losing those I love. How can I live in a world without my Sonny?'

'Our time here is temporary. Loved ones become invisible to us, then we too blend our spirits with the Great Creator. Let the sacred voices

Who Disturbs the Kūkupa?　　　271

echo through your life, Atarangi. They will show you the way.'

The farm dog, Kete, appeared above the sand hill.

'Hello, you.' Ata reached out. 'Did you sneak away from the milking to find us?'

'She keeps an eye on you, that one.'

'Look at her tummy. I think Kete is having babies.'

'Lucky girl. Why don't you take her home? I'm sure Hēmi will be pleased to see you.'

A flush crept over Ata's cheeks. 'I know what you're doing, Auntie.'

Miriama shrugged and gave her old lady's giggle.

━◯◯◯━

Their herb stocks needed replenishing before the coming winter. Wherever Sonny went, he carried dried sage, thyme, oregano, lavender and garlic cloves in a leather pouch tied to his belt. Chest infections and rheumatism were common complaints among cave dwellers, and hunters were prone to all kinds of cuts and scrapes. He liked having something to brew up in a pot as an inhalant or antiseptic wash, and he was proud he'd been assigned the role of cave expert on all things medicinal.

The next day Sonny went out in search of dittany. Alena had sung the praises of this special herb. She said it was a curative for stomach problems and wounds, ailments frequently visited upon soldiers. As for infections, everyone claimed it was a miracle worker. In the ancient world, dittany was a sorcerer's herb, believed to prove hearts in love and valour. Whatever its uses, he should search for a few leaves of this rare plant. If Alena recommended dittany, that was good enough for him. *Who knows when I might need its magic?*

Sonny took his pack and rifle and told his friends he would be gone for two nights. Mo and Lucky offered to come with him, but he explained the places he was going to were very remote.

'It's better we don't disturb their steep slopes.'

He'd been told dittany grew anywhere between the White Mountains and the isolated ravines of the south coast. It occurred to him this elusive

     Kayleen M. Hazlehurst

plant might even be found in the Imbros Gorge on the way to Sfakia, or closer to Preveli further east.

Since the sacking of the monastery, German posts had been positioned to guard the southern paths and beaches. Sonny planned to slip past those guards, undetected. He doubted there'd be surveillance in the neighbouring hills and gullies. This foraging gave him a chance for one last glimpse of the place where he spent two happy nights with the monks.

Ahead there could be months of fighting, and he was no longer certain Crete was where he should be languishing. His dream of Atarangi and the albatross had been a powerful sign. He needed to gather all the things necessary for a long sea journey.

For several hours he headed south-east, across country, climbing and sliding over the rough terrain and collecting an assortment of medicinal plants, but still no dittany. He felt the rhythm of these dry hills—of days unchanging, as they had been for the stick gatherers and shepherds for centuries. In the afternoon he returned to the main path, painfully aware that his boots were once again in tatters. After an hour of walking, he heard voices.

He ducked up a bank and parted the bushes. Twenty yards further on two armed guards stood with their backs to him, smoking outside an improvised shelter. It was safe to risk leaping across the path and down the slope. Clay and loose stones allowed him to hurtle downwards on his backside, using his legs to slow his momentum.

After a few yards he wriggled to a stop and checked his limbs for grazes, wondering whether there was a less injurious way of descending. To his left, a narrow track arched over a ridge above a straight drop. Small mammals used it to reach the waterway, but would it hold the weight of a man? Above the mouse path was a tumble of rocks and shrubs, where the stones were less likely to skitter away. A broken neck at the floor of a gully was not the kind of exit Sonny wanted from Crete.

He assessed the stability of each footstep until he was able to slide down the last incline on the seat of his sturdy new breeches obtained from the last airdrop. Summer had slowed the river, but the water was clean enough to refill his bottles. From here he would hike along the riverbed, estimating he would emerge at the coast somewhere west of Limni Beach.

Few humans had passed this way, yet he half expected to see evidence of an old campfire, a stone axe or bronze blade, or scratched markings on the cliff walls. There were none of these, but on a damp bank under the shade of the cliff he was astonished to find a flourishing patch of the velvety-leafed herb he'd been seeking.

~

Sonny dropped his things at the cave entrance, allowing plant cuttings to spill from his pack.

'Hi-ho.' The Australian waved at him from the back wall where he was lounging. 'Find what you were looking for?'

'Yeah, I got everything I wanted.' Sonny rolled the stiffness out of his shoulders and went to sit with Lucky by the fire. 'I think I've got us a boat.'

'No kidding?' Lucky said, surprised. 'What kind of boat?'

'A small landing barge. I'm not sure of its condition but—'

'A landing barge!' Mo sat up sharp. 'They're bloody primitive, mate.'

'I know. I've seen better canoes.'

'I've seen better inner-tyre tubes.'

'A boat is still a boat,' Lucky said.

Lucky was right. A boat was definitely still a boat. In recent months, there had been no available vessels within twenty miles in either direction on the south coast. Nothing that wasn't well guarded. Nothing that vagrant soldiers could beg, borrow or steal.

'Trouble is, there's little else, Mo.'

'We'll fix her up,' Lucky said. 'What needs doing?'

'Pretty much everything.'

Mo joined them. 'Where did you find this old thing?'

'In one of the sea caves near Sfakia. Some of our blokes must've planned to come back for her—'

'But never did,' Lucky interjected. 'So she's ours!'

'Looks like it. Waves lapping around her. Bottom with six inches of sand.'

     Kayleen M. Hazlehurst

'Bloody hell.' Mo crouched and rubbed a palm over his forehead.

'It's not that hopeless. Someone stashed the engine on a ledge at the back of the cave.'

'Was it rusted?' Mo asked.

'Dry as a bone. Take a look for yourself.'

'Suppose I could give it a once-over.'

'What tools do you need?'

'I can scrounge tools from the villagers. But finding fuel and oil, that will be hard.'

We can ask around. Trade them for meat.'

Lucky looked at his hands. 'I work with engines. I fixed Dad's tractor on the farm.'

'Is that right?' Mo gave the modest Kiwi a slap on the back. 'Hidden talents, eh? You dark horse. Then I reckon you'll be our fix-it man from now on.'

Lucky's face turned beetroot. Being useful pleased him no end.

—✺—

Two boxes were being prepared. One for food and the other for practical items. So far, they had gathered silk cords from parachutes, knives, wire cutters, and a hammer and spanner in case of engine trouble. There were several lengths of thick rope, some rags, fishing lines and tackle. Sonny had squirrelled away spare blankets and the men joining them would bring their own coats. Nights were going to be cold.

He had his reservations. Outfitting a flat-bottomed boat to ferry destitute men four hundred miles across the Mediterranean in winter was probably the worst idea a man ever had. For the voyage, Sonny needed to foresee every possible calamity. They could be struck by lightning, swamped by a giant wave, lose their bearings. If all went well it would be a five-day crossing, but what if it stretched out? How long could they survive without food and water? The worst of it was having to keep these fears to himself.

Dried meat and bread would provide their staple nourishment. Additional supplies included some pears and walnuts, a few figs and raisins, and as many oranges as he could find. Lucky dug into his pack and pulled out four army biscuits and a tin of bully beef. The biscuits had turned green with mould.

'You keep the biscuits, Lucky. But we'd be glad to share your tin of bully beef. It must be the last one on Crete.'

'Sure, Sonny. Put it in your food box. I'll lend you my teaspoon.'

Water was their most vital resource. There was no shortage on the island, but bottles and containers were scarce.

To be successful, this venture required the ingenuity and faith of their Cretan friends. Apart from food and fuel, the soldiers desperately needed their prayers. Maritime people understood this. The island was sprinkled with wayside chapels dedicated by fishermen to their saints. Surrounding Crete were angry seas and jealous gods who expected to be appeased.

It was strange to think he might be returning to his battalion. Would he be flung straight back into battle or sent home? Home was rarely far from his mind. Hēmi would want to take him out hunting. Atarangi would be waiting to marry him.

Deacon interrupted Sonny's brooding by placing a hand on his shoulder and a whiskery face by his ear. 'Moseley and I are going hunting. Do you want to come?'

Sonny caught the familiar smell of tobacco and turned to gaze into the grey-black eyes of his leader.

'Sure, I'll come with you. Are we getting meat for the villagers?'

'Yes, and some for ourselves.'

'I'll skin the beasts tonight.'

 Kayleen M. Hazlehurst

~36~

The Villagers

They floated the barge where it was and left it hidden in the sea cave. It took them four days to scoop out the sand, refit the engine using a block-and-tackle pulley, and to check the metal hull for leaks. To avoid rumours, which might cause fifty hopefuls turning up on the morning of their departure, Sonny enlisted the aid of his closest friends.

Makos and Deacon were best placed to choose the right men to come with them. Makos was familiar with everyone between Souda and the upper villages. Deacon knew every remote herding settlement and rebel cave throughout the mountains. They were each asked to find four men who knew how to keep their mouths shut.

At one time their landing barge could have transported thirty combat troops from ship to shore, but twelve was all Sonny was prepared to take to Egypt. It wasn't only a question of food and water. The barge had been abandoned for months. He was neither confident of its manoeuvrability, nor certain of the extent of its corrosion.

He would leave it up to Makos and Deacon to warn the escapers of the risks and to guide them to the location of the hidden boat on the appointed day.

———◦∿◦———

They were making their way towards the next village.

'Hey, Lucky,' Mo said, 'unless you want your throat cut, remember to keep your grimy paws off the girls. Those knives their men carry aren't just for skinning sheep, you know.'

'Shut up, Mo.' Lucky turned aside.

Sonny, who doubted his countryman had much experience with girls, put his hand on Lucky's shoulder. 'What's a man to do if the ladies can't resist this good-looking boy?'

'That's right,' Lucky said defensively. 'What if they want to touch me? What then, eh?'

'Then I suggest you sit with their fathers or brothers.' Sonny gave him a wink. 'Sooner or later someone will offer you a bride.'

'So I've heard,' Lucky said mournfully.

Mo widened his eyes. 'Do you know anyone who's taken up an offer of marriage?'

'Give it time,' Sonny said. 'Our blokes are well blended into the countryside. I reckon one or two of them will never leave.'

'Not me,' said Lucky. 'I want to go home.'

Makos guided them to the schoolmaster's residence where they would spend the night. Basil Vasilakis had studied medicine before the war, Makos explained as they walked to the outer edge of the village. When financial difficulties stopped him from completing his medical degree, he had taken a teaching post on Crete.

The 'good doctor' was a closely guarded secret and a treasure to the community. He allowed few challenges to defeat him and could stitch wounds, set bones and deliver babies as well as any qualified practitioner.

They came upon a grand house with a shaded balcony set among the trees. A side path led to rooms at the back where the local children received daily lessons. A thin, bespectacled man in a worn three-piece suit and collarless shirt greeted the Anzacs at his doorway. After a quick glance down the street, Basil ushered Sonny, Lucky and Mo into the kitchen to meet his elderly father, Pávlos Vasilakis, and his wife and daughter, Helena and Emilia.

When they asked Basil about the school he confessed the curriculum was closely monitored. He was required to tutor all subjects in German— reading, writing, arithmetic and geography. Basil scowled. 'I'm even forced to teach the propaganda our masters have dressed up as history.'

Every member of the household contributed something to the school. His wife, Helena, who was bright-eyed despite her resigned manner, taught

     Kayleen M. Hazlehurst

cookery and sewing to the girls. Grandfather Pávlos trained the boys in carpentry and other useful skills. Fearless Emilia, the daughter with chocolate-brown hair, led her brood of children to a shed in a secluded part of the woods to impart the now 'illegal' language of Greek.

The family was rapt with interest as the Anzacs revealed plans for their imminent flight to Egypt. They had come down from the hills in search of provisions. Anything suitable for a long sea voyage.

Mo stared down at his hands. 'What we need most is fuel and oil,' he told them. 'Although we've no idea how we will find them.'

On hearing this, Basil Vasilakis sent his wife and daughter out to fetch the priest.

When Father Joseph entered with the two women Basil's face broke into a smile.

'Ah, my dear friend!'

Basil told them this man was a 'true patriot'. An excellent priest to the settlements of the Omalos Plateau, whose advice was sought by high and low alike. Around the dining table they spoke of the Occupation. German reprisals had been brutal and military raids were increasing. There were concerns for the men in the mountain regions. Anyone caught helping the Allies, or participating in the Resistance, was shot and their homes reduced to rubble. The Cretans had set up warning systems along the paths and trails to alert each other when the enemy was on the move.

'Tell them about the night they attacked us,' Helena urged her husband.

Basil hunched over the table to trace a circle with his finger.

'At the café we heard a detachment of German soldiers was going to surround us that very night. The women were weeping and waving their hands. "The Nazis are coming to kill every one of us," they wailed.'

Helena crossed herself.

Grandfather Pávlos pointed to the slopes behind their house. 'People scattered into the hills, but a few remained behind.' He looked fondly at the priest. 'After some squabbling, Father Joseph agreed to go with the larger group on condition enough of us remained with the elderly, and the mothers with small children.'

'We begged Papa to come with us,' Helena said, her eyes moist, 'but he said he was too old for climbing hills.'

'Yes,' Basil agreed. 'Our dear Papa stayed to keep guard, so the rest of us could slip away. We climbed the mountainside and slept among the boulders for a couple of hours. Soon word spread among us that armed troops were pouring over the Pass. "Awake, poor souls. The Germans are upon us," we told each other.'

'In the moonlight we heard the approaching clatter of the soldiers,' Emilia said, 'and we sent up prayers for our little village.'

Pávlos carried on with the story. 'The soldiers were shouting instructions and going from house to house. Then they drove us all into the church.'

'Oh, no!' Helena cried, reliving the horror. 'They're going to burn alive our dear ones in God's Holy Place!'

'I won't let them!' Father Joseph wrenched at his cassock. 'I'll go down there and offer myself as a sacrifice!'

'Wait, Father!' Basil put his hand on the priest's chest. 'We may need you yet!'

Poor Mo swung his attention from one enactment to the other. Overcome by the drama, he let out a roar. He picked up his rifle as if he would have gone down there himself.

Pávlos took control of the narrative. He placed a reassuring hand on Helena's arm. 'No, my dear. I think the purpose was to keep our people in one place. One by one we were taken out and interrogated while they searched our homes.'

Lucky's chin was almost scraping the table. 'What were they looking for?'

'Weapons. But we had them well hidden.'

Basil stiffened his spine. 'We heard shots and feared they were executing our people. Then all went quiet. At sunrise a boy came to tell us the soldiers had gone. We hurtled down the hillside to find a few people had been beaten, but no one was badly hurt.'

    Kayleen M. Hazlehurst

It had become apparent the Germans were searching for Colonel Papadakis and the Englishman who was accompanying him.

'They wouldn't find them,' Pávlos said. 'Aleko helped the colonel and his family escape to Egypt last August.'

'How did you dissuade them?' Mo asked.

'I asked to speak with the commanding officer. "Herr Major" I said most humbly. "Last night your soldiers were shooting at two naughty schoolboys who were running away. Not that feckless Papadakis and his treasonous friend." The officer moved in closer, his eyes shining, as if he'd found himself a Judas. "Do you know where they are? Can you show me?" I looked at him sorrowfully. "Sir, these villagers are just poor but honest peasants. We do not keep such grand company. But may I offer you a goat horn of ouzo before you go?"'

'Strewth,' said Lucky. 'What happened?'

'The officer put his nose in the air and walked away, as if talking with a mere peasant was beneath his dignity. An hour later he and his men were gone.'

Everyone laughed at the grandfather's cunning, but Helena gave a weary sigh. 'We later heard our courageous women had hidden the weapons under their skirts. It was a miracle they weren't searched.'

Father Joseph got to his feet. 'Yes, we got off lightly. Others have not been so fortunate.' He turned to the Anzacs. 'I will get what you need for your boat ... There is a police sergeant I know in Chania, or maybe I'll find a few sympathetic fishermen ... Come back in three days.'

Sonny grasped the priest's hand. 'We will never forget your kindness.'

Still awake on the matted floor of the classroom, Sonny listened beyond the rasping breaths of his sleeping comrades to the songs of frogs in the forest pools.

He went over the story of survival told to them that evening. The calm of the old men who gave no challenge to an aggressive enemy. The courage of the wives and mothers who feigned indifference and hid the weapons. Their frail bodies offered up to the stick and boot. It had been the best strategy. The Germans did not like being made out as fools. In a vengeful raid the atmosphere might be very different—tinder dry, ready to ignite into carnage.

Sonny woke to the alluring smells of baking. His host joined him in the hall as they walked to the kitchen.

'Later I'll show you the place where I'll leave your fuel,' Basil said.

'Choose somewhere outside. I might be coming through at night.'

'Fuel is heavy. Do you have a donkey?'

'Āe. Makos will be with us.'

'Good.' The man pointed towards the forest. 'I'll hide it behind Emilia's shed.

A meal of barley bread, with fresh cheese and figs, had been laid out. Basil waited for the women to leave the room, then he spoke with urgency. 'The Germans have become devious, sending spies posing as Englishmen to play on our sympathies.'

'Surely no one has fallen for that,' Mo responded.

'Some have, and they've paid dearly for it. Be careful who you trust, my friends.'

Sonny waited, sensing his host had not finished.

'They've been making reconnaissance flights,' Basil went on. 'We fear they are planning large-scale incursions into the White Mountains.'

'Duly noted,' Mo said bitterly.

Lucky turned to Sonny. 'We'll take the path to the coast at night, won't we? Push the boat out before dawn?'

'That's the plan.'

'You would be welcome to spend your last evening with us.'

'It's safer for everyone if we stick to the hills.'

Helena came out of the kitchen carrying two napkins, folded and tied. 'Bread and honey for you today, and a bag of walnuts for your sea journey.' She reached up to pat their cheeks, her eyes glowing with tears. 'Such dangerous times for you. God keep you safe. Father Joseph said he would hold a special service on your behalf. Please know you will be in our prayers.'

Sonny accepted the food bundles. 'This is wonderful, Helena.'

'You can be sure every morsel will be appreciated,' Mo said.

   Kayleen M. Hazlehurst

Lucky grinned. 'Every morsel by hungry men.'

Sonny nodded at Helena. 'Please tell Father Joseph we will need all the prayers he can muster. You will all be close to our hearts while we are at sea.'

Emilia came over to offer Sonny a thin book. 'My school atlas is not very special, but it may help.'

Sonny accepted the gift. 'A schoolteacher's atlas will certainly help, Emilia.'

Pávlos shuffled in, clutching a pair of polished boots. 'Your boots are falling apart, Sonny. You can have these, if they fit.'

'I can't take a man's boots,' Sonny protested.

'*Oh*, but they are spare. I only wear them to church.' The grandfather placed the footwear by Sonny's feet. 'How many Sundays does an old man have left? I'm sure your feet will make better use of them.'

Sonny measured the Sunday boots against his feet and bent to try them on. The leather had relaxed over time and his feet slipped in easily. He looked at the smiling faces around him. 'How can I not do well with such a magnificent pair of boots?'

———∞———

A bitter wind was blowing. Deacon stood at the cave entrance, looking down into the valley. There was an alertness about him, suggesting something had caught his eye in the afternoon light.

Sonny put down his bone needle and thread of silk, drawn from a parachute cord, to study their white-haired leader. Notwithstanding the hardships of cave dwelling, Deacon kept his clothes clean and mended, his beard and moustache trimmed. He expected the same standards from his men and would not have them going around in ragged garments.

Sonny came to Deacon's side. 'What is it?'

'Someone is coming.'

Below them, a figure was darting along the narrow track. The boy waved and began the slow climb up the escarpment.

'Tobias.' Sonny offered his hand to help the young messenger onto the rim of the cave. 'What brings you here so late in the day?'

'Bad news, Uncle.' The runner bent to catch his breath. 'There are troops moving towards the upper villages. The priest sent word …'

'Come warm yourself, my son.' Deacon placed Tobias beside the fire and sat opposite to watch his face. 'How many soldiers?'

'About twenty. Father Joseph thinks they're looking for trouble.'

'A rogue group … This could be a problem.'

Lucky poked the embers. 'Especially if they have something to prove.'

'Unless they are scouts,' said Sonny. 'Were they hiding and sneaking about?'

'The priest thinks they are intent on something.'

Lucky stared at Deacon. 'Are they acting on their own, do you think?'

'Sounds like it.'

Mo was observing them from the back of the cave with the tautness of a wound spring. It was a quality Sonny admired in the Australian. His alertness and stillness in a crisis, which often came with a brutal clarity. 'Someone's unhappy they didn't get blood the last time.'

Deacon let out a ragged breath.

Sonny immediately thought of his friends. He feared the villagers had become overconfident since the last incident. They might take fewer precautions with a smaller group of soldiers. 'Did they appear drunk?'

Tobias lifted his shoulders.

Sonny considered the consequences of a belligerent group returning to where they'd been outfoxed by the local Cretans.

Deacon's eyes were the blackest Sonny had ever seen as he snapped out his commands.

'Put out the fire … Get the guns.'

<hr>

Miriama was working her hoe in the garden, plunging the blade into the soil like a soul possessed. The problem she was facing was how to ensure the safe passage of her eldest son into a future where he and their lineage would continue to flourish. The duty of the senior women was to propose unions that guarded the seeds and the gardens. Bloodlines were kept pure by good marriages and healthy children.

Kayleen M. Hazlehurst

She recalled the myth of the dog-headed men who kidnapped women and took them away to their caves—or was it a myth? She herself had delivered a child with a deformed jaw to a couple who had ignored the whakapapa advice that their families were too closely related. For so many reasons, Atarangi was an ideal wife for Hēmi. Now, with scores of Northland men lost in this war, an even greater strain had been placed on the elders to make suitable matches.

The sun was close to setting when she heard the beating wings of her kūkupa returning to their roost in the pūriri tree. As she watched the incoming sea mist, she noticed a figure with a knapsack walking towards the village. He had the stride of a man who was coming home, yet the apparition was not quite touching the road.

'Sonny!'

Miriama's hoe fell away as she collapsed to the ground.

37

November Oranges

Their leader watched them sort through the weapons.

'Arm up well, men,' Deacon said, then he drew aside the young runner. 'Go home, boy. This is not for you.'

Tobias puffed himself up. 'I am a man, not a boy. Why can't I guard your back, Uncle? Carry your messages?'

A smile crept over Deacon's lips. 'All right, but no guns. And keep out of our way. I don't want you getting shot.'

'Unless you call me, you won't even know I'm there.'

The men grabbed all the weapons and ammunition they could carry. Sonny wished he'd got his hands on a tommy gun. He touched the obsidian in his pocket, an item now precious to him, and took a handful of cords. He didn't have a bayonet but he could tie a blade to the end of a stick.

TEN CRETANS WILL DIE FOR EVERY GERMAN KILLED. This Nazi declaration, displayed on noticeboards and dropped in leaflets, was part of the insurgents' spiritual landscape. Enemy threats made the rebels more daring. The Resistance would remain firm.

'What will we do?' Sonny asked Deacon.

'If it's sport they want, then sport we will give them. There won't be a trace of Nazis left on this island.'

Five heavily laden men and one shepherd boy had to negotiate the foothills before the fading daylight made walking difficult. Paulos crouched on the ledge to watch them go. He'd been left to guard the cave and to survey the terrain as the band came and went. One gunshot from Paulos would send a warning. Tobias, who loved these tracks like old friends, led the way at a fair pace.

     Kayleen M. Hazlehurst

It was common to see the dark figures of rebels slipping through these hills. They passed by the shepherds' huts without disturbance. Tobias did not stop to tell his family where he was going. They'd have guessed he was with Deacon's men.

On reaching the last fold in the ranges, the men looked down. Stretched before them was the Omalos Plateau. Helped by an ascending moon, they expected to reach the upper settlements in good time.

In this subtle light, the straw-gold glow of the grazing land against the grey surrounding rocks cast a dream-like quality over the plain. As they passed through the grassland, Sonny sensed they were crossing from the safe fortress of the mountains into a world where evil-doers willed them harm.

They camped near the first village and woke refreshed. Sonny retrieved his field glasses to scan the road. There was no sign of Germans.

'The soldiers have stopped somewhere overnight.'

'We'll push on,' Deacon responded.

A man bowed by a bundle of sticks passed them by in sad-eyed silence. As they neared the second settlement, Sonny offered to scout the area. Sufficiently tanned and bearded, he would be taken for a Cretan.

Deacon cautioned Sonny to be on his guard and pointed to a grove of trees. 'We will hide there until you return. Get some food for us. We'll look for a creek or a spring in the forest.'

After half a mile Sonny entered a cobbled alley, realising he was thirsty. People had withdrawn into their homes and the town was strangely quiet. He had a few coins and hoped he might find a café. When a resident ambled up the street carrying a basket of oranges, Sonny respectfully lowered his eyes. 'Good morning, Uncle. How are you today?'

The man hesitated as Sonny did his best not to ogle the oranges.

The Cretan answered with a slow smile. '*Englaishe?*' he whispered.

Sonny looked up and dipped his head. The man put a finger to his lips and beckoned him to follow. After winding their way through the narrow lanes, Sonny was ushered into a house filled with the welcoming aroma of olive oil and garlic. The kitchen was cramped, but clean. In the corner, a wooden hand press, a contraption the size of his mother's washing machine, stood on a base of old bricks.

The orange merchant, who said his name was Leo, crouched by his window and pointed down the street. Two hundred yards away twenty young Nazis, some stripped to the waist, were sunning themselves outside a tavern. Each soldier gripped a glass of the local beverage and rested his other hand near a gun.

'How long have they been here?'

'Two days. They've got machine guns …'

'No one is safe.' Sonny ran his tongue over his cracked lips. 'May I have some water, Uncle?' This time his eyes grazed off the oranges.

Leo moved to the table and put his hand on the basket. 'Would you like these? November oranges. Our last crop of the season.'

Sonny beamed. 'We would be glad of them.' He helped Leo pour the entire basket of fruit into his knapsack.

'You have come with more men?'

'There are six of us.'

Leo hunted through his larder. 'Here, take these.' He handed over two loaves and a dark bottle with a cork. 'My special olive oil that I prepare with garlic. You can eat it with bread or apply it to wounds.'

'Greatly appreciated.'

'I would offer you a place to stay, but I expect you want to report back to your friends.'

'Yes. They will be eager for both your food and news. I should not be discovered here, but your kindness travels with me.'

Leo went with Sonny to the door. 'Can you help us, dear *Englaishe*, if these Nazis give us trouble?'

'We will try.'

Sonny discussed his findings with the others. Things didn't look good. People were cowering in their homes while armed Jerries primed themselves with liquor.

Lucky was incensed. 'These are not the ordinary German army?'

 Kayleen M. Hazlehurst

'I don't think so,' Mo said. 'I heard crack mountain troops have arrived in Crete. This could be them. My guess is they'll want to shake things up in the villages, then press on for the higher regions.'

'We have to stop them,' Lucky blurted.

Sonny rubbed his forehead. 'If these raids are to crush Cretan opposition they won't be taking prisoners.'

'Executions,' Deacon said darkly.

They all lapsed into silence.

After a few minutes, Deacon turned to Sonny. 'Would you trust your orange merchant to take care of the boy?'

Everyone looked at Tobias, who had fallen asleep under the brushwood after a meal of oil soaked bread, followed by two sweet oranges.

'Leo is a good man. I would trust him.'

'There's our answer. The boy can be our lookout. Bring us news.'

'What do you think, Mo?' Lucky asked.

'It's a good plan. Tobias is a fast runner. Who would notice a young shepherd boy?'

Sonny slept until morning, having taken the earlier watch. He was looking through the leafy canopy to the pale autumn sky. Below the forest, and beyond the parched grass and cobbled streets, there were houses occupied by frightened Cretans. After breakfast, Deacon and his men had set up their positions, calculating the soldiers would leave by this road and wanting to draw gun fire away from the residents.

They were well camouflaged on the outskirts of the village. Trees in the fullness of yellow and russet leaf reminded Sonny of the dappled overlay of Atarangi's eyes. Autumn had once been his favourite season. The joyful time when he and his brothers went pig hunting. Now he lay in wait for another prey, thinking their odds weren't bad. *Four each. That's all we have to knock off.*

Mo stalked the perimeter, looking down at the village. Deacon focused on the rise in the road. Sonny listened for signs—the quietening of crickets, a sudden flight of birds, anything that might announce the coming of enemy soldiers.

Mo would get the first sighting and they waited for his cue. When they heard gunfire coming from the village, they strained to see the tall Australian lumbering towards them.

'What is it?' Deacon asked in a hoarse voice.

'Some rounds fired ... People fallen in the street ...' Mo answered in short, sharp breaths. 'Huns are rounding up the rest ... There's a crowd coming this way.'

'Keep under cover,' Deacon ordered. 'Watch for my signal.'

Their thin line of defence was stretched the length of the grove. Lucky took his place behind an oak between Mo and Sonny. Deacon stood with Deo—father and son, guarding each other's backs.

A cloud of pigeons burst into the air and swung across the rooftops. With the tramping of feet, strange broken shadows rose above the hill and spread over the road. It was a spectacle they hadn't expected. Forty men and youths were being driven by armed soldiers. Trailing close behind was a group of sobbing, beseeching women.

They held their fire as the adult males of the village were lined up along the bank of a dry creek bed in front of the execution squad.

Deacon glanced at his men and raised his arm. *Wait.*

Sonny heard scurrying feet. Tobias had skirted back into the grove with half a dozen boys, each placing extra guns and ammunition at their feet.

'Good lad,' Sonny said. 'Quick now, take your friends and go.'

Tobias beckoned to his friends, and they slunk away.

Deacon gave the signal. *Now!*

The rebels aimed their rifles and fired. Five soldiers fell.

The Germans, realising this was an ambush, swung their guns to the left. Deacon's men dropped to the ground, rolled to the right, and fired again. Streams of bullets zipped into the forest and splintered the bark of trees.

Three more volleys brought down half of the execution squad.

In the confusion, the hostages crouched like foxes and scuttled on hands and knees along the gully into the waiting arms of their women.

One soldier turned his gun on the escaping civilians and got it in the

Kayleen M. Hazlehurst

neck. Those remaining were firing wildly at the attackers they could not see. Well-aimed bullets appeared to be coming at them from all directions. Two ran and were shot in the back, the rest cast aside their weapons and sank to their knees. They were all felled.

Deacon's men had agreed that no survivors would return to tell of the attack. The rebels had their own message for the Germans. *Hunters of Cretans will vanish into the mountain mists.*

Sonny felt the wind on his ears. Heard footsteps. Tobias. The sturdy legs of the shepherd boy and his friends were pounding the earth behind him. He stopped to speak with them.

'I must fetch the doctor. Can you find Father Joseph and ask Makos to bring his donkey?'

The boys gave him cheeky grins and veered off like a flock of birds.

Minutes earlier, Sonny had looked along the treeline to check on the others. A shot had caught Mo in the thigh. He was swearing at Lucky, who was attending to the injury with a first-aid kit. Mo did not appear to be in any immediate danger. The person most seriously hurt was Deacon, who was bleeding badly.

He looked down in pity at this loved leader. The bullet must have missed Deacon's heart but was lodged in his chest. The gaping hole exposed the sharp edges of a shattered sternum. Sonny tore a sleeve from his own shirt and knelt beside the distressed son.

'Here,' he said, pressing the ball of fabric into Deo's hand. 'Hold this tight on your father's wound. If we can stop the bleeding it might not be as bad as it looks.'

Deacon was gasping in agony. He reached up and grabbed Sonny's forearm with surprising strength.

'Friend, I must ask something of you.'

'Anything, Deacon.'

'Take Deo.'

'What?'

'Take Deo to Egypt … I beg you.'

'Papa, no!' Deo's cheeks flooded with tears.

'Beloved son, you were the finest comrade a man could want.' Deacon coughed again and more blood trickled from the side of his mouth. 'You must leave this wretched island and live.'

Sonny rose slowly to his feet and choked back his own tears. 'Hold on, Deacon. I'm going to run for the doctor. He will patch you up in no time.'

Deacon stroked Deo's head, resting now against his shoulder. 'May God go with you,' the leader said. He looked more serene than Sonny had ever seen him.

As Sonny left to find help, he saw people returning. Girls came carrying milk for the fighters. Matrons brought buckets and brooms to wash the cobblestones. Everywhere there was blood. It had soaked into the clay of the bank, splattered over the grass and stained the road. Men with shovels had charged themselves with burying the evidence.

A massacre had occurred here today—but this time the dead were not Cretans.

<div align="center">~~~</div>

For the hundredth time Sonny reviewed his list. *Water, blankets, tools, revolver, atlas, compass, torch, fishing lines, hooks and sinkers, ropes, oars, salted fish, bread, biscuits, dried goat meat, fruit and nuts.* He needed more bandages and some lengths of wood. Splints were something his mother always took on a boat, in case she had to set a broken arm or leg.

Rumours of Deacon's defence of the village had sprinted over the high plains and peaks, by way of the Cretan telegraph. Every rebel band throughout the ranges was arming up in anticipation of retaliatory raids. Sonny was racked with worry. The enemy did not yet suspect their elite troops had met an ill fate. Once they did, no one would be spared their fury.

Their cave hideout was no longer safe. With their leader gone, it seemed fitting they should disband. Paulos said he would join the rebels in the Amari Valley after the others had made their escape. Sonny steeled his resolve to move forward the date of their departure. Preparations were nearly complete, and the chosen men were pressing him to put the barge to sea.

        Kayleen M. Hazlehurst

The good doctor had removed the bullet from Mo's leg and stitched the gash, but Sonny wanted to make sure the leg was healing. Nothing could have been done to save Deacon. By the time Basil and Makos arrived on the scene he had passed away. Caesar was given the saddest task for a donkey—to bear the body of a renowned Cretan to his home in the mountains, where he would be laid to rest between earth and sky.

———•———

While the November sun still provided warmth, the nights were getting cold. That evening they talked around the fire about the sea life in the Mediterranean.

Paulos mentioned squid, dolphins, green turtles and giant leatherbacks. 'You might even see a whale,' he said.

'What about sharks?' Mo asked.

'Sharks are rare. But you should be able to catch a few fish from the boat.'

'Trouble is,' Lucky commented, 'we won't be able to cook what we catch.'

'They'll dry in the sun,' Paulos advised.

Mo liked the idea, saying Aborigines in Australia had preserved meat this way.

Sonny listened while the others chatted. Deo was curled on his bed in the corner, refusing to speak to anyone. This grieving boy was now Sonny's responsibility. On open seas the greatest danger was the weather, and the first few miles leaving Crete had its own perils. The boat might prove unseaworthy, the engine could break down, or they might encounter a patrol vessel. Even the most careful planning could not protect them from everything.

'Give Gavdos a wide berth,' Paulos said, as if in answer to Sonny's private forebodings. 'It's the last of the occupied islands. Eighteen miles west of there is Gavdopoúla, an uninhabited islet where you can land if you run into trouble.'

Mo adjusted his leg, his face showing pain. 'And after that …'

'After that, you're on your own.'

For forty-eight hours Sonny waited. He went to the cliffs to check the sea traffic and to watch the movements of the guards at their posts. Activity on the south coast was irregular at this time of year. No one appeared concerned with the stretch of water in front of their sea cave, west of Preveli.

Messages were sent out to the escapers. 'We leave at daybreak.'

A group of ragged but resilient men tramped through the hills with an entourage of their Cretan friends. Paulos and Deo were at the head of the party, alert and fully armed, guiding them on the treacherous tracks in the moonlight. Then came Makos, with Caesar on a lead, and Sonny behind them keeping an eye on provisions. Caesar carried two baskets stuffed with food and tools, with a pile of coats and blankets across his back. Further behind, the Cretans supervised two more donkeys burdened with the heavy fuel. Lucky insisted on being at the farthest end of the procession, guarding the rear. With him limped Mo on a homemade crutch, carrying his own pack and rifle.

Walking through the Cretan hills, where gusts of salt air blended with the scent of wild thyme, there were moments for melancholy. Yet, Sonny was proud that these stragglers of reduced means were still strong in spirit.

Nobody expected the landing craft to be so difficult to move. This was no fancy marine tractor on wheels. It was a flat-bottomed steel trough meant for amphibious landings. The men had done well in digging out the base, but it now rested in a shallow pond of cave water.

It seemed every well-wisher within miles had turned up to see them off. *Talk about keeping things quiet.* At least willing shoulders and backs were there to help haul the tub from its hiding place and shuffle it down the beach.

There were tears and embraces, words of thanks, and last-minute crusts of bread thrust into the hands of leavers. Sonny had witnessed these emotional scenes during other evacuations, but it did not prepare him for the pain of his own leaving. Put simply, the escapers were gutted to say goodbye to the families who had cared for them during their time on the run.

 Kayleen M. Hazlehurst

Loaded and ready to go, two of their group pushed oars against the sand while helpers waded in to guide the hulk beyond the breaking waves. They drifted out on the current. The engine would not be started until the crowd had dispersed and the barge was well away from the shore. Men hung on the edge of the vessel to drink in their last vision of Crete.

Sonny raised his eyes to the hills. There, thirty more of their friends lined the cliff top—rifles in hand, ammunition slung across their chests, their dark clothing catching the wind. Beside the rebels stood two monks and a priest, their black cassocks hitched up to access the pistols in their belts.

As the first rays broke over the sallow hills, glints of light reflected back to the wayfarers from the silverwork of knives and the barrels of guns.

part five

38

The Thirteenth Man

1943

Sea fog gave them cover as they paddled the barge from the shore. Soon it would lift, making them wish they had one more shrouding hour of darkness. There was a stillness among the men, each traveller needing to dwell on his own leaving.

Sonny went over the names of the men assembled with them on the boat. Besides Mo, there were two other Australians. Tony Nelson and Lloyd Masters, who'd grown up in the country town of Bathurst, had enlisted on the same day with the 2nd Australian Imperial Force. The best mates were put with the 2nd/11th Battalion and had set out together after the withdrawal from Rethymnon.

The third New Zealander to join them was Alvin Rogers. Sonny and Lucky welcomed Alvin as a fellow Kiwi, even though he was not a member of their own battalions. The older man, previously employed in the Whangārei Postal Service, was familiar with the communities of the Far North. On discovering this, Sonny hoped he and Alvin might trade a few stories in the days ahead.

Among the British soldiers was Sergeant Sykes from Birmingham, whose father and grandfather had worked in the metal trades. Arthur Sykes struck Sonny as a man who took his responsibilities as an NCO seriously. The second Brit was Roland Franks, a sapper, whose engineering skills should help keep the barge moving. Bernie Patterson, a man of diminished teeth but much banter, had been an army cook. Poor Bernie was unlikely to get his hands on a frying pan until they reached land.

Sonny knew little about Omar, a Palestinian, and Ahmet, a Turkish Cypriot. Both men spoke a little English, but they sat in the corner of the boat looking out of place. Sonny knew he would have to work at making them feel part of the group. As volunteers with the British Army, and fellow soldiers in the fight against Hitler, these lesser-known countrymen still deserved his respect. Deo made up their number to twelve.

The beach had emptied as figures melted into the colourless hues of rock and brush. One party remained. At the foot of the cliff two men stood beside what could only be a donkey. Makos and Paulos were keeping watch to make sure their friends got away without incident.

Each passenger carried his own gear and water bottle. Two years in hiding had brought them low. They were gaunt, bearded residues of their former selves. Men who'd lived with the peasants and shepherds were in better condition than those who'd stayed close to the starving towns. Sonny would have to gauge the health of all of them to identify who was sick and who was wounded. He didn't want anyone dying on this trip.

Roland Franks came to his elbow. 'Time to start up, old boy. We need to put as many miles as we can between us and land.'

'Righto. Can you give Lucky a hand?'

'Which one is Lucky?'

'The Kiwi bloke over there. He's checked the engine and says it's okay.'

Sapper Franks glanced to one side. 'I don't want to step on anyone's toes.'

'That's fine, Roland. Lucky will be glad of your help.'

From the minute they set out Deo stuck close to Sonny. As their band leader lay dying, Sonny had made Deacon a promise to see his son safely to Egypt. Strong loyalties developed during wartime, but from Deo's perspective a rebel's allegiances were written in blood. The young fighter wanted to know everything that was going on between the men on the barge.

Ten miles out to sea, and the water was getting choppy, but the engine kept pushing them through the waves. Roland Franks laid a rough chart on the floor to sketch their course from Crete to North Africa.

'We should avoid Tobruk or any part of Libya,' the sapper said, pointing to a peninsula. 'If we come to shore south-east of here, we'll

 Kayleen M. Hazlehurst

be in Egypt. Sidi Barrani is not too far from Alexandria. There's a road along this coast. Likely, we'll run into some of our chaps who can get us to Cairo.'

Sonny searched his pack. 'A schoolteacher gave me this atlas.'

Roland flipped over the pages. 'Yes,' he said, deciphering the Greek. 'See here. This is where we're headed.' They put their heads together to estimate distances.

Someone let out a shout. 'Object to port!' Bernie hollered.

Bernie Patterson had set himself on 'crow's nest' duty, with Arthur helping him scan the waters. Sonny and two others took out their binoculars to see what Bernie had sighted. Something to the left was bobbing in the water. As they came closer they saw a man draped over a log the size of a small tree. Then an arm went up.

'He's alive!' Arthur cried. 'Lucky, slow the engine!'

Tony had grabbed a strong rope and his friend Lloyd was leaning over the side, dangling a wooden plank.

'Crikey, mate,' said Lloyd, stretching to reach the floater. 'Where did you come from?'

'Looks like you're on your way to Australia,' Tony said.

Sonny turned to Roland. 'This is going to be difficult.' The side of the barge was steep and the man looked severely weakened. 'Who knows how long he's been paddling out here?'

Bernie stripped off to his shorts and singlet. 'I'm the smallest. Lower me on that rope and I'll grab him.'

'Can you swim, Bernie?' Sonny asked.

'Don't need to. My friends here won't let go of the rope. Will you, fellas?'

Tony raised his eyebrows. 'Lose our cook, are you mad?'

They tied the rope around Bernie's waist and gave it a tug.

Mo stepped up. 'Give the rope to me. Arthur, help me anchor this thing. Think of it like a tug of war. Ahmet, you and Omar grab the other end.'

Bernie clambered down the side of the barge and took hold of the log. 'Don't worry, chum. We've got you. What's your name?'

'Harry,' the man croaked. 'I need water.'

'Hey, chuck us some water, will ya?' A bottle tied to a piece of fishing line was lowered. 'Here matey, have a swig of this,' Bernie said, putting it to Harry's lips.

The man drank greedily until water ran from the corner of his mouth, and Bernie gently retrieved the bottle.

'Okay. Do you think you're strong enough to pull yourself up the side of the barge? Here, use my rope … That's right … Doing well … Now reach up. Those Aussie boys with the long arms will pull you in.'

Lucky reversed the motor to keep the barge from pulling away.

'Say, Bernie,' Sonny called down in his most courteous voice. 'If it's not too much trouble, do you mind handing up that tree? We'll send down another rope.'

'Not at all, Captain … Happy to oblige … I'll do it right before I drown.'

After the rescue of the thirteenth man, Sonny was given the honorary title of 'Captain'. Harry Gibson, an English airman, had sunk in a leaky boat during his third attempt to escape from Crete. Everyone agreed it was a miracle he was still alive. At the end of the day the sergeant, who owned a prayer book, offered to hold a service to give thanks and to bless their boat—proudly named the *Dittany*.

⌁

Another letter had come from Winifred.

Api saw how her correspondence weighed upon Hēmi. A year ago, she had left for Hobsonville to train with the Women's Auxiliary Air Force. Then, after some months of working in Hamilton, she was transferred to Air Force Headquarters in Wellington. The couple had seen each other a few times, but it was obvious her life had taken a different turn.

Winifred's letters were always cheery, making the war effort sound exciting. She had made new friends. Girls who went to dances and picture shows together. In contrast, Hēmi's life on the farm seemed dull and uneventful. With Sonny and Tama lost, and most of his generation gone

Kayleen M. Hazlehurst

to war, the situation had somehow beaten down the brother left behind. Guilt, Api supposed.

Over the milking, Hēmi confessed how much he missed the challenges of his army training, before they sent him back to the farm.

'Will you answer this letter?' Api asked.

'I don't know, Dad. Probably not this time. I think Winnie has a new life now.'

'I'll send off a note. Winifred's a good girl. We don't want to hurt her.'

'Say hello to her for me.'

'Have you given some more thought about Atarangi?'

Hēmi did not reply.

'You know Mum is keen to make the match?'

'I know.'

'Watch out, Hēmi. Your mother will start organising your wedding.'

'Does Ata even want me?'

<center>~~~</center>

About twenty-five miles out, motoring at about five knots while they tried to slip past the last island of Gavdos, they heard a heart-stopping hum. A reconnaissance plane was searching the coast for anything suspicious.

Nothing about them looked innocent. They weren't a patrol boat, a fishing caïque, or even a trading vessel going about its business. Who wouldn't be suspicious of a landing barge heading for the open sea?

Mo and Roland stood beside Sonny and they stared at the sky.

'What's the worst they can do to us?' Sonny asked Roland.

'Spy planes fly at high altitudes beyond the range of our rifles. Their purpose is to report on the sea traffic, but they can also act as strike aircraft.'

'You mean if they don't like the look of us?'

'Yeah,' Mo interrupted. 'If they don't like the look of us, we're dog meat. Ask Harry.'

Their newly acquired airman, who now sat under a pile of blankets, looked a little less blue around the gills. A strip of dried goat, with some raisins and nuts, seemed to have sorted him out.

Who Disturbs the Kūkupa?

'We have company, Harry. What do you think?'

Harry studied the plane. 'It's a Junkers 86. You can be sure he's seen us. He won't waste a bomb but he might try a few bursts from his guns.'

Mo fingered his rifle. 'Yeah, but to do that he'll have to come low.'

'No, mate,' Sonny answered. 'We won't stand a chance. Let's hope he's not interested.'

'Perhaps we should give him the Nazi salute,' Mo offered.

Sonny laughed. 'When I was sailing to Crete the Luftwaffe came calling. So I ran up a Nazi flag and waved at the pilot.'

'Cunning bugger. Did it work?'

'I'm still standing.'

They looked at the skipper in the steering hut. Lucky was focused like a maniac on getting them past Gavdos before they were seen.

'How far do these blighters fly out to sea, Harry?'

'Anyone's guess … Thirty or forty miles.'

'Better warn Lucky.'

The German bomber dropped down, banking to give the pilot a better view.

A bargeman could have been carting produce or wood. Instead, they were a handful of worthless escapers waiting to be used as target practice. *If only I'd brought a tarpaulin to hide under. I can almost hear the bastard laughing.*

'Take cover!' Sonny commanded as the plane lined up for a return sweep. 'Roll to the sides!' He saw Lucky working the rudder. No one had more raw instinct than this country boy. Lucky would swerve without capsizing them.

'Incoming!' Bernie warned.

Bernie and Roland crouched beneath the forward ramp. The others thrust their bodies against the armour-plated walls of the barge.

'Heads down!' Roland yelled.

Bullets staccatoed across the water in front of them.

Lucky veered to port, so the rest of the bullets skimmed along the side and passed beyond the stern. Sonny heard the *crack, crack, crack* of lead on steel and prayed nobody was hit.

 Kayleen M. Hazlehurst

Dittany became her own beast. She dug her hooves into the sea like a trusted mare, sending a surge of water over her side. Lucky spun the wheel, correcting the balance of the stalled vessel, and then ploughed ahead.

'He's turning!' Bernie screamed. 'Stay down!'

Sonny imagined how enraged the pilot must be, having failed in his first strike.

Something in the atmosphere changed. Voices stilled. Time slowed. Motion became laborious. Had the pilot regained his humour? Had he seen that this game was no longer sporting, or had he been called away?

For whatever reason, at the next pass the aircraft started to climb. They gazed in stunned silence as the last snarl of the plane faded back into the clouds, not yet realising Crete was forever behind them.

~39~

Due South

On the fourth night, they entered the belly of the whale. The sky was so dark Harry Gibson was struggling to find even the North Star to guide them.

'Bloody clouds,' Harry said to no one in particular.

They needed to head due south, but this didn't help much with no sightings of land. There were four modest compasses between them, but after months of corrosion and trauma, no two of them agreed. As an RAF navigator, Harry knew all about faulty compasses and the problems they caused. The airman preferred to put his trust in the sun and stars. He used a sextant when he could get hold of one, which wasn't in this instance.

Sonny wished his own father had taught him celestial navigation. The seafaring skills he had learned were limited to managing a boat between the landmarks of the shore and coastal islands. Besides, the night sky in the South Pacific was quite different from that in the northern hemisphere.

Harry had stuck a knife into a plank of wood. In daylight he could determine their direction from the thin shadow of the blade cast by the sun. 'If we hold our course,' he said, 'we should be all right.'

The voyagers had settled with their coats and blankets across the deck. Sonny examined the starless sky. He thought about his lost mates, and the lives he had taken, feeling the weight of death upon his soul. *What a terrible thing it is to kill.*

He reached into his pocket and withdrew a fistful of shelled walnuts. He had saved them to stave off the gnawing hunger before trying to sleep. Their attempts at fishing from the barge had been unsuccessful. Whatever

　　　　Kayleen M. Hazlehurst

was working against them, engine noise or the line dragging too close to the surface, unless they caught something very soon they would run out of food.

'Can you spare a couple of those nuts?'

The voice in the dark was Mo, resting near him. Big men suffered the most on short rations. Sonny reached over to drop the remaining nuts into the man's hand.

'You owe me.'

'Righto.'

'How's the leg?'

'Throbbing.'

Sonny fetched his torch. 'Let me have a look.'

Mo cried out as they turned down his trousers. Blood and yellow fluid had soaked through the doctor's bandage. When Sonny pulled back the dressing, he was shocked to see Mo's stitches had broken apart.

'Bugger!'

'Must have happened when I took that dive for cover.'

Sonny was thankful more of them hadn't been hurt during the aerial attack.

'What's up?' Lucky came to sit beside them, having handed steering duties over to Roland.

'I need to give this thing a wash. Mo, can you take off your trousers so we can keep them dry for you? Lucky, get me some seawater while I help Mo.'

'Sure, Sonny.' Lucky attached his tin mug to a piece of string and dipped it overboard.

From his medicinal herbs, Sonny extracted a clump of dittany. 'Here, Mo. Chew this but don't swallow.'

Mo's thigh was fiercely hot, but the wound looked less angry after it was washed.

Sonny held his hand under Mo's chin. 'Okay. Spit out that wad for me.'

Lucky knelt down, holding the torch. 'What've you got there?'

'It's that special plant I told you about. I'm going to pack Mo's wound with it.' He took the masticated leaves and pulled them into the shape of a round plaster to cover the hole in Mo's thigh. 'You can swallow the juice now, it will do you good.'

Mo swallowed as instructed. 'Poisoning me is a high price for a couple of nuts.'

'If I'd wanted to poison you, I'd have done it weeks ago.'

'Thanks!' Mo watched the wad being applied to his leg. 'What's that supposed to do?'

'Heal infection.' Sonny bound the wound with clean rags. 'I'll give it another wash tomorrow. Sorry, I've got nothing for the pain.'

'I've got something,' Lucky said, and he crept off with the torch.

Mo looked over his shoulder. 'Bet that boy has a hidden flask of ouzo.'

'Let's hope.'

At breakfast they opened their only tin of bully beef. All the bread and dried meat had gone. Sonny figured fish at the centre of the Mediterranean were deep-sea dwellers. *That's why they're so hard to find ... What I could do with a long trawling net.*

Half a mug of water, a handful of dried figs and two teaspoons of the bully beef each. They had all become weak, and despondency was setting in. During the day they sat around like limp sheep or stared morosely at the horizon. Any energy spent talking was about either food or home. Arthur and Roland, in addition to keeping watch for ships or floating debris, had been assigned to guarding the water bottles.

Another concern was the engine. For miles it had chugged along without complaint, but close to sunset on the fifth evening it spluttered and stopped. Roland and Lucky went to have a look. Before they stripped down the engine, Sonny checked their fuel supply. He lifted the canister and gave it a shake. The last person to fill the tank hadn't mentioned they'd run out. He unscrewed the cap and poured in the dregs.

When the engine whined but refused to start again they stood around watching each other's faces.

'So that's it,' somebody said at last.

It was a magical night, drifting under a dome of stars with silver-peaked

     Kayleen M. Hazlehurst

waves rising above amethyst dips and troughs. Even the silence was enchanting, for a time. Yet the brutal truth was far different. They were moving at a slow pace, more south-west than south, and could easily continue this way without ever reaching land.

Sergeant Sykes pulled himself to his feet and took out his black book. 'We'll think of something, lads. Would you like me to say some prayers? Bernie, hold the lamp for me, there's a good chap?'

They all bent their heads.

O Almighty Lord. Forgiver of sinners. Punisher of the wicked. Take pity on Thy poor servants and show us Thy way. Keep us safe, that we might strive for peace and justice in the name of our Lord, Jesus Christ. Amen.

After a few prayers the atmosphere lightened. Hearts had been kindled with a flicker of hope. The sergeant was right. The Divine may or may not look kindly upon a handful of starving seafarers, but from now on they would have to depend on themselves.

Alvin Rogers led them in a couple of hymns. Before the war, Alvin had been a church organist when he wasn't being a postmaster. 'Awake My Soul'—*Praise God, from whom all blessings flow*—was sung with fervour. This was followed by 'Abide with Me'—*Heaven's morning breaks and earth's vain shadows flee.*

Then came the popular songs. 'There'll Always be an England'—*Wherever there's a cottage small, beside a field of grain*—rendered loudest by the Tommies. 'Goodnight Sweetheart'—*Till we meet tomorrow, sleep will banish sorrow.* This was crooned by everyone, with few dry eyes.

Sonny studied these sentimental soldiers. They might sing songs, but every one of them would slay the enemy of his God—as long as in death, he was not alone.

Sonny leaned his back against the siding.

'Let me tell you a story,' he said. 'Once we had a horse …'

Mo got to his elbows. 'Hello. A horse story …'

Sonny waited while the others got comfortable. 'It was really my mother's horse. She had ridden it to school as a girl. When she married my father the horse came with her. By the time Mum was a young mother the horse had retired. He was a wise old animal with a sense of humour who didn't mind children scooting around under his feet.'

'Did this 'orse have a name?' Bernie asked.

'Old Hōiho, we called him. Old Horse. Sometimes Dad would hold the little ones on his back and walk them around the house. Hōiho considered himself one of the family. He enjoyed looking through the windows and eating the flowers.'

'Sounds like a character,' said Roland.

'What this horse loved the most was teasing my mother,' Sonny continued. 'One day, when Mum was hanging out the washing, Hōiho lay on the grass and put his legs straight up in the air. Mum let out a shriek and came running over. "Hōiho! My dear friend, are you in pain? Have you died?"' Sonny put on a voice to imitate his mother.

The listeners chuckled and sighed.

'We all raced into the paddock and stood around his old wrinkly body and the dogs sniffed his tail. Someone poked the horse in the ribs and his bottom lip trembled. Then it fluttered to show off his yellow teeth and he opened one eye. Mum gave Hōiho a shove. "Oh, you cheeky one. Get up, you old bag of bones." Us kids were laughing and rolling around with the horse on the grass. I don't know how many times he pulled that trick on my mother.'

Sonny's account of Old Horse had set them vying to tell their own tales.

'Did you hear about the shepherd who outwitted the Germans?' Tony asked. 'Soldiers were taking children into forced labour, carting them off in trucks. A load of them were stopped by a mob of sheep. The guards were shouting at the shepherd, demanding the road be cleared. While the old Greek made a woeful attempt at moving the sheep, the children were hopping off the truck like fleas and dashing for the hills.'

'But the Cretans weren't so easily fooled.' Lloyd commented. 'A man in torn uniform hobbled into town pretending to be a British officer. He

     Kayleen M. Hazlehurst

spoke English and was begging for food and shelter. The sharp-eyed residents saw he lacked the British gait and decided he had eaten too many German sausages.'

'We heard,' Arthur said. 'The villagers grab the imposter by the throat and thrash him like a donkey.'

'Yeah. They dragged him to the nearest garrison, all the while scoffing at the "British dog" and declaring their loyalty to the "great German Reich". The commandant could only smile weakly and thank them for their trouble.'

Now the men were howling with laughter and holding their skinny ribs to stop the pain.

40

The Albatross

Seven ladies bustled into the hall, each carrying armfuls of flowers, fronds of fern, strips of flax and rolls of raffia. The craft group and their friends were busy with preparations for the wedding ceremony. Beyond the doors, propped open to invite in the evening air, there were other women seeing to the banquet tables. As this was an aristocratic marriage, they expected many visitors of high rank to attend. Everyone would be welcomed onto the marae for the celebrations, and it would be an auspicious day.

'The church flowers are done,' declared one of the seven as they entered to rounds of greetings, 'and we have saved a few for the hall.'

Someone took the leftover flowers into the kitchen to be arranged into jars taken from under the sink. The best vases, along with the best blooms, had already been given to the church.

Tomorrow the wedding service would be conducted by the Anglican minister. This would be followed by a priest's blessing—an invocation imparted by Miriama to ward off evil spirits and to invite the atua to preserve the young couple in good health and prosperity. The children of the dance group were to perform in costume and, most likely, there would be outbreaks of singing among the adults. Despite their sorrows, there was great excitement that Atarangi Tahiri, a puhi woman, and Hēmi Wirima, of rangatira birth, were to be wed.

Miriama had prepared Hēmi's feathered cloak, and the flowers to crown the bride's flowing locks had been delivered to Nan. The making of the garland had been supervised by Miriama, with the help of two ladies, at a secret place away from the eyes of men. It had been made with flowers closest to Atarangi's heart—white lacebark, fluffy clusters of white rātā, and delicate clematis picked from the forest vines. This war had wearied them all but Miriama anticipated that in a year from now a new child might bring the promise of a brighter future.

It was unusual for a bride to visit the hall the night before her wedding. The women preferred to keep the fruits of their labours hidden until they were revealed to the young couple on their wedding day. The arrival of Atarangi had not been foreseen. As she stumbled through the open doors, drunk with anguish, the state of the girl alarmed them.

'Where is she?' Atarangi demanded.

'Old one, you're needed,' someone called into the kitchen.

Miriama came out carrying a spray of flowers for the table. 'Hello. I thought you'd be resting. Is Nan with you?'

'No. I came to see you.' Ata took Miriama's hand. 'E pou, I don't think this is a good idea.'

The women stopped what they were doing and held their breath.

'Are you having a change of heart, Atarangi?'

'You know I love Hēmi, but I can't make a good life for him.'

'And what is a good life?'

Ata touched the petals of the flowers. 'I'm sure you're going to tell me.'

'A good life is to care for others and to not wreak havoc upon the universe.'

'I don't see how choosing my own husband can cause any kind of havoc!'

'Our choices can be our friends, or they can be our enemies. How do we know the difference?'

'That is easy,' the girl answered flatly. 'Choices that harm us are our enemies.'

'Āe. And there are some that appear to be our friends, and some that are not so friendly.'

Ata looked away. 'You say this about alcohol, but I know you're not talking about drinking. So why don't you say what you mean?'

The women had now clustered around to listen. Some with their hands on their hips, others anxiously touching their faces.

Miriama considered her words. 'One way to measure the worth of a friend is to observe how they treat the things we value. If a man would treasure the widow of his brother, surely this is true fidelity?'

'I was *never* Sonny's wife.'

The women muttered agreement among themselves.

'Atarangi has never been married,' Mata said.

'Āe, she is nobody's widow,' protested Heti.

'Does marrying the betrothed of a brother still apply?'

'Why does it have to, if the girl is unwilling?'

Ignoring these interruptions, Miriama pressed on. 'Hēmi is a perfect husband for you, dear. Does he not share your love of the whānau and your love of the land?'

'I tell you, I'm *not* the right one for him.'

'*Ah,* I see. You're sticking up for Winifred. That girl has gone—'

'You are *assuming* this. She may come back.'

'The poor boy cares for you, Ata, and he respects who you are.'

'Hēmi doesn't have a clue who I am! Do you think I have no choice in love, Miriama? You think this sacrifice is my only pathway to happiness?'

Some of the women gasped. Never had they heard Atarangi address an elder by their personal name. But it wasn't the first time they had seen a bride come unstuck. On such a night, all would be forgiven.

Miriama flinched and lowered her voice. 'This marriage is your pathway to greatness. Happiness may or may not follow, but you will always have a choice.'

The girl was staring at them, wild-eyed. She dismissed the tearful faces of the aunties and swept her hand over the wedding preparations.

'Choice is *exactly* what I *don't* have. I was supposed to marry Sonny!' Weeping now, Atarangi fled from the hall and down the steps.

'Wait, Ata. Please wait.'

Miriama rushed to the doorway to watch the slender figure running away in the moonlight. She heard the distant cry of an owl and turned to her friends.

'We must go after her. It's too late to be alone on the cliff.'

The women gathered their skirts and set off with Miriama, the seven who had prepared the church flowers and two others from the craft group. The older ones, whose knees could no longer endure running, stayed to finish

     Kayleen M. Hazlehurst

the hall. Fearful for Atarangi, and frightened themselves of the dark, the bride-rescuers hurried away without even a lamp to guide them.

The path behind the houses narrowed as it went uphill. Straw-like grasses, caught in the glow of the moon, provided a guiding line for their feet. As they made their way up the sandy path and onto the ridge the track became an indistinct ribbon of blue. There was no sign of Atarangi. The black night of Hinenuitepō seemed to have swallowed her up. The women looked around and called out the name of the loved one.

Miriama noticed a movement. 'Over there!'

The girl stood alone against the indigo light, staring out to sea, as if she willed from it a different destiny.

'Sonny is alive … I know he is!'

Miriama stepped forward. 'Oh, my dear, I'm so sorry. Please come away from the cliff. We can talk …'

More begging words came from the aunties, who dared go no closer.

'Dear one, please come back where it's safe …'

'Come away. Come away. This is too dangerous …'

'You can't see where you're standing …'

'Let us help you. Everything will work out …'

'But I promised to wait for him!' Ata's voice raised a pitch. 'Sonny, where are you!'

Miriama stretched out her hand as she heard pebbles and soil crumble away.

'Ata, come back. *RIGHT NOW!*'

A startled nesting bird took flight from a lower ledge, making Atarangi twist back as the seabird swooped by.

Uttering the faintest of sounds …

Her hands brushing against an updraft of ocean air …

She fell.

———

At daybreak on the sixth day, Sonny glanced up at the sky. The rays of the rising sun had fired the feathers of an albatross, brilliant gold, as it passed overhead in slow, steady curves.

41

Fluke's Turtle

An albatross crossing over the boat was all the evidence he needed. The ocean bird would be heading for land. By its direction, he could see they had swung too far west. Mo raised his rifle, but Sonny floored him with a footy tackle.

'Crikey. Watch the leg.'

'Kill the albatross and you kill the guide.'

Mo looked abashed. 'Sorry, mate. I'm just a bushie. What do I know about seabirds?'

'We have to turn the boat, Mo. I'm going to push it from the water.'

Deo insisted on joining him. Everyone agreed, Sonny and his Cretan friend were both strong swimmers, and the Australians were the best ones for pulling them back in.

A barge was difficult enough to control, but now they had lost their steering. Sonny and Deo, standing in their underwear with long ropes tied around their waists, waited for Tony and Lloyd to lower them over while Harry confirmed again which way was due south.

'We'll turn her nose from the right,' Sonny told Deo.

Mo watched them lean back and crawl feet first down the side. 'Let me know if you need help.'

'Thanks, Mo. Two of us should do it.'

'Have you got a knife?'

'What for?'

'Who knows?'

Sonny locked eyes with Deo. He had never seen a bandit unarmed. Deo indicated he had a knife stowed at the back of his leather belt. Sonny's own knife was still on the deck. Side by side they plunged in, made breathless from the shock of the cold, then they manoeuvred their

Kayleen M. Hazlehurst

way towards the front, pulling their tethers with them. There, they pressed their shoulders and forearms on the steel, kicking hard against the water and rolling the hulk over several ranks of waves until it faced further east.

'That should do it,' Harry called down.

There were cheers from those who had found the strength to stand and watch. They trod water while Sonny patted the bottom of the barge to make sure it was solid.

Deo lunged at a floating sea sponge and tucked it into his belt. 'Could be useful.'

Sonny looked further out. 'Thought there weren't sharks out here.'

'There'll be a few. Why?'

'What's that coming at us? Should we make a quick exit?'

Deo scanned the water. 'Don't know. Hasn't got a fin.'

'Mo, have you got your binoculars? What's that thing out there? Is it a body?'

'No, mate … It's a bloody big turtle … Looks dead.'

Deo reached to untie the rope from his waist. 'I'm going to get it.'

'Deo, no!'

'Don't be a fool!' Tony shouted. 'If you lose your rope, you'll never catch up with us.'

'Hang on, I've got an idea,' Sonny said. 'Tony, toss me your end of Deo's rope. That will double his length. For God's sake, Lloyd, don't let go of my rope.'

Tony deftly dropped Deo's rope into Sonny's hand and called down, 'We'll keep a good grip on you, old son.'

The activity below was stirring some interest. If sea scavengers had left a boatload of hungry men a little turtle meat, there was some hope for them.

Lucky's head appeared above the ledge. 'Hey, you might have enough rope to reach it.'

'Better be quick,' said Mo.

Sonny tracked Deo, holding the boy's rope as he pierced the waves with a slick style of overarm.

'*Ti diáolo!*' Deo swore and slashed his palms on the surface.

'What the hell!' Sonny's heart did a flip when he saw Deo streaking back. The upside-down turtle was motoring towards them. Something was propelling the dead thing. Churning up the water. Breathing in short, sharp snorts.

Deo reached for his knife.

'Wait Deo, what kind of fish …?'

Behind the upended shell came the earnest face, flattened ears and frantic paddling of a black dog with his jaw clamped onto a flipper.

The mutt was a young sheepdog like those kept by the shepherds. On Crete Sonny had seen the poor wretches from the destroyed villages, all lost and starving. Kiwi soldiers occasionally took pity on them. Had this dog fallen overboard or been a survivor from a capsized vessel? It was a sure sign that other escapers had passed this way.

'Okay, boy, I've got you.' Sonny scooped the animal into his arms while the dog continued to paw at the air. 'How long have you been swimming around, eh? Damn it, if you haven't got yourself a turtle. Mind if we share a bit?'

Sonny shunted the turtle over to Deo, who stuck his blade into the carcass before they swam back to the barge.

'Which one's dinner?' Mo asked as two men, one dog and a half-eaten turtle fell in a misshapen heap on the deck.

Sonny scowled. 'Not the dog. That's his turtle, and he's just bought himself a ticket.'

Alvin put one hand on his chin and examined the new arrival. 'That's one fluky dog.'

'Another mouth to feed,' someone grumbled.

Lucky bent to pet the mutt. 'Don't worry, Fluke. You can be our fishing dog. Nobody will eat you then.'

Sonny turned his eyes skywards. A monstrous head of cloud was rearing in the east, and the air was becoming raw and chilly. It reminded him of another squall, at another time in the Cyclades. A shot of fear passed through him. According to his father, storms at sea never bode well, but an ocean tempest was completely beyond his experience.

He remembered what a Greek fisherman had told him. Waves at the centre of the Mediterranean could reach as high as mountains.

    Kayleen M. Hazlehurst

~42~

Fitful Winds

When Sonny first looked south there was barely a haze on the horizon. Now, in the morning's wet light, he saw a breeze had got up and he was eager, along with Arthur and Roland, to keep the barge travelling in the right direction.

Roland pointed to the back of the boat. 'We have to create some drag. It's better than drifting for days or being spun about by fitful winds.'

'What do you suggest?' Sonny asked Roland.

'We could use an oar for steering.'

'As long as we don't lose it overboard.'

Arthur shrugged. 'What choice do we have? Unless there is a thick plank somewhere.'

They looked through their stack of wood, finding nothing suitable.

'When we land our oars might be all that stand between us and the rocks.'

Arthur ran his fingers through his hair. 'How about tying something to the rudder. Make a tiller?'

Roland frowned. 'The rudder is fixed to the steering shaft and we lost control of that when we lost the engine.'

'Okay, we'll use an oar,' Sonny said. 'Tie it with a slack rope to the stern.'

Others were coming over to listen to the debate.

'Holding ourselves against this wind will be a battle,' Harry commented. 'If we could catch it somehow.' He gave the log that had been his life-raft for twenty hours a respectful tap with his boot.

Arthur's smile broadened. 'My Aunt Molly's bloomers, they would have made excellent sails. Massive woman.'

The others agreed that cotton bloomers might well have done the trick. 'What about blankets?'

'Eh?'

'Blankets will catch the wind,' Mo repeated. 'We only have to figure out how to rig them.'

Sonny nudged the log. He had manufactured a tree mast once before on Gyáros. That strange uninhabited island with its befriending seals. *It's not enough to fix the steering. To cut through waves, a boat needs power.* Roland had said it plainly. 'Fitful winds'. You either harnessed them, or you were blown off course.

He looked around at the ardent faces. 'Come on, fellas. Let's build us some sails.'

Sustained by their meal of turtle meat they got on their knees, tools in hands, chattering and using the deck to plan out their next great feat of engineering. The longest crosspieces scavenged from the woodpile were attached to the twelve-foot log with nails, reinforced with wire and ropes.

They tested the weight of the blankets. There was room to stretch out six, but should it be four? Would the frame be robust enough if the blankets became drenched with spray or rain? Would the first strong wind tear down the sails or blow out the excess water? They had one chance to get this right.

Someone suggested they use bootlaces to stitch together the blankets. Half of them worked on this, threading the ends of the laces through the thick woollen cloth and tying the ends.

It took their combined strength to raise the craggy log and heavy sails. While four held the mast firm, the others lashed it to the loading ramp. They stepped back. When the thing didn't fall over there were joyous shouts and whoops. Even the dog joined in.

The effect was instant. Sails curled and billowed. Blankets pulled taut. Bootlaces tightened. The boat paused and corrected itself. Then their brilliant *Dittany* sprang forward and flew off like a startled duck.

They ran before the wind, making up for lost time. Dehydration was their

     Kayleen M. Hazlehurst

greatest enemy. This 'lost time' was more a measure of how long they could survive without water. The answer was—not long. Death would come to them in forty-eight to seventy-two hours.

Roland was sure they had covered only two thirds of their journey. He reminded them that some of this distance they'd drifted west. 'I would say we are one hundred and twenty miles from the North African coast.'

Sonny had a sinking feeling. *This is still a hell of a long way.* Although they were clipping along with their sails, they would run out of rations well before they made landfall. Not that he was one to declare doom. People on this boat had guns and might decide to use them. If their last meal had been sea turtle, it stood to reason that the fish would return. They could drink fish blood, that's what he would tell them.

He bent to give Fluke a scratch. 'Come on, boy. We could do with a bit of your luck.'

The storm came from the north-east. Flashes of silver split the sky, leaving the air crackling. Within minutes the raindrops splashed down. Excited men looked for anything that might hold fresh water—plates, mugs, tins, hats, boots. They turned their faces to catch the drops in their parched mouths. Where water ran in rivulets across the deck Deo sopped up the precious liquid with his sea sponge and squeezed it into the necks of bottles.

A new wind was driving a black curtain across the sea, whipping the waves into spray that stung their eyes. Then they were hit by an explosive torrent of rain. Three men crowded into the steering hut. The rest took shelter under the narrow gunwale. Terrified, the dog wedged himself between Sonny and Lucky. Minutes earlier the animal had been seen skittering across the deck and it looked like he'd hurt his leg.

'You're a smart dog,' Lucky said, gripping Fluke by the scruff of the neck to stop him from being flung overboard. They were all frightened and soaked to the skin.

There was little point trying to navigate in fifteen-foot swells and no hope of steering the barge with an oar. These were real waves with rolling peaks and deep gullies. *Landing craft are not built for this,* Sonny thought, as the barge nose-dived into another rise and slapped down on the next fall.

Any of these waves could swamp them, or the crashing impact on the hull could break them apart. *If we capsize it will all be over.*

～

The old woman saddled the horse and rode alone to the foot of the Brynderwyns. People were still searching for Atarangi. Api and Hēmi had left early with a group of boats to look for the girl's frail body. Miriama had gone back to the forest because this sacred sphere was the only place she could find solace. *Tāne, comforter of birds and man.* The dog Kete had followed her, but Miriama sensed a storm brewing, and as she tied the horse to the fence she ordered the dog to go home.

She entered the forest and set out on the rough track, stumbling past the moss-covered trunks and fallen logs. Kauri and ponga drew in around her, forest birds flew near and low cloud streamed down from the mountain like a river of tears. Her lamentations so pierced her soul that she failed to feel Tāne's ferns and branches grasping at her skirts and scratching at her arms.

Hand over hand, she climbed until she crossed onto the sharp rocks of the summit. A tower of cloud had settled above the peak. With her back thrust against the rocks, she scanned the rough fields back to the coast, where rain was sweeping in from the sea.

'O Mountain,' she called out. 'Hear the voice of this white-haired one.'

Great Tūmatauenga, here is my life.
If bones must be broken, let them be my bones.
If hearts are to be torn out, gladly I offer you mine.
This mother calls you—already she has sacrificed.
Consume me, Mighty Tū, and save the life of my sons.

O Waters of Tangaroa … O Winds of Tāwhiri-mātea …
Launch the great canoe and set it forth from the harbour.
Steer it past the singing rocks and beyond the enemy's spears.
Let mountains be thy markers and seabirds be thy guides.
Find the way the ancestors once discovered,
with the Spirit held fast.

    Kayleen M. Hazlehurst

Peals of thunder rolled across the sky, making the mountain groan, carrying the inner voices she'd been taught to trust. *O faithful daughter, we have heard your lament. With you, we are well pleased.*

She felt a warmth by her leg. Kete had secretly followed her and was pulling at her skirt to come away before the rain and wind hit the mountain. *Who can question the loyal heart of a dog?*

—⁓—

The outer sails were flapping, and the mast was kicking from side to side.

'Fluke, stay here with Lucky.'

Sonny pulled himself along the metal railing, avoiding the same flying debris that had injured the dog. His internal compass told him they were being blown west again. Their only chance was to angle the barge across the waves. A slight adjustment would make all the difference to where they ended up—too sharp, and they would be hit broadside and flip.

He gauged the slope and speed of the churning hump of water behind them. Then he reached up to tilt the sails.

Something stirred deep within his being and from his chest came the resonance of a sacred chant. Sonny called out to Tāwhiri to turn back the ferocious winds and to Tangaroa to grant them a kinder sea. This close to death, how could a man's heart be heavy?

Dittany surfed across the wave, slanting in a new direction. As Sonny stared at the turbulent water he saw the silvery fingers of his atua rising up to guide them.

The Winter of their Resolve

Dittany sat motionless on the sea, blanket sails limp as foam trailed along the sides in creamy swirls. They woke cold and wet, stiff from exhaustion. During the night the wild winds had swept past them. There were no clouds for predicting the weather, no currents to indicate in which direction the land lay. No tohu. No signs from the gods. They were alone under an empty sky, with nothing but the certain madness of a salty sea all the way out to the horizon.

Sonny stumbled over the prostrate bodies to retrieve the fishing gear from the steering hut. It was their ninth day at sea, and around him were the haggard faces of the severely malnourished. Eyes were disappearing into dark sockets, all the voyagers were suffering from stomach problems and, since the storm, Sonny worried about pneumonia. His own cough had returned and there was pain deep in his chest. With few provisions or medicines left to sustain them, his priority was to find some fish.

What will I use for bait? … Fluke's turtle. Sonny took out his knife. From the leftovers, he cut away some juicy pieces of entrails and tips of flippers to fix on his hooks. Now, with the boat drifting at less than one knot, he could sink the lines into twenty feet of water where he hoped the fish would be.

After tying the lines to cleats on the decking, Sonny called the dog. 'Come here, boy. You can help with the fishing. Tell me when we get a bite.'

'Need a hand?' Lucky came up to him.

'Thanks, mate. Could you watch the lines while I get around the men? If we don't catch something today, we're …'

'I know. We're history … Never fear. Fluke and me will catch us some fish. You'll see. At least we've got ourselves a bit of rainwater.'

Sonny couldn't help smiling at Lucky's understatement, considering

Kayleen M. Hazlehurst

the drenching they'd received the night before. 'Āe, at least we've got that.' He stepped back from the gunwale. 'There you go. Four lines, eight hooks. Yell if you need me.'

'Right.' Lucky fixed a determined expression on his face. 'What did you use for bait?'

'Turtle bits.'

'You're a magician, Sonny.'

'I wish.' His thoughts turned again to Tama. In recent days, Sonny had felt his brother's energy around him. Their time together on Mount Olympus came back to him in fragments. The day they sighted the bronze eagle. Tama showing off in the rock pool. Their last moments together before the spirit people ushered the boy away.

He rubbed his eyes. They had been bothering him. Too much sun. *Hey, little brother. Any chance of sending us some fish?*

Sonny did his rounds again. He spent time with Alvin and Bernie, who had chummed up and seemed to be helping each other. Mo's leg was on the mend and he had gone back to his old ways of joshing the others. Tony and Lloyd were sharing memories of growing up in the back-blocks of Australia. It was hard going for everyone, but good humour and kindness were keeping them alive.

'Are we lost again, Harry?' he asked as he flushed out a nasty gash for the airman. Last night, Harry had cracked his forearm on the side of the boat while trying to dodge a flying hammer. Sonny realigned the two edges of skin and wrapped the wound in a piece of washed rag. He had a needle, but no thread left to stitch it.

'God, I hope we're not lost.' Harry studied Sonny's face. 'How's my arm?'

'Bruised, but I don't think you've chipped the bone.'

'Bloody sore.'

'At least your face isn't wearing a hammer. Keep it moving, you may need that arm.'

'I will, thanks. I'm concerned about the Palestinian.'

'What's wrong with him?'

'Yesterday he was groaning and holding his stomach. He's gone quiet since the storm.'

'I'll take a look. Come with me.'

Sonny lifted Omar's eyelids, finding his eyeballs had turned back.

'Any idea what's wrong with him, Ahmet?' Harry asked the man's friend.

The Cypriot looked away.

Sonny glanced at Harry. 'I hope you didn't eat any more of that turtle? It's gone rancid. I told everyone to stay away from it.'

'Turtle smells bad ... No eat turtle.'

'Good. For a minute I thought it was food poisoning.'

'Appendicitis?' Harry asked.

Sonny pressed Omar's lower right abdomen. Omar groaned but did not cry out as Sonny would have expected with an inflamed appendix. 'No, it's something else.'

'Thirsty,' Ahmet said. 'Every day Omar begs for water.'

'We're all thirsty,' Harry muttered.

'What have you been giving him?'

'Ahmet help.' The Cypriot waved his hand towards the sea. 'Plenty water.'

Sonny wiped his forehead. '*Bloody hell*, you've been giving Omar seawater!'

'Don't you know drinking seawater can kill a man?' Harry demanded.

Ahmet cringed and his face crumpled with misery. 'I make mistake.'

Sonny gripped Ahmet's shoulder. 'I'll sit with you both tonight. Don't be afraid.'

As they moved away, Sonny bent his head towards the Englishman. 'There's nothing we can do, Harry. The man's too far gone. His organs are shutting down.'

When they went to check the fishing lines, Lucky greeted them with shining eyes. At his feet lay two red mullet, a mackerel, a small shark and something that looked like seabream.

'There's fish here, Sonny! All we had to do was slow the boat long enough to drop a line.'

 Kayleen M. Hazlehurst

The catch was divided between the men and eaten raw, especially the shark's liver. Fluke got the fish eyes and cheeks, with a few licks of rainwater, and the guts were held back for bait.

Ka ki te puku, ka manawanui.
A full belly makes a brave heart.

They were all revived by the meal. Everyone except Omar, who could no longer eat. That night the Palestinian sank into a coma, and died four hours later. With the death, Ahmet spiralled into grief. Nobody knew much about the lives of these two soldiers, but Sonny was sure they had watched each other's backs during the fighting.

Arthur Sykes conducted the burial at sea and those who were strong enough assembled to offer solace. Deo sat beside Ahmet, explaining the service in a soft Greek voice. The Cypriot was too stricken to speak. The poor man blamed himself for his friend's death. As the body plunged into the sea, Ahmet raised a wail that brought Sonny sharply back to the first days of his escape—memories of the keening wind on top of Mount Olympus, and of his own remorse after Tama's passing.

Hope evaporated in Ahmet's eyes on that day. The danger was obvious, yet Sonny allowed the task of fishing to divert his attention. When he heard the shout, it was too late. Ahmet was sitting on the edge of the barge, tears streaming down, screaming his rage at the sky and brandishing his pistol.

A single shot. One bullet to the temple and Ahmet released himself from his painful world. He fell backwards, palms raised in a question, into the embracing hush of the sea. Few things shocked Sonny more on his journey than this one wasted life.

They entered their tenth day.

Under the moon the water in front of the boat was at its darkest blue, tempered with streaks of sea fire. Now the colour was changing. The phosphorous glow of a million tiny marine creatures brightened it to a brilliant green.

'Mo, take a look at this. Deo, Lucky, Harry, come and see.'

The five of them stared at the scene. The night breeze seemed not quite resolved whether to push them on or to leave them there to drift to eternity.

'Christ,' Mo said, as he faced the luminous ocean. 'It almost makes you believe in heaven.'

'Do you think this is the pearly gates?' Lucky asked, wide-eyed.

'I'm not dead!' Deo glared and gripped his pistol. He looked like he might shoot St Peter if he dared to appear.

At the centre of their vision the sea began to roil and churn. Froth and bubbles boiled up and expanded into a hump of white water.

'What is it?'

'Dunno.'

'I'll be damned!'

The first thing to rise was the conning tower. Then the colossal body of a submarine burst onto the surface, with streams of water cascading over its dark sides.

'It's a submarine!' Lucky yelled. 'Wake up everyone. It's a sub! It's a sub!'

Dittany rested her battered shell against the formidable steel structure. Greek sailors rushed out carrying ropes. A man leaned over to address them. He was plain-clothed but had the air of a senior officer.

'In a spot of bother?' asked the spokesman in an upper-crust British accent.

Submarines regularly offloaded and recovered commandos and Secret Service agents from Crete. Was this one of them?

Mo stood up proud. 'Nothing we can't manage,' he said. 'Which way is Egypt?'

The man laughed. 'We're going to Alexandria, if that would help. Care for a lift?'

'Hold on, I'll ask the Captain.' Mo turned to Sonny with a huge grin.

'Much appreciated,' Sonny answered. 'We've eleven survivors and one dog.'

'The crew will give you a hand. Welcome to the RHS *Papanikolis*.'

     Kayleen M. Hazlehurst

Once on board the Greek vessel the escaping servicemen were shown the greatest kindness. It seemed the Royal Hellenic Navy was as pleased to have found them as they were to be found. They were wrapped in blankets and given hot cocoa and sandwiches.

As the submarine dived to a safer depth with its prized cargo of lost soldiers, Sonny called out to his teina.

Look Tama. I am a whale. I flick my tail and make the waves lash against the warships. I am a whale and I am coming home!

From his bed in Alexandria, Sonny was watching light filter through the tall windows of the British General Hospital. Dozens of soldiers were convalescing in this ward. Some he knew, most he didn't.

Pleurisy, they said. How long had he fought through the pain and the fever, straining for every breath? During his delirium, images of childhood flickered across his eyelids. The setting sun turning summer hay to gold. Atarangi's laughter as he chased her through the paddocks. The sweet curve of her neck.

As heat raged through Sonny's body he relived every tree and every bird song, every dewdrop on every spider's web and every shriek of gull. If the fever hadn't killed him, this longing for home would surely have done him in.

Now he was waiting for breakfast. It wasn't so much that he was hungry as he was looking out for the nurses. He remembered them coming and going, delivering this or that remedy to the soldiers. The rustle of grey-and-white uniforms, the caring eyes and quick smiles. The excited chatter about a new wonder drug that had saved a couple of badly wounded soldiers. Today he was much better and looking forward to the food. Scrambled eggs, suet puddings, hot soups and steaming mugs of tea. He welcomed them all. Like the other Kiwis, he enjoyed teasing the girls.

After the RHS *Papanikolis* slipped into port, covered trucks had rushed them to the military hospital. They were each asked not to mention their venture to anyone, so as not to jeopardise the escapes of other men. The survivors of this particular crossing from Crete, Sonny now realised, had cheated death by mere hours.

The army authorities bent over backwards to help them, delivering letters and packages to the hospital and providing paper and pencils for their replies. They were assured that military dispatches would report the news of their arrival in Egypt. Families of the boys believed missing or dead would be told they had been found. There was even talk about them being sent home.

Sonny turned to his friend in the next bed. 'How are you doing, Mo?'

'Spoilt rotten. Loving every minute of it.'

'The operation on your leg went well?'

Mo tapped his plaster cast. 'Removed some chips of bone and tidied me up nicely.'

'What happened to Fluke, do you know?' Sonny asked.

'Some army blokes came and took him away. I told them his story.'

'They'll look after him at the camp?'

'Too right, mate. He'll be a bloody celebrity.'

'Are the others okay?'

'We survived, mate. And we owe it to you and your boat.'

'Nah. We pulled together, that's how we came through.'

'With a little help from Providence, eh?'

'Didn't I tell you that dog would bring us good luck?'

Mo gave a deep-throated chuckle. 'Jeez, you Kiwis. Stark raving, the lot of you!'

Sonny grinned. 'Maybe we are.' *Or maybe we were formed by the hand of a different god.*

Sonny scribbled a few words to his parents to explain he was under medical care in Alexandria. He apologised for his long silence. The action of putting pencil to paper was difficult, as if he had forgotten how to write a letter.

After their first encounter with the enemy in April 1941 he and Tama had become separated from the battalion, he told them. His hand

     Kayleen M. Hazlehurst

trembled as he related how Tama died in his arms on that stormy night on Mount Olympus. He described his journey through Greece and the Aegean Islands until he reached Crete and how, one night in January, having set sail for Egypt, a small group of escapers were rescued by a Greek submarine. *Give my love to Atarangi. Please tell her I will write.*

After removing the second cord from his neck, Sonny slipped Tama's dog tags into the envelope.

Sonny looked over the ship's railing, captivated by the lather of white as it streamed away from the bow. The doctors had declared his party unfit for service. They were to be sent back on hospital ships to their countries of origin. For this group of battlers, the war was over.

Earlier in the week their English friends had departed on the HS *Somersetshire.* Two days later the HS *Wanganella* whisked away Mo, Tony and Lloyd, bound for Sydney. The rest of them were to journey home on the splendidly decked-out New Zealand hospital ship, HS *Maunganui,* presently anchored off Port Tewfik.

On their last day Deo, the strongest among them, had come to say goodbye.

'I will join the British Army and fight for the freedom of Crete,' Deo told Sonny.

'Deacon would be proud of you. You'll make a fine soldier. Maybe even an intelligence officer, eh?'

'Let's see what they offer me.'

'Find Abbot Agathangelos. I heard he was working for Intelligence in Cairo, though I doubt he'll be flapping around in his robes and beard.'

'I'll look closely at every large man I see.'

With particular sadness, Sonny watched Deo walk away, knowing this young lion would give his last drop of blood for his beloved Crete.

Twenty-two months on the run could change a man's perspective. Yet Sonny's own heart had never left Rangitakō. That place where a breeze carried down the scent of the forest, where sun-dried linen waited for him at the end of a working day, where there were people who loved him.

'How are you doing, fella?' A Kiwi soldier with a bandaged head and a missing right hand came to join him at the ship's railing. The amputee lifted his stump and grinned. 'Goes to show what happens if you chew your fingernails.'

Sonny smiled. 'My mother warned me about that.' He wondered whether he would have been as good-natured under the same circumstances, but at that moment he was truly glad to be alive.

'Looking forward to going home?' the soldier asked.

'Yes, brother. I'm going home to marry my best girl, Atarangi.'

    Kayleen M. Hazlehurst

~44~

Homecoming

Hundreds of men were making their way north. Servicemen and medical orderlies flowed around Sonny on the Wellington wharf, and later as he eased his way along the railway platform to the last door of the train. Those who'd been treated on the hospital ship, and survived, were less crook than when they first boarded in Egypt. The wounded hobbled to their seats or were lifted in wheelchairs onto carriages—if not in high spirits, then at least with a renewed sense of purpose. When the engine shunted forward and chugged out of the station, Sonny braced himself against the press of bodies. The seats would empty at successive stops and soon there'd be a space for him beside a window.

Once settled, Sonny scanned the faces around him. His thoughts were with the outnumbered defenders trying to hold on to Greece. The skies filled with thousands of mushroomed parachutes. The slaughter of civilians, and the savage response of the Cretans. All this, he had left behind. The people who had shared their meagre resources and risked their own lives to save his. *What decent man turned his back on his friends?*

This homecoming should bring him joy, but instead he felt shame. *Why did so many men die and not me? Am I even worthy of Atarangi's love?* Part of him hoped she had married somebody else. He rested against the window, letting the sway of the carriages rock him to oblivion.

—⁂—

His parents had been watching the road for days. A letter had arrived over a week ago and by its date they saw it had taken two months to reach them. Miriama had held the envelope close to her heart. When she tore it open something slid from its pencilled pages. She screamed as Tama's dog tags fell to the ground.

They had been wrong about everything. It was their youngest who had died on Mount Olympus. Sonny was alive and convalescing in a military hospital in Alexandria. 'How unwell is he?' they asked themselves. 'Will they send him back to war, or home to New Zealand?'

After Atarangi's death the whānau had spiralled into despair. Only Sonny's letter had lifted them out of it.

'Shall I go to the bus stop?' Api asked.

'You've been there every day.'

'I'll take the dogs, just in case.'

Miriama agreed. The dogs would give their returning son such a greeting.

Api looked at her, worried. 'Should I tell him the news right away?'

Miriama paused to consider how they were to tell Sonny about Atarangi. 'We'll take him to the river for a cleansing ceremony.'

'Then we will tell him?'

'Āe.'

'You know he'll blame us for Ata's death. That wedding palaver ...'

'It's me he will blame, Api. Ask Hēmi to join us. Sonny needs his brother's support.'

Rather than wait for the country bus, Sonny hitched a ride on one of Wilson's freight trucks. The lorry had been dropping off produce at the Auckland Railway Station and the Pākehā driver recognised him.

'Hello, matey!' Kenny Sinclair, a man too old for the army but still of working age, leaned from his window. 'Sonny Wirima, isn't it? Are you going home, lad? Would you like a lift to town?'

'Kia ora, Mr Sinclair, that would be great!'

The rural township was eighty miles north. From there, it was four miles by dusty road to the Māori village. When Sonny walked over the rise and caught his first sight of Rangitakō lands, after two and a half years away, his heart gave a sigh.

Children came running, then more people poured from their houses. The way the women wept over him, the way they touched his scarred face and sunken chest, he could see in their eyes he was not the man they once knew.

On his arrival home his family whisked him off to the river. He was grateful for their prayers and intercessions, sensing some of the darkness lifting. The polluting tapu of killing being washed away. After the cleansing ceremony his parents sat him down on the riverbank and told him his fiancée had fallen into the sea. Somehow, he wasn't surprised. His soul had known this from the moment he saw the albatross.

In his dreams that night he saw Atarangi drifting on the liquid surface. Her beautiful young body and flowing hair suspended on a platform of rope, made buoyant by flotations of cork.

Sonny woke in his old bedroom thinking about Satanas. The fearless resistance leader he'd once glimpsed at the rebel camp in the Lasithi Mountains. This morning he had a thumping headache and felt grit behind his eyes. The head battering taken at Dulag Krete still bothered him. No part of him wasn't in pain. *Would Ata have wanted to see me like this?*

He lay in bed studying the ceiling as a dull light crept through the window. Hēmi had stayed close by him the whole of the previous day. They'd strolled over the fields, talking about the animals and recent developments on the farm. Nothing more was said about Atarangi's accident, and little was spoken about Hēmi's own girlfriend.

'How is the lovely Winifred?' Sonny had finally asked.

'Seems busy. She enlisted with the WAAFs ...'

'The airforce. Good old Winnie. Be proud of her, brother. You must miss her.'

When Hēmi turned away Sonny realised the subject was too painful. If he wanted to know what had been happening while he was away he would have to ask around. There were plenty of unanswered questions. *Why was Ata on the cliff that evening?*

Before he left Crete a rumour had been circulating the island about the great insurgent, Antoni Grigorakis, or 'Satanas'. A man fierce in both reputation and deed. The rebel leader paid the British infantry commander, Brigadier Chappel, a visit on the evening the Royal Navy planned to evacuate troops from the Heraklion region. The British were burning documents and getting ready to depart before midnight.

Satanas was said to have placed a fatherly hand on Chappel's shoulder. Speaking gently, he petitioned the Brigadier to leave behind their weapons, so the Cretans would be able to carry on the fight.

'My son, we know you are leaving,' Satanas said without bitterness. 'But when the time is right the British will come back to help us.'

Chappel was so moved by this encounter he collected all the guns and ammunition he could from his men and handed them over to Satanas.

Sonny heard his mother calling from the kitchen.

'Breakfast is ready. Come and eat.'

Api and Hēmi were at the table in their milking gear—woollen jumpers pulled over cotton shirts, above heavy wool trousers and leather belts. They looked up expectantly at him from their bowls of porridge.

'Rest for another day,' Miriama urged Sonny. 'Regain your strength. Don't take any notice of those two, they just want another pair of hands.'

'I'm okay. Do you still have my old work clothes and gumboots?'

'Your clothes are in the wardrobe. I bought you new gumboots last week.'

'We'd be glad of your company,' Hēmi said.

Sonny wondered what kind of company he would really be.

Api's eyes crinkled at the sides, as they always did when he was trying to be kind. 'Can't you hear those dogs? They've been whining themselves silly all morning to see you. You'll have a few stories to tell us, no doubt.'

They were talking in the yard after the milking while the cows meandered back to the pastures. Morning sunlight brushed the road, turning the backs of the Jerseys mellow gold.

Hēmi took a long drag on his cigarette. 'Would you like to come fishing with me today?'

'Don't we have work to do?'

'We can catch a late tide. A couple of snapper for our tea, hey?'

'If you want.'

'What did you eat while you wandered those hills? Do you mind me asking?'

 Kayleen M. Hazlehurst

'No, I don't mind. I lived on whatever I caught—ducks, rabbits, deer. Sometimes I found a nest of partridge eggs or snared a couple of game birds.'

'Knocking around the cowshed should be easy after that.'

Sonny shrugged and turned away. 'I'll shut the gate on the cows.'

It was a careless gesture, one that would hurt his brother's feelings, but he didn't have the energy to explain any more.

Hēmi entered the kitchen and swung his pail of milk onto the bench.

'He's not the same, Mum.'

Miriama fixed her eyes on him. 'What do you mean?'

'Something's gone out of him. It's like he's not here.'

'Give him a chance,' she replied. 'His heart is broken.'

'Yeah, broken over Atarangi, or broken over Crete?'

Api put aside his mug of tea. 'Horrific things went on out there, Hēmi. Don't you be hard on him. We have no idea what he's been through.'

'Fair enough. I asked him out fishing. Thought he might like some time on the boat.'

'That's good, son. We have to ease him back into it.'

'Ease him back into what, Dad? What sort of life does he have with us now? What if it's not enough?'

'The land will heal him,' Miriama answered in a firm voice. 'Sonny loves Rangitakō. This is where his heart beats.'

Their father let them off the afternoon milking, saying he would ask one of the cousins to help. As they pulled out from shore Sonny gazed back at the shining fields, the pockets of forest, and the distant shapes of the Brynderwyns behind. Since the rescue, when he and his friends came so close to dying, his days had become a blur. Even the time of year was wrong.

It was the end of the New Zealand summer, with the early signs of a change of season. He thought of other autumns. Winds blowing crumpled leaves across narrow pathways. Mountain tracks pierced with blue-grey rocks. The sway of baskets on the back of a donkey named Caesar, whose breath was sweet from hay and who never failed them on difficult trails.

Hēmi grasped Sonny's arm, jolting him back to the present. 'Are you okay?'

He looked around. They had reached their fishing spot in the main channel and the anchor had already been dropped. There wasn't much to see, just the coastal cliffs and a couple of islands.

'Sorry, I was remembering ...'

'Remembering what? Help me to understand. What was it like fighting on Mount Olympus ... Losing Tama?'

'I can't share my grief with you. I wish I could.'

'That's all right. I don't expect you to.'

Sonny looked over the side of the boat for a mislaid splinter of memory in the blue water. He smiled at his brother. 'I can tell you something,' he said. 'Tama and I were out scouting when we sighted an eagle. We were on the far side of a gorge, the Mavroneri.' He raised his hand to show the passage of flight—picturing in his mind the beautiful bird soaring above the peaks of Olympus.

Hēmi settled beside him to listen.

'Tama asked me how eagles built their nests,' Sonny went on, 'and we talked about watching hawks from our hills as kids.'

'All of us kids loved watching the hawks.'

'Then Tama told me that if he died he would come back as one of those big birds. He would fly up and up, close to heaven. And, you know, I'm sure that's what he did. Someone was watching over me as I walked through those mountains.'

'That's a nice memory of Tama. I'd like to have a memory like that myself.'

'I'll give it to you. Consider it a gift, brother.'

'Thanks ...' Hēmi gave him a friendly punch on the arm. 'What about Crete? You were there for nearly two years. What were you doing all that time?'

'*Ah,* Crete was different. That was a war by stealth. It was a war of cunning and survival. I tried to help where I could.' He stopped talking, as images of lost friends brought an ache deep in his chest.

'One day you'll tell me the whole story.'

 Kayleen M. Hazlehurst

'Yeah, one day.' Sonny went to the fishing box. 'Are we going to throw over these lines? I've been looking forward to a meal of snapper.'

'Bait's under the seat.'

'Would you like to hear about Fluke, our fishing dog?'

'You've got me there! Who wouldn't want to hear about a fishing dog?'

—⁓—

On the far hills they were using the horses to move sheep. The dogs were working the rear, with directions from the saddle. For three months Sonny had been labouring beside his father and brother, sensing his strength drawing in. Hēmi was a competent whistler when it came to commanding dogs. It was something Sonny had never mastered.

Hēmi rode Dancer, the new stallion, and Sonny had Sal. The young one kept touching noses with its mother for reassurance, making Sonny smile. After witnessing human trust so badly broken during the war, the fellowship between animals was helping to restore his faith.

They dismounted to close the last gate and rested against a log. Unlike the home paddocks of rye and clover, the land between the steep hills at the rear of the property consisted of wild grasses growing between patches of tussock and bracken. Romneys, a hardy breed of sheep, were more than capable of finding enough feed in the backcountry.

Hēmi dug into his shirt pocket to take out a packet of smokes.

Sonny accepted a cigarette. 'You handle the dogs well. Got your whistles down pat.'

'It took a bit of work.'

'On Crete, mountain shepherds used to talk to each other across ravines by this ancient language of moans and whistles. When enemy soldiers reached the remote regions, they could never understand why the villages were empty.'

'I can make whistles like that.' Hēmi turned his head towards the hills and tried out a couple of bird calls, grinning when he heard a faint echo. 'Yeah, we'd work out a warning system if those Jerries or Japs ever came here.'

'You would ride like the wind from town to town delivering messages.

You'd be good at that, Hēmi.'

'I reckon.' The dogs were sucking up for attention and Hēmi gave each a head-scratch. 'We can go hunting tomorrow, if you like.'

'Sounds good.'

'Were there poaka in Greece?'

'Domestic pigs, mainly, owned by villagers or farmers. Might have been some wild ones in the forests, though I never saw one. I didn't have dogs to help me flush them out.'

'Wild pigs are good at hiding.'

Sonny gave a slight chuckle. 'One fella told me the Māori cooks got so desperate they decided to nick a domestic pig. They put the carcass on a stretcher and covered it with a blanket to sneak it past the villagers.'

'Ēhe!'

'The women came rushing out of their cottages, weeping and laying flowers on the fallen soldier. All the while our men plodded along, looking glum as they carried away Sergeant Pig to the pot.'

When they stopped laughing, Hēmi said, 'You boys got into some mischief, eh?'

'Oh, we did. Hey, we should get a sow and piglets for the farm. Expand a bit.'

Hēmi jerked his thumb at the neighbouring property. 'The whānau are thinking of buying the land behind here. The Pākehā owner got himself killed on his tractor and his widow wants to sell.'

'What size is the property?'

'A hundred acres, give or take. The land is going cheap.'

Sonny swatted at an annoying fly. 'How would we get the cash?'

'A few of us thought we'd go scrubcutting or shearing for a while. Pay it off piecemeal. What about you, Sonny?'

'What about me?'

'Don't you get a soldier's payout from the government?'

'I haven't seen any payout. What does Dad think?'

'He says buying land is a young bloke's game.'

'Yeah, well. So is soldiering, and the war's not over yet in case you hadn't noticed.'

    Kayleen M. Hazlehurst

~45~

Reinforcements

A letter arrived for Hēmi that morning, and his face had a glow. It seemed Winifred had leave time and was due home on the afternoon bus. Her message must have come with words of love and peace pigeons, because the bridge between them had somehow been mended.

A year had passed since anyone had seen Winnie. Api was especially pleased, and the dogs darted about as if they sensed something was happening. Only Miriama was quiet, leading Sonny to suspect that a letter from their mother had propelled the event.

'Winifred's mother has not been well, poor thing,' she murmured, hinting that this was the reason for the visit.

Sonny took his gun and the dogs and went into the bush to get out of the way. He'd been doing a fair bit of this since he'd come home. Sometimes he would sit for an hour on a fallen tree, listening to the birds.

The next morning Winifred came to the house carrying an assortment of flowers. She wanted to lay them on the cliff in Ata's memory, she said. Would the brothers join her?

Api examined the flowers. 'Dune flowers were Ata's favourite.'

The three friends arrived at the grassy bluff above the cliff and stared out at the glittering sea.

'Is this where she fell?' Sonny asked Winifred.

'Nobody knows, exactly. But she loved to sit here to be with you, Sonny.'

'Ata told me in her letters she had a special place.'

'She used to bring the dogs.' Hēmi gave his eyes a savage wipe. '*Damn and blast!*'

Winifred put her hand on Hēmi's chest and wept there for a minute.

Sonny watched them in silence until they pulled apart. 'Is there something I should know? What the *blazes* was Ata doing here at night on her own? No one will tell me … Did she throw herself off the cliff? … Did she die because of me?'

'No, Sonny. It was an accident,' Winifred responded. 'We *have* to tell him, Hēmi.'

'Tell me what?'

Hēmi's shoulders slumped. 'If it was anyone's fault, it was mine.'

'Your fault!' Sonny clenched his fists and took a step towards Hēmi. 'What did you do to her, you bastard?'

'Sonny, wait!' Winifred got between them. 'Listen to me, please.'

Hēmi turned his back on them. 'Go ahead. Tell him. If he's still wild, he can push me off the cliff.'

'Don't be silly. Nobody's pushing anyone off the cliff. They tried to force Hēmi and Ata into marriage, Sonny. The old people. Ata ran away the night before the wedding.'

Sonny sank to his knees, his whole body shaking. 'Because they thought I was dead.'

Later, Sonny cornered his mother in the kitchen.

He lowered his voice and checked his father wasn't listening. 'They told me,' he said. There was a chill to his tone but he couldn't stop himself. 'It was your idea, wasn't it? You convinced the kaumātua to chuck Atarangi and Hēmi together, even though they didn't want to marry.'

He saw her eyes darken with pain. 'I was not your enemy in this, Sonny.'

'No? Who asked you to interfere in my life, you and those meddling aunties?'

'It wasn't meddling. We were making do with what we had. I was trying to help Ata and Hēmi—'

'Your ambition got the better of you! It was your ambition for a Wirima to marry a Tahiri! That's it, isn't it?'

Api came into the room and stood beside Miriama, staring his son down. Sonny turned and walked away, shouting back at them, 'I blame you both for this!'

'Āe, I'm sorry, dear,' Miriama said, her voice barely audible. 'It was my fault our loved one was lost.'

On Sunday evening the brothers went for a walk on the beach. Winifred had returned to her job in Wellington and Hēmi seemed more encouraged. The moon was rising when they lay on the soft sand to study the pinholes in the dusky-blue dome above.

Hēmi said, 'When we were kids, Mum used to recite for us the genealogy of Creation. Do you remember?'

Sonny thrust himself up. 'Don't talk to me about that old crone and her teachings. That's how she kept Ata under her thumb.'

'Ya' reckon?' Hēmi sat up with him. 'I never saw that girl do anything she didn't want to. Not the Atarangi I knew.'

Sonny ran a finger through the sand. 'No, you're right. Ata was her own spirit.'

'She was one of the great souls, everyone saw it. If she had lived, her life would have been special. Don't blame Mum for wanting to protect her. It was the war that mucked things up for our family.'

Sonny choked back his grief. 'I just wanted Ata to be with me.'

'She will be. Like Mum was with you, all the time you were away.'

'I guess I knew that.'

Hēmi lay back on the sand. 'Come on, brother. Tell me the story of Creation. First there was the Great Abyss, followed by Chaos …'

Sonny looked back at the sky. 'Then came the many Stages of Night …'

'Followed by the Expansion of Energy,' Hēmi said. 'That was my favourite …'

'Which begat Shape and Form …'

'Time and Space …'

'Life and Light …'

'Tell me, Sonny. Where does the war fit into all of this?'

'That's pretty bloody obvious. War represents the end of Creation.'

'The end of Te Ao Mārama. Do we start going backwards into Chaos and the Great Abyss?'

'I'm pretty sure that's what our side is fighting against.'

'Let's hope our side wins.'

'You can't imagine what it was like going into action,' Sonny said, feeling a sudden urgency to explain. 'I would look out in the morning and wonder how many of my cousins and friends would see the setting sun. Whether the next one to die would be me. Even now, I feel bad about deserting my mates.'

'How could you have known the Anzacs were going to take off in the dead of night? You didn't desert them, you were left behind.'

'Maybe.'

'You're still in grief over Atarangi. Dad and I hoped the farm would help, but we can see you have lost your anchor.'

'I'll admit, working the land has made me stronger. But I cannot stay, Hēmi. I can't leave my mates fighting out there on their own.'

'I know, teina. I know you have to go back.'

Hēmi was sitting on his bed reading Winifred's letter again. They were still friends, but she had made it clear she wouldn't leave her post at the Department of Defence. *Let me do this*, she had written. *Once the war is over I'll come home. I promise.*

He put aside the letter and went to open his wardrobe, standing there for a few moments. Then he reached in to brush his hand over the army uniform he'd worn for such a short time during his training in Palmerston North.

—❧—

The Dutch ship SS *Nieuw Amsterdam* was due to sail from Wellington with the Tenth Māori Reinforcements on 21 July 1943, destined for Port Tewfik in Egypt. It was unusual for a Māori soldier to volunteer to re-enlist after being discharged. But the army needed men, and after his months of farm labouring Sonny believed he was fit enough not to be turned away.

Māori soldiers shared an understanding. Many may have joined the army for adventure, to escape poverty, or to defend their lands, yet there was another compelling reason. It was something explained by the myths and the whakapapa. The ancestors had projected their minds beyond the stars to obtain knowledge. Earth, Sky and the Underworld were all caught up in this net. The purpose of a good man was to protect the world from the blanketing darkness.

On the roadside the women were weeping. Sonny, dressed in full uniform and carrying a single pack, stood waiting for the Auckland bus. All week his mother had begged him not to leave. Asking why he would return to military service when the government didn't require it. Making dire predictions. Today half the community had come to see him off. As the bus came into view his mother fell to her knees, with two older women supporting her outstretched arms.

'Oh, my boy, please don't go back to the war!' Miriama cried, setting off more tears and wailing. 'I have seen … I have seen … If you go you will never return to us!'

Other recruits were waiting on the bus. They were on their way to the training camp or destined, like Sonny, for the reinforcements ship. It took all of his resolve to walk away.

His father stepped out from the crowd, clutching his hat. 'Are you certain about this, Sonny?'

'I'm sorry, Dad. What happened in Crete could happen here.' He looked around but couldn't see his brother. 'Say goodbye to Hēmi for me.'

'I'm proud of you, son,' Api said, gripping Sonny's hand. 'Don't you worry about the farm. It will be here for you when you get back. God keep you safe.'

Sonny climbed on board and took a seat. His eyes turned from the scene on the roadside as the bus pulled away.

The huddled onlookers gasped. The vehicle had gone barely a hundred yards when it jerked to a halt. Then it slowly reversed and stopped a few yards from the gathering. The door opened and Sonny descended the steps. He walked back to his mother. Putting his hands under her armpits, he lifted her to her feet. He and his mother stood face to face, a mirror of each other in willpower and determination.

Sonny bent his head to her. 'I have to go, Mum. I'd rather die facing the enemy on my feet than have you face them on your knees. Trust me on this. We must turn back the darkness at its source.'

An expression of shock crossed his mother's face, then a flash of comprehension. Miriama straightened her back and stood taller. 'Haere ra i runga i ngā manaakitanga e tama,' she said. 'Go with the blessings of our Creator.'

Sonny kissed her cheek and held her in a long embrace. 'Soldiering is what I do best, Mum. I won't let you down.' He reached to grip his father's right shoulder in a hongi, then he strode back to the waiting bus.

Api was holding the crook of Miriama's elbow. 'We can do this,' he assured her.

Miriama sighed. 'Men always travel for love.'

The weeping had stopped when the bus pulled away for a second time. Instead, there came heartfelt singing from the well-wishers on the roadside. This was answered with exuberant arm waving from bus windows and a rich swell of baritone voices from the young men.

All eyes were on the trail of dust when Miriama spun around to search the group.

'Where is Hēmi? Has anyone seen him?'

A girl came running towards them. 'I saw him, Auntie,' she said, stopping to catch her breath. 'Hēmi got on the bus when no one was looking ... He was in uniform.'

~46~

The Sappers—the Road to Rome

1944

Walls shook as pigeons took flight. All night the sky had been pierced with Verey lights. The broken cottage, where six of them had lain in a chilled and restless sleep, would not withstand another bombardment. Corporal Sonny Wirima clenched and stretched his shaking hands. They looked like claws, so raw and numb from the icy cold they were hardly a part of him. He reached for his rifle and roused the men. Other groups on patrol were in the vicinity. They would all have to move before shellfire started again.

The 2nd New Zealand Division had joined the Allied advance into Italy after a hard-won victory in North Africa. Axis forces were entrenched across Europe where the Gustav Line ran for a hundred miles south of Rome. In the depth of winter, the Allies were trying to break through the defensive front to come to the aid of an Allied beach landing, sixty miles further north, at Anzio.

When the Kiwi troops were brought up to the line they entered a pastoral valley bordered by a thirty-foot-wide river. Beyond this were the steep uplands and peaks of the Apennine Mountains. Sonny's map showed the road to Rome, Route 6, curving around the mountain chain and passing through a gap between the ranges. Protecting this narrow gateway into the Liri Valley was Monte Cassino.

The men's attention was drawn to the high barren rock with its ancient abbey set on the summit. Built from massive cubes of stone, the Benedictine monastery was larger than any of the houses of worship Sonny had seen in Greece.

At the base of the hill was the town. The streets of Cassino were almost unrecognisable. Above the rubble and bomb craters, the rock face and damaged buildings were now fortified with enemy bunkers. It was assumed Germans also occupied the monastery. Allied officers reckoned Fritz was using this elevated site for surveillance—scrutinising their every move. This was a battlefield none of them could have imagined.

'The whole show is set up to the advantage of the other fellow,' they told each other.

Germans were a familiar foe to Sonny. He knew they started their day with a hearty breakfast and was hoping this would give their boys time to dash over the pitted landscape. Six men of his section were clustered under a sagging roof, waiting for the sky to lighten. They would leave as soon as their dark surroundings turned to dim outlines, and they could see where to put their feet.

Hēmi was crouched like a tiger, ready to spring out from their hideout. Sonny knelt down beside him. 'Easy, brother.'

'How are we supposed to get around these buggers?'

'There's only three ways. By road, railway or river. None of them are terribly flash.'

'I should have known there'd be rivers.'

At Piedimonte d'Alife, where the Māori Battalion welcomed the new recruits from the Tenth Reinforcements, the fighting units had been put into training for river crossings. It was here that Sonny had been promoted to corporal. Now, forty miles north-west of Alife, they were on short rations and being tormented by snow, sleet and rain.

Rawiri, a stocky thirty-five year old, spoke in a slow, rough voice. 'Nothing is good around here.' He wiped a hand over his dust-smeared face, making him look like everyone's uncle. Rawiri could relate the story of Cassino better than anyone.

Tuteri, a cheeky youngster who'd lied about his age to join the army, was trembling beside them. 'What do you say, Koro? Can we take this place?'

'The Americans tried to do that two weeks ago,' Rawiri answered. 'The roads were so bad their tanks got bogged down. You've seen the wrecks.'

The Māori Battalion had heard about this failed attack on their arrival. In mid-January the US Fifth Army, along with some French and British

 Kayleen M. Hazlehurst

troops, suffered crippling losses in a full-scale assault. South of Cassino the US 36th (Infantry) Division were nearly wiped out trying to cross the Gari River in small boats.

'Those poor Texan boys would have been sitting ducks on the water,' Peta said. He turned to his younger cousin. 'You'd better watch out, Ted. There'll be gunmen everywhere.'

Ted widened his eyes. 'If the Americans couldn't break through, what chance do we have?'

They lifted their faces to where the abbey was emerging in the early light. As the shadow of the mountain fell over the town the presence of the fortress was bitterly felt.

The Kiwis were sent to relieve the Americans in the first week of February. Their camp behind Monte Trocchio, a prominent ridge shaped like a loaf of bread, overlooked the marshland and mangled trees of the Rapido Plain and the three-mile stretch back to Cassino. Assembled under the New Zealand Corps were also British, Indian and Gurkha soldiers.

A few of their boys had decided to occupy the abandoned dugouts and trenches on the hillside, giving them a good view of the terrain. When the NZ 27th (Machine Gun) Battalion went to explore the area in front of the ridge, they found it strewn with American corpses. Their Pākehā brothers brought back the bad news. The ground was strung with barbed wire and sown with mines, readied by the enemy as a killing field.

For eleven days they were sent out on fighting patrols. As artillery shells whistled overhead, and Jerry's six-barrelled mortar fire echoed around the hills, they trod light-footed among the vacated trenches, deserted farmhouses and clumps of river willows to determine enemy locations and strengths. What the boys discovered was disconcerting. Wherever there was something to hide behind, there were Germans. By counting the flashes, they calculated German machine-gun nests housed six to eight Spandaus. With dawn coming they needed to leave their hideout and get back to headquarters to report their findings.

Sonny sensed the lingering presence of the people who had once occupied this ruined cottage. Dust-covered belongings lay among the crumbled masonry—the wind-up gramophone, the cracked mirror and family photograph, the twisted frame of an iron bed bleeding white feathers from its mattress. Footprints of the lives that were lost.

He'd heard stories about civilians being caught up by the fighting. Women and children searching for food and shelter. A sobbing mother cradling a limp infant in her arms. An old man bent over a walking stick, oblivious to the dangers. At Galatas, Kiwi soldiers had hurried these souls away before the street battles began. What had haunted them most were the churches filled with the sound of weeping.

Had there been scenes like this at Cassino in the months before the Allies arrived? Ordinary people whose peaceful villages had become a frontline. Sonny could barely think about it. *This isn't right.*

Ted was tying a woman's shawl around some things he'd pinched from the house.

'Leave that stuff and come over here,' Peta snarled.

Sonny raised his hand. *Stop.* He sliced his index finger across his neck. *Silence.* The others froze to listen. All they could hear was the low moan of the wind. He directed the cousins to stand on the opposite side of the opening. Eyes watched for more signals. Sonny lifted two fingers, dropped them, and lifted them again. *They must leave two at a time.*

Peta and Ted volunteered to go first. Rawiri and Tuteri second. The remaining two braced their rifles on the stone walls, watching their mates' backs as they ran across the open space. Twenty yards between each pair. If one fell, the other one could help him. The last pair to leave, before the snipers emerged from their weasel holes, were Sonny and Hēmi.

Reconnaissance must have convinced their commanding generals, Freyberg and Kippenberger, that a frontal assault should be avoided. Half a mile south was the Cassino Railway Station. The primary mission of the New Zealanders was to capture that station, they were told. This task was assigned to two companies of the 28th Māori Battalion.

In the meantime, every possible weapon would be used to distract the attention of the German garrison. The moment the 28th seized the

     Kayleen M. Hazlehurst

railway station, the 4th Indian Division would attempt to take Monastery Hill and the high ground behind. It was an ambitious plan.

—⁓—

Torrential rain had put everything under an inch of water. Added to this, the enemy had diverted rivers and side streams into a treacherous cross-hatch of canals and ditches.

The engineers, the sappers, had their work cut out for them. For nights they tried to drain the ground and clear it of mines and booby-traps. They inspected the railway line for damage from exploding shells, discovering twelve demolition sites that required bulldozing, culverting and bridging to make a safer route.

The train track had been built on a raised bank, and the idea was to convert this embankment into a road for the heavy armour. To this new battlefield the New Zealand Division had brought in anti-tank guns and one hundred and fifty Sherman tanks. The sappers had one more bridge to finish before the armoured regiment could send support weapons through to the Māori infantry, and all this digging and building had to be done in darkness.

The double assault on the Cassino Railway Station and Monastery Hill had been planned for the night of February 13, but there was a delay. Hampered by precipices and deep ravines, the Indian Division was not ready. General Freyberg must have realised he'd given the Indians an impossible task, although no one expected the general to take matters into his own hands. Something big was about to happen at Cassino.

All the men were told was to make themselves scarce.

On the morning of the 15th, they heard a rumble.

'American bombers!'

The planes came in wave after wave. Eight groups of nine aircraft. Mitchells and Marauders and the huge, four-engine, Flying Fortresses. Their bombs struck the monastery and hillside in hideous blue flashes, sending columns of debris and black smoke high into the air. Between the bombing runs, the artillery pounded the mountain to mop up any Germans the planes might have missed.

The men had gathered to watch the spectacle from Monte Trocchio. Among rounds of cheers, there were words of exhilaration tinged with terror.

'Bloody brilliant, mate!'

'How d'you like that, eh?'

'Now we've got you pinned down!'

'Hope those Yanks know which hills to hit.'

Everyone laughed.

'Else we'll all be done for!'

One or two missiles did go awry, one hitting a cemetery. Dislodged boulders were hurled as far as the river, scattering men from their gun posts and just missing battalion headquarters. Instinctively, the observers all ducked.

Later that day, an eerie silence fell over Cassino. The brothers stared back at the shattered husk of the abbey in the deepening twilight.

Sonny leaned in to speak. 'And they call *us* savages.'

Hēmi smiled wryly. 'Āe. I'm not sure what all this bombing achieved.'

'I bet it didn't touch those gunners in the hills.'

'Yeah. They'll be there to fight us tomorrow.'

'I feel sorry for the monks. What did they ever do to us?'

'I don't know, Sonny. As long as it shortens this bloody war.'

'Where's the honour if our side plays dirty?'

'Is any war honourable?'

'The ancient Greeks used to think so.'

Hēmi gave a snort. 'You're not a mad old Greek, brother.'

Sonny grinned. 'Might be heading that way.'

—⁂—

The second day after the monastery bombing, February 17, the Royal Sussex and Indian rifle regiments positioned in the hills were ready to do the unachievable, putting the Māori Battalion back on schedule. In the late afternoon the Māori troops assembled for a briefing. Captain Matarehua

     Kayleen M. Hazlehurst

Wikiriwhi would lead B Company, and Captain James Henare would lead A Company. Their first objective was to seize the railway buildings and the area around the engine sheds.

Once the enemy had been quelled at the station, B Company was instructed to move north to the scattered buildings on the sunken road leading north-west back to the town. They were to go from house to house until they had removed every German. The job of A Company was to secure the left flank, including a series of mounds south of the station, known as the Hummock.

'Fasten onto the strengths of each other,' their officers urged them at the briefing. 'Show courage. Do your best to shield your brothers. Our purpose is to eliminate the fanatical followers of Hitler. If the price of freedom is high, so be it. Remember who you're fighting for. Remember your people at home.'

Yes, Sonny thought, *home is where every heart will be.* How he would love to go down to the creek to catch an eel on a summer's day, or to watch for a pheasant on a hillside in autumn. This region of Italy had its own beauty, great slabs of cliffs and snowy peaks, but it hadn't passed his notice that Cassino was devoid of birds. *I don't blame them. They have retreated from this place of death and its thin, bony trees.*

The officers ordered them to remove all identification patches from their uniforms. (So as not to alert the Jerries the Māori Battalion was sneaking up on them, they all reckoned.) This was followed by a meal of mutton stew and potatoes with rough bread. Afterwards they stood for a short church service and to contemplate the night ahead.

The Christians among them were mostly Anglicans, Catholics or Ringatū. When he enlisted Sonny wrote 'Church of England' in the space on the form. The local Anglican minister had been friendly with the Wirima family. As the battalion padre was absent a member of the Ringatū Church led the prayers. 'Let us pray for our advance,' Lieutenant George Takurua said. Ben Hake then intoned a strengthening karakia, and Lieutenant Colonel Young closed with some bolstering words. Sonny understood this desire to seek Divine help before battle. The two hundred men around him would not have wanted it any other way.

A biting wind stung their faces as they set off at dusk, picking their way over ditches and creeks and trying to stay within the white tape the sappers had laid. They trudged single file along the fast-flowing river, over the Rapido at the railway crossing, to reach the starting line in good time. Captain Wikiriwhi and his men got there at 21:20 hours. Captain Henare's company, who'd been slowed by barbed wire, arrived ten minutes later.

Nearby, the sappers were working flat-out on the embankment. Meanwhile, the Allied field regiment continued to make a fuss to cover any road construction noises, and their mortar and machine-gun platoons provided fitting distraction.

A slice of moonlight, cold and pitiless, fell on the sappers. Batteries of mortar bombs woofed around them, sending up geysers of mud and water. A couple of shells must have hit their mark, because the Māori soldiers could hear screams.

'Bugger this, I'm going up there,' Sonny said to Hēmi. 'Come with me.'

Hēmi emitted a low bird-whistle to get the Lieutenant's attention, and he tilted his head in a question. Stealth was needed to capture the station, so nothing was going to be happening until things had quietened. The answer came back in a cautious hand signal and a narrowing of eyes. *Okay, you fellas can go. But don't be long.*

Tuteri scampered ahead of them towards the railway line where a pall of smoke and dust hung over the causeway. All colour and texture had been leached from everything and the smell was sickening. In this ashen light, the first thing they saw was a bulldozer blown off its caterpillar tracks. Dazed and injured engineers were helping each other draw back from the construction equipment. A few sappers lay dead or dying. One writhed on the ground, holding his stomach, with half his guts spewing out.

In the distance Sonny saw figures running towards them, the white armbands of stretcher-bearers flickering in the moonlight. He knelt to look intently at the man with the abdominal wound, not recognising him, yet knowing he would not survive. In the dim light he could see the twisted agony on the man's face. Sappers were unarmed and their work

Kayleen M. Hazlehurst

was dangerous. The job of the Māori Battalion was to protect them. In this, they had failed.

'For Christ's sake, shoot me!' the Kiwi begged in a hoarse whisper.

Sonny heard the release of the safety catch on Tuteri's rifle, but Hēmi put a deterring hand on the muzzle. Sonny held the sapper's gaze. 'Help is coming, my friend.' He gripped his bloody hands. 'Do not be afraid, Pākehā. You are not alone.'

He chanted a quiet karakia and the other two bowed their heads as he called for more powerful assistance. With a ragged sigh the sapper's eyes fluttered and closed for the last time.

Only the Gods—The Battle for Cassino

They waited, watching the station under a patch of clear sky. The Germans were shooting at anything that moved on the landscape. Enemy detection of the engineers had already drawn mortar fire from the lower slopes of Monte Cassino. The Māori soldiers ducked when a cascade of flares burned across the sky, but flares also worked in their favour.

Sonny felt a hand clutch his elbow.

'Look over there.' Hēmi pointed to the narrow frontage of the rail yard. Someone had strung a length of ugly concertina wire across the entrance.

Sonny glanced sideways. Further along the line a couple of brave men were rushing out between the flares with wire cutters. Brave, because snipers were active. They stayed out of sight while they cut openings at the far ends of the wire. Sonny eased up his rifle and scoped the area for telling glints of metal.

The companies moved forward. Captain Wikiriwhi leading Te Arawa on the right side of the embankment. Captain Henare leading the Ngā Puhi on the left. They hadn't gone far when a mortar shell exploded near B Company. The blast flattened Wikiriwhi, ripping off his helmet and knocking an aide unconscious.

A runner brought them news. There'd been cuts and scrapes. The captain had sustained a gash in the leg and was now at the dressing station, but he was expected to take back command within half an hour. Wikiriwhi was lucky to be alive. A sharp object had lodged in the bulky No. 38 wireless set strapped on his chest, shattering the valves and ending contact between the platoons.

A swollen stream had obstructed the progress of A Company. Earlier, the telephone cables linking Captain Henare with headquarters had been severed by long-range shelling. With communications cut, the battalion now had to rely on their men as runners. Isolated, with reserves running low, they needed to send out an urgent request for more ammunition.

They hunkered down in shell pits, trying to ignore how hungry and cold they were. Sonny reflected on what had just happened. If the assault on the sappers was the first sign of disaster, losing contact between HQ and the platoons was the second. The success of this battle depended on the Allies getting reinforcements through to the Māori Battalion by morning.

All the elements seemed to be against them—rotten weather, flooded rivers, the road-builders under constant fire. Before the sun rose above the spine of Italy the Māori infantry would have to capture the Cassino Railway Station with only the gods on their side.

Sonny adjusted the weight of his knapsack and calmed his mind, asking Tama to be his eyes and ears. The railway complex was five hundred yards away. Tracer bullets criss-crossed the night sky. Mortar bombs and artillery shells fell beyond the station. Three sappers had been killed, possibly more, and the road construction crew had withdrawn. The two machine-gun posts at the entrance to the station were now the battalion's major concern.

The fighters pushed forward, scattering themselves among the scant cover. With the earth waterlogged, and having to dive so often into muddy ditches, it was a wonder they hadn't grown gills. Sonny might have had mutinous thoughts, had the words of Bandouvas not come back to him. 'Our anger will become the fuel for good,' the rebel leader had declared to his followers from his mountain retreat. *Surely this is our night for rage.*

When A and B Companies merged for the attack, it was with the knowledge that every man present was prepared to die for his brother. The snap of steel as bayonets were fixed. The click of safety catches on rifles. The metallic sound of magazines clipping into tommy guns.

At 23:00 hours they were told to charge.

'Run … Drop … Run,' their commanders ordered. 'Zig-zag where you can.'

It wasn't much of an order, but nobody needed one. With a deep growl, they rose as one body and sprinted across the last section of open ground.

Sonny saw Ata's black hair loose on her bare shoulders and fire rose in his heart. They leapt forward, guns blazing. The Germans, who now knew they were here, met them with violent bursts. Three men fell near Sonny, two slain outright. Young Ted was dragged by the collar to a wall. Peta pressed his hand urgently on his cousin's wound but seconds later he was shot himself.

Another man tripped an S-mine. Most mines sown in this area had gone off during the monastery bombings. Not this one. A lethal ring of ball bearings exploded outwards.

At two hundred yards the men came to the concertina wire. Some passed around the obstacle where it had been cut. Where it hadn't, their training kicked in. Two soldiers fell onto the wire and the others jumped over them. Dark figures hunched over bayonets. Grenades ready to throw within a few strides.

Sergeant Walsh dashed forward to hurl the first grenade, liquidating one of the gun posts and copping a chestful of bullets. Māori fighters didn't take kindly to their leaders being killed, especially when that man had sacrificed himself for the younger soldiers. They descended on the second gun post with terrifying efficiency.

'Auē! … Auē! … Auē!'

'Maoris!' Germans yelled. If the war cry hadn't startled them, being at close quarters to assailants with bayonets had. Fingers froze on triggers. Gunners turned to run or flung themselves under benches.

The battalion flowed through the marshalling yard like a torrid river. Skirmishes were going on in every corner of the station. Groups engaged with pockets of German infantry. Fists, wrestle holds, rifle butts. Screams and howls washed through the building when the unyielding were dealt the blade. Of those who died that hour, Sonny was most aware of the dreadful sucking sound as bayonets were withdrawn from bellies. It was something he would never forget.

On the western approaches, the Allies were stonking with artillery and

     Kayleen M. Hazlehurst

hammering with mortars. Against this noise and clamour, fighting at the railway station continued until the job was done. When the station went quiet there were bodies strewn everywhere.

Dead Jerries … Dead mates … Blood seeping silently into drains.

The two companies were digging in at the station. Prisoners huddled on the floor under guard, unshaven and exhausted, looking hopeful that no Māori would stick an unarmed man with a bayonet. Tuteri sauntered over and gave one of them a poke with his rifle, making him squeak.

'Oi!' Hēmi said. 'Leave those jokers alone.'

'They look like kids.'

'Well, so do you, as it happens.'

'A Jerry is a big man behind a machine gun,' Sonny muttered.

'Not so big now, eh?' Tuteri said, glaring.

The German youth winced and drew out a crumpled packet of cigarettes with a shaking hand.

'Will you look at that, he's offering me a smoke.'

Hēmi shook his head. 'Get out of there, Tuteri. You can't fraternise with the enemy.'

'Bet he's got a mother out there somewhere.'

'That's the trouble with war. Everyone has.'

At moonrise, 03:00 hours, the captains established a control centre in the machine workshop near the engine turntable. The siege had cost them dearly and the night was not yet over. One third of their fighting men were down, including Lieutenant Takurua, who only hours before had led their prayers.

Thirty-six men lay on the forecourt, either dead or in shivering misery. Northerners lying side by side with men from the Bay of Plenty. More of the wounded were being delivered on the backs of their friends. One soldier shot in the leg had been carried on a seat made by two mates joining arms. So many grey faces, moaning and crying out.

During a lull, the stretcher-bearers raced to get the injured to the Bren carriers who'd been assigned to transporting them to the regimental aid post. The RAP wasn't poorly equipped, but with six cases of jaundice and the recent torrent of casualties, the messages coming back indicated that the medicos were overwhelmed.

Sonny and Hēmi were standing around with a group from A Company talking in low voices and keeping an eye on their officers.

'We can't take the Hummock tonight,' Henare was overheard saying to Wikiriwhi. 'There aren't enough men. We'll have to wait for the armoured regiment.'

'Can you spare us a few, Jimmy?' Wikiriwhi asked. 'We're moving out to clear the houses.'

'I'll send you some.' Henare paused. He'd been wounded at El Alamein, but the desert war had not prepared him for Cassino. With no tanks behind them, the battalion was far more vulnerable. 'Shades of the Battle of Ōrākau and Rewi Maniapoto?' Henare said sadly. 'Āke, ake, ake.'

Wikiriwhi gave an ironic laugh. 'Āe. We will fight on forever and ever. Until every last one of us is gone.'

Henare dipped his head. 'We'll hold the station while you're gone, Monty.'

B Company had taken control of the buildings and engine shed, and A Company had emptied the yard and gun posts. It was obvious Captain Henare was determined not to lose such hard-won ground. He walked stiffly towards his men.

'I want twelve of you fellas to go with Captain Wikiriwhi.'

Sonny met Hēmi's intense stare. *Should we go?* The distances were short—eight hundred yards north-west to the houses, and four hundred yards to the Hummock. It would mean more street fighting. If things went their way, the houses could be taken first, followed by the mounds to the south.

The night before the attack Hēmi had confessed he'd had a dream about their mother.

'What do you think it means, Sonny?'

'Nothing. She's sending us prayers and protection, that's all.'

Anyone who claimed he wasn't afraid during combat was a liar. Courage was not to deny fear, it was to use your mind to turn fear to your advantage. He had often called on his parents when he needed their strength.

Father Jacob was speaking to him now. *'And your gods, Sonny. Are they still with you?'*

'Āe. We are chosen by Tū and blessed with the vital force of fighting men.'

'The bringers of righteous fire?' The priest's words, not his.

Right now, Sonny wanted utu. For Tama, who lost his life so young. For Peta, who died saving his cousin. For Rawiri, who disappeared somewhere behind them after a mortar attack. He wanted retribution for all the people of Greece and Crete who had shown him kindness. For his lost friends and their bereaved parents—he was doing this for them.

The air snapped and tremored from gunfire and bombs. Sonny hadn't seen a single animal or bird for days. This place was more desolate than Egypt and lonelier than Crete. His mother once said that if all the world's creatures perished, humans would die from sorrow. Cassino was the strongest point in the Gustav Line. Tū had sent the Māori Battalion here to kill the monster at the centre of its molten heart.

They'd been split into groups of five or six and told to fan out. As they crept along the road towards the houses Sonny signalled his group to hold back. He turned his head in quick movements, right and left. Listening. He lifted his nostrils to the wind, detecting traces of tobacco and human sweat. A shift in the atmosphere sent a prickling sensation down his spine. Whether by fall of shadow or flash of light, he knew the enemy was near.

The forward groups hadn't seen the enemy post overlooking the road. A machine-gun nest had been positioned above the rim of a wall. Once the firing began the boys on the road didn't stand a chance. They fell in waves, one after another.

Hēmi turned desperately to Sonny. His gun had jammed and Sonny was faster than anyone at dismantling and reassembling a rifle. They swapped guns and within seconds the rifle was restored. They stopped to stare back at the road where B Company had been. So many had fallen. *This is slaughter.*

Spandau fire raked the ground in front of them. In the next sweep three of A Company were hit, then the two Ngā Puhi close to Hēmi.

'Oh, Mum!' Hēmi cried out.

Sonny felt the heat of the bullet sear through his brother's flesh. Hēmi's hand was stemming the blood on his thigh. The shock of it put Sonny into a strangely solitary place, where senses and sound were muted.

'No, you don't, you bastards!'

Sonny sprinted to the wall and thrust his body against the raw stone. He clawed his way upwards, seeking out chinks between the blocks until his knuckles were bleeding. Near the top, he dug his feet into two grooves and hung on with his left hand. He reached into his pocket to pull out his last grenade, removed the pin with his teeth, and threw it over the wall.

A single shot rang out.

He couldn't have known a sniper was behind him. Couldn't have known the German was there. The marksman might have winged him, might have shot him in the back. Instead he had gone straight for the head.

Sonny's helmet fell away as the bullet pierced the metal.

> His eyes are open as he plunges backwards—the sky
> to the south is a cascade of stars. In an instant he is
> drifting on a luminous sea in the company of the very
> best of men; lazing on a sand hill with Ratty and their
> brother fugitives; nestling among the roots and leaves
> of an old pōhutukawa tree, his coat clasped tight
> around Atarangi. And there is his mother. She stands
> beside a sacred river where light speckles the ripples—a
> myriad fleeting souls—just before he hits the ground.

     Kayleen M. Hazlehurst

~48~

The Dedication Ceremony

1947

Currents of warm air stroked the broad earth. The old woman rearranged her skirts on the grass and smiled around at the children. She had collected more scraps of information to share with the learning circle.

> *She cradles their image behind her eyes,*
> *their spirits in the palms of her hands.*
> *Safe there. Not ready to let go.*
> *'I will tell you their stories, moko,' she says.*
> *'These tiny salients.*
> *These small mementos of months, unknown.'*
> *And she asks: 'Who are these men*
> *who would fight mountains for Tū?'*

A year ago, January 1946, the men of the 28th Māori Battalion had returned to Aotearoa—some to the bosom of their families, others to marry. In two days there would be a dedication ceremony for those who had failed to come home.

'The war is over, dear ones, and we must honour the fallen,' Miriama told the mokopuna. 'On Sunday we will gather to unveil the memorial and to lay wreaths.'

The older ones, who had known their brothers and fathers before the war, stared straight ahead. The younger ones lowered their heads. *The children are angry*, she thought.

'We may voyage over great oceans, but like the great albatross we always return.'

'Not all of us,' an older boy retorted.

'Āe. Though their hearts may ache, not all of our seafaring birds come home. It is these departed ones that we remember. Stand close to your whānau, moko. They need your support.'

Miriama was as stricken by this sadness as those around her. No public affirmations of valour could replace lost sons. Healing would come slowly, or not at all, where minds were wounded. *Whose world will ever be normal again?*

Two fat wood pigeons flew over the war memorial outside the marae grounds and settled on the pūriri tree at the back of the church. From their bough the birds turned their heads, this way and that, to observe the milling crowd.

Civilians, officials and churchmen were welcomed with a pōwhiri onto the marae, along with army representatives in dress uniforms, some in wheelchairs. The memorial dedication that followed included prayers and solemn speeches, and the haunting notes of the last post. Later, the guests were invited to join their Ngā Puhi hosts for lunch at the hall.

Miriama exchanged a few passing words as she made her way to the church cemetery where a group of relatives lingered. She acknowledged her kūkupa in the pūriri tree with a respectful nod. Her atua were here. If a bird appeared at a ceremony it was a sign that the Divine had come to bear witness.

Her tokens of affection—sprigs of fern with flowers and berries bound by cords of flax—were placed beside the plaques for Tama and Sonny. A third maimai aroha she laid on Ata's grave. Atarangi was the only one of her three lost ones whose body had been recovered.

People clustered close to listen to Miriama's comforting words.

When the air is soft and warm,
the land breathes like a sleeping child.
When harsh winds blow, the world awakens.
Seas roll, waves froth and foam.
Leaves ripple and grasses feather and swirl.
How do we withstand these scattering winds?

 Kayleen M. Hazlehurst

Where is our strength?
It is in the power of our forests.
Our noble kauri and tōtara. Our rimu and pūriri.
See how they stand as a single body.
How they sway in unison, yet do not break.
So it is with our people, our valiant tangata whenua.
Today we honour them, but we do not say goodbye.
They will be with us, as our atua are with us.
They will be our gods of peace
and our gods of wrath.
Forever, and ever, and ever.

As Miriama turned to leave she touched Hēmi's shoulder in a blessing. Her eldest son and his pregnant wife had been standing beside her, holding hands. Hēmi was leaning on a walking stick, supporting his leg. His injuries still caused him pain, but the couple had been able to assume responsibility for the farm, sparing Api.

Only a day ago, Hēmi and Winifred had been in her kitchen discussing how the war in Europe had ended, and how her eldest son was rescued by stretcher-bearers in Cassino, and thankfully sent home. The equally ferocious war over the Pacific with Japan was resolved by dropping atomic bombs on the people of Hiroshima and Nagasaki.

Miriama was not impressed. 'So, the scientists have learned how to tear a hole in the cloak of the universe!' She slammed the teapot on the kitchen table, making everyone jump. 'And do they know how to stitch it back together?'

Hēmi reached to touch her arm. 'A fair question, Mum.'

Winifred's eyes glazed with tears. 'I'm so happy Hēmi came home to us, but this war has brought sorrow to everyone. I have seen it in the lives of my friends.'

Now, as Miriama walked from the churchyard, she felt a quiet presence. A Pākehā in uniform was standing there as she latched the gate behind her. Her heart sank with pity when she saw his ruined face. Jagged scars ran from his eye to his jawline, as if someone had hitched the right side of his face into place with the best effort of a needle and thread. Despite this damage, there was a glow of gratitude and goodness in this young man.

'Were you waiting to see me?' she asked the stranger.

'May I speak with you, Mrs Wirima? I think I knew your son. Sonny saved my life on Mount Olympus.'

'I see. What is your name?'

'Nathan Smith. "Gunner Smith" your son called me. He invited me to visit him at Rangitakō when I got home. I was unwell at the time and his words gave me hope. I wanted to let him know that old Smithy survived.'

'Sonny died at Cassino.'

Smithy blinked and directed his gaze towards the cemetery. 'I'm so sorry. That wonderful man carried me on his back to find me a doctor. May I thank you instead?'

'Come, dear. I will take you home to meet his father. Api is too frail now to venture out, but he will be pleased to see you. We will have a cup of tea and you can tell us the whole story.'

———〰———

At Rangitakō, craftmaking and weaving had declined during the war years, although in recent months there had been renewed interest for the craft group to meet again at the hall. Talking helped to heal grief, and it was natural for women to talk.

At their next craft day the tohunga—medium to the gods and interpreter of the sacred lore—was asked to explain the meaning of the great wars, and why the Māori people had suffered such terrible losses. For illumination, she turned to the seers of the past.

'Our Creation Myths have taught us that Out of Darkness comes Light,' Miriama said, as she applied strips of flax to the basket she was weaving. 'This is known by all.'

There was a quiet chirruping of agreement.

'Less understood,' Miriama continued, 'is the principle of service.'

'Tell that to my children,' said a mother of six.

'Āe … Āe …' The women chuckled and sighed.

     Kayleen M. Hazlehurst

Miriama smiled at her friends but assumed a more serious tone. The message she wanted to convey was of grave importance. 'The element of self-sacrifice can be a powerful force for regeneration. This great mystery is seen in a warrior's last breath during battle. If blood is spilt to protect the innocent, a wave of energy is released into the earth to bring forth fruitfulness.'

The weavers stopped to consider the significance of this teaching.

An elderly widow walked to the end of the table. 'To give your life for others is a rare gift,' she said, returning to her chair with a handful of flax.

Handkerchiefs were extracted from bodices and pockets to wipe away tears.

'What about our enemies,' one woman contended, 'have they suffered like we have?'

'They lost the war ...'

'Their mothers must have suffered ...'

'All aggressors suffer ...'

Miriama seldom spoke about the enemies of Māoridom, many and varied though they were. 'From the moment of our birth into the physical condition certain truths affect us.' She tipped her head mindfully towards the church for the benefit of the Christian ladies. 'Sin,' she said, 'or to breach any sacred thing under the protection of the atua, will create a noxious vapour. The same dark energy that corrupts the souls can spread pestilence and famine throughout the nation.'

'Only prayer and cleansing can wash away the darkness ...'

'Our priests have known this for centuries ...'

'As for these aggressors, let me say this,' Miriama continued. 'Cowardice and dishonour bestow unbearable shame upon the people of mana. The abuse of power invites severe retribution from the gods. Isn't this what our enemies discovered?'

The women nodded and murmured among themselves.

'Nobody wants to be accused of cowardice ...'

'Particularly not our soldiers ...'

Miriama raised a finger. 'Yet, we can be sure our boys served their people well.'

'They were brave until the very end ...'

'We will never forget their sacrifices ...'

After more eye patting, the women's voices began to rise and blend into a soulful waiata. At the end of the singing, Miriama stood to address them.

'My friends, I see your hearts are broken. My guidance is to put aside your sorrow and activate your mauri ora. Remember Rongo-mā-Tāne, the god of peace. Cultivate the earth and dedicate yourselves to your whānau and hapū. It is the duty of the grandmothers and grandfathers to place a light at the feet of the young. Teach the mokopuna to become caretakers of the natural world. What greater gift of life can there be than this?'

'Kia ora, Miriama.'

'Thank you, old one.'

'Kia ora.'

'Kia ora.'

For the children of the learning circle, Miriama had other words.

'Be one of the great-souled chiefs,' she urged the dreamers. 'All species were put on this earth to help us. Without guardianship there would be only death and decay. When a tree is felled in the forest to make a canoe, does not Tāne need placating? Listen to me, moko. We have all come from the same stream of light. Be part bird, part fish, part thread of flax in the weaver's hand. In the spider's web, or in the smallest speck, we see the patterns of the universe.'

—◆◆◆—

Some months after the dedication ceremony Winifred gave birth.

It had been fifteen long hours of labour—one night, and half a day. Miriama's hair was wild and loose about her as she handed the perfect infant to its father.

'Your beautiful firstborn, Hēmi.'

Engrossed with love, Hēmi watched the tiny fingers of his boy wrap around his forefinger. He turned to Winifred, who was holding their second son. Twins. She looked happy.

'You did brilliantly, Winnie.' He moved to the side of the bed to lift

    Kayleen M. Hazlehurst

wisps of hair from her damp face. 'I couldn't be prouder of you.'

Winifred beamed at him from her crumpled bedding. 'I wasn't expecting two.'

He laughed. 'Neither was I. We're so lucky, taupuhi.'

Miriama went to touch the girl's arm. 'You did well, little mother, there'll be much celebration in the community.'

She looked at the door where more people were crowding to come in. After a delivery, once mother and child were seen to be safe, the midwife usually slipped from the room to allow others to press forward.

'Wait, Mum,' Hēmi said. 'We have something to ask you. Winifred and I hoped … We were hoping to name the baby after …' He glanced at Winifred for help, not wanting to show a preference.

Winifred stroked the head of the second child. 'Now we have two boys, may we name them after Sonny and Tama?'

Miriama was taken aback. 'A precious gift,' she said. 'Such naming will please the tūpuna and I know Api will be pleased.'

In the late afternoon of the twin birth, the old woman dressed in a black dress and woollen shawl walked towards the sea cliff. Her role was to help her people in times of birth and death, and all of life in between. Miriama was not here to hoe the garden or to pick the vegetables.

When she reached the cliff top, she raised her hands in a karakia. A chant of thanksgiving to the atua for the blessings of new life. Ocean air wrapped her loose hair and dark clothing around her. She was bent, but she was not broken.

'Who disturbs my kūkupa will answer to me,' she said, staring defiantly out to sea.

A mist was descending from the mountain, erasing every feature of the forest and the land. Against the white clouds she pictured the faces of her lost children and heard their voices on the wind. Words of love between Sonny and Atarangi … Promises they would always be together … Snatches of Tama's impish laughter.

Far off, she could see the silhouette of an ocean liner making safe passage across the shoulder of the world.

Acknowledgements and Author's Notes

No thumbnail account can adequately describe the heroism of the 28th Māori Battalion in the Allied fight for the liberation of the Free World during World War Two. At the Olympus Pass, the infantry helped to hold back the full force of the German Army as it swept into Greece. In the Italian Campaign, their fierce attempt to capture and hold the Cassino Railway Station was the second of four major battles that occurred before the Allies were able to breach the Gustav Line. Of the Māori Battalion, A and B Companies lost sixty percent of their men on that fateful night—one hundred and twenty-eight men killed or wounded, out of two hundred.

There are many stories about these tough but kind-hearted soldiers. Most intriguing concerned their close friendships with the civilian populations they had come to protect, and the moral support they received from their families at home. The German Commander, Field Marshal Erwin Rommel, encountering Māori fighters for the first time in Egypt, was reputed to have said: 'Give me the Māori Battalion and I will conquer the world.'

Historical figures and events in five countries appear in this book (New Zealand, England, Egypt, Greece and Italy). I am indebted to official records and first-hand accounts held at Archives New Zealand, Alexander Turnbull Library, National Library of New Zealand, New Zealand Electronic Text Collection (NZETC) Te Pūhikotuhi o Aotearoa, Auckland War Memorial Museum, New Zealand Papers Past, and the website of the 28th Māori Battalion Organisation.

Of the books, reports, articles, diaries and sites I surveyed, I would particularly like to acknowledge the works of Lt. Col. Arapeta Awatere, Sir Antony Beevor, John Carr, J. F. Cody, Artemis Cooper, Harry Dansey, Wes Davis, Thomas J. Dunbabin, Major H. G. Dyer, Geoffrey Edwards, Dr Peter Ewer, Xan Fielding, David Filer, Sir Wira Gardiner, Maria Hill, Megan Hutching, Michael King, G. C. Kiriakopoulos, Gavin Long, Rev. Māori Marsden, Jim McDevitt, Sir Āpirana Ngata, Matthew Parker, E. B. 'Scotch' Patterson, George Psychoundakis, Christopher Pugsley, Murdoch Riley, Samuel Robinson, Dr Monty Soutar, Dame Anne Salmond, and Major H. R. C. Wild.

My thanks go to the war historians John Carr and Peter Ewer for checking the final draft; to Tom Dunbabin (nephew of Thomas J. Dunbabin, and editor of his uncle's field notebook) for his advice on wartime Greece and Crete; to Lesley Marshall, Hilary Johnson, Renell Judais and Ian Howe for their editorial assistance; to Rahera Shortland and Basil Keane for their translations from English to Māori, and to Christos Papadopoudos for his translations into Greek.

Many Māori leaders helped me during my original New Zealand research, most particularly my mentors Sir Patu (Patrick) Wahanga Hohepa, Dr Ranginui Walker, Hon Matiu Waitai Rata and Sir Hēnare Kōhere Ngata. Without their simultaneous translations and guidance none of my work would have reached fruition. A special thanks also to Auntie Girlie Paul (Iraihi Kataraina Sullivan), who nurtured me like a second mother during my childhood, and left a lasting impression on my heart.

To my husband, Dr Cameron Hazlehurst, my deepest gratitude for his constant support and encouragement.

Kayleen M. Hazlehurst

Kayleen Hazlehurst is a fifth generation New Zealander who grew up beside the Mahurangi River on a farm established by her Scottish ancestors in the 1840s. In her early twenties she travelled to Canada and worked with Canadian Indian communities in the Northwest Territories and in a remote Inuit village in Labrador. For her doctorate with the University of Toronto she returned to New Zealand to follow the 1981 election campaign of Matiu

Rata in his bid to win Parliamentary seats for the new Māori political party, Mana Motuhake (*Political Expression and Ethnicity*, Praeger 1993). During this time Sir Hēnare Ngata encouraged her to write about the Māori Battalion.

Kayleen became a Bahá'í at the age of nineteen and devoted her life to the principles of world peace. In Australia she was employed for fifteen years as a researcher and policy adviser on justice and human rights issues. She was awarded a Rockefeller Fellowship with the Virginia Foundation for the Humanities and Public Policy and a Visiting Fellowship at the University of Durham.

Married to the historian and biographer Cameron Hazlehurst, she divides her time between Aotearoa New Zealand and Australia where she and her husband continue to work on their writing projects. Her two novels *A Caramel Sky* and *Who Disturbs the Kūkupa?* are family sagas with themes of love and war in authentic historical settings.

'Au, e Ihu', 'The Soldiers' Hymn'

As discussed in *The New Zealand Folk Hymns* online collection, 'Au, e Ihu', 'The Soldiers' Hymn', is a well-loved hymn of the Māori people. It was sung by the men of the 28th Māori Battalion before they went into battle, and at the battle's end. It is No. 94 in the Anglican Māori Hymn Book.

Au, e Ihu, tirohia	At me, O Jesus, look
Arohaina iho rā	show compassion.
Whakaaetia ake au	Allow me to come within
Ki Tou uma piri ai	your embrace at the time of distress,
I te wā e ake ai	When these angry waves
Enei ngaru kino nei	seem to assail me,
I te wā e keri ai	When the storms
Enei awha kaha mai	get stronger.
Tiakina mai ahau	Take care of me
I te wā e rurea nei	when all around trembles,
Aratakakina e koe	You guide me
Roto te marino nui	towards lasting peace
Aua au e waiho noa	Do not forsake me,
Awhitia mai rā e Koe	would you embrace me
Hīpokina iho au	cover me
Raro i ou parirau	beneath your wings.
Rānea tonu ana mai	There is much abundance
Tau aroha atawhai	of your love.
Kaha ana mai ko Koe	Your strength
Ki te muru i ngā hē	washes away all evil.
Puna o te orange	Fountain of life
Whakahekea tenei wai	Let this water cascade forth
Kia pupū i roto nei	and bubble from within (me)
Tae noa ki te mutunga	unto the end.
Amine	Amen

English translations by H. T. Rikihana.

    Kayleen M. Hazlehurst

Led by Padre Huata, the Māori choir sing 'Au E Ihu' at a memorial service on
Crete, 30 September 1945, in honour of the men who died there in 1941.

*The Maori Battalion was in Northern Italy at the end of the war, helping persuade
Tito that the port of Trieste did not belong to Yugoslavia.*

*Well before the first day of peace dawned the battalion marched to the parade ground
and in complete silence waited the arrival of Padre Huata. Then, as at the end of so
many campaigns, the troops sang the hymn 'Au E Ihu'.*

*Back in the battalion lines the Maoris set about breaking down the hostility of
the Slav population, and the next two months were taken up with wharf and guard
duties in Trieste.*

*Then in early September it was announced that memorial services would be held
at war cemeteries near the principal battlefields and that Crete would be visited first.*

*Colonel Henare was asked to detail the guard of honour, who would also act as the
choir. Twenty-five men from the different tribes and of the main religious denominations
were selected and went into rigorous training in ceremonial rifle drill, haka, action songs
and hymn singing.*

They embarked at Naples on 27 September 1945 and landed at Crete two days later. During the dedication ceremony, Padre Huata farewelled the Maori dead on behalf of the Maori people. Similar ceremonies were later held at the Cassino and Sangro military cemeteries and the men lying in smaller plots at Coriano Ridge, Faenza, Forli, Padua, Monfalcone and Udine were visited by Padre Huata and a small party before the Maoris left Italy. The Maori Battalion commenced its return to New Zealand on 6 December 1945 when it entrained at Florence then embarked on the Dominion Monarch *at Taranto on 26 December.*

The Dominion Monarch *arrived in Wellington Harbour on 23 January 1946, and berthed just after midday at Pipitea Wharf, in almost the same berth as the Maori Battalion had departed from in the* Aquitania *nearly six years previously.*

Source: New Zealand Folk Hymns, *Māori songs and Kiwi songs,* http://folksong.org.nz/au_e_Ihu/index.html; and summary from 28 Māori Battalion, *Aotea Quay,* http://28bn.homestead.com/history19.html.

 Kayleen M. Hazlehurst

Poems, Songs, Chants and Speeches

Composed by Kayleen M. Hazlehurst
English to Māori translations by Rahera Shortland
Translations editor, Basil Keane

Three Poems

1.

What sad spirits, to fall so far from their people.
To lie, forgotten, on some distant soil.
To not take flight over cliff and dune to that place where
sea kelp swirls and flax leaves twist and knot.

Kātahi ngā wairua pōuri, e hingahinga i tawhiti nei i ō rātou iwi.
Te takoto, te warewaretia nei i runga whenua o iwi kē.
Te kore e rere ā-pari, ā-taipū ki taua wāhi
e āwhio ai te rimurapa, e takawiri e pūtiki ai te rau harakeke.

2.

Where are the young men
to be inspired by the feats of their ancestors?
Where are the leaders who will shape their lives
by the virtues of the great chiefs?

Kei hea ngā taitama
Hei whakaawe i ngā mahi rangatira ā ō rātou tūpuna?
Kei hea ngā kaiarataki hei tauira i te oranga
me ngā horomata o te rangatira rongo nui?

3.

So, little flycatcher.
Will you come out to boldly challenge me
when I approach the place of Hinenuitepō?
Or will I be renewed like the moon and restored to life?

Nō reira e te kaihopu ngaro iti.
Ka māia tō puta mai ki te takitaki i ahau
I ahau ka tata atu nei ki te kāinga o Hinenuitepō?
Ka whakaorahia mai anō rānei pērā i te marama hōu?

Will you laugh and dance
when I come alive in the sunlight?
Will you love me when I come to you at dawn?
Hah! And they said Māui would never return!

Ka kata ka kanikani rānei koe
Ina ora mai anō au ā te whitinga o te rā?
Ka aroha mai koe ina hoki atu au ki a koe i te ata hāpara?
Ha! Me tā rātou kī mai, e kore a Māui e hoki mai!

Songs, Chants, Spontaneous Speeches
Waiata, Karakia, Kōrero tene

I.

A Traveller's Song

I am a traveller.
I walk upon the earth with other travellers.
We stand upon the shoulders of Tiki.
The soil gives her fruits, the sea his kaimoana.
The winds of Tāwhiri-mātea rage over the land.
The oceans of Tangaroa encircle the earth.
All creation is soaked with the tears of Rangi.
The forests are cloaked with the mists of Papa.
I rise up on the love between Rangi and Papa.

     Kayleen M. Hazlehurst

I walk on the mists.
I reach for the universe.
We live and die together.

He kaipōkai hāereere ahau
Kua takahia e au te ao me ngā kaipōkai whenua
Kua piki mātou mā runga i ngā pakihiwi o Tiki.
Kua homai e te one āna hua, e te moana āna kai.
Pūkeri ana te whenua i ngā hau a Tāwhiri-mātea
Hōrapa ana ngā moana a Tangaroa ki te ao.
Mākū katoa te ao tūroa i ngā roimata ā Rangi.
Kōpakina ana ngā ngahere e te kohu i a Papa.
Ka mārewa ake au mā runga i te aroha Rangi rāua kō Papa.
Ka hīkoi au mā runga i te kohu.
Ka toro atu au ki te ao tukupū
Ka ora ka hemo tahi mātou.

2.

Song of Homecoming

Verse One

I am troubled,
And I can stay here no longer.
I will go to another place to prepare my leaving.
My love, I hear you calling, 'Come back to me.'
The waves are breaking,
Soon I will sail on more friendly seas.
I will return and there will be a great homecoming.

E rarua ana au,
Kāhore au mō te noho tonu i konei
Ka haere au ki wāhi kē ki te whakarite i taku wehenga atu
E te tau, e rongo ana au i to reo karanga, 'Hoki mai ki ahau.'
E whati mai ana ngā ngaru,
Ākuanei he au te moana ka hoea e au.
Tērā he hokinga nui ā taku hokinga mai.

Verse Two

Ah, to see the pīwakawaka,
As she flits and turns in flight.
How she fans her tail and mocks me with her spinning.
My love, I hear you calling. 'Come back to me.'

Arā, kia kite i te pīwakawaka,
Ka rere porotēteke ana
Ka tawhiuwhiu tana hiore me te takahuri o te taunu i au.
E te tau, e rongo ana au i tō reo karanga. 'Hoki mai ki ahau.'

Verse Three

Dear one, we are far apart.
My pen slips and breaks with longing.
If my words never reach you, know I have died for love.
Remember the promises we made.
The promises we made as we lay
like plaited straw under the pōhutukawa tree.
My love, I hear you calling. 'Come back to me.'

E te tau, kei pāmamao tāua
Ka paheke ka whati ana taku pene i te koingo noa
Ina kore aku kupu e tae atu ki a koe, mōhio mai i mate au i te aroha
Kia mau ki ngā oati i oti i a tāua.
Ngā oati i a tāua e takoto tahi ana
ānō he whiringa kakau i raro i te rākau pōhutukawa.
E te tau, e rongo ana au i tō reo karanga, 'Hoki mai ki ahau.'

Kayleen M. Hazlehurst

3.
Miriama's Plea

Great Tūmatauenga, here is my life.
If bones must be broken, let them be my bones.
If hearts are to be torn out, gladly I offer you mine.
This mother calls you—already she has sacrificed.
Consume me, Mighty Tū, and save the life of my sons.

O Waters of Tangaroa ... O Winds of Tāwhiri-mātea ...
Launch the great canoe and set it forth from the harbour.
Steer it past the singing rocks and beyond the spears of the enemy.
Let mountains be thy markers and seabirds be thy guides.
Find the way the ancestors once discovered,
with the Spirit held fast.

Tūmatauenga, anei taku oranga.
Ki te whati he kōwi, meinga ko ōku kōiwi.
Ki te tīhorea he manawa, anei tōku te hoatu mārire nei.
E karanga ana te whaea nei ki a koe—kua ea ke tāna whakahere.
Kāinga ko au e Tū mana nui, ka tohu ai ko te oranga o aku tama.

E ngā wai a Tangaroa ... E ngā hau a Tāwhiri-mātea ...
Uakina te waka nui ka tuku ai kia tere i te wahapū.
Urungitia kia pahure i ngā toka kawe waiata, ki tua i ngā tao a te hoariri.
Meinga hei ngā maunga o pouwhenua, hei ngā manu o te moana o kaiarahi.
Hora noa te ara i kitea ai e ngā tūpuna,
e mau ā-wairua tonu nei.

4.
Miriama's graveside speech

When the air is soft and warm,
the land breathes like a sleeping child.
When harsh winds blow, the world awakens.
Seas roll, waves froth and foam.
Leaves ripple and grasses feather and swirl.
How do we withstand these scattering winds?

Where is our strength?
It is in the power of our forests.
Our noble kauri and tōtara. Our rimu and pūriri.
See how they stand as a single body.
How they sway in unison, yet do not break.
So it is with our people, our valiant tangata whenua.
Today we honour them, but we do not say goodbye.
They will be with us, as our atua are with us.
They will be our gods of peace
and our gods of wrath.
Forever, and ever, and ever.

Ka ngāwari, ka mahana ana te taiao,
ka hāhā te whenua ānō nei he tamaiti e moe ana.
Pupuhi kaha ana te hau kerekere ka oho ake te ao,
Oioi ana te moana, pūkeri, pūpūhuka ana ngū ngaru
Rērere ana ngā rau, āmiomio ana ngā kura.
Me pēhea te whakatau i ēnei hau kerekere?
Kei hea tō tātou kaha?
Kei ō tātou ngāherehere
Kei roto i ā tātou tōtara, a tātou rimu me ngā pūriri.
Mātaki atu e tū mai rā anōnei he tinana kotahi.
E pīoioi kotahi ana, e kore mō te whati.
He pērā anō ō tātou iwi, ō tātou tangata whenua toa.

Naianei e whakanuia ana, engari e kore e poroakitia.
Ka noho tonu ki a tātou, pēnei i ō tātou Atua.
Kō rātou ō tātou Atua Maungārongo
ō tātou Atua o te riri.
Mō ake tonu, mō ake tonu atu.

     Kayleen M. Hazlehurst

Who Were They?

Regional Distinctions of the 28th Māori Battalion Infantry Companies

A Company Northland: Ngā Puhi and Te Aupōuri tribes and sub-
tribes

B Company Rotorua, Bay of Plenty, Taupo, Coromandel: Te Arawa
and Tūhoe

C Company East Coast, Gisborne, East Cape: Ngāti Porou,
Rongowhakaata

D Company Southern North Island and South Island confederates,
Waikato-Maniapoto, Taranaki, Hawke's Bay-Wairarapa,
Wellington, Chathams, and Stewart Island: Ngāti
Kahungunu and others

Secret Service Agents on Crete

Between 1941 and 1943, the period of this story, several British Secret Service
agents infiltrated Crete. Their mission was to help Commonwealth troops escape
after the fall of Crete, and to support the Cretan Resistance. Each operated with
undercover names and their identities were seldom revealed to the local people.
The real intelligence officers briefly encountered by Sonny and his friends were
as follows:

'Yanni' Major Jack Smith-Hughes (RASC, SOE).

'Siphi' (originally 'Michalaki'), Captain Ralph Stockbridge (Field Security,
ISLD).

'Aleko' Major Xan Fielding (Cyprus Regiment, SOE). Alexander Fielding was
born in India to a military family and gave long service in the subcontinent.

'O-Tom' Captain Thomas Dunbabin (SOE leader on Crete), Oxford archaeologist in Greece and Crete, born in Tasmania, Australia.

'Michali' Captain Patrick Leigh Fermor (Intelligence Corps, SOE).

'Skipper Poole' Lieutenant Commander Francis Poole (SOE).

Other important agents who came before or after this period—such as 'Vasili', the famous New Zealander Sergeant Major Dudley Perkins, known by the local people as 'The Lion of Crete'—could not be mentioned here.

OSO Office of Special Operations, wartime intelligence agencies

British Directorate of Military Intelligence, Section 9 (MI9)

ISLD Inter Services Liaison Department (MI6)

RASC Royal Army Service Corps

SOE Special Operations Executive (MI9)

Kayleen M. Hazlehurst

Glossary

āe	yes, agreement, to give assent
ai!	gosh! yikes! oh! exclamation of surprise
āke, ake, ake	forever and forever, forevermore
Aotearoa	Māori name for the country of New Zealand
ariki	paramount chief, aristocrat, lord, firstborn in high ranking family
aroha	love, compassion, sympathy, charity
atua	The gods who created all things in the universe, including humankind. Deity, supernatural being, guardian ancestors. Many trace their whakapapa from deified ancestors. Some atua have visible representations, such as birds and mountains. Sometimes referred to as the Powers.
auē!	to cry, howl, wail, groan
Ē he!	gosh! crikey! I'll be damned, an exclamation of surprise
e ipo	beloved one, darling, my friend
e kare	my dear, an affectionate term of address to a friend
e pou	my teacher, mentor, grandmother/grandfather (shortened form of Pōua)
haka	to dance, fierce dance with chant, cultural war dance
hāngī	earth oven for cooking food on hot stones
hapū	sub-tribe, clan
hāpuka	groper or grouper, large fish with wide mouth.
hoki	marine fish
hongi	act of greeting, salutation, to press noses
ihi	Essential force, psychic power, vitality, quality of excellence which increases by close association with the gods. The energy that goes before Māori warriors in an attack
iwi	tribe, nation, extended kinship group, people of common ancestry
kai	food

kaimoana	seafood, shellfish
kākāriki	parakeet birds, brightly coloured
karakia	prayers, incantations, ritual chants
karanga	a woman's welcome call onto a marae
ka pai	very good, well done
kaumātua	respected elders, older men and women of status
kauri	largest native tree in the New Zealand forest
kērangi	harrier hawk
kia ora!	Hello! cheers, best wishes, good luck
kina	sea eggs, common sea urchin (a delicacy)
kiore	rat, mouse
Kiwi	nickname for New Zealanders, taken from the flightless kiwi bird
kohekohe	native tree
korimako	bellbird, an olive-green songbird
koro	grandfather, term of respectful address to an older man
kōtuku	white heron, rare bird with white plumage
kūkupa	native wood pigeon
kūmara	a starchy root vegetable, otherwise known as sweet potato
maimai aroha	tokens of affection (e.g. clematis garlands at funerals)
mākutu	black magic, to bewitch, curse or cast spells
mana	spiritual power, prestige, authority granted by the atua
mānuka	New Zealand tea-tree, common native
Māori	indigenous people of Aotearoa New Zealand
Māoritanga	Māori culture, lore and customs
marae	gathering place, complex of buildings with courtyard, community facilities
maunga	mountain
maunga-ā-rongo	peace making
mauri	life force granted by the gods, inner essence allowing all entities, ecosystems, social groups, trees, birds, animals, rocks and objects to exist
mauri ora	vital life force, one's get up and go, to become involved in things
mihi	speech of greeting, to acknowledge, to pay tribute
moko	traditional tattooing on the face or body, a sign of status and identity

   Kayleen M. Hazlehurst

mokopuna (moko) grandchildren, descendant, term of addressing children, shows fondness

noa free from tapu, ordinary, unrestricted

Pākehā New Zealander of European descent, person of foreign origin

pipi flat shellfish, cockles, or clams, that live in the sand

piupiu ceremonial skirts made of flax

pīwakawaka fantail, small flitting bird with fanned tail

poaka swine, wild pig, pork

pōhutukawa trees found in coastal regions, that produce large red flowers in December

poi a ball, a dance using a ball on a string in rhythmic patterns

ponga native tree fern, with silver and green fronds

pōrangi mad, insane, deranged, beside oneself with grief or despair

pōwhiri welcoming ceremony, chant to beckon guests onto a marae

pūhā small leafy plant, eaten cooked as a green vegetable

puhi a woman of noble birth, a virgin

pūkeko purple swamp hen

pūriri large native tree with red berries and flowers that attract birds

rangatira to be of high rank, ennobled, esteemed, chiefly

rangatiratanga chieftainship, chiefly authority, attributes of a chief

ruru morepork, brown spotted native owl

tangata whenua people of the land, the local people

tangihanga (tangi) funeral, rites for the dead held on the marae

tapu sacred, restricted, forbidden, set apart

tarakihi marine fish

tātua belt

taupuhi darling, beloved, my love

Te Ao Mārama the world of life and light, world of the living

teina younger brother of a boy, younger sister of a girl, cousins of same gender from a more junior branch of the family. 'Little brother', an affectionate term.

tī-tī mutton birds

tohu signs or marks of guidance, to point out

tohunga	expert, priest, healer, someone who is proficient
tohunga wahine	female expert
tōtara	large native tree with prickly olive-green leaves
tū	to fight, engage, oppose
tuakana	elder brother of a boy, elder sister of a girl, cousin of same gender from a more senior branch of the family. 'Protector', a term of respect.
tuatara	a lizard native to New Zealand, an ancient spiny-backed reptile
tūpuna	ancestors, grandparents, forebears (tīpuna, eastern dialect)
utu	vengeance, retribution, reciprocity that ensures balance
waiata	song, to sing a psalm or chant
waiata aroha	song of love
waiata tangi	song of mourning, lament, a prolific class of traditional songs
wairua	soul or spirit of a person that exists beyond death, distinct from the body and the mauri.
waka	traditional canoe, vehicle, spirit medium
wānanga	place to discuss and teach genealogical knowledge, philosophy, cultural rites and ceremonies, and religious lore
whare wānanga	house of learning, school or forum of higher knowledge
whakamā	to be ashamed, embarrassed, bashful
whakapapa	genealogical table, to place in layers, to recite genealogies, origins
whānau	extended family group, once the primary economic unit
wharawhara	a silvery, grass-like native plant.
wharekai	dining hall on a marae
wharenui	meeting house, main building on a marae, decorated with carvings

Kayleen M. Hazlehurst

ATUA

Io   Primary Creator, Supreme Being

Elemental gods

Primal couple

Ranginui (Rangi)	Sky father
Papatūānuku (Papa)	Earth mother

Offspring of Rangi and Papa

Rongo-mā-Tāne	god of the kūmara and cultivated foods, god of peace
Tāne-mahuta (Tāne)	god of the forests and birds
Tāwhiri-mātea (Tāwhiri)	god of the winds, clouds, rains, snow, storms
Tangaroa	god of the sea and fish
Tūmatauenga (Tū)	god of war, god of humans
Tiki	Tiki, a demigod figure, was represented in Māori mythology as either the son of Rangi and Papa, who created the first man by mixing his own blood with clay; or he was the first man created by Tūmatauenga or Tane. Tiki is said to have founded the archaic Māori language. As he appears in many Polynesian cultures, it may be presumed Tiki conducted sea voyages. It is possible the concept of Tiki was based upon an early, or several early, pioneers in ocean travel and settlement throughout the Pacific region.
Hinenuitepō	daughter of Tāne-mahuta, great woman of the night who receives human spirits after death and shepherds them to the underworld